SHADOWED HEARTS

AND

SECRETS

T.M. CARUCCI

First paperback edition February 2026

Cover design by Atra Luna Design

ISBN 979-8-9944825-0-6 (paperback)

Published by T.M. Carucci

PLAYLIST

I love listening to music, especially while writing. Even on those days I have writer's block, I would throw on my headphones, listening to music while I crochet, and before I knew it, a scene would play out in my head like a movie, or I guess you could say, a music video. A lot of these songs have truly brought the scenes to life for me, to the point I would play the songs on repeat while writing. So, I am happy to share the playlist with the inspired song for each chapter. Enjoy!

Chapter 1: "Superbeast" by Rob Zombie

Chapter 2: "Watching Over You" by Smash into Pieces

Chapter 3: "Had Enough" by Breaking Benjamin

Chapter 4: "Coming Undone" by Korn

Chapter 5 "It's All Inside My Head" by Nightcall, Nocturne

Chapter 6: "Cry Little Sister" by Marilyn Manson

Chapter 7: "Shatter Me" by Lindsey Sterling (featuring Lzzy Hale)

Chapter 8: "Dirty Little Secret" by The All-American Rejects

Chapter 9: "Precious Things Lay Hidden" by Pater Gundry

Chapter 10: "All The Small Things" by Blink-182

Chapter 11: "Take on Me" by King Vagabond

Chapter 12: "Papercut" by Linkin Park

Checkout the whole playlist on Spotify: SHaS Playlist

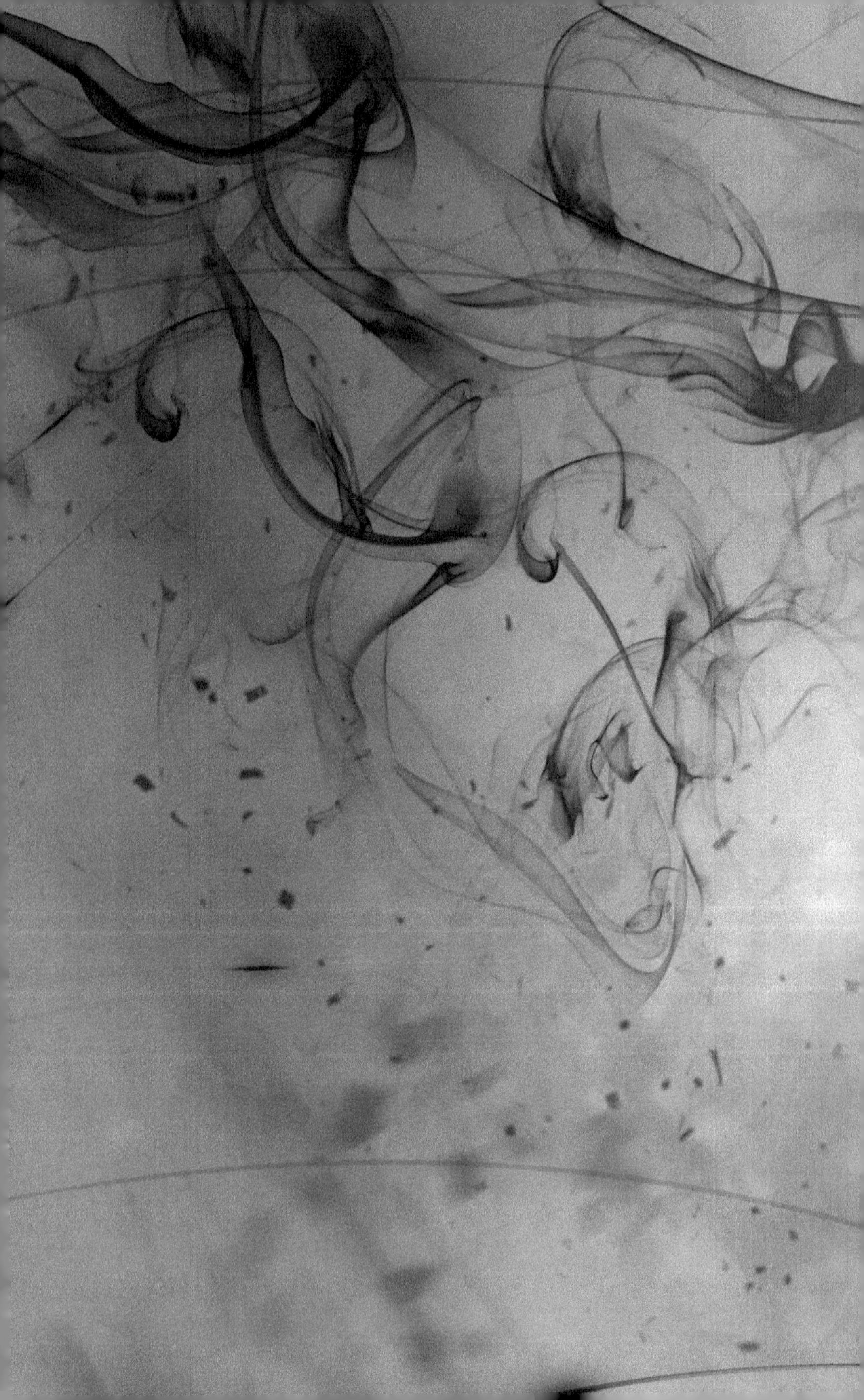

CHAPTER 1

Ravenna

I t's a clear night tonight.

Damn it.

I should've guessed, considering how cloudless the day was. But a part of me had hoped the clouds would roll in, cover the moon, give us the shadows we need. Instead, the sky is glittering with stars, and the full moon hangs high, flooding the forest floor with its silver glow.

Perfect. Just what we need. More light for the monsters to see us coming.

Outside the gates of the kingdom, we moved through the field and made our way along the thinning edge of the forest, six shadows wrapped in worn leather and quiet purpose.

Though we are the king's Royal Slayer Squad, we didn't wear the royal colors of sky blue and silver or polished steel like the royal guards do. We wear scarred black armor molded by necessity and built for survival.

Codrin Hardtblade, our squad captain, moves with grit and control. His black armor is stripped down, worn and battle-touched. His storm-gray eyes sharp along the iron mask that covers half his face, its etched detail of teeth and fangs still giving him the weight of command. His dark auburn hair falls loosely over his brow, and the only weapons he carries are the sword at his side and the promise in his gaze.

Codrin keeps his back to us as he signals for us to fan out. Without question, we move quietly along the tree line of the Nothingness Forest, hugging the edge of the shadows. I square my shoulders, the layered pauldrons pressing into my muscles, twin belts strapped tight across my hips, my double-blade axe slung low at my back.

The name *Nothingness* is a lie. There's everything in this forest, from twisted creatures and night-borne horrors to trees that move when no one's looking. Some say they trap the unwary. Others say the forest swallows you whole and keeps your screams tucked under its roots.

If you get lost in there, you'd better hope whatever kills you is quick.

Codrin decided we didn't need to double up tonight. There's been little activity for months anyway. So, only six of us are spaced out across about seven hundred yards. We take cover where we can just inside the tree line, eyes peeled for movement of anything trying to slip from the forest into the kingdom unseen.

I make my way along the forest line, the tall grass rustling beneath my boots. The cool familiar weight of my axe rests in my palm. Its twin crescent blades curve like silver moons, edges sharpened to clean, deadly arcs. Delicate engravings trace along the neck of the weapon, etched into the dark iron in sweeping patterns that almost resemble wings.

The grip is wrapped in dark leather, worn smooth from years of use, and the shaft bears the quiet memory of battle of scuffs along the silverwork, a faded nick from a deflected blade, and the faint shadow of old blood in the grooves. Princess by birth, slayer by blood. I don't wear a crown. I wear this.

Where others favor swords or hammers, I choose the axe because it demands more than skill. It demands resolve. There is no fencing with this weapon. No flourishes. Just weight, momentum, and the will to wield it without hesitation.

My weapon. My shield. The one constant I trust when the night grows sharp.

I crouch low in a patch of tall grass, hidden from both forest and field. From here, I can see deep into the blackened trees and over the open stretch behind me, where Theiahold's castle looms in the distance like a sleeping beast.

The summer wind shifts from its usual warmth to cold. Too cold. Like something stirs the air that shouldn't be awake.

The ice chilling wind comes from the Nivalis Requiem Summit and slithers out of the forest, tugging at the grass, bending the branches with a hollow whine. I shiver as it cuts straight through my leather armor, straight into my bones. No matter the season, the Nothingness Forest is always cold. Like the trees themselves breathe frost.

Trying to keep my mind busy and my body from freezing stiff, I adjust the mask over the bottom half of my face. Made of a special lightweight iron alloyed with ashenbane, the mask fits perfectly along my jaw and over my mouth. Bobby, our talented blacksmith, designed it to look like a snarling demon mouth, jagged teeth bared, and it's more than just for show. It protects us from the soul-suckers, the ones that drain you with a single breath. Ashenbane burns demon flesh on contact and makes the iron stronger than steel. It's why all our weapons are made of the same material.

I adjust the reinforced leather of my cuirass, sleek and black, molded to my form like a second skin, yet suffocating at times. I pat down my gear. Daggers. *Check.* One strapped to each side of my ribs, two at my waist, one at each thigh, and a small bear claw blade tucked into the back of my belt. Just in case.

Time creeps by. Nothing moves in the forest. Nothing shifts the grass. The quiet is beginning to itch under my skin.

Most nights, I'm grateful when patrols are uneventful. But tonight?

Tonight, I *need* something to fight.

The sharp crack of a twig to my right yanks me out of my thoughts, heart instantly slamming against my ribs.

Finally.

I shift, eyes darting to the sound, my grip tightening on the shaft of my axe. The smooth, steady blade catches the moonlight with hunger.

The tall grass rustles. I freeze, breath held, pulse pounding. Whatever's coming thinks it's hunting me.

Big mistake.

I've faced worse than demons. I was seventeen when my father, King Zephyr Rosewyn, shoved me into the Royal Slayer Squad as a punishment for refusing the first suitor. He would not release me from the squad until I begged for forgiveness. So, since then, I've fought monsters that would drive lesser warriors mad. This one won't be any different.

"Hey…" The whisper slithers through the grass.

I exhale. Loud. Annoyed. You've got to be kidding me. Like I said, *worse than demons.*

Zavier pushes through the tall blades like a creeping snake, he crawls up beside me, unbuckling his plain iron mask and tossing it aside as he stretches out on his side like we're here for stargazing.

"I came to check on my girl," he murmurs with a smug grin, looking like he stepped out of a war portrait. His gear is always spotless, his sword gleaming, and his blond hair slicked back in place.

I grip my axe tighter.

"Bullshit." I snarl. "What are you doing here?"

He shrugs, plucking at the grass. "Been thinking about you lately."

"Well, that makes one of us," I mutter, keeping the blade angled low beside me.

"Oh, come on, Princess." He pouts like a child. "I know you still think about that night."

"No. Actually, I don't."

Four months ago, I needed an escape. Mother's constant matchmaking. Father's rage after I rejected yet another suitor, ending with a backhand that still bruises my memory to this day. I wasn't thinking clearly. Zavier was there. Willing. Easy. Forgettable.

He was a mistake I buried the moment the sun came up.

He, apparently, still thinks he's *un*forgettable.

"Hear me out." He runs a hand through his wavy dirty-blond hair.

"I don't have to listen to anything you have to say."

He shifts onto all fours, crawling closer like a beast stalking prey. "You know you want my cock inside you again." His hand brushes my thigh.

I recoil, disgust rising like bile. He's only a few inches taller than me, but his presence suddenly feels enormous. His biceps straining under his sleeves, hazel eyes gone dark with hunger.

He doesn't like being told no. And judging by the look in his eyes… I'm not sure it's an option anymore.

Zavier rises to his knees. "You don't have to act like such a bitch," he snaps.

I chuckle, low and sharp. "Fuck off, Zavier. You haven't crossed my mind since that night. And trust me. You are nothing to brag about."

His hand snaps forward, seizing my throat. His face is suddenly inches from mine.

"You'll regret saying that little princess. It's not like you're some perfect little saint."

"Zavier…" I gasp, but his fingers tighten more, cutting my words short.

He pulls me close to his chest and unbuckles the straps from my mask. It falls to the grass.

"There, now I can use that pretty little mouth of yours." He grins, his eyes darkening.

I gasp, choking, grabbing his wrist. My axe slips from my grip.

He slams me to the ground.

Time fractures. All I hear is my own breath clawing for space. My mind blanks, then snaps back, screaming.

"Get off me!" I rasp, shoving at his chest, his weight crushing the air from my lungs.

"Don't bother fighting, Princess," he growls, grinding his hips against mine. "I always get what I want."

I struggle, every muscle burning with fury.

He's heavier. Stronger. But he's too focused on control. On power.

"You're going to love this just as much as you did the first time."

Something rustles behind him. Followed by laughter.

Giggling?

Zavier stiffens. His hand loosens and I suck in a deep breath. Shoving him off me. Hard. He stumbles back. His eyes wide, darting in all directions.

"What was that?" He reaches for the sword hilt at his side.

But before he can draw it, something grabs his ankle.

With a startled grunt, Zavier's body jerks backward, dragged out of the tall grass like a sack of meat.

Gone.

I crouch low, listening to struggling, an ear-rupturing screech pierces the air, and then silence.

I don't move. I don't breathe. I just stare at the place where he vanished, wondering if the forest just claimed him… or if something worse did.

The grass shifts again, rustling low around me. I bring my axe close to my chest and crouch, eyes darting through the darkness, listening to movement from every direction.

I'm surrounded.

Codrin and Athan Brexen are northwest, still a few hundred yards out. Maybe I can run. Maybe I can scream. No. My only option here now is to fight.

I've taken down many demons before. I can do it again.

I slide a dagger from the sheath at my waist and grip the blade, holding the point between my fingers. Low to the ground,

I pivot slowly, breath held.

Movement. Right. Then left. Then behind me.

Rustling closes in on all sides.

Three… maybe four.

I press my body lower into the grass, heart thundering. Their footsteps are light but deliberate.

A shuffle to my right.

I don't hesitate. I hurl the dagger. A shriek rips through the air, so piercing it echoes like a crack of lightning, followed by a thunderous crash as something massive collapses to the earth.

The other footsteps scatter, retreating.

Then, once again… silence.

I stay low, waiting. Listening.

Nothing.

After a long, tense moment, I rise, stepping out from the tall grass. My gaze lands on the demon.

Still breathing. Barely.

I approach with slow, calculated steps. My dagger juts from its chest, the handle quivering with each of the creature's rattling breaths.

I search the forest grounds, but Zavier is nowhere to be seen.

I spot a trail of thick black blood leading back into the tree line.

"Thanks for the heads-up, asshole." Rolling my eyes, I shift my gaze back to the snarling demon at my feet.

Slatier demons.

Of all the monsters in the Nothingness Forest, the Slatiers are the cruelest. You don't hear their footsteps. Their laughter is the only warning giving you time to run.

"Looks like it's just you and me big guy."

It lets out a wet snarl as I rip the dagger free of its chest. Its thick black blood splatters across my arm and cheek, its open wound sizzling from the burn of the iron blade.

I drop the dagger to the ground, grab my axe with both hands, and raise it high.

The demon's glowing yellow eyes lock on mine, wide and wild.

"Burn in the Void," I growl.

Then swing.

The blade slices clean through its neck. Blood sprays my face as its head rolls along the grass, its body limp. I wipe the hot blood from my face with the back of my sleeve, chest hea-ving, adrenaline still thrumming. I retrieve my dagger from the ground and clean it across my pants before sliding it back into its sheath.

Behind me, footsteps pound the ground. Loud and fast.

I draw in a deep breath, axe raised, leather groaning beneath my fingers as I spin around.

Only to stop an inch from taking Codrin's head off.

"Fuck!" he shouts, sliding to a halt, slipping and landing flat on his ass in the dirt.

"Shit, Codrin!" I snap, lowering my axe. "A little warning

next time?"

I reach out and help him to his feet. He rips his mask off, chest rising with every breath, lean, curved muscle tight with tension. Those storm-gray eyes of his lock on mine, full of that damn mix of concern and judgment.

Athan comes barreling up behind him. His heavy shoulders heave as he bends forward, bracing one hand on his knees, his massive war hammer thunking to the ground in the other. Some of his wavy dark brown hair has come loose from his man-bun. Cardio was never his strong point. Not that you'd expect it from a six-foot-six wall of solid muscle. He's built like a war-horse, and right now, he's wheezing like one too.

Close behind. *Of course.* Is Talon Rosewyn. Prince of Theiahold. My twin brother. He jogs up beside Athan and drops silently into his usual slayer stance, shoulders squared and sword angled low. His silver-streaked brown hair barely grazes his shoulders, and his icy blue eyes. The same color as mine. Flick over my body, checking for injuries.

"Geez, Rave. Bit early to be trying to decapitate the captain, don't you think?" he mutters, removing his own mask and securing it to his belt.

I run my tongue along my inner lip and pivot on my heel, making my way back to the tall grass in search of my mask.

"Zavier said you were being attacked," Athan huffs between gasps as his eyes fall on the headless demon.

"I *was*," I mutter, teeth clenched. "And now I'm going to kill him for leaving me here to fend for myself."

I keep my eyes fixed on the ground, using the blade of my axe to move aside the tall grass.

"Where the fuck is it?" I grumble under my breath. I swear if I don't find my mask, it will be one more thing I'll truly make Zavier pay for.

"Leaving you?" Codrin arches a brow. "He was at his post. He said he saw demons heading your way."

I stop in my search, head snapping up to meet Codrin.

"Where is he?" I spit. "He's a fucking liar. He snuck over here and almost."

I clamp my mouth shut. No. They don't need to know. What happened months ago is none of their business. And what almost happened tonight…

That's mine to deal with.

"He was dragged off. Then got away without so much as a heads-up. Ran like a scared little coward," I snap my voice sharper than I mean it to be.

I continue searching for my mask, feeling Codrin watching me for a beat too long. Not pressing but not missing a thing either.

"As of now, he's back with Miles," he says finally. "I'll talk to him after you both give your reports. But if Slatiers are crossing the border, we've got bigger problems."

"Um… guys?" Talon's voice cuts through the tension, low

and urgent.

We all turn to him.

"We've got company."

He gestures with his head, crouching into a ready stance, sword rising. A cold jolt spikes down my spine as I turn back to the trees.

Two dozen sets of glowing yellow eyes blink through the darkness.

The shadows shift. Thick leathery bodies materialize between the trees, more clambering silently into the branches above us. Their rough black skin blends with the forest sha-dows, but the delight in their eyes, their hungry, feral slits, glows like fireflies in hell.

Laughter bursts through the dark like a cracked violin string, sharp, erratic, and far too deranged to be human. One drops from a branch. Another slinks forward on all fours.

They're everywhere. Circling. Hunting.

Slatiers don't just kill. They *play* with their prey.

They range in size from half my height to some towering at nearly seven feet. But all of them… armed with claws as long as my forearm and twice as sharp as my axe.

Talon tightens his grip on his blade. Athan's jaw clenches.

"Damn..." Athan breathes. "That's *a lot* of Slatiers."

"No, shit," Codrin mutters, eyes narrowing. "We can't outrun that many. Not yet."

My heart pounds in my ears.

He raises his sword. "On me. We take down as many as we can."

I raise my axe across my chest, muscles tensing. Talon takes Codrin's left and Athan takes the right beside me, a glint of mischief in his piercing cognac eyes like he relishes the fight ahead.

Branches snap behind us.

In unison, we raise our weapons, ready to strike whatever is trying to sneak up behind us.

Two figures emerge from the shadows, blades drawn, faces grim.

Miles Fenrickson and Zavier Walheld.

I let out a relieved breath, lowering my axe only slightly.

"Just in time for the party, boys." Athan gives a crooked grin.

"I like to make an entrance. What can I say?" Miles spins his twin blades, silver flashing sharp and fast. Twelve inches of trouble in each hand. Dark curls frame the dark skin of his angular face beneath the mask. He's lean and quick, all sharp lines and speed, built more for slicing through shadows than holding a front line. "Didn't want to outshine you, big guy."

Blade already drawn, posture rigid and precise, Zavier rolls his eyes as he steps past Miles without a word, moving with elegance, like every step is rehearsed and maybe it is. Steering clear of me, he makes his way to the far opposite end, taking position behind Talon. His eyes harsh and analyzing as he sweeps over the shadows of demons before us.

The demons shriek a chorus of bloodlust tearing through the trees.

One lunges.

Codrin's sword flashes. Clean. Brutal.

The Slatier's head rolls into the ferns, black blood hissing against the dirt.

A second drops from above, snarling.

Talon pivots mid-step, blade driving up through its chest. The impact lifts the demon off its feet before it crumples. Blood spatters across his face and perfectly fitted black armor but he doesn't flinch.

Another, barrels toward Codrin. I open my mouth to warn him.

But Athan is on it with a quick swing of his hammer. Crashing into the demon's leg with a bone-snapping crack. The thing drops with an ear shattering shriek.

Athan steps in, calmly planting his boot on its throat and the unmistakable sound of bone crunches beneath the weight of his boot.

"Another day, another demon," he huffs.

The forest erupts. Slatiers pour from the trees. Their claws flashing, jaws snapping, limbs like shadows with teeth.

One drops from the canopy straight toward me.

I swing up hard, my axe biting deep into its ribs. The shock of impact jolts up my arms. Black blood sprays across my boot as the demon spasms and drops to the ground lifeless.

Another rushes me.

I duck low, pivot, and slice its thigh wide open. It howls, stumbling as Zavier's blade appears beside me, sliding beneath its ribs with a swift, merciless motion. One twist, and it's done.

Zavier flashes me a snarky grin before turning the thin blade of his sword on another oncoming demon.

Yeah, he's not getting a thank you from me.

Above, branches snap. More shadows shifting through the canopy.

"They're regrouping!" Miles calls.

One dives at him. He sidesteps with ease and buries both blades into its spine. The thing collapses with a hiss of steam from its lungs.

"There's too many," he breathes.

Two more launch at Athan. One from the front, another from behind.

The first one meets his hammer midair. The second claws at his side, drawing blood.

Athan doesn't even wince as he swings around and grabs it by the throat and slams it against a tree so hard the bark splits open. He's the strongest of us, and he damn well knows it.

I duck under another lunging Slatier and twist upward, my axe cleaving straight through its midsection. I can feel the heat of its blood spray the side of my face, but I don't stop.

"Talon. Left!" Codrin's voice cuts through the clash.

Talon turns just in time to block a claw aimed at his throat. He stumbles back, boots skidding through the dirt, before regaining his footing and driving his sword deep into the demon's spine.

The forest is alive now. Shrill cries echo in every direction. Shadows shift in the treetops. Claws tear at bark. Their yellow eyes light up the night like lanterns. There are too many to count.

My pulse hammers in my ears. *Fuck!* This is spiraling… fast.

I glance at Codrin. His face is blood-smeared but focused, scanning the field like he's counting us, measuring every second we have left.

"We can't hold this line," I growl through clenched teeth.

"Hit hard!" Codrin shouts, slashing down another demon as it lunges for him. "Head west. Regroup at the gates!"

My stomach twists. Run?

I don't want to. But he's right. Another minute here and someone *will* die.

His eyes meet mine. Gray and burning. "I expect to see you all there."

Athan gives a sloppy salute. "Yes, sir, Captain Sunshine."

Another Slatier crashes down between them. Codrin turns, slicing clean through its chest before it hits the ground. His blade black with blood.

Then he sucks in a breath, deep and sharp.

"Move!"

We run.

Boots slam against dirt. Branches whip past. Weapons flash around us.

The Slatiers scream in delight, shrill and wild as they give chase.

I hurl myself over fallen logs, vault over tangled roots. The shadows blur into streaks of black and silver under the moonlight.

The Slatiers' claws rip through earth and bark.

I hear the rustle and pounding of my teammates' footsteps, but then I lose them. Athan and Miles, gone. Talon and Zavier. Out of sight.

But Codrin is fifteen feet to my left, sprinting hard.

I catch a glimpse of a Slatier moving faster on all four of its long limbs. Its skin like obsidian bark, barreling straight for him. Its claws outstretched ready to strike.

"Codrin!" I scream.

He glances back barely dodging the swipe of its fingertips as it grazes his boot.

"And don't slow down." He barks to me as he surges forward.

I press harder, lungs screaming, feet barely touching the ground.

Up ahead, Talon appears in a break between trees. Still running but fighting too. His blade arcs mid-sprint, sending a demon crashing into a trunk with a sickening crunch of bones and bark.

"Ravenna!" Codrin's voice slices through the wind, sharp and urgent.

I glance over my shoulder.

Five of them, bounding, snarling, and right on my heel.

I pivot hard, zigzagging through the trees, trying to shake them.

But they're relentless.

They shriek with glee behind me. Excited by the hunt. Chasing me down like starved wolves.

One lunges at me.

The air shifts beside me and I stumble, only to catch myself as its claw slices past just grazing my sleeve.

I push harder, branches whip across my face. Roots snag at my boots. I veer sharply left, then right. Ducking low beneath a thick limb as I try to lose the pack at my heels.

Their pounding footsteps don't falter.

My lungs burn. Every step is a battle.

Moonlight flares as I burst into a small clearing.

Codrin cuts across my path, eyes sharp.

"Ravenna!" he shouts again, his eyes locking on the demons behind me.

Before I can answer, one about my size leaps. I see it too late.

Its weight crashes into me from behind, a solid wall of bone and muscle slamming me to the ground. My chest hits hard. The impact knocking the air from my lungs, and my axe flies from my grip, landing with a dull, distant thud.

The world tilts sideways. A jolt of pain shoots up my spine. Dirt grounds into my mouth, my nose, stinging my eyes.

I try to breathe, but claws clamp around my ankle and yank.

I lock my jaw against the scream and shove the pain aside, scrambling for anything to hold on to as I'm dragged backward, my armor scraping against the forest floor.

The demon's full weight slams into my stomach, driving the last of the air from my lungs in a ragged gasp. A sickening crack pulses through my shoulder as claws punch through the thick leather of my right pauldron, raking deep into the muscle beneath.

Pain explodes like fire across my chest. I scream out of fury.

Its breath hits me next, hot, fetid, and foul, burning across my cheek as its face presses in close, drool sliding down its chin to drip against my skin.

"Delicious," it rasps, voice warm, twisted.

Its teeth snap, inches from my face. I flinch back, heart hammering, vision strobing with white. My hands scrabble for a weapon. Anything.

"Not like any human," it croons, chuckling a wet, rattling sound that vibrates through my skull.

My fingers close around the hilt of a dagger at my hip.

I don't hesitate.

Iron flashes as I drive the blade up beneath its jaw. The Slatier shrieks, a horrible gurgling cry, like a wild boar choking on its own blood.

I wrench the blade free with a twist. Hot fluid sprays across my face. Its body spasms once. Then goes still.

I shove it off me with a grunt and scramble to my knees, every breath a sear of fire. But I barely have time to recover. Another Slatier is already surging toward me.

A blur of movement. Iron slashes through the air.

Codrin barrels into the demon like a charging bull, his sword cleaving through its ribcage.

The creature collapses, twitching, black blood soaking into the dirt.

Codrin spins, grabs my arm, and yanks me to my feet. "Stay with me!"

We run, my hand snatching up my axe from the grass as we go.

I don't look back.

I don't need to. Their shrieks chase us through the trees.

Codrin doesn't let go, his grip firm around my wrist as he cuts through the terrain, leading us downhill where the forest thickens.

"We're getting close," he calls over his shoulder, breath ragged. "Just a bit further!"

Another Slatier crashes through the trees on our right. Codrin jerks me left, keeping himself between me and the threat.

We burst out of the woods into another clearing just as Talon and Athan break through the opposite side.

"Over here!" Talon waves us on.

Miles and Zavier appear from the tree line, bleeding but breathing. We regroup. Panting. Clothes torn. Weapons slick with black blood.

But alive.

The demons don't follow. Melting back into the forest, swallowed by darkness. Only their laughter lingers. High. Mocking. Triumphant.

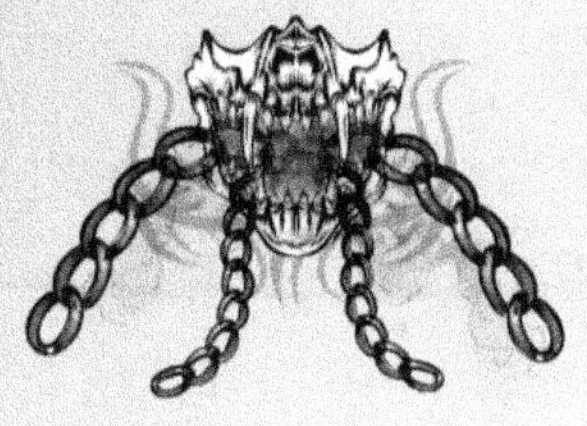

CHAPTER 2
Codrin

"Everyone okay?" I ask, breath still heavy as I brace my hands on my knees. Sweat drips from my brow, mixing with dirt and grime.

"Yeah," Athan huffs, ripping off his mask, etched with symbols that resemble the tattoos covering his chest and arms. He wipes a sleeve across his forehead.

"No," Talon grumbles.

"What? What's wrong?" My tone shifts instantly to captain mode, edged with concern.

"I lost my mask," Talon says with a huff, dropping his arms dramatically to his sides.

"Oh, no. You poor baby." Miles pushes out his bottom lip.

"Are you serious right now?" I sheath my sword with a little too much force.

"It took Bobby *months* to get that thing to fit my jaw just right." Talon crosses his arms like a sulking child.

"Then go back out there and get it, if it means that much to you." Athan chuckles, throwing a punch to Talon's arm.

Talon exaggerates the blow, stumbling a step back. "Why don't you be a gentleman and go get it for me?"

He lunges forward with a return punch, but Athan just stands there unfazed.

"I'm not the one whining like a big baby." Athan hooks an arm around Talon's neck and yanks him into a playful headlock.

I run my hands down the scruff of my face as I watch Talon swing wildly, fists flying, as the two of them lock in a roughhouse scrap.

"I don't think you're getting out of that one, Talon." Miles chuckles, his sharp brown eyes flickering with just as much mischief.

Glad to see even after tonight's ordeal they can still make light of the situation.

"Will you two *knock it off!*" I snap.

Athan immediately releases Talon. They straighten like chastised schoolboys, arms rigid at their sides.

"Sorry, Cap," Talon mutters, suddenly very interested in the ground.

He and Athan side-eye each other, barely holding back matching grins. Sometimes I wonder if I'm a babysitter more than the captain of grown-ass adults of the Slayer Squad.

I turn my attention away from them and spot Ravenna, standing off from the group. Tense. Favoring her right arm.

"You, okay?" My voice softens as I move toward her.

"I'm fine," she mutters, clipped and dismissive, as she turns away too fast. But I catch it.

The tear in her sleeve. The red blooming beneath the edge of her pauldron. Instinct tightens my spine. I step in and gently catch her uninjured arm, pulling her into me before she can pull away.

"No, you're not."

She tries to shake me off, but I hold firm, dragging her into better light.

She hisses through her teeth as I lift the leather carefully, revealing the deep gashes across her shoulder that look raw and angry.

"Shit." The word slips from my lips without thinking. "I told you not to slow down."

She scowls, defensive, but her shoulders tremble for half a second. I know it's not from pain but pride.

"I didn't slow down," she snaps through gritted teeth. "I chose not to leave you."

My jaw drops but I can't seem to form the words I truly want to say. Instead, I turn back to the group.

"Who else needs to see a wound-binder?" I sweep my eyes over each slayer, trying to pick out any injuries on the others. "Athan?" I know he got slashed by a demon claw.

"Nope. I'm good." Athan gives me a toothy grin.

My eyes sharpen on him.

"Serious. I still have a bottle of that fast-acting ointment in my room from the last one. So, no worries."

"Fine. We're done for the night then," I announce, raising my voice for the others. "Everyone back to the barracks. No reports tonight. Get cleaned up and get some sleep. Training in the morning." There's a wave of grumbles, but I ignore it. "I'll inform the king in the morning. Guards can double patrol until then."

No one argues further.

"As for you," I point to Ravenna with a stern finger. "I'm taking you to the nearest cold-handed magic-wielder with a bone needle and a bad attitude."

She whirls on me. "You take me to someone with cold hands, I'm stabbing you with my *cold* blade."

"Careful, Princess. That almost sounded like flirting… with an officer no less," Athan chuckles as he walks past us with a sly smirk.

I step into her space. "Now *go.*"

She mumbles something very unprincessly under her breath as she turns on her heel and stomps off.

As we pass through the iron gates of the city, the flickering street lanterns cast long shadows across the cobblestone. It feels too calm, too quiet. Like the world is pretending nothing just happened.

"So, those little shits haven't been sighted in months." Athan tosses his hammer over his shoulder as he strolls by my side.

"I know," I reply. "We'll be increasing night watch immediately."

"Goody. Sounds fun. Anything else?"

I shake my head, and Athan gives me a quick pat on my

back as he shuffles ahead with Talon and Miles.

We make our way up the main road leading straight to the castle gates. Ravenna keeps her distance from me, and her scowl deepens as it flashes toward Zavier, who trails a couple of feet to her left with a smug arch in his brow and a slow flick of his tongue across his bottom lip, like he's savoring something.

I let out a warning cough to him and the look vanishes in an instant. His gaze darts away, replaced with his usual hangdog slouch, eyes fixed on the ground.

My jaw tightens, fingers curling slightly at my sides. I don't say anything, but I don't look away from him either.

"Back the fuck off, Codrin," Ravenna hisses under her breath, her eyes narrowing on me over her shoulder. Her voice is sharp, quiet, for only me to hear. "I'll deal with him later."

I blink at her, caught off guard.

That tone. That choice of words. The fire behind them.

Something happened. Something bad.

I know her and Zavier have some history, but it's nothing to write home about. But I don't think Ravenna knows that I know. As for tonight, this is something new, and it's driving me insane wondering what the hells happened between the two of them. Either way, as the captain, I need to make sure things don't get out of hand. I make a mental note to talk to her about just kee-ping her distance from Zavier. This will be the last time I group them up on patrols as well.

When we reach the main castle gates, the guards posted at the entrance snap to attention.

"Slatier demons," I tell them quietly. "Twenty or more. We took care of half or so but there were too many. Spread out beyond the tree line. Patrol routes need to double for the next forty-eight hours. Remind the inner wall watch to keep runners on rotation."

The guards nod, their faces paling just slightly.

I know some of these guards rarely, if ever, have dealt with demons. But what do they expect when the kingdom is just miles from the Nothingness Forest?

Athan, Miles, and Zavier break off toward the barracks as we cross the courtyard. Athan gives me a nod of respect, Miles following close behind. Zavier keeps his head low, saying nothing.

Good. I'll deal with him tomorrow.

I turn and cross the courtyard where the Rosewyn twins stand, waiting beneath the torch-lit tower entrance. Ravenna doesn't wait for me as she turns her back and makes her way inside, cradling her injured arm.

Talon waits, only to chuckle under his breath as I near.

"What?" I try to hide my tone of annoyance, already suspecting what he's going to say.

"You really know how to piss her off don't you," Talon says as I follow him into the castle.

Ravenna is already halfway down the corridor, her footsteps echoing angrily off the stone.

"Maybe if she wasn't so damn stubborn, I wouldn't come off as such an ass to her," I mumble under my breath just as Ravenna shoots a narrow eye at me over her shoulder. *Shit.*

"I think she heard you," Talon leans in to whisper.

"Hm…"

My eyes don't leave her back as we make our way down the large empty corridor. The castle has such a different feel at night after everyone has gone to bed, except the few night shift guards who clink past us in their polished silver armor, their sky-blue capes flowing behind them as though carried on a ghost breeze. The iron sconces hold flickering candles along the walls.

Talon veers off toward the main stairs with a quick wave and mouths, *"Good luck."*

"Thanks," I deadpan, already dreading what's next.

I quicken my steps to catch up to his sister, who still hasn't said one word.

"You doing okay?" I ask as I walk at her side.

She gives me a side glare with a deep exhale. "I'm fine, Codrin." Irritation laces her voice.

"Are you going to tell me what happened out there?" I press.

She stops in her tracks, her eyes blazing up at me. "Well, as far as I could tell, we were ambushed by Slatier demons."

"That's not what I mean, and you know it," I snap, more than I mean to as I turn to face her. "I am your captain, and I have a right to know what's going on with everyone in my squad."

"There are just some things you don't need to know, *Captain*," she says, spitting the last word at me.

My fingers curl into fists at my side as I try to not let her snappy attitude get under my skin.

Silence settles around us as we stand off, waiting to see who'll cave first. Her icy blue eyes blaze straight into me, straight into my very soul. Even the shadows seem to shrink up the walls, keeping their distance from the rising tension.

I've known Princess Ravenna Rosewyn for over seven years. And ever since King Zephyr threw her into the Slayer Squad five years ago, the only woman in a squad of twenty men, I've seen what she's really made of. She's not some pampered noble with an axe. She's got fire. More than any of us sometimes. I don't blame her for it.

It's not just being her captain that makes me protective of her though. There's something else. A pull I can't explain. Maybe it's sympathy. Maybe it's more. All I know is, I want to be the one who catches her before she ever hits the ground.

"How's your shoulder?" I finally ask, letting the subject drop.

"It's fine," she hisses through her teeth.

Stubborn.

We continue down the corridor and veer left, passing large tapestries of gods and goddesses bound to their elements. A guard nods as he walks past.

At the end of the hall, a wooden door hangs open. The soft clatter of movement and low voices drift from within.

Ravenna quickens her pace, but I'm right on her heels as we step inside.

The room opens wide, rows of beds line the far wall, privacy curtains half-drawn between them. Cabinets stretch along the left side, and a door at the back leads into other chambers.

One of the binders has her back to us, standing on her toes to reach the top shelf of a cabinet. Her red robes mark her as a blood-hand, skilled in poison extraction and handling major blood loss. Not what Ravenna needs.

I scan the room.

A male binder with dark brown hair and dark blue robes strolls past. Demon wounds. Perfect.

"Hey, Zeek," I call out. "Where's Irk?"

Ravenna stops and spins to face me, her brows drawing tight.

I shrug. "Told you."

Zeek eyes Ravenna's cradled arm, then glances back at me. "He's in the back. Anything I can help you two with?"

Ravenna's mouth opens to speak but I'm faster.

"No offense, but I'd rather Irk take a look at her shoulder."

Ravenna's mouth snaps shut.

Zeek grins, too knowingly. "Got it." He disappears through the back door.

"I am *not* seeing Irk," Ravenna growls.

I lean down to eye level, a wicked grin tugging at my mouth. "Oh, yes, you are."

She runs her tongue along the inside of her cheek, her lower lip bulging slightly. Holding back whatever smartass remark is about to erupt.

The door creaks open again, and Zeek steps back into the room, followed closely by Irk.

The old binder moves with the calm authority of someone who's spent a lifetime elbow-deep in blood and bone. His dark brown skin is weathered with age, creased in deep lines around eyes that haven't missed a thing in decades.

His hair is mostly white now, with only faint streaks of original brown left. A sharp white mustache and goatee frame his mouth, and despite the years, there's still muscle in his tall frame, more than enough to wrestle a slayer down if he has to.

His dark eyes flick between the two of us like he's already tired of whatever drama just walked through the door.

"You gonna keep standing there bleeding, or can I get on with my night?" He strides to one of the beds and stops at the foot of it, arms crossed, waiting.

I place my hands on Ravenna's shoulders and lean in. "Have fun."

"I hate you," she mutters and jabs her elbow into my stomach.

I grunt, trying to recover before either of them notices, but too late. Zeek chuckles. Even the blood-hand girl across the room smirks.

"So, what happened this time?" Irk asks, dragging a cart of supplies closer as Ravenna slumps onto the bed.

"Just another encounter with a lovely demon," she grumbles, flopping back with a grunt.

"No need to get hissy with me, Princess," Irk says, not even looking at her yet. "I've seen worse attitudes sewn into corpses."

Irk rolls up his sleeves with a grunt and grabs a cloth from the cart. "Off with the pauldron. Unless you want me to cut it off." He reaches for a set of tools without waiting for her to comply.

Ravenna sighs through her nose, unbuckling the straps with one hand while keeping her gaze fixed on anything *but* him. She tosses the leather armor behind her, and it falls to the po-lished white marble floor.

He presses his fingers around the torn edges of her shoulder, shifting the fabric of her sleeve aside. The moment his cold fingers touch the wound, her jaw flexes, just for a second, but she doesn't flinch.

"I haven't seen claw marks like these in a while," Irk says, more to himself than anyone else.

Ravenna's voice is clipped. "We were ambushed."

He grunts again, eyes narrowing as he presses along the gashes. "You're lucky this is all that happened."

She grits her teeth, keeping still. She refuses to show pain, but her eyes flick to mine, steady and defiant as if daring me to look away. I don't.

Irk doesn't either. "You planning to hover all night," he asks without looking up, "or let me do my job?"

Before I can answer, Ravenna chimes in flatly. "He can stay. You might need to tend to him after."

Irk raises a brow, gives me a slow once-over. "He doesn't look injured."

"Yet," Ravenna snaps back, flashing me a tight, smug little grin.

Irk lets out a low chuckle, more gravel than sound. "Alright, shirt off. I'm going to need to stitch some of these."

Ravenna's grin widens, eyes flicking toward me with wicked delight as her fingers slip to the hem of her shirt.

She grabs the edge and starts to pull it up, slow, unapologetic, her gaze locked on mine.

Just as the fabric rises to the edge of her chest, I whip around, turning my back with a muttered curse.

A heartbeat later, something soft smacks my back. I glance down to see her balled-up shirt at my heels.

Behind me, I hear Irk moving tools around on his tray without pause.

"Make yourself useful, Captain," he says, not even looking up. "Grab those scissors over there."

I clear my throat and step forward, eyes on the table, doing everything in my power not to turn around.

I reach for the scissors but stay exactly where I am.

A pause.

"I'm going to need you to turn around, Captain," Irk drawls. "Unless you plan on tossing them over your shoulder and risk taking out the princess's eye. Even your aim can't be that good."

Shit.

I slowly turn, breath hitching the moment my eyes land on her.

She's seated sideways on the edge of the bed, torso bare save for the bra hugging her chest, simple, unforgiving and infuriatingly perfect.

But my mind snaps backward.

Two years ago, I charged into this same wing with her limp in my arms, bleeding and broken. Myself covered in her own blood.

Wound binders, blood-hand binders, even field binders rushed toward me, wrenching her from my grasp as I stood frozen. Watching helplessly as they hauled her into the back room. I stood there motionless, bleeding from wounds I didn't remember getting. I barely even remember Talon and Athan being there with me.

Hours passed before Irk emerged from the back, his expression grim but calm. "She'll survive," he said.

We'd been ambushed by Slatier demons then too. But that time was worse. One of them nearly sliced her open from chest to hip. The binders stitched her back together. Gave her a tonic that kept her in a deep sleep for almost six months while she healed.

But I never left her side.

Every day, I sat beside her bed. Every night, I held her hand and rested my head on her mattress, whispering prayers to gods I didn't believe in.

Now she sits before me, strong, stubborn and alive. No scar cuts down her torso. Got to love magic sometimes. No trace of how close I came to losing her. Just smooth, pale skin and a silver braid slung over her shoulder, bloodied but breathing.

She knows.

She remembers.

Just one glance and a twitch of her lips, that almost-smile and I know she hasn't forgotten.

I've fought demons. Survived wars. Endured the king's wrath.

But nothing. *Nothing* has undone me like this woman has.

"Some time tonight would be nice," Irk snaps, jerking me back to reality.

"Right." I step closer and hold out the scissors, jaw clenched tight, doing my damndest to keep my eyes on her shoulder.

Irk grabs them, and the blade snips through the thread with a quiet snap.

Now that I'm facing her, I can't bring myself to turn around, to look away from Irk's steady hands sewing the edges of her wound back together. My cheeks burn. And Ravenna's eyes, godsdamn it, they never leave me.

Irk makes another stitch and cuts.

I don't look down, not fully, but I still see her in the corner of my eye. The curve of her chest rising and falling with each breath, steady and controlled despite the pain. Her fingers curl tightly into the thin blanket beneath her, knuckles pale, every time Irk presses into a deeper gash.

I keep still. Keep breathing through clenched teeth. Try not to notice the tremble that runs through her each time the needle sinks in. Before I even realize it, my hand creeps forward, reaching for hers. Trying to offer some measure of comfort as the needle pierces her skin again. But I wrench them both behind my back and clasp them together so tightly my knuckles ache.

Fifteen minutes feels like a lifetime.

And then Irk finally exhales and sets the needle and scissors aside.

He pulls a small clay jar from the tray, pops the lid, and scoops out a thick, pearlescent cream that glows faintly in the candlelight. It smells clean and sharp but strange, like cooled steel and crushed herbs.

"This'll burn a little," he mutters, smoothing it gently over the stitched wounds. "But it's the good kind of burn."

Ravenna flinches slightly. "It always is," she mutters through gritted teeth.

I know that cream. We all do. Every slayer knows that smell. Knows what it means.

It was developed by the castle mages under King Zephyr's

orders years ago, designed specifically for the slayer ranks. A potent, fast-acting healing salve brewed with magic and mage-blood infusions. Cuts that should take weeks to close are reduced to days. Sometimes less than one. The king made damn sure his slayers could be patched up and thrown right back into the fight by morning.

Irk doesn't bother explaining. He just nods to the jar. "You know the drill."

Ravenna reaches out and takes it, still holding back a wince. "I know."

"Apply it again in the morning. And at night. For a week," Irk says, covering the stitched wounds with bandages. "You'll be sore, but you'll be good by morning."

Ravenna nods once. "Got it."

Irk gives a satisfied grunt, wiping his hands on a cloth. Tossing the cloth onto the cart, he wheels it away without another word, the tools clinking softly as he disappears through the back door.

I bend down, grab her discarded shirt off the floor, and toss it at her without warning. It smacks her square in the face.

"Get your shirt back on," I mutter.

She yanks the fabric off with a scowl and a dramatic sigh. "You could've *handed* it to me, jackass."

I raise a brow. "Figured you could handle worse."

As she slips the shirt over her head, she shoots me a wicked grin. "Don't pretend you didn't enjoy seeing the girls."

I turn toward a tray of tools on the side table to hide the heat creeping into my face. "You're insufferable."

"I try." She turns, tugging the shirt down over the bandages.

She shifts on the bed, leaning to the side and reaching down, her head hanging over the edge, one arm stretched out toward the floor, fingers clawing for her pauldron.

"Seriously, Ravenna. Do you have to make everything so difficult?" I huff, watching her struggle. Her face reddens as blood rushes to it. Her fingers barely graze the leather.

"I got it," she insists, still reaching.

I stomp around the bed and lean down at the same time she manages to hook her fingers through the strap. She yanks it up just as I reach for it.

She sits back upright, armor in hand, smug as ever. "See?" she says, smirking like she just won a battle.

I roll my eyes. "You're impossible."

"Only on days that end with *day*," she quips, slipping the pauldron into her lap.

I let out a long breath and jerk my chin toward the door. "Let's go, Princess Trouble."

"Sure thing, Captain Annoying."

She hops off the bed without missing a beat, her steps light, almost victorious, as she moves past me and out into the corridor.

I follow, slower, more out of habit than choice.

Gods, she's infuriating. Stubborn, reckless, mouthy as all seven hells. And yet somehow…

Still, the only thing that feels like solid ground.

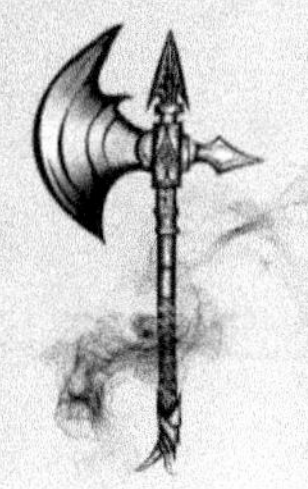

CHAPTER 3

Ravenna

"**G**ood morning, Princess."

Colette's soft, familiar voice stirs me from a restless sleep. I blink open one eye to find her gliding into the room, a silver tray balanced in her hands, steam curling from the coffee kettle. The clink of porcelain and the subtle scent of honey and citrus fill the air as she makes her way to the small table by the fireplace.

Short and slightly round, Colette moves with the quiet efficiency of someone who's done this a thousand times before, her humming gentle, like a lullaby meant to coax me into the day.

"Did you sleep well?" she asks, pouring coffee with care. "Looks like another beautiful morning. Best enjoy it before the sun becomes unbearable."

I groan and throw an arm over my face. Sunshine is the last thing I want.

With a heavy heart and a pounding head, I sink deeper into the mattress, trying to ignore her cheerful voice. Colette has been with me since I was in a swaddling cloth. Though older than my mother, kinder too, she is warmth and steel, sass and sense. The only woman in this castle who ever truly felt like home.

I hear her cross to the window. The scrape of curtain rings

precedes a flood of golden light. I hiss and pull a pillow over my face.

"Your father wants a word with you before training," she says casually, as if the words weren't laced with dread.

Another groan escapes me, this one more guttural. My father. First thing in the morning. Of course. As if I hadn't had enough of him lately. Maybe I can use my injured shoulder as an excuse to skip the day altogether, but even I know it isn't bad enough to justify that. And training is the least of my problems.

"What is it this time? A royal decree? A scolding? Or did Father finally fall off his high horse?" I mutter from beneath the pillow.

Colette laughs, the sound soft and musical. She moves to the wardrobe, her deft fingers selecting my usual black training gear. "You won't know unless you go see him," she says, hanging the clothes neatly over the back of the chair near the hearth.

I peek out just enough to glare at her.

She doesn't flinch. Instead, she strolls over and yanks the pillow from my grip, tossing it aside. "Eat breakfast, my dear. I'll return shortly."

Once she leaves, I sit up with a reluctant sigh, letting my feet hang over the bed. No matter how much I want to stay curled up in bed, Colette always manages to get me moving.

My shoulder aches, a dull, tight pull under the skin where the gashes were. The muscle is still healing, but the sharpness is gone. Just tension now, like something mended but not forgotten.

I peel the bandage back, wincing slightly as it tugs my skin. The stitches are gone. Quickly dissolved overnight like Irk said they would. What's left behind are thin, angry lines already beginning to scar.

I reach for the small jar of cream on the bedside table, unscrew the lid, and smooth the cool salve across the marks. The cool cream stings but fades quickly, replaced by a faint warmth.

Pushing off the bed, I stand, rolling my shoulder once, testing it. Still tight. But manageable. I make my way over to the tray Colette left.

The smell of warm biscuits, spiced sausage, and fresh eggs should have been comforting. But it only turns my stomach.

I pick up the cup of coffee she poured, watching the steam rise in elegant spirals. The sharp, dark, almost bitter scent of wakefulness in liquid form tickles my nose. I take a sip, letting the warmth spread through my chest, but it does little to settle the nausea curling in my gut.

Making my way across the room, I settle in front of the window. My room sits high in the tower. Overlooking the courtyard and town. But my gaze shifts beyond the main gates of Theiahold and passes the open fields until they merge into the forest. In daylight, the Nothingness Forest seems peaceful, almost as though it's sleeping. Calm, like you could take a stroll through the trees and enjoy their beauty.

Yeah, that's never happening. As I watch, several trees move from one spot to another. A warning that this damn forest never sleeps. That no one is safe when entering the Nothingness. Even though most of its creatures hide or sleep, or whatever the hells they do during the day as they wait patiently for the sun to set and the night to take control, there are still creatures who roam the forest grounds in sunlight. Hiding in the darkest of shadows, waiting for any mortal who dares enter to pass by.

Fog covers the mountains of Nivalis Requiem Summit. Its perpetually snow-covered, rocky tops peak high over the trees. Just the look of that place sends a cold shiver down my spine.

Turning away from the window, I turn my mind to other things. More comforting things. Like the way Codrin looked at me last night. The way his jaw clenched every time Irk pressed down too hard on my shoulder. How he wouldn't meet my eyes—except for when he did and then couldn't look away fast enough.

I chuckle at the memory and make my way back to the small table, setting the cup down with more force than necessary. As if things aren't already tangled enough with Zavier's violent posturing and my parents parading suitors before me like it's some royal sport.

Appetite gone, I push the tray aside. The day's barely begun, and already, I want it to be over.

Half an hour later, there's a knock at my door. Quickly slipping on my boots, I rush to the door, a smile materializing on my face to greet Colette, only for it to drop before it even fully forms.

"Oh, it's you." My shoulders drop, and I walk away from the door, leaving it open for Madame Adelaide. "What do you want?"

"I am here on behalf of your father. He requests to speak with you. Or have you forgotten since Colette told you earlier?" she snaps, her lips pressing into a sharp, pale line.

"I didn't forget. Just thought Colette was coming back. I can walk myself down a corridor to the library. I think I still remember where it is." I tap my finger to my chin as though trying to think hard.

"Mind you, a princess does not snap off to their elders." Her eyes scan me up and down. Her lip curls as if the very sight of me leaves a bitter taste in her mouth. She never liked the idea of a *princess* joining the Slayer Squad. However, she would never speak aloud against my father's orders for me to join.

It's not like I had a choice in that matter.

I drop my arms to my side, rolling my eyes. Our father's head housekeeper is an ever-present force, like a storm cloud that never quite clears the sky. Always looming, always watching.

Her expression remains as blank as ever, masking everything but the coldness in her dark green eyes. "Follow me, Princess." She turns on her heel, her nose in the air.

I roll my shoulders back, forcing myself to appear unbothered, though the uneasy feeling creeping up my spine tells a different story. Closing my bedroom door behind me, I follow her.

My mother is strict, but Madame Adelaide is worse. A relentless enforcer of propriety, etiquette, and tradition. She's had it out for me since childhood, always seeking opportunities to catch me misbehaving, being "unladylike." My place among the slayers? Just more fuel to the fire.

I keep my gaze locked on her back as we make our way down the steps to the main floor, noting the tight bun atop her head, white from age but not a single strand out of place.

Her crisp sky-blue servant's dress and pristine white apron put my always-tangled silver braid and usually sweat-streaked training leathers to shame.

"Why does Father want to see me?" My voice comes out steadier than I feel.

Madame Adelaide doesn't stop, doesn't even glance my way.

My composure wavers. I try to maintain my mask of calm indifference, but beneath it, my heart kicks against my ribs.

I fidget with the edge of my sleeve, hoping it quells the knots tightening in my stomach, twisting into something far worse than fear itself.

Father never requests to see me. Or Talon.

When he summons us, it's with the Slayer Squad. Always for orders. More night patrols. Training reports. Recruitment demands.

But never me. Never alone.

Madame Adelaide stops so suddenly that I nearly slam into her back.

"When the king requests to speak with you," she hisses, her eyes sharp as thorns, "you nod your head like a lady and do not question it." Her hands clasp tightly together as she rolls her shoulders back, posture as stiff as ever.

I nod, more to be a smartass than anything, as she turns away, continuing down the corridor.

"Such an ungrateful, brat," she mutters, just loud enough for me to hear.

I stick my tongue out at her.

Making our way down the corridor in silence, the morning sunlight streaming through the floor-to-ceiling windows, casting long golden beams across the stone floors. A gentle breeze stirs against my damp skin. We reach the library's massive doors. Dark wood carved with ancient runes. The weight of my father's presence crushing me before I even step inside.

Madame Adelaide pauses, then pushes the heavy door open. She snaps her fingers at me, motioning me forward.

Anticipation spirals in my gut. Unease slithers beneath my skin. I straighten my back, force a thin smile, and step through the threshold.

The door clicks shut behind me, sealing me inside.

The musty aroma of aged leather and parchment wraps around

me, thick and suffocating. My footsteps echo softly as I move deeper into the library, my eyes adjusting to the unusual dimness.

The thick curtains, normally left open to welcome daylight, are drawn tight, smothering the room in shadows. A shiver snakes down my spine, my gaze drifting toward the darkened corners where the candlelight does not reach.

Something feels off.

My eyes flick upward. The second-floor balcony, usually a place of quiet study, is shrouded in darkness. As if the room itself is hiding secrets, unwilling to reveal them to the outside world.

The only source of light comes from two towering candlesticks near the desk, their glow faint and flickering, casting twisted shadows across the walls.

I scan the room. My father is nowhere in sight.

With a slow inhale, I move toward his once-meticulously organized desk, now cluttered with books and scattered parchments.

Frowning, I lean over the desk, squinting in the dim light. My gaze catches on a rough sketch scrawled across aged parchment, the words scribbled beside it speaking of an ancient gemstone, lost to time.

I lift another parchment, this one stealing my breath. A weathered sketch of a three-headed hellhound, its massive maws dripping with blood. Dread coils in my gut.

A low, deep voice shatters the silence. "Your father is not here, Princess."

I jolt back, the parchment slipping from my fingers as I whirl toward the shadows. Quickly composing myself, I narrow my eyes at the far side of the room. "Where is he, then? I was told he would be here."

I already know the answer before the figure even steps forward.

Lord Bartholomew Mastro.

My father's right-hand man. His grand vizier. The one he always sends in his place.

Of course, Father isn't here. He never is.

"He had other important matters to attend to." Bartholomew's nasally voice drifts through the cavernous room, bouncing off the towering shelves.

I crane my neck, scanning the second level, searching the shadows. A scoff slips past my lips. "More important than speaking with his daughter?" How disappointing, but not surprising.

Father will do anything to avoid speaking with his own children.

I cross my arms over my chest, exhaling sharply through my nose. I don't even care that the action makes me look like a sulking child.

Bartholomew shifts. The movement is off, not where I expect it.

My brows furrow. "Well," I sigh, dropping my arms. "If my father is too busy to speak to me, then I'll discuss this matter with him later." I turn toward the library doors, already done with this conversation.

"You are set to wed the King of Veilstead."

The words slam into me.

My steps falter. My lungs rebel, refusing air.

"Veilstead?" My voice trembles despite myself as I pivot back toward the darkened library. The kingdom that sits on the other side of Nivalis Requiem Summit? What the actual fuck?! A kingdom where the sun never shines and its cold and always snows there.

Bartholomew emerges from the spiral staircase, arms heavy with books. He moves with calm indifference, as if his words aren't currently shattering my world.

"Yes." He sets the books onto the desk, barely sparing me a glance.

I curse under my breath.

"But why?" The question escapes me before I can stop it, my arms flying out at my sides.

That kingdom has been at war with us for nearly two hundred years. Since the rise of darkness. It was only a little under eighty years ago, they finally withdrew their forces. But not before razing the surrounding lands of Theiahold.

My great-great-grandfather once ruled over seven kingdoms. Now? Only three remain. And that includes Theiahold.

And even with the northern threat gone, we are far from safe.

Dark magic still seeps into the land. Creatures of nightmares still prowl the Nothingness Forest miles beyond our borders. That is why the Royal Demon Slayers exist.

To fight back against the horrors that refuse to die.

"King Alaric Vyrenhartmir has agreed to your hand in marriage to unite the kingdoms." Bartholomew delivers the words as if discussing the weather.

He opens a book, flipping through the pages. Casual. Unconcerned.

My entire body goes cold. I stumble back, my boot catching a pile of books. My heart pounds. My breath shallows.

I drop to my knees, stacking the books clumsily. My hands grip the last one too tightly, knuckles white as I glare at Bartholomew.

"This has been made official as of last month, Princess."

My breath halts.

A month?

They looked me in the eye at dinner every night for a whole month and didn't bother mentioning they'd promised me to a monster?

Bartholomew sets a book down with a deep sigh, stepping toward me, his sharp, polished boots echoing against the library walls.

When his hands land on my shoulders, my skin practically crawls. His sky-blue eyes, so bright against his dark brown skin, search mine with feigned sympathy.

I rip away from his grasp.

"Don't touch me." My voice shakes, but I straighten my spine, chin lifting. "I will not marry this monster."

Bartholomew looms over me, unmoving. His eyes darken, almost black in the firelight, glinting like polished onyx.

"Oh, but you will, Princess." He adjusts the cuff of his sleeve with practiced ease, his expression calm, unreadable. "You will, indeed. It is your duty, not just as a princess, but as the key to securing this kingdom's future. This marriage will bring unity, strength. It will ensure Theiahold's survival."

My lip curls. "That's what this is all about? For my father to gain more power." Anger rises like fire in my chest. "We know this king isn't even mortal. He's a blood-sucking killer."

"*Enough.*" Bartholomew sighs, turning his back to me, scratching at the short hairs of his goatee. His dark brown and black attire is pristine, perfectly fitted. Controlled. Just like him. "You and King Alaric are to be wed, whether you like it or not."

He barely spares me a glance as he shuffles through the parchments on the desk.

My stomach twists. I feel like my heart has been ripped from my chest. My words die in my throat, but my mind races.

How dare my father decide my fate without so much as a warning. Without facing me himself. Of course he wouldn't. Of course, he sent Bartholomew to do his dirty work.

Because my father is a coward. And *he knew* I would never accept this.

I tighten my grip on the book in my hand, the hard spine biting into my palm. I want to hurl it at Bartholomew's head, wipe that uncaring look off his face. But he doesn't even glance at me.

Instead, he waves me off. "That is all. You are dismissed."

Without another word, he vanishes into the shadows of the library.

Frozen in place, my gaze fixates on the empty space where Bartholomew stood. I always knew it was my duty to marry for political gain. But this? Not only is my father marrying me off, but he's throwing me into the clutches of a monster.

A vampire. A king no one has seen in over one hundred years. And for what? Power.

That fucking bastard. Tears blur my vision, but my rage burns hotter, hurling the book across the room. It slams into the shelf where Bartholomew disappeared, toppling smaller tomes with a sharp thud.

But it isn't enough. None of this is enough. They planned this. All of them.

My father. My mother. Bartholomew. Even that old bitch, Madame Adelaide. They plotted behind my back. They knew I would refuse.

Of course I refuse!

I grab another book, chucking it across the room. The pages tear from the spine, scattering like dead leaves.

The Veilstead king is a monster.

And now?

I belong to him.

"I. AM. NOT. SOMEONE. YOU CAN PAWN OFF!" I scream as I hurl another book.

Then another. And another.

But no matter how many books I throw, Bartholomew remains hidden from sight.

My breathing is ragged, shallow.

"This is my life." The words come out as a choked whisper.

But still no response. Bartholomew is gone. His absence sending my rage into a downward spiral.

I seize a pile of parchments from the desk and rip them from their stacks, scattering them across the library like fallen leaves.

Without thinking, I storm toward the double doors. Throwing them open, I spin back just long enough to unleash my fury.

"You're a fucking coward, Bartholomew!" My scream shatters the heavy silence.

I slam the door behind me, the sound echoing violently down the corridor.

I press my back against the wood, gasping. My lungs strain for air.

My body feels like it's on fire. Sweat drips from my brow. My chest tightens as a suffocating darkness closes in around me.

Bells chime in the distance, reminding me of the hour.

Shit! Now I'm late for training.

My heart drops, unexpectedly to the pit of my stomach to the thought of facing Codrin. I can't find the strength in me to tell him what my father has planned.

Pushing off the door, I quicken my steps, but not fast enough to rush to training. The longer I can delay going, the better.

CHAPTER 4

Ravenna

"Rosewyn! Get your shit together! Or I'll have you running laps the rest of the day."

My teeth grind together as I resist the urge to throw my axe at Codrin. He's been snapping at me throughout most of our training, and right now, it's taking every ounce of self-control not to snap back.

Last night, he was making lovesick eyes at me, and today, he's got the rage of a thunderstorm in those gray eyes of his. Talk about a mind fuck. It seems Codrin's the one who needs to get his *"shit together."*

Then again, I really shouldn't be bitching. He's the captain of the *Royal* Slayer Squad. *My captain.* And here I am the damn princess whose father owns this squad. There's no winning this. Codrin and I can't act on how we feel for each other — if there are any feelings left between us at all.

"Your stance is all off. You are such a thorn in my ass, Rosewyn." He grumbles, running a quick hand through his messy dark auburn hair, the sharp lines of his heart-shaped face only making him look more annoyed. And that ever-present five o'clock shadow gives him an older yet aggravating look.

"Oh, trust me, Captain. You'd know if I was in your ass." I

smile and wink, twirling my axe, I launch at him again, but...d*amn it.*

He chuckles through a toothy grin, and I swear I see a slight sparkle graze his gray eyes as he smoothly side-steps, proving his point with infuriating ease.

I exhale sharply through my nose, glaring daggers at him. Two hours. Two miserable, sweat-soaked hours in this blistering heat, and I still can't land a solid hit on him. The somewhat cool breeze rolling in from the sea does little to ease the sweat trickling down my spine. The muscles in my right shoulder burn.

Half the Slayer Squad is already lounging in the shade, cooling off after their sparring round with Codrin. Meanwhile, I'm stuck here unable to focus, and a part of me just wants to scream. To tear down the walls of this castle stone by stone until someone listens. Until someone understands I'm not some pawn to be passed off between kings like a bargaining chip. I want to fight. Gods, I need to fight. But the reality is cold and sharp: this isn't just about me anymore. It's about Theiahold. About survival. Power.

But what if there's some truth to what Bartholomew said? That my marriage to King Alaric will protect the realm?

And who am I to challenge that? A princess, yes, but still just a daughter expected to obey. Expected to bow, smile, and seal an alliance with her vows.

But what if I don't?

What if I run?

Would it even matter? Could I truly escape the reach of two kings, one mortal, one immortal, and the weight of their expectations?

Or worse… would I doom my kingdom just to save myself?

Because maybe the real fear isn't losing my freedom…

Maybe it's realizing that I never had a choice to begin with.

"Focus," Codrin barks as he points his sword at me, yanking me from my thoughts. His sun-kissed skin glistens with sweat as he shifts into a defensive stance.

I wipe the salty sweat from my upper lip with the back of my sleeve, squinting against the sun's relentless glare. The black leather of my uniform clings to me like a second skin, trapping heat like a furnace.

End me. End me now.

Just throw me to the demons.

Whose brilliant idea was it to make these uniforms completely unbreathable?

Letting out a slow, hot breath, I force a smile and take a sidestep, searching for an opening. "I would focus better if you would keep that hole in your face shut," I say, dancing my brows up and down.

Codrin's gaze sharpens, reading my movements before I even make them.

I twirl my axe. Gripping the handle, I square my stance, locking on Codrin. My silent challenge is clear. *"Make a move, Captain. I dare you."*

He doesn't. He just holds his stance effortlessly, fluid and unreadable. *Damn it,* he's been doing this longer than I have. Six years longer, to be exact. Of course, his form is flawless. Of course, he moves like a lethal extension of his weapon.

I roll my eyes. And, of course, he takes his role as our captain way too seriously.

"Come on, Ravenna! Take him down!" Athan's voice rings from the sidelines, followed by cheers from our teammates on the opposite end. Even Codrin's closest friend is rooting for me, not him.

Codrin's jaw ticks. His stone-cold glare flicks toward Athan, warning him to shut up. His attention snaps back to me.

"Prove me wrong, then." His low, gravelly challenge is accompanied by a slow, deliberate stroke of his fingers along the stubble of his jaw. A smirk tugs at his lips.

Cocky bastard.

Fine. Let's play.

I circle him, muscles coiled, breath tight in my chest. The sparring area feels smaller than usual, as if the air itself is waiting for me to fail, yet again. My arms ache from the last few rounds, each strike from him landing like iron against bone.

Codrin stands tall, relaxed, with that ever-present certainty in his storm-cloud eyes. He's always been quicker. Stronger. Better.

But not today.

I feint left, drawing him into the movement. He takes the bait, his blade slicing through empty air where I should've been. I twist at the last second, my shoulder screaming, but I ignore it as the world narrows to the rhythm of my feet on packed earth, the hiss of breath in my lungs. Then I drop low.

My leg sweeps out, fast and clean, catching him mid-step.

For a heartbeat, time stutters.

His balance falters, eyes widening, just a flicker, just enough. And then gravity claims him.

He hits the ground hard, the breath knocked from his lungs, his back flat against the dirt.

Silence follows.

The ring around us stills. Even the wind seems to pause.

I stand, panting, sweat trickling down my spine. My hands shake, not from fear, but from something else. From disbelief. From adrenaline. From victory.

Codrin stares up at me, stunned. And slowly, he smiles.

I brace my hands on my knees and lean over him. "Looks like I win this round," I say, offering him my hand, trying to keep my grin in check. "And that's with an injured shoulder."

Codrin lets out a breath, still winded, but a faint smile tugs at his lips. "Glad your shoulder is better. You're getting faster."

"And you're getting slow," I shoot back, fingers closing around his as I help him up.

Our hands linger just a second too long.

He meets my gaze, something unreadable in his eyes. "Or maybe I just let you win."

I snort. "Sure. Keep telling yourself that."

His chest rises and falls in steady breaths, his usual stoic demeanor slightly shaken.

"Excellent work," he murmurs. Towering over me, his gray eyes darken as he raises his hand toward me. For a moment, I think he might stroke my cheek or brush some loose hair aside. I suck in a breath, my stomach taut with anticipation. It hovers awkwardly in the air until he finally pats my shoulder and walks past me.

"I think that's it for today," he calls over his shoulder.

I take in a deep breath and turn toward the sidelines, ready to shake off the match and what I thought was a split second of a moment, when a familiar, nauseating presence steps into my path.

Zavier.

I barely have time to react before his arm snakes around my waist, yanking me into his side.

"Release me, Zavier," I snarl, gripping my axe tightly at my side.

"Relax, Ravenna," he murmurs, his lips too close to my ear. "I was just thinking, maybe we can start where we left off last night." His breath is warm against my skin, his voice dripping with amusement.

A chuckle rumbles from his chest as his lips brush my ear.

Rage rises within me, and in one swift movement, I slam him to the ground. Before he has time to process what happened, I drive my knee between his shoulder blades, pinning him down.

His back coils under the pressure, taut with defiance, like a predator too proud to yield.

Cheers erupt around us. The squad circles in, forming a loose ring, their boots kicking up the dust. Some clap, others whistle, voices blending into a rowdy chant.

"Take him down, Princess!"

"Twist it harder. Make him beg!"

"Damn, Zavier, didn't realize you liked it so rough!"

Laughter ripples through the group.

To them, this is just sport. A friendly brawl between two warriors. Nothing more.

"Five silver says she makes him tap out!" one shouts, crossing his arms with a smirk.

"Oh, please," another slayer scoffs, shaking his head. "He'll wriggle out of it. Ten silvers says he flips her over first."

"You're both idiots," Miles chuckles. "Ravenna's got him pinned like a damn trophy kill."

The others laugh, their cheers fueling the rowdy energy.

But to me? It's not a game.

My fingers tighten around Zavier's wrist, forcing it higher. His arm strains against the unnatural angle, muscles coiling in resistance. He growls and bucks beneath me, his shoulder twisting in a desperate attempt to throw me off.

He nearly succeeds.

My balance slips for a breath but only a breath. I slam my weight back down, knee digging between his shoulder blades, grinding him into the dirt.

I push his arm higher, forcing his muscles to strain. His jaw clenches, teeth grinding as he stifles a wince.

I want to break it.

I want him to feel pain. The same kind of raw, searing pain he's inflicted on me. Harassing me this past month, last night. Not taking a fucking hint.

He was never anything to me. Never a lover. Never a mistake I cared about. Just a drunken miscalculation.

I lean into his ear, hissing through my teeth. "Is this what you had in mind, Zavier?"

My fingers hold his hair in a death grip, driving the side of his face into the dirt. My other hand twists his arm unnaturally up his back, his hand almost to his ear.

He doesn't matter.

Break his arm. The thought slithers through my mind, dark and demanding.

He deserves it.

"Fucking bitch," he spits, fighting harder now, wild and uncoordinated. Rage burns through him, but it's not strength.

It's *fear*. He knows he's losing. I twist his arm higher. His fingers twitch, his shoulder shrieking beneath my grip.

Good.

The squad's cheering fades into the background. The world narrows to just me and him. My heart pounds in my ears. The heat of my rage rises with every passing second, the pulse of something darker, more dangerous, lurking beneath the surface.

"Don't you ever fucking touch me again," I growl.

He bucks one final time, a desperate, furious heave, but I don't budge. I own this moment.

His breath hitches, and for the first time, I feel it: the crack in his armor. The humiliation bleeding through.

He knows he's lost.

I press, and there's a tension, a warning, coiling in his shoulder like a trap about to spring.

Zavier's wincing only steers me closer to the edge.

A little more. Just a little more pressure.

Will he scream?

Pop.

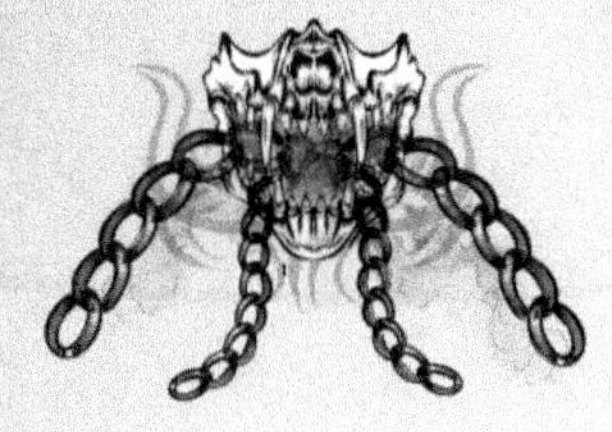

CHAPTER 5

Codrin

"That looked brutal," Athan comments, his brow arching as I near him on the sidelines.

"Yeah, well, last night didn't help. Didn't sleep well," I mutter, massaging my left shoulder. "And will you please put a shirt on?" I throw a hand up.

"I'm working on my tan." Athan laces his fingers behind his head as he settles back against the tree. The chain of his pendant around his neck falls to the side of his massive, heavily muscled chest, marked with subtle scars from countless fights and tattoos that sweep across his chest, shoulders, and arms, symbols of his heritage and battles long past.

"Don't you need to be in the sun for that?" I shake my head, ignoring Athan as my mind drags me back to last night in the binder's wing. Her shoulder torn open, blood on her skin, and me doing everything I could not to reach for her.

She didn't say much, but her eyes said enough.

And I… I was too close. Too aware.

Of her breath. Her pain. The way she still smirked even when stitched together by a grumpy old binder.

She's a princess. I'm the captain of the king's Slayer Squad. That line between us? It's carved in stone, cold and unforgiving.

Letting myself feel anything is a mistake. One that could destroy us both.

And then there's the other reason. The one I don't speak aloud. The one I've buried so deep, it's a wonder it hasn't torn its way to the surface already.

There are truths I can't afford to let her see. Things that would turn everything between us into ash.

So no, it couldn't go further. Even if part of me wanted it more than anything.

"Didn't sleep well? Is that your excuse for my sister kicking your ass?" Talon's words cut off my thoughts.

I shoot Talon a look.

He smirks, shaking his head. Like he knows something he's not saying. I know Ravenna keeps stuff from him. He's too overprotective of her, and he would probably kick my ass if he knew what I really thought of her.

Cheering fills the air from across the field, I look over my shoulder to see just about every slayer circled around, howling and clapping over something.

"What's going on over there?" Talon turns to the crowd.

"Boys being boys I take it." I shrug a shoulder, turning away and sheathing my sword, tossing it to the ground beside Athan.

But Miles's voice cuts through the noise.

"Ravenna's got him pinned like a damn trophy kill."

What?! I whip my gaze to the sideline. No sign of her.

"You have got to be fucking kidding me." I huff, already breaking into a sprint across the field.

I swear, I need to keep a leash on that girl. She's got a fire in her. Reckless when pushed, and too damn proud to back down from a fight.

The others might see wrestling as a game, but if she's throwing someone to the ground, it's not for fun.

And if it's who I think it is…

Hells.

This won't end well.

Pushing through the crowd, I find Ravenna in the center of the circle of slayers, pinning Zavier to the ground on his stomach. She has his arm twisted so far back that she can break it at any second.

"Ravenna!" I shout, my voice lost amid the cheers. "Ravenna! Let him go!"

Everyone is so hyper-focused on the fight before them that no one notices me standing in the center, trying to break it up.

"RAVENNA!" I shout louder.

But she doesn't notice either. Her eyes are dark with rage, her teeth clenched so tight I can see the muscle in her jaw tic.

Fuck!

Without hesitating, I bolt toward her, slamming into her. Not giving her time to react, to register what's happening, I tear her from Zavier, arms wrapping around her waist, locking her in a crushing grip. Too late, if that popping noise was any indication.

We crash into the ground like a war hammer striking stone. Her back smashes into the dirt, my body pinning her down. A sharp gasp rips from my throat as air rushes from my lungs. Dust kicks up around us, and the squad's cheers morph into stunned silence.

For a moment, she freezes, blinking rapidly, breath ragged. Her icy blue eyes dart, unfocused, like she's trying to reorient herself, to make sense of up and down. Then they sharpen. Focus. Narrow.

Her teeth bare, her hands clench into fists. Even as she's still trapped beneath me, she trembles with the instinct to strike.

I grab her wrists and pin them to the side of her head.

Gods, she's still trembling. Not from fear though. No, she's burning with fury.

"Ravenna!" My own blood is boiling over the edge.

Still on top of her, I brace on my forearms, caging her in, my chest heaving. Every muscle is wound so tight it aches.

Her eyes meet mine, and she swallows hard.

My weight pins her down, but the fury behind my eyes holds her still like iron pressed to skin, impossible to move through. My breath saws through clenched teeth.

My jaw grinds. A vein pulses at my temple. Every muscle in my body is wound tight, straining with the effort not to lash out. Not at her, but at the fire she's just lit in me.

She hurt Zavier. And right now, I don't know who I'm more furious with. Her or myself for letting this happen.

I should've seen it coming.

I *knew* something happened between them last night.

But I didn't say a word. Didn't pull Zavier aside. Didn't check on her earlier.

Went straight from the king's damn war meeting to training like it could all wait.

And now here we are.

The squad shuffles around us, realizing this isn't just a playful fight anymore. The chanting dies. Laughter evaporates.

"Get back to the barracks. *Now!*" I bark at them.

Boots scrape against the dirt as bodies shift away. A few exchange glances before making a quiet, hasty retreat. Like prey catching the scent of a predator.

The fire inside me claws for release, hot and wild, but I shove it down, burying it beneath layers of control I'm not sure I can keep much longer. My breath drags in slow, uneven pulls as she lays beneath me. I can tell she's livid and defiant; none-theless, beautiful in a way that only makes it worse for me to even think in such away at this time.

Every part of me is tense, burning with the effort not to lose it. Trying not to say something I'll regret. Not to feel too much.

Long moments crawl past before the fury dulls enough for me

to move. I grip her bicep firmly, maybe too firmly and haul her to her feet. My hand stays there, wrapped tightly around her like I need the contact to ground myself. Like letting go would mean unraveling completely.

Behind me, Talon takes a step forward, his eyes locked on one person.

Zavier.

Zavier has staggered to his feet, with the help of Lucas. He cradles his arm close to his side, his shoulder visibly out of place.

Fuck.

Pain warps his features, but he tries to mask it with a sneer.

A satisfied smirk tugs at Ravenna's lips.

"Crazy bitch," he mutters, low but audible.

Talon steps forward, fists clenched. "Zavier, get the fuck out of here before I finish what she started."

Ravenna rolls her eyes at Talon, a sharp exhale escaping her lips. Her cheeks stay flushed, fury still pulsing just under her skin.

Zavier lifts his good hand in mock surrender, but there's defiance simmering behind his hazel eyes as he backs away. He's injured but far from humbled.

Ravenna takes a hard step forward, but I hold tight, pulling her back. "Lucas, get him to the binders."

Lucas nods and guides Zavier away.

I tug Ravenna's arm, forcing her attention back to me. "What in Hella's fire was that about?" My grip tightens slightly, my fingers digging into her bicep.

She bares her teeth at me. "He deserved it."

"You need to calm down."

Her eyes fly wide. "He was…"

"I don't care," I cut her off, my voice sharper than I mean it to be. But I can't stop now. Not with my heart still pounding and the image of her nearly breaking Zavier's arm burned into my skull. I *do* care, more than I should, but I can't let that show. I'm still her captain. "Control your anger for once."

It's not just about Zavier. She attacked another slayer, in front of the entire squad. That alone could get her hauled in for disciplinary action. And whatever twisted history there is between them, she's keeping it from me. That burns more than I want to admit.

And worse I'm being a damn hypocrite.

Her jaw drops, and her body stiffens in my grasp, as though I physically punched her.

"Fuck you!" She spits the words out like venom, ripping her arm from my grasp.

My shoulders drop, and my voice softens. "I'm sorry. I shouldn't have said that."

She doesn't let me finish.

She pivots hard, her silver braid lashing across my face like a whip. "Spare me the lecture, *Captain*." She doesn't wait for a response. Just walks away, her chin held high. Her steps sharp, like every inch of her is daring me to follow.

I watch her retreat, the words still echoing in my head. Not *Codrin*. Not even *friend*. Just *Captain*. And gods, that one cuts deeper than I care to admit.

Ravenna's pissed, and I deserve it. I did not handle any of this the way I should have. Whatever Zavier did to set her off, the hurt on her face now… that's on me. And somehow, that feels worse.

I follow her and Talon to the shade. Keeping my distance from Ravenna. Giving her enough space to hopefully cool off.

"I swear one of these days I'm going to knock his ass out." Talon stalks over with a waterskin in hand.

Ravenna shoots him a glare through thick, dark lashes. "I don't need you fighting my battles, brother." Her words come through clenched teeth, the lingering anger from Zavier and probably me still boiling under her skin.

Talon ignores her. He arches his brow, his icy blue gaze, a mirror of his twin sister's, drifting past her to me.

I shrug my shoulders in defeat. I'm not going to question her right now.

Ravenna's jaw tightens as she glances back at me, the flicker of accusation in her eyes sharp and brief before she turns back to Talon. She shoves her axe into his arms and snatches the waterskin from his hand. Tilting her head back, she takes a long, deliberate drink.

"Don't get into fights, and maybe neither of us would have to save your ass," Talon mutters, gesturing between himself and me. But his tone isn't biting. It's brittle. Like he's trying to joke through the fear he won't always be able to catch her in time.

"Keep me out of this," I say, raising my hands in surrender.

"Keep you out? You're the one who tackled her like a wild beast." Talon chuckles, shaking his head.

Ravenna's eyes narrow at both of us over the rim of the waterskin. Before she can retort, Talon yanks it from her grip, splashing water across her face.

She sputters, coughing as water runs down her chin and swiping at her face with the back of her sleeve, shooting him a murderous look. "What the hells, Talon!"

Talon snickers, tipping the waterskin to drink.

I cough back a laugh, but Ravenna catches me with a cold glare. I shift uneasily and snatch the waterskin from Talon's hands mid-motion and take a long pull myself.

"Hey!" Talon lunges, but I pivot fast, blocking him with a shoulder.

"Asshole," he mutters under his breath, arms crossing over his chest.

Too busy enjoying the cold water sliding down my throat, I don't notice Ravenna moving, until she punches me square in the stomach.

I double over, choking mid-swallow. Water sprays from my

mouth as I cough and sputter in every direction.

"Oh, shit, Rave!" Talon gasps with a laugh.

Laughter erupts from the few team members nearby, all of them clearly enjoying the show.

"I think he kind of deserved that one, man," Miles calls, slapping his knee, howling.

I don't say a word, just level him with a look that could cut glass. His smile drops instantly, mouth snapping shut as he turns away.

"Get back to the barracks," I bark, coughing out the last of the water. "Or you'll be running laps around the courtyard till nightfall."

Miles and the others bolt without another word, feet pounding against the dirt.

Athan makes his way over, shirt back on, his war hammer gripped in one hand, my sword in the other.

"Looks like she's got you officially beat."

Athan's broad shoulders shake with laughter as he hands me my sword. His dark brown hair pulled back in his signature man-bun, muscles flexing beneath worn training leathers. Always the mountain of the group, towering and solid, but with a grin that makes him less intimidating and more annoyingly charming.

"Yeah, yeah." I straighten, snatch the weapon, and strap it to my waist

"You all think this is funny, don't you?" Ravenna snaps. Arms crossed tightly over her chest, she shifts her weight to one side, brows furrowed deeply. "You have no fucking idea the shit I'm dealing with, and clearly, none of you fucking care."

"What are you talking about? What's going on?" I take a step forward, pulse kicking up as my mind scrambles to make sense of her words.

Ravenna's arms fall to her sides. She storms toward me, closing the space between us. Her mouth opens, ready to unleash everything, but clamps shut again.

"It doesn't matter," she huffs, averting her gaze.

"Ravenna," I take a step forward, concern tightening in my chest. "What's going on?"

All eyes turn to her. Talon takes a cautious step forward, but she sidesteps him without a word.

When her gaze finally lifts to mine, it knocks the breath from my chest. Her icy blue eyes are dull, lifeless, void of that usual fire, and her bottom lip trembles.

"What is it?" Talon presses, stepping closer.

I reach for her hand, and she lets me.

Talon glances at our joined hands, his jaw clenching as he shoots me a sharp glare, but says nothing. I don't care. Right now, it seems Ravenna needs that connection. Something to help ground her to whatever is truly troubling her at this moment.

"Father is marrying me off."

Talon shrugs. "That's nothing new."

But I see it. I see it written all over her face, this isn't just *nothing*, this is *something new*.

She darts her pained gaze to her brother, causing Talon to go rigid.

"To whom?" his eyes soften with concern.

My stomach knots.

Her fingers tighten around mine. Her throat bobs as she swallows.

"King Alaric Vyrenhartmir." Her voice is a whisper, and even saying it aloud makes her flinch, as though the name itself cuts.

"Damn," Athan mutters behind me.

The grounds around us stills. Even the birds fall silent.

"What?!" Talon explodes, arms slicing the air as he starts pacing tight, furious loops, rage rolling off him like heat. "The king of the fucking vampires? Are you serious?!" He grabs a fistful of his hair, pacing harder. "After everything he's done, everything he *is*, how the hells could Father agree to this?"

The air vanishes from my lungs and refuses to return, choking me. My pulse hammers behind my eyes. The familiar name hits like a blade to the gut. I force my face into something unreadable, even as memories I thought were buried claw their way toward the surface.

Not here. Not now.

Ravenna doesn't flinch. Doesn't move. Just stares at the ground, looking like she's trying not to collapse.

The weight of it all hits me like a punch to the chest. Their father has been trying to marry her off for years. And Ravenna, fierce, stubborn, and downright impossible has always found a way to slip the noose. To fight back.

But this?

This isn't something she can outrun.

Not when the cage is gilded in politics and sealed with blood.

Not when the name *Alaric* makes something cold coil around my spine.

She's being given to *him*.

Talon stops pacing and whirls around, his chest rising with a deep inhale. He's trying to rein it in, to stay level.

But I know him too well. That rage is still boiling, just waiting to erupt.

I can't mask the concern etched across my face. I glance at Ravenna and gently squeeze her hand.

"We'll figure something out," I say quietly, offering her anything. *Everything*. To hold on to.

She exhales hard, tilting her head, her eyes narrowing with something frayed and tired. "Really? Like what?"

I shrug. "I'll kidnap you. Take you far away from here. No goodbyes. No looking back."

A grin tugs at my lips, just enough to tease some light back into this moment.

She rolls her eyes, but there it is. That faint pull at the corner of her mouth, a whisper of the Ravenna I know. The one who fights, who never bends.

And gods, I understand now.

Why she went after Zavier like that. Why her fury burned so hot. I'd been so quick to judge, so sure I was right. But I didn't know. I didn't see.

The guilt settles low in my chest, sharp and unrelenting.

Still, I smile back. Pretend the weight isn't there. Because for now, she's still here. And I'll hold on to that for as long as I can.

She squeezes my hand once in return. Then let's go.

And just like that, the smile vanishes.

"It doesn't matter anymore," she murmurs. "I knew I'd have to marry… someone." She hesitates, her voice dropping lower. "I just wish it was with…"

Her words trail off with a slow exhale.

I wait.

I want her to finish. Gods, I want to hear it. The thing I've only let myself imagine be spoken aloud.

But she doesn't. And I bury the hope before it can take root.

There are bigger things at stake now.

Magic lives in every corner of these lands. Some of it pure. Some of it twisted and cruel. The mages here in Theiahold are healers, herbalists, gentle wielders of elemental power. But the magic festering beyond the Nothingness Forest is something else entirely.

The Summit is different. Veilstead isn't just another kingdom. It's a realm swallowed whole by shadow.

And now, her father wants to bring that darkness here.

But why?

I glance at Talon. He's pacing again. Talon's ash-brown hair clings to his furrowed brow, damp with sweat from training and his rising temper. His tall, athletic frame moves with restless energy, every step carving deeper into the dirt beneath his boots.

He's not letting go.

"Tonight, we'll talk more," I say. "For now, let's just take it easy."

"Take it easy? Are you kidding me right now, Codrin?" Talon snaps.

"Talon," Ravenna cuts in, her voice firm. It halts him mid-stride. "Stop. Please."

"There's nothing you can do right now anyway. King Zephyr is holding court all afternoon," I remind him. "Unless you plan to confront him in front of the entire nobility?"

"Why shouldn't I? The prick deserves it."

"You know damn well he'd flay you alive for that insolence. And he'd probably order the binders not to tend your wounds, just to make it hurt even more. You'd be laid up in a sickbed for weeks."

He clenches his jaw, shoves his hands into his pockets, and kicks at the dirt. "Fine," he mutters under his breath.

"Come sit down, take a breather." I reach for her hand again, relieved when she doesn't pull away. Her fingers slide into mine, and I guide her to the shade of a nearby tree.

Talon grabs his sword from the ground and heads out into the middle of the field, Athan follows, hammer slung over his shoulder, a knowing grin on his face as he goes to help a friend burn off some steam. Talon spins his sword, as though bleeding the anger out, once, twice, and they begin their drills. The rhythmic clash of iron cuts through the silence like thunder.

I lean back against the tree as Ravenna settles beside me, then shifts closer until her body presses against mine. Seeking warmth. Comfort.

I don't even realize I stilled until my lungs remember to move again. My shoulders relax. For the first time in hours, a flicker of calm settles over me.

She silently lifts her head slightly, her eyes searching as they meet mine, only to steal the breath from my lungs.

Then her hand moves, slow and tentative, brushing a lock of hair from my brow. Her fingers graze my cheek, light as silk, and the touch burns.

I almost lean into it. Almost catch her hand in mine and hold it there, like a fool chasing warmth. But the moment slips through my fingers, leaving only the ache behind.

"I'm sorry I punched you," she whispers.

I chuckle softly. "I deserved it."

She brushes a kiss against my cheek. Her lips linger half a second too long but long enough to ignite heat that spirals low in my gut.

I almost turn. Almost close the distance. But the moment ends before I can reach her plump lips.

Even after everything. Her temper, her stubbornness, that damned fire she wields like a blade. I still want her. And gods help me, I think I always have. No matter how reckless, how maddening, how impossible she can be… she's the only one who's ever made the noise in my head go quiet. When she's close, the world feels a little less cruel. A little more like something I could survive… if she's beside me.

Across the field, Talon stops mid-swing. His brows furrow, his gaze locked onto us. Slowly, he raises his sword and points it at me.

A silent warning.

I'm breaking every unspoken *hands-off-your-best-friend's-sister* code, and I can't help the grin that twitches at the corner of my mouth.

I lift my hands in mock surrender. "What's with the look, Talon?"

His glare sharpens. Grip tightens. But he doesn't speak.

"Stop being a prick, Talon," Ravenna shouts.

His jaw flexes, his knuckles go white around the hilt of his sword, but he says nothing. Just turns away and continues training.

Each swing of his blade heavier, sharper than the last.

I know him. This isn't over.

The sun dips lower, setting the sky ablaze in hues of orange and violet. Athan has long since left, but Talon remains. Alone.

Swinging.

Striking.

Ravenna gives my waist a gentle squeeze. Then, softly, so softly only I can hear, she whispers. "Tonight."

One word.

But gods, it carries everything. So much meaning. So much restraint. So much we both know we can't afford.

I close my eyes. Just for a breath. "Tonight," I whisper back.

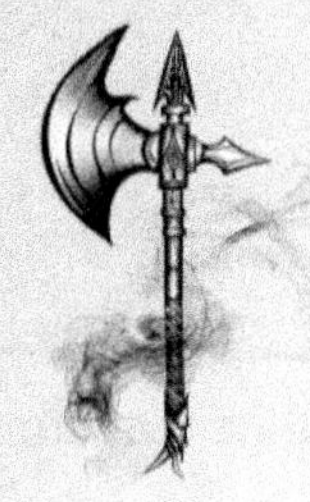

CHAPTER 6

Ravenna

The cool evening air kisses my cheeks, stirring me slightly awake. I don't know how long I was out for, but I'm in no rush to move from my current position, my head resting on Codrin's chest, listening to the soothing rhythm of his heart beating in my ear.

There's a safety in his closeness I didn't realize I'd been aching for. Like for once, I can breathe without bracing for the next storm.

"She's not going to marry that monster." Talon's voice is low, the concern in his tone telling me to keep my eyes closed.

Codrin's reply is hushed, trying to not wake me. "Is there truly anything you can do to stop your father?"

"I'll figure something out." Determination rumbles in Talon's voice. "I'll lock his fat ass up in the East Tower." They both chuckle.

The tower still stands on the east side of the castle, overlooking the sea. But there is no entrance into the tower—most likely sealed up, since it was last truly used over one hundred years ago. During the war, mortals would capture *creatures* and lock them in the tower to burn as the sun rose over the horizon. Picturing our father locked in that tower and left to rot brings a snicker to my lips.

"I see someone is awake." Codrin shifts as I sit up, stretching.

The sun has completely set, the stars emerging one by one over the calm seas, glistening like a jeweled tapestry, countless secrets held beneath its surface. My mind replays the evening's havoc.

Shaking away the memory, I turn my gaze from the sea to Talon, who sits nearby, arms draped over his knees, his trusty sword at his side. His ash-brown hair has grown longer than usual, falling into his eyes despite the silver-streaked strands he constantly pushes back. The silver catches the starlight, faint echoes of my own full head of silver hair. A reminder that no matter how different we've become, we were born from the same fire, and he's carried more than his share of the burn.

We have been inseparable our whole lives, even if some memories have blurred with time. Though we're twins, Talon's always taken on the role of over-protective brother like it's his sworn duty to keep me safe, no matter the cost.

"What time is it?" I say with a yawn.

"It's late," Talon replies. Grabbing his sword, he gets to his feet and sheaths it.

"Mother and Father won't be pleased we missed supper," I note.

Codrin gets to his feet, brushing the grass and leaves from his pants and straightening his shirt. He extends a hand to me, helping me to my feet.

"Thanks." My voice is a whisper as I arch my back in a languid stretch, my spine curving with a crack of released pressure, arms high above my head.

"Who cares?" Talon growls. Missing supper is the least of our parents' concerns, knowing Talon has a few choice words for them, mainly our father.

As we ascend the stone steps leading to the castle's side door, Talon glances over his shoulder, his jaw tightening. A flicker of unease passes over his face before he schools his expression.

My stomach knots. What is he worried about? I follow his gaze, glancing over my shoulder to find Codrin a few paces behind us. He moves with careful ease, his stride measured, as if ensuring he doesn't get too close but not too far either. The flickering torchlight along the path, casting shadows across his face, but I don't miss the way his eyes briefly lower, as if considering something unspoken.

I whip my gaze back to Talon as I step past him in the doorway. "What did you say to him?" I hiss, punching his arm lightly.

"Nothing. And, *ouch*," Talon mutters, rubbing the spot with a dramatic grimace.

I roll my eyes. *Liar.* I know Talon has said something to Codrin while I was sleeping. I just wish I knew what.

Curiosity gnaws at me, and I risk another glance over my shoulder. This time, Codrin's eyes meet mine and for a second, something flickers there. Hesitation, regret, maybe even guilt?

Just as quickly, his expression shifts, and he offers a tight, unreadable smile.

I force a small smile in return before quickly facing forward, my thoughts churning as we continue down the corridor. The click of my boots on stone echoes louder than it should, filling the silence between breaths. I should be planning what to say when I see them. Mother with her careful words and watchful eyes, Father with his fiery will already set in stone. But instead, my mind spirals.

Do I confront them? Beg for a different path? Or pretend I'm fine, play the dutiful daughter and hope there's still a way out before the crown is forced on my head?

Would they even listen?

I shake the thought, but it lingers like everything else I can't seem to let go of.

We stop short, nearly colliding with Athan as he rounds the corner, his face flushed, strands of dark hair sticking to his forehead as he pants out a breath.

"Prince. Princess," he says, struggling to steady his voice. "We've been *searching* for you two since you missed supper. I can have the kitchen prepare something if you'd like."

I grin slightly at his hesitation on the word *searching*; he knew where we were.

"Don't bother. Where is our father?" Talon demands, stepping forward.

"Your parents are in the council room." Athan shifts his weight to one leg.

"Good." Talon's shoulders go rigid, nostrils flaring. Though Athan is a head taller than Talon and could easily toss him with a flick of his wrist, he lets Talon push past him without another word.

I linger for a moment, offering Athan an appreciative squeeze on his massive bicep, which my hand doesn't come close to fully enclosing around. This isn't just for delivering a message. It's for everything he does.

"Of course, sweetie." His warm cognac eyes sparkle with mischief as he winks.

I release a short breath, giving him a tight but genuine smile before turning to follow my brother. My pulse quickens with each step.

Behind me, Athan shifts awkwardly. "Shall I…"

Codrin steps forward, patting Athan's shoulder, a silent reassurance. He shakes his head slightly, and Athan wisely swallows back whatever words were about to leave his mouth.

I can feel the storm brewing inside my brother, his fury reverberating in his every step. *Geez, and they say I'm the one with anger issues.* The weight of his boots striking the stone floor is enough of a warning to *stay the fuck out of his way.*

The flickering candles nestled in iron sconces along the corridor cast jagged shadows across his face, sharpening his already rigid expression. The mere mention of our parents has ignited something fierce inside him. His hands clench at his sides, tendons taut beneath his skin as he fights to keep himself from unraveling. I catch his glance, silent but weighted with meaning. No matter what happens, we face this together. And no matter how many times I have told my brother that he doesn't need to fight my battles for me, at the same time, I am thankful he doesn't listen.

Codrin steps up beside us, his nod small but steady. Whatever tension lingered between him and Talon before, my brother doesn't seem to care now. His expression softens slightly, a flicker of unspoken appreciation in his eyes.

We near the towering council chamber doors. Without hesitation, Talon raises his arms and shoves against the massive wood. The doors slam open, crashing against the stone walls with a force that sends a resounding boom through the chamber.

"WE NEED TO TALK! Right now!" Talon's voice thunders, his always clean-shaven jaw clenched and icy blue eyes flashing. My twin brother looks every inch the fierce prince raised for war, not politics. His combat boots strike the stone floor with each determined step as he storms toward the council table, his fury palpable.

I follow, matching his pace, fury simmering just beneath my skin. Every stomp of his boots echoes through me, stoking the fire already burning in my chest. My breath comes shallow, fingers curling into fists at my sides. I don't try to calm him. I don't want to. His rage is mine too. Just another storm I'm fueling with every step, every thought of what waits.

Talon's voice cracks across the room, hard and fast. "What in the seven hells is the meaning of you sending my sister off to some monster?"

Our father, King Zephyr, sits at the head of the long council table, his fingers drumming impatiently against the polished wood. His dark brown eyes, almost black and void of mercy, fix on his son with a quiet intensity. The sharp angles of his face are partially concealed by his thick, gray beard, trimmed with strict precision, much like the man himself. His graying slicked-back hair, never a strand out of place, frames an image of unyielding discipline and authority.

"It is in the best interest of the king and his kingdom," Bartholomew says smoothly. Seated to our father's right, his long fingers interlace on the table, and his gaze falls on Talon like a vulture waiting to pick apart the bones of a fallen beast.

To our father's left, our mother sits in perfect, practiced stillness, her focus elsewhere. She barely acknowledges the discussion, her attention instead on a young servant boy pouring wine into her goblet. The flickering flames of the fireplace catch the rich green silk of her gown, the golden threads woven along the hem, sleeves, and bodice shimmering like sunlight trapped in fabric.

Her golden-blond curls cascade in loose waves down her

back, framing a regal yet unreachable posture. Between us stands an invisible barrier built through years of strained interactions, unspoken disappointments, and misaligned expectations. The weight of her disapproval is not new, but it sits heavy on my chest all the same. A familiar presence. A shadow that never quite fades.

Behind our father stands General Kazimir Hawk, commander of the royal guard as well as the Royal Slayer Squad. His polished armor reflects the dim candlelight, his gray cape swaying behind him like mist rolling over a battlefield. He shifts slightly, a single armored boot scraping the stone floor. His thinning white hair blends into his pale, wrinkled skin, but his sharp blue-green eyes hold the cold steel of experience. A man who has seen, and enforced, our father's will for decades.

"Fuck off, Bartholomew. I wasn't speaking to you," Talon snaps.

Bartholomew's brows furrow as he turns his head away, but I catch the twitch of his mouth. A hint of restrained satisfaction. He enjoys seeing Talon lose his temper.

Father leaps to his feet, the heavy wooden chair scraping against the floor with an echoing screech, causing me to jump slightly. Talon doesn't so much as flinch. A storm rages behind Father's dark eyes; his patience stretched to its breaking point.

Our father rules with an iron fist, his name spoken in equal parts fear and forced reverence throughout the remaining three Everlight Realms. He believes himself respected and renowned, but I see the way people whisper in the shadows, the nervous glances in his presence. His hunger for power has grown insatiable, sending tremors of fear through the kingdom.

He's launched military campaigns against neighboring regions, claiming their resources "for the good of Theiahold" while leaving scorched earth and orphaned villages behind. Dissenters, scholars, or advisers who question his rule mysteriously vanish, their families silenced by fear or exiled under vague charges of treason. And he's dismantled the council of elders, rewriting laws to give himself full authority. No vote needed. No checks. No balance.

As if we didn't already have enough demons to fight, one also sits on the throne.

He expects Talon to inherit his ruthlessness, to follow in his footsteps as a formidable ruler. One forged by war, not softened by diplomacy. Talon wasn't just trained, he was thrown into the heart of war, over and over and over again. Not to groom him for leadership, but to harden him past the point of return. To mold him into a weapon loyal only to our father's command.

It's his twisted way of securing the throne: not by shielding his successor, but by drowning him in fire until even death recoils at his name. And if Talon dies? Then he was never strong enough to wear the crown in the first place.

And as for me? My place has never been beside my brother in battle, not in Father's eyes. I might wear the Royal Slayer crest, but I was never truly meant to serve. Father made no exceptions when he commanded my enlistment. Not because he wanted to test me. He sent me to the blood-soaked training yards not as a soldier-in-the-making but as a pawn in his game of obedience. A daughter defiant is more dangerous than a son too soft.

And now, he harbors a different aspiration for me: to see me wed to another powerful ruler. A pawn in his endless pursuit of power.

The pressure has always been there, shaping Talon and me into something useful, necessary, controllable.

But we were never meant to be controlled.

Talon marches forward, slamming his hands against the council table so hard that the polished wood rattles beneath his palms. He leans in, his jaw tight, teeth bared like a wolf ready to rip into his prey. "She will not marry that king."

Father lets out a harsh, guttural laugh, sending a chill down my spine. He pushes forward, placing his hands against the table, his lips twisting into a cruel smirk as he brings his face nose-to-nose with his son. His breath is hot, reeking of the spiced wine he's undoubtedly indulged in throughout the evening.

"Yes, she will." His voice is unwavering sharp, cold iron. "And in doing so, I will go down in history as the greatest ruler to save what is left of the Gildensun Kingdom."

He steps forward, eyes burning with that dangerous gleam he wears like a crown. "For centuries, we've stood divided.

Light and shadow. Metal and fang. This marriage will do what no sword, no treaty, no bloodshed ever could. It will end the war before the next one begins. It will bind Theiahold and Veilstead, fire and night, into a single, unbreakable reign. *Mine.*"

He sweeps his gaze across the room, jaw tight with conviction. "While other kings build armies, I build empires. While they carve borders, I erase them. And long after I'm dust and ash, the histories will remember me. Not as a tyrant, not as a butcher, but as the sovereign who tamed two worlds."

His eyes narrow on me. "And your name, daughter, will be the hinge upon which that legacy turns."

A muscle twitches in Talon's jaw. I know that look. The barely restrained fury, the loathing in his narrowed eyes. That look he saves for only one man. The man he despises calling Father.

But Zephyr is no father. He's a bloated, self-indulgent tyrant who craves power more than he ever cares for his own children.

"You will go down in history as nothing more than a mad king who let greed and power blind him," I snap, stepping up beside Talon. My pulse hammers in my ears, but I refuse to let my voice waver.

At the corner of my vision, I catch Bartholomew slipping away, sliding down the length of the table, eager to remove himself from the growing firestorm. *Coward.*

Father's gaze snaps to me. Slowly, his dark eyes rake down my body, scrutinizing every piece of me in silent disapproval.

Those words are going to cost me.

Dearly.

I resist the urge to fidget. Instead, I defiantly hold his gaze. I won't cower before him.

Father's lip curls. As though he knows what I'm thinking. He can see right through my shield of defense and crush it with one swing of his mighty fist.

I steel myself, locking my spine straight as his gaze bores into me. I will not shrink away. I will not let his disapproval chip away at me. Not anymore.

Then, a muttered whisper, barely audible. "What a disgrace."

My head snaps toward my mother. The words have barely passed her lips before she takes a sip from her goblet, her lashes casting a shadow over her distant, unreadable gaze. She shakes her head, fingers tightening ever so slightly around the delicate stem of the glass.

The weight of her disdain settles over me like a lead cloak. After all these years, I should be used to it.

"Bite your tongue, daughter," my father's voice booms, dragging my attention back to him. "Or I shall cut it out myself."

He steps forward, nostrils flaring, his frame towering over me like a beast preparing to strike.

I hold my breath as his fingers twist the heavy ruby ring around his meaty finger. The ring is nothing more than another reminder of his wealth and authority, the decades he has ruled this kingdom with an iron fist.

A flash of movement catches my eye, and I see Codrin take a single strong-minded step forward, poised to intervene.

Father's gaze snaps to him. "You are dismissed, Captain Hardtblade."

Codrin freezes mid-step, his hand flexing at his side, itching toward his sword.

General Hawk turns to him sharply. "The king gave you an order, Captain."

Codrin's jaw clenches, his shoulders square. "I feel it is in my best interest…"

"Leave. Now," Father barks cutting him off. His expression darkens, his face flushing red with fury.

Talon turns slightly, giving Codrin a small, reassuring nod. "It's fine. Go."

A part of me wants to run to Codrin. Wants him to grab me in his arms and take me away from this awful nightmare. But my feet stay planted to the ground, unable to move.

Codrin hesitates, his fingers twitching at his side. But there's nothing he can do. His throat bobs as he swallows his anger, bowing stiffly and backing toward the door, his gaze never leaving the unfolding storm before him.

The door clicks shut.

I hear it before I feel it. A sharp crack of impact fills the silence of the room. Followed by pain that explodes across my face where my father's massive hand strikes me, his ring splitting the skin of my cheekbone. My breath catches, the world tilting sideways as I drop to my knees.

A sharp ringing pierces my left ear, my cheek burning, searing, throbbing from the strike. My fingers curl against the wounded skin, but my hands tremble from the building rage mixing with pain.

For a breath of a second, the room falls deathly silent. Only to be filled with the unmistakable hiss of drawn swords.

I snap my gaze up to find General Hawk, sword drawn, its polished ashenbane iron glinting in the light of the fire. The blade's tip rests precisely at the hollow of my twin brother's throat. "Stand down boy," the general hisses.

Talon grips his sword so tightly, his knuckles are bone white against the still-sheathed hilt.

The air knots in my throat. Did he try to draw his sword on our father?

I stand on shaking legs, trying to offer comfort to my brother by letting him know I will always be at his side.

Tension crackles in the air, thick as the scent of burning wax from the candlelit sconces along the wall.

Father lets out a low belly laugh. A sound so cold it sends ice through my veins. He enjoys this. Seeing his son's life threatened is nothing more than a game to him. *Sick bastard.*

"I got this, General."

I take a small step forward, ready to fight.

Talon's arm sweeps across my front, a firm barrier. His body rigid, unmoving, careful not to press too hard into the blade resting at his throat.

Still, his icy blue gaze finds mine. His eyes soften, a silent plea, an unspoken command.

"If anyone is going to be punished, it will be me."

I shake my head, my hands trembling at my sides. But Talon is resolute. Gently but firmly, he pushes me behind him.

"Stay back," his touch warns. *"Let me take the brunt of this."*

Father draws his own sword.

I gasp. The room swallows the sound as iron meets iron, Father's blade pressing over General Hawk's, pinning it harder against Talon's throat.

My stomach twists. My hands ball into fists at my sides, but I know better than to act.

Two swords. Two sharpened points pressing into my brother's skin.

Talon holds firm, his chest rising and falling in slow, controlled breaths. But I see the tension, the fire burning beneath his skin. He's fuming. Barely holding himself together.

General Hawk withdraws his sword, stepping back. But he doesn't go far. His eyes linger, his presence still a looming threat at our father's side.

I press a hand against my brother's back, feeling the heat radiating through his shirt.

Would Father actually kill him?

No.

He needs an heir. Doesn't he?

But pain. Pain is a different story. Pain is a tool. Pain is Father's favorite game. The many scars across Talon's back, the lash marks still etched into his skin, are proof of that. And Father making sure those marks were never to be erased.

"Pain is what makes a man," our father has told him many times. "Pain is what will make a great leader out of you."

Even as a boy, even for something as simple as stealing a biscuit from the kitchens, Talon was whipped.

And now, our father is testing him again.

A bead of sweat slips down Talon's temple. I feel the tension curl in his muscles, the nerves on edge.

Still, he refuses to break eye contact. He shows no fear.

Father sneers. "You dare challenge me? I am your king. I have been fighting battles, killing demons and creatures of unspeakable sizes, since before you were even born."

His sword presses harder into Talon's skin. A thin trickle of red slips down from the point, a single line of defiance against cruelty.

Bartholomew, still at the opposite side of the table, looks on with wide, disbelieving eyes. His fingers dig into the chair's backrest, his knuckles bone white.

The blade is already at Talon's throat, but Father doesn't

stop there.

His hand tightens on the hilt. He draws the sword back with a shout, ready to strike.

Talon doesn't flinch, not even as the edge glints in the candlelight, ready to split him open.

A sob tears from me. *No.* This isn't a threat. This is intent.

"Are you done playing?" Mother's voice cuts through the scene like a dagger through silk.

Everything freezes. Father's arm still hovers midair, blade cocked, fury etched into every line of his face. He wasn't done. Everyone knows it. The only reason Talon is still breathing is because the queen intervened.

And I feel it.

The final crack in whatever loyalty remained.

This man, our father, would spill his own son's blood to secure power. Would trade his daughter like a pawn to rule both day and night.

There's no going back now.

Mother sits, unbothered. Her cold gaze slides over the drawn weapon, more concerned about decorum than her own son's well-being.

Father ignores her. His gaze stays fixed on Talon. "You would do well to know who you're up against before you even think of using that sword."

Then, his dark gaze shifts to me.

His grin widens into a slow, predatory smile spreading across his face.

"And as for your sister…" His words slid from his lips, thick with spite. "What I do with her is none of your concern."

His sword slides back into its scabbard with a soft, hissing sound. But the weight of his stare remains.

A challenge.

A warning.

A promise.

"Bastard," Talon mutters, his jaw tight, his body still tense. His fingers retreat from his sword's hilt, but they linger close, ready to strike.

I feel it too. The unshakable sense that our father might test him again.

"Leave." Father's voice cracks through the air like a whip. "Now."

Talon spins sharply on his heel, his arm wrapping around me as he guides us from the room.

Mother's voice follows us, disapproving but empty. "Do you feel better about yourself now?"

"They need to learn. And how I teach them is of no concern to you."

Talon's steps slow. Turning back to the room, his eyes blaze like fire, unrelenting and wild as he holds our father's gaze before slamming the door shut.

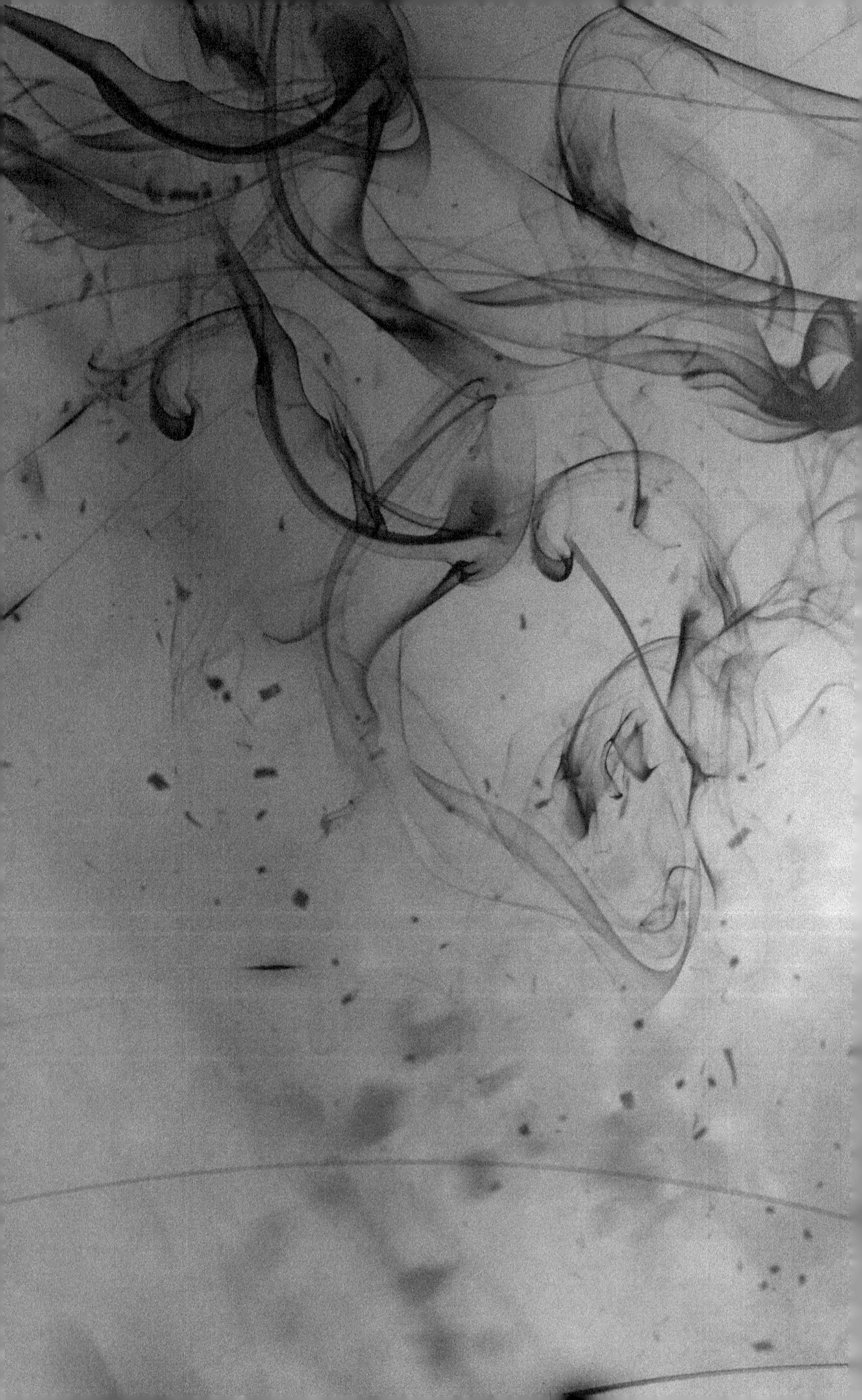

CHAPTER 7

Ravenna

Talon and I move through the dim corridor, our boots barely making a sound against the cold stone floor. The silence is suffocating, heavy with the remnants of our father's rage.

My anger swirls inside me like a dark, churning storm. My blood still feels hot in my veins, simmering with fury. I can't imagine how Talon feels, his anger bottled up too well every time I steal a glance in his direction.

His hand rests at the small of my back, a silent attempt to ground me, to offer comfort. But not even Talon's presence can stop the tremors running through my body.

I keep my gaze ahead, but I can't ignore the line of dried blood streaking down my brother's neck. A grotesque reminder of how truly fucked up our family is. Our father wouldn't have hesitated.

Not for a second.

If I had stepped in, I would have only made it worse. The look in Father's eyes wasn't rage. It was something far darker. He didn't merely threaten Talon; he drew his sword back to strike, fully prepared to spill his own son's blood. That wasn't anger. That was the kind of evil that chills bones and silences rooms.

Stopping at my bedroom door, Talon pulls me into a brotherly hug, dragging me from my thoughts. I return the hug and force a weak smile before slipping into my room, shutting the door with a soft *click*.

I cherish the proximity of our rooms, with Talon right across the hall from me. A setup he fought for when we were younger.

I used to wake in cold sweats, my screams echoing down the halls, convinced that shadowy creatures crawled across my ceiling. And every time, Talon came running. Wooden sword in hand. My fearless protector. But he can't chase this monster away. King Alaric is real. This marriage is real. And I have never felt so alone.

With a long, slow breath, I kick off my boots, letting them land haphazardly. I collapse onto the plush rug before the fire, stretching out, letting the heat wash over me.

The flames dance, casting erratic shadows across the ceiling. They twist and leap, forming dark shapes that almost look like figures, watching.

Rubbing a hand over my face, I wince. My cheek still throbs from my father's brutal slap, the skin tender beneath my fingertips. The impact of his heavy ring still burns, sending a dull ache through the side of my face.

I force myself to my feet, dragging myself to the vanity. My reflection stares back at me, hollow-eyed and weary. The bruise on my cheek is already darkening, a small cut tracing the curve of my cheekbone.

"Thanks, Father." I grumble aloud clenching my fists, nails biting into my palms.

"Weak."

The unfamiliar voice whispers around me.

I snap my head up, my chest rising and falling with every shaky breath as my eyes search around the room.

"Pitiful." I jump in my seat as the unfamiliar voice comes again as though speaking right in my ear.

"Is someone there?" I swallow hard.

Only the crackle of the fire response.

"Great. Now I'm hearing things." Shaking my head, I turn back to the vanity mirror, my eyes falling on my reflection. I trace a finger over the faint scar marring my right cheek. Another one of father's delightful backhands from years ago, when I skipped lessons. Hells, even my wrist still aches sometimes from where Father nearly crushed the bone for using the wrong utensil at a royal dinner. And last year, the bastard dragged me down the hall by my hair for refusing yet another suitor. And through it all, Mother sat there, blank-faced. Uncaring. Almost…bored.

My chest tightens, fury rising like bile as the memory of this evening starts to choke me. The vision of Father's sword at Talon's throat flashes behind my eyes. The arranged marriage. Mother's indifference. A deep, stabbing pain burrows into my ribs of self-hatred, raw and unrelenting.

Too fragile to fight her own battles. This time the unfamiliar voice rings in my own head. Its words curling like smoke, thick and poisonous, winding its way around my thoughts until it's all I can hear.

Always in need of saving. The voice, low and laced with disdain, threads itself through my mind like it belongs there.

My pulse pounds. Not true. I can fight my own battles. I have so many times before.

But the voice only laughs in my head. A twisted, dark thing that feels like claws raking against my skin.

My breathing picks back up. My heart pounding against my ribs. This voice. It's words. Where is it coming from? I can hear it whispering in my head. Infecting me with its cruel words. But it speaks such volume. Such truth. My own thoughts feel tainted, polluted by something darker and yet I welcome it as a red haze blurs around my vision, heat burning through me like a wildfire. The world narrows, sharpens, all my anger funneling into one point.

A scream rips from my throat.

I don't remember slamming my fist down. Just the violent clatter of perfume bottles rattling, one tipping over, spilling sweet-smelling liquid across the vanity.

But it's not enough.

My reflection stares back at me, pale, tear-streaked, chin

trembling.

Pathetic. Weak. A nothing. The voice sinks its claws in deeper, mocking, jeering.

"FUCK YOU!" I scream, my fist collides with the mirror. Glass bursts in all directions, tiny shards slicing across my knuckles.

The pain is sharp, but it feels right. Like punishment. Like validation.

I stumble back, panting. Blood drips from my knuckles, staining the vanity. My breath comes in ragged gasps, each one tasting of iron and desperation.

"Shit!" I choke out, my voice a cracked, hollow sound. I really let my own thoughts get to me this time.

Rushing to the washroom, I snatch a hand towel and sweep the larger shards from the vanity into my trembling palms. The jagged edges slice against my skin as I make my way back to the washroom, blood dripping onto the porcelain sink like crimson rain. It doesn't matter. None of it matters.

I drop the pieces into the sink with a clatter, my blood smearing across the glass like ink spilled on parchment. The sting in my knuckles intensifies, searing and raw, but it feels distant. Like my pain is no longer mine.

Shattered fragments litter the sink. But it's the reflections that draw me in.

A thousand splintered versions of me. Broken. Shattered. Weak.

My eyes stare back from each piece, but they look wrong. Hollow. Betrayed.

You are nothing.

I freeze. The voice is clearer now. Not a whisper but a presence. Tangible. Ruthless.

My eyes drift to the washroom mirror. My reflection stares back, but something feels… off. It's subtle at first. The tilt of the head. The slow curl of its lips.

Not mine.

Shadows crawl around it. Thickening.

My breath snags in my throat. Panic claws at my chest, but I can't look away.

The reflection's eyes darken, shifting from icy blue to deep, blood red.

Dark. Bottomless. Like spilled wine soaking through silk. Like death.

And then it speaks.

"You don't get to choose." The words are soft, caressing. "You never did."

A violent shudder rips down my spine.

"No." The word cracks from my throat, but the reflection only smiles, a sliver of madness curling at its lips.

"You fight and scream," it purrs, the voice silk and shadow. "But for what? It's already done."

The air thickens, pressing against me, strangling me. My pulse roars in my ears, each beat a countdown to something inevitable.

The reflection leans closer. The breath against my ear is real. Hot. Suffocating. And there's no one there. "You belong to it now."

"It?" My voice shakes on a whispered breath. What does that mean?

"You think they'll save you?" the voice mocks, curling around my thoughts like a constricting vine. "Athan? Talon? Codrin?" The names are spat like rotten fruit.

"They're all powerless."

The world tilts, the room spinning like a maelstrom. My hands grip the sink's edge, knuckles bone white. But the voice doesn't stop. It doesn't relent.

"You cling to their promises like a drowning girl gasping for air." It laughs, low and vicious. "But you will drown, Ravenna. And no one will come to save you."

Pain twists in my chest, sharp and cold.

"Codrin?" The voice hisses his name, drawing it out like it enjoys the taste. "He's gone. Abandoned you. Left you to burn."

My own voice is barely a whisper. "No, he hasn't. He won't."

"Wait and see." The reflection's grin widens, teeth gleaming like knives. "He can't protect you. He *won't* protect you."

The words twist through me, slicing deeper than any weapon. I try to tear my gaze away, but I'm locked in. Entranced. Overpowered.

"You will kneel before it." The voice promises, each word a dagger carving itself into my soul. "You will become it's—"

"No." I cut the reflection off, my voice cracking through clinch teeth, my jaw aching. The denial feels fragile, weak but I will not become some passion to the king of darkness.

The air is thick and icy. It crawls down my throat, suffocating me from the inside out.

A sob claws its way up, raw and burning.

"I won't."

The reflection tilts its head again, eyes burning with a hungry crimson glow. The grin widens, feral and triumphant. "You say you won't now. But you'll beg for it before the end."

"No! I WON'T!" I shriek.

Everything inside me snaps.

A scream tears from my throat, hoarse and wild. I grab the largest shard from the sink and hurl it at the mirror. Cracking the mirror, the piece shatters on impact, the pieces exploding outward like glass rain. Splinters scatter across the floor, glittering like spilled diamonds.

I stagger back, chest heaving.

Silence.

I squeeze my eyes shut, my nails digging into my palms until pain blossoms.

This isn't real. This isn't real. This isn't real.

But when I open my eyes, the mirror is nothing but a mess

of broken glass. My reflection fractured and normal. The crimson eyes are gone.

I really let today get to me. The stress of everything. From nearly breaking Zavier's arm to my father's rage to this stupid arranged marriage with a vampire king. My mind got the best of me by playing tricks on me.

I let out a shuddering breath. Relief floods me, warm and suffocating.

But then I see it.

A single shard, sitting in the sink, almost untouched by the rest.

A sharp breath stutters past my lips.

Because in its reflection, the crimson eyes are still watching me.

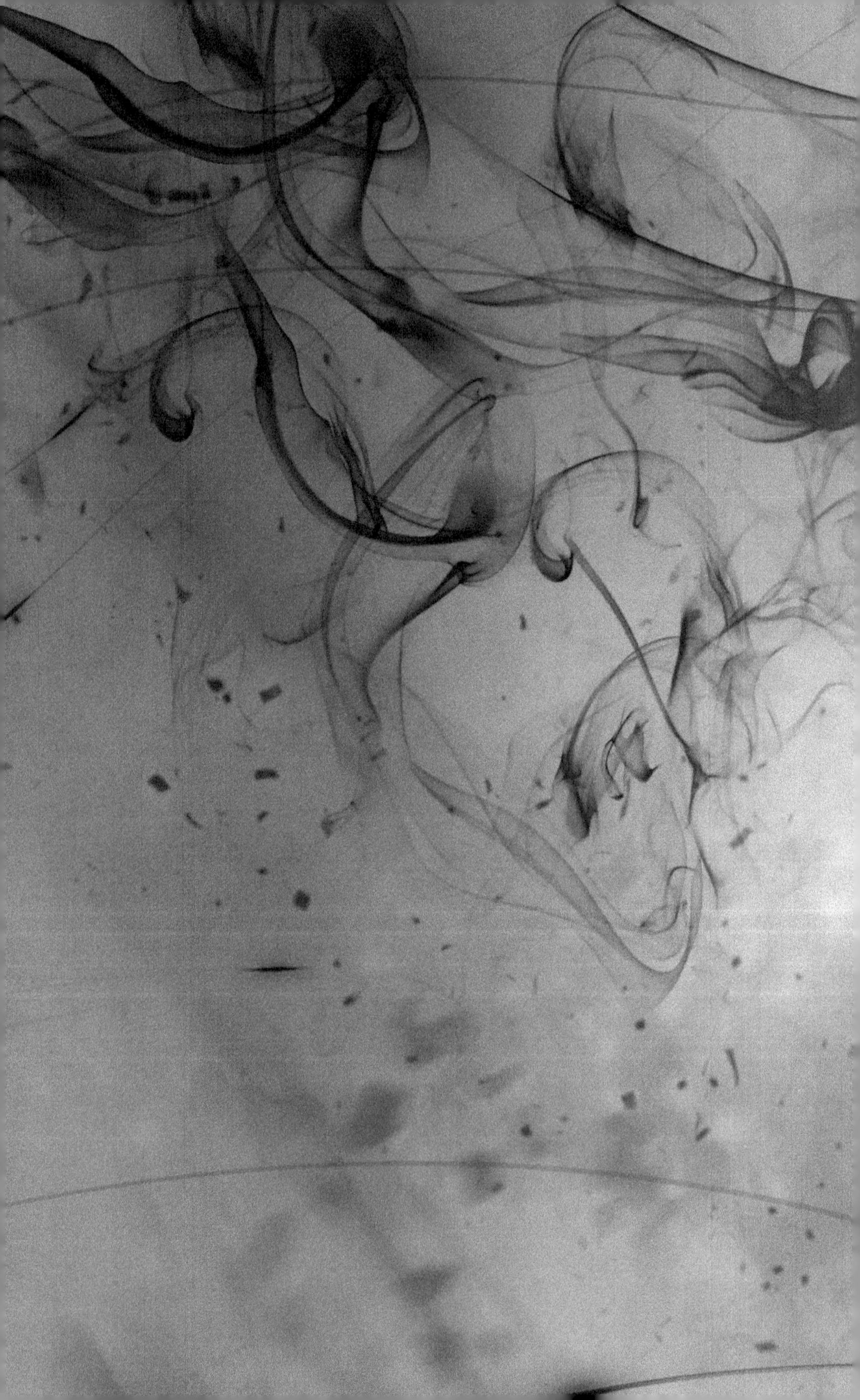

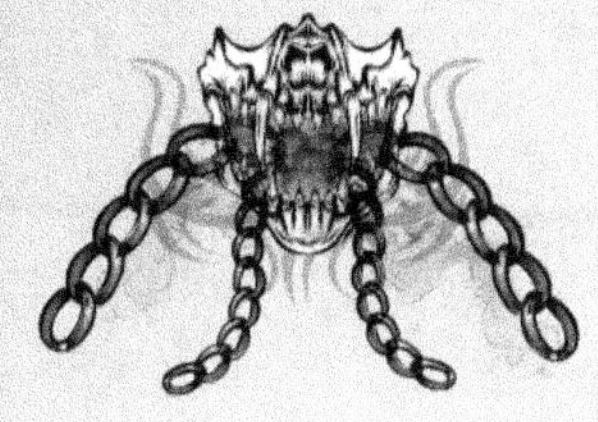

CHAPTER 8
Codrin

I speed down the corridor, drawn toward the twins' rooms like a force is pulling me. Both doors are shut, but my gut tells me where I need to go first.

Talon would scowl at me for going to Ravenna's room before his, but something is off. That feeling started the moment I reached the floor of the tower. Like she needs me.

"She doesn't need you," I mutter under my breath, shaking my head. "You're just pathetic."

A humorless chuckle slips from my lips. Me calling myself pathetic should probably be a sign. Still, I knock softly, rocking on my heels as I wait.

The door swings open within seconds. Before I can even speak, Ravenna's fingers curl into my shirt, yanking me inside.

The door slams behind me, and our bodies collide as Ravenna wraps her arms tightly around my torso, pressing her head against my chest.

"Are you okay?"

"Hug me, damn it," she replies quietly but firmly.

I don't hesitate. Though she's wrapped in just a towel, her hair still damp, tells me she just got out of the shower only minutes ago. My arms encircle her, my chin resting atop her head. She holds tighter, like she's trying to ground herself, like I'm the only thing keeping her from falling apart.

Or I'm just reading way too much into a simple hug.

Her heart pounds against my ribs, too fast, too erratic. She tightens more, pressing her body closer.

Gods, this woman.

The heat from her body seeps into mine, and with it, the slow, creeping realization that she's far more rattled than she's letting on.

I take a slow, deep inhale. She smells of fresh lilacs and jasmine. I shouldn't be thinking about this. But she is every bit as intoxicating as she is untouchable.

Her breath fans against my collarbone, her pelvis brushing too close…

Fuck.

I pull back before my body betrays me.

Hands cupping her shoulders, I force a smile, willing my pulse to slow.

"What happened after I left?"

Ravenna closes her eyes and tilts her head away.

I pull her chin back toward me so I can see into her beautiful icy blues. Are there tears forming there that she refuses to shed?

"Talk to me," I whisper.

"I can't. Not yet." She sucks in a breath and steps out of my hold, too quickly, spinning on her heel and making her way across the room to the wardrobe. Yanking the doors open, fabric flies over her shoulder, landing haphazardly on the bed.

I only saw the beginning and now the aftermath. Enough to know something went horribly wrong. Then they shut me out. Ravenna won't talk. And the way she avoids my eyes? That says more than anything. Something happened in that council room. Something bad. And I can't help her if she won't let me close.

"Talon is joining us, right?" Ravenna's voice breaks through my scattered thoughts.

"Um… yeah," I stammer. At least, I assume he's coming with us. I didn't stop at his room to ask him first.

"Good. I think we all need a drink tonight." She gathers an armful of clothes and disappears behind the folding screen in the corner.

Forcing my gaze away, I exhale.

I *should* step out and give her privacy, but staying in her room a little longer? I'm not passing that up.

My gaze drifts around the room, absently taking in the disarray. A few books partly stacked, partly tossed on the nightstand, boots kicked aside.

Then, I see it.

The vanity mirror.

Shattered.

My stomach tightens.

Glass litters the surface, catching the firelight in jagged, fractured reflections. I step closer, careful not to crunch the shards underfoot.

"Ravenna, what happened here?"

The sounds of movement and rustling clothes behind the folding screen stop suddenly.

"What?" Ravenna peeks out from behind the screen. "Oh, that. That stupid thing broke when I was trying to adjust the mirror."

I arch a brow. Adjusting the mirror?

I've caught her in enough lies over the years to know her tells. Her too-casual tone. Her eyes just a little too wide. And avoidance. Proving my point, she disappears again before I catch her expression.

And deflecting.

Before I can press any further, she curses under her breath.

"These pants are so… fucking… tight."

I huff out a laugh. "Need help?"

"Shut up." Her head bounces from behind the top of the screen.

I turn to face the screen. "You sure you don't need help."

I freeze mid-step as she stumbles out from behind the screen, hopping as she yanks the fabric over her hips.

My mind blanks, as if a fog has swallowed every coherent thought.

Gods help me.

Her pants are partly down, hugging half of her perfectly

round ass.

And then, as though the gods are enjoying my torment, she begins to hop, her firm ass bouncing before me.

My knees buckle beneath me. I am going to die.

What was I thinking about before? Shit. I force my gaze away, throat closing in on itself. Shoving a hand into my front pocket to adjust.

After a long, torturous moment, she finally gets her pants all the way up.

"There we go," Ravenna sighs as she sits on the edge of her bed, pulling on her calf-high black leather boots. Completely unaware of what she just put me through.

Pushing off the bed, she walks past me, her fingertips barely grazing my waist, causing a shiver to bolt through me.

She has no idea what she does to me.

Desperately trying to avoid looking at her, she retrieves a brush from the vanity drawer. Her face squinches with pain when the brush snags at the tangles in her hair. With a frustrated huff, she gives up and tosses the brush back in the drawer and weaves a loose braid instead.

She doesn't acknowledge the damaged mirror. Doesn't so much as glance at it.

Something is wrong.

"Ready!" Ravenna snaps a pose, hands on her hips, giving me a heartfelt smile. For a split second, it looks forced.

Shaking off the thought, I close the distance between us.

Her silver braid spills over one shoulder, nearly blending into the soft, loose white blouse that hugs her frame. The snug leather pants accentuate every muscle, every curve of her legs.

"You look amazing." I brush a stray lock of her hair behind her ear.

She flinches as my fingertips graze over her cheek, and that's when I notice it. The small cut and already-forming bruise along her cheekbone. Fury hits me instantly.

"Did he do this?" I know the answer. I just want to hear her say it.

Her jaw locks. "It's fine," she mutters, brushing my hand away.

No. It's not fine. It will never be fine.

King Zephyr Rosewyn. Even the thought of his name leaves a sour taste in my mouth. There are not enough words to describe the type of bastard he is. And the aftermath of what he does to Ravenna can turn even the sweetest man feral.

"Let's get out of here." She grabs my hand and drags me toward the door.

But as she pulls me away, my gaze flicks once more to the shattered mirror. Something about it lingers. Something about her lie doesn't sit right. I just don't know why.

Yet.

We step into the hall to find Talon leaning against the wall, one foot propped up, hands buried in the front pockets of his pants.

"What were you two doing in there?" His eyes flick from Ravenna's wide smile to me. I look away, failing to hide my flushed cheeks. "You both look suspicious as hell."

"Nothing!" I blurt too fast, wiping my sweaty palms on the front of my shirt.

Ravenna just snorts, waving him off like he's being ridiculous.

"You read too much into things." She tosses a mischievous glance as she strolls down the corridor. "Codrin was just helping me change."

I freeze, jaw dropping.

"You've got to be kidding me," Talon growls, pushing off the wall, his jaw clenched so tight I can almost hear his teeth grinding. My friend vanishes in an instant. Replaced by the fierce, overprotective brother I should've seen coming.

"That is *not* what happened!" I step back with both palms raised. "Tell him, Ravenna!"

No response. Just her laughter echoing down the corridor.

Thanks for the backup.

"Are you two coming?" she calls, her voice carrying a taunting edge.

The warm candlelight crowns her in a gold-silver halo, her silver braid swinging mockingly with each step. She disappears down the hall, leaving me to fend for myself.

Talon steps forward and I brace for the hit.

But it doesn't come.

He pauses, narrows his eyes at me, then pivots with a sharp exhale and stalks after his sister.

I gather what little pride I have left and follow once there's enough space between us. We descend the stairs in silence, weaving through the empty kitchen until we reach the back door. The cool breeze of summer's night greats us, rustling our clothes with unknown promises, and maybe, if I survive Talon, a shred of freedom.

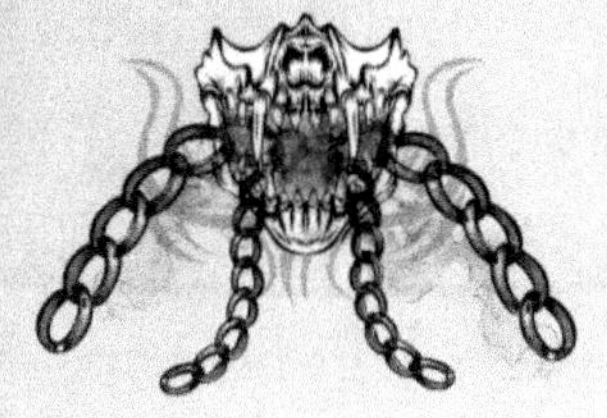

CHAPTER 9

Codrin

The quaint town surrounding the castle feels like an entirely different world at night. During the day, townspeople scurry about, the scent of fresh bread wafting from the baker's shop mingling with the rhythmic clinking of metal from Bobby's forge, where he shapes our swords and slayer masks. But now, in the hush of evening, lanterns cast a warm golden glow along the cobblestone streets, illuminating the weathered charm of buildings lining our path.

The air is thick with sea salt and the mouthwatering aroma of roasting meat as we stroll through the quiet town.

We pass a few royal guards along the way, each giving us a respectful nod. Their numbers have doubled along the walls and through the streets. After my brief conversation with King Zephyr earlier this morning, he threw the responsibility onto me without question or concern, and honestly, that lack of interest doesn't surprise me.

In the distance, near the lower shores of town, I catch sight of the great ships at the harbor. Their silhouettes stand starkly against the star-speckled sky, masts reaching like spires into the heavens. They looked like something pulled straight from a tale of old majestic creatures gliding across the waves, ready to carry their passengers into legend.

What would it take to step aboard one of those vessels? Ravenna at my side, the wind at our backs, setting sail into the unknown. A different life. A freer one. One where her future wasn't bound by politics and bloodlines, and I wasn't shackled to duty. Just her and me, chasing the horizon.

Stone crashes against iron, the sudden sound shattering the calm. I flinch as I'm dragged from my thoughts.

Another rock flies, this one from Talon's hand, colliding with a precarious stack of iron scraps along a narrow alley. The clatter echoes like cannon fire against the buildings.

"Talon, *seriously!*" Ravenna's eyes flash with heat as she marches over and punches her twin in the arm. "Grow up."

"*Talon, grow up,*" he mimics in a higher pitch, smirking as he falls into step beside me. Talon grins, rubbing his arm for dramatic effect. "Did you see that? I think that qualifies as sibling abuse. Aren't you going to do something about that, *Captain*?"

"I'm off duty," I say with a low chuckle. "What she does to you now is your problem."

"Come on, man. I need backup."

"After the death glare you gave me ten minutes ago? Hard pass." I shoot him a pointed look. "I'll sit this one out."

"That was *brother* Talon you were dealing with. Now you've got *best-friend* Talon." He pats a hand against my shoulder like he's making a deal.

"Lucky me," I mutter, raising a brow at him.

We head down a dark alley, Talon rushing ahead toward a warm, inviting light seeping through a slightly ajar door. He grabs the large, worn-down wooden handle and swings the door open. Lively chatter, clinking mugs, and the uneven notes of a piano spill out into the night.

"My lady," Talon bows, holding the door open for Ravenna with a dramatic flourish.

"Why, thank you, kind sir," she replies, strolling past him into the bustling tavern.

Talon claps a hand to my shoulder as I follow behind. The door thuds shut behind us, sealing us into the tavern's familiar chaos.

The scent of stale beer mingles with the musk of aged wood and sweat. A group of drunken men slam their mugs together in a raucous cheer, their slurred voices blending with the discordant tune pounding from an old, battered piano in the corner. The keys rattle with every uncoordinated strike, the music more noise than melody, but somehow, it fits the room's rough edges.

Dusty chandeliers hang crooked from the ceiling, their amber light casting long shadows over the scarred faces of card players. The dim glow renders their eyes black and bottomless, their expressions flickering between hope and quiet desperation with every turn of a card.

Women dressed in low-cut, silky skirts drift between tables, their movements smooth, practiced. Flirtation drips from their voices as they vie for attention. In the far corner, a staircase curves upward into the shadows, leading to small upstairs rooms reserved for long stays… or short visits. I spot one woman guiding a drunken man up the steps, her hand curled around his belt, his feet barely working.

Despite the reputation of the place, it feels almost like a second home. Over the last year, we've gotten to know most of the women, on a respectful level, and the staff. The regulars respect us, give us our space. And in return, we always claim the same booth in the back corner, dimly lit, tucked away from prying eyes.

The floorboards creak beneath our boots as we pass the bar. Simon, the bartender and our dear friend, leans casually against the counter, regaling Willis, an older gentleman, with one of his infamous fishing tales. Willis, already swaying and hiccupping between sips, downs another drink like it's the first of the night.

Simon gives us a wave mid-sentence, never missing a beat. The old man slams his empty mug on the bar, laughing dryly, only to nearly tip off his stool before catching himself and sitting up straight like nothing happened.

Near the back corner, two familiar voices echo over the din of conversation, arguing good-naturedly over a card game.

"BAM!" Miles leaps to his feet, slapping his cards face-up on the table. "Full house!"

"Hmm…" Athan scratches his thick, well-kept beard, eyeing

the cards. "As cute as that is…" He lays his own cards down slowly. "Four of a kind beats a full house. So. BAM!" He grins, leaning back in the booth like he's just won the kingdom.

"What?!" Miles's shoulders slump, and he drops back into his chair with a groan. "Dang it."

I step aside to let Ravenna slide into the booth first. She scoots across the bench, settling close to Athan and resting her head on his shoulder. He leans his head gently against hers in greeting.

"Hello, sweetie," Athan murmurs, patting her cheek and pressing a soft kiss to the top of her head. "Feeling better?"

"Will after I get a few drinks in me," she says with a small smile.

"Having fun, Miles?" I ask, sliding in beside her.

"Yep." Athan grins wider as he gathers the cards and starts shuffling again.

"Noooo," Miles groans, muffled behind his hands.

"I got next game." Talon grabs the chair beside Miles and spins it backward, straddling it with his arms propped on the backrest.

"I'm out." Miles drops his hands from his face. "Maybe you can win some of my money back for me."

His flushed face gives away how unlucky his night has been.

"No, you're not. Play another round." Talon elbows him.

"Oh, no, poor baby," Ravenna teases, reaching across the table for his hands. "Is Athan not playing fair?"

Miles pouts his lip and bats his eyes at her.

"No one takes advantage of my baby boy." She pats his hands

in mock sympathy.

Being the youngest in our group, Miles is used to the teasing. He grins, bright and proud, then narrows his honey-brown eyes at Athan. "See? I knew my girl would have my back."

"*Your* girl?" Athan leans back and throws an arm around Ravenna's shoulder, tugging her close. "I think she's sitting next to *me*."

"Only so she can keep you in check."

"Yeah, okay. Talon, deal." Athan removes his arm from Ravenna's shoulder and smirks at Miles as he waits for the cards.

Talon starts shuffling, a wicked twinkle in his eye. Cards slap onto the table, and the game begins again.

In the middle of their card game, one of the tavern's younger barmaids strolls over, gracefully balancing five frothy beer mugs on a tray.

"Enjoy, you all," she says sweetly, carefully placing the mugs on the table.

She turns to leave, but Talon snags her hand, gently tugging her back toward him, brow arched with mischief. "Where do you think you're off to so fast? Don't I even get a proper hello?"

"Hello, Talon," she sighs. Her faded brown dress and cream-colored apron do little to flatter, but her amber eyes shine brightly beneath a curtain of thick, dark brown hair. Her skin, kissed by the sun, glows in the candlelight.

Talon flashes a roguish grin and pulls her onto his lap, arms looping casually around her waist. He playfully nuzzles her neck as she lets out a shriek.

"Talon! Knock it off," she giggles, trying to push him away. "I'm working."

She wriggles out of his grip, smoothing her apron, but not before shooting him a half-annoyed, half-affectionate smile. Then she's gone, vanishing through the swinging door into the kitchen.

The table falls into stunned silence. We all watch Talon's eyes follow her until she's completely out of sight.

Ravenna casts me a wide-eyed look.

Miles sits slack-jawed.

Athan just grins, full of teeth.

Talon turns back toward us and grabs his beer like nothing happened.

"What?" His eyes, far too round, flick up, and the faintest smirk plays at his lips.

"Is there something going on between you two?" I ask, lifting a brow.

"Maybe," he mutters into his mug, glancing at the kitchen door like it might reopen just for him.

The four of us exchange a look. Ravenna shrugs and reaches for one of the mugs.

Talon's no stranger to flings, but there was something different in the way his eyes lingered on her. Softer. Focused. Something almost... vulnerable. A dangerous thing, given his status. I tuck the thought away as the table stirs back to life, everyone reaching for their drinks.

Miles raises his mug. "Cheers to the best sons of bitches a guy could ask for."

"Agreed," Athan says, and we clink our mugs together.

I take a long swig. The beer is stale but cold and just what I need after today. I set the mug down with a breath, catching Ravenna out of the corner of my eye.

She's still drinking.

Talon, Miles, and Athan all set their mugs down, but Ravenna tilts hers back farther, draining every drop in one impressive, unapologetic gulp.

She exhales sharply and sets the empty mug down. Her weight shifts forward as she meets our impressed, mildly stunned gazes with a raised brow.

"Would you like another one?" Talon laughs. "Or should we just have Simon bring out a whole barrel?"

"If you're offering, I'd be happy to take one." Ravenna wipes her mouth with the back of her hand.

"Damn, sweetie," Athan chuckles. "Don't need you showing us up."

We four clink mugs again, spilling over the rim, and race to drain them.

I slam my mug down just a heartbeat before Athan, then Talon, then Miles.

Ravenna rolls her eyes, but the curve of her lips betrays her. She's smiling. Maybe just a little. But I'll take it.

This is what she needs. What we all need.

There's not much I can give her, not truly. But I can give her this. The laughter. The distraction. A moment of joy. And maybe, for tonight at least, that's enough.

CHAPTER 10

Ravenna

After winning three rounds of cards with the guys, the night rolls on in a haze of laughter, drinks, and the faint fuzziness induced by beer.

Talon and Miles must really be feeling it because they've had twice as many as I have. Both sway in their chairs and keep laying down the worst hands of cards.

I'm not sure how many he's had, but Athan can drink any-one under the table. I can tell he's drunk. His voice climbs with every sentence, but he's still all warmth and wide smiles. Codrin, on the other hand, has been taking his time, milking his fourth beer, which is more than half full.

"I win again, boys." Athan downs the rest of his beer, slamming the empty mug onto the table with such force that it wobbles and rattles the empty mugs. "Sure, you want to play another round?"

"Nope. I'm out." Miles leans back in his chair, defeated.

"One more round," Talon hiccups, "I know I can beat you."

"You okay there, Talon?" Codrin asks with a tight grin.

"I…" *Hiccup.* "Fine…" *Hiccup.*

"He's gone," I whisper loud enough for Talon to hear.

"No…I'm not." He stares at me with glazed eyes.

I roll my eyes at him and look away. Codrin's interest in Talon's drunken state has been replaced by something else. He sips at his drink, staring across the room. I follow his gaze to two older ladies standing near the bar, leaning close to each other, their shoulders shaking. Meira, a barmaid in her mid-thirties, is talking with a slightly older woman whom I don't recognize. The woman looks as though she's been crying, her eyes bloodshot, her hands tightly gripping a handkerchief as though she is trying to strangle it. I can't hear what they're saying, but I watch Meira point at our table and then give the woman a comforting hug. The woman shuffles away, leaving the tavern as Meira makes her way over to our table, carrying more beer on the tray.

"What was that about?" Codrin asks as she sets the mugs down on the table.

Her lips press into a tight line, but her electric-blue eyes soften as she lifts them to look at Codrin. We've known Meira since we started coming here a year ago. I truly admire the woman. There's something about the way she moves. Her chin high, shoulders squared that dares anyone to try her patience. And plenty have. They don't usually try twice.

Shaking her head, her voice low, she says, "You know Magdelene Meler's two sons went missing last month, along with the Eldern boy." Meira lets out a deep sigh. "Apparently, now Magdelene's daughter is missing as well."

Both Codrin and Athan sit up straighter.

"Delia is missing? When?" Athan asks, leaning in.

I scoot closer and lean in as well, the noise around us dulling to a hum.

Codrin has been fighting nonstop, sending Father reports and addressing the matter in meetings. Father brushes it off every time. They're of age; I think even a couple of years older than me. He says they're just typical runaways. "Cowards probably jumped on a ship to escape their true purpose for this kingdom."

Supposedly, they were to join the Slayer Squad the week following their disappearance. But Codrin doesn't believe they just ran away and has been visiting with the families to get as much information as possible.

"Last night. She was last seen here in town." Meira clicks her tongue, sparing a quick glance at Athan before looking back at Codrin. The barmaid lets out a shaky breath, dropping her head in despair. "Is the king doing anything about this?"

"I sent him all the reports…again last week. We even had meetings to address the concerns on the missing boys and *other things* these past few days." Codrin slumps back, his shoulders sagging.

No need to mention Slatier demons and scare her or cause an outcry through the town.

"Hm." Meira is unimpressed with the whole matter, I know what she thinks of my Father, and I don't blame her. She turns on her heel, the tight curls of her long brown hair bouncing behind her as she heads back to the kitchen.

"First Delia's brothers and their friend go missing, and now her," Athan taps his finger on the table. "Something isn't sitting right if you ask me."

My stomach tightens. I never met Delia or her brothers, but Codrin has really taken this to heart over the past month. And still, my father shrugs it off like a petty inconvenience.

"I know." Codrin leans past me, speaking to Athan. "No one has shown up dead or alive. It's like they just vanished. The king isn't doing anything about it. He hasn't spoken with any of the other two kingdoms, either. Problem I'm having is he tells me it's not in my job description. It's for his royal guards to deal with. And we sure as hells know LT isn't doing shit about it."

"And you're surprised by this? It's Ulric. He's just there to look pretty in his armor," Athan sneers. "Every time he opens his mouth, I consider retiring early."

I chew on my bottom lip, considering the situation. Codrin has implored many times to send out search parties or to investigate where they were last seen. But knowing my father, that's not going to happen.

Codrin reaches an arm behind me and pulls me close to him, giving my shoulder a gentle squeeze. "I'm working on it. I promise. The king might not care about them, but I'm not going to ignore the problem," he whispers in my ear, but the words fall flat, sounding more for his own comfort then mine.

"What if more go missing? What do you think is happening to them?" I glance up at him, searching his face for reassurance, for something solid to hold onto in the swirl of uncertainty.

"I don't know yet, but I'm going to find out."

I catch Codrin glancing over my head at Athan, but I don't say anything.

The tavern quiets down as it begins to empty. Some of the swaying drunks still sing as they make their way out the door, a few making their way up the stairs with a lady.

The pianist starts up another tune, and Talon jumps from his chair so fast the chair flies back, hitting the wood floor with a thump.

"Hells, yes! I love this song!" Talon bellows and rushes to the piano.

Miles pushes off from his chair and stands, swaying briefly before placing both hands on the table to steady himself. His eyes stare off to nothing, the dark skin of his face ashy as though he's ready to upchuck at any moment. But he recovers and makes his way across the tavern to Talon, knocking into a few chairs and a table along the way.

Codrin and Athan fall silent as the three of us watch Talon and Miles, arms slung over each other's shoulders as they sing. Very off tune. And sway to the music. Some of the other drunks join in, singing and dancing. Even a few hard-focused card players clap and cheer. The melody spills from the corner piano, quick and jaunty, keys clinking like laughter over tankards.

The pianist doesn't miss a beat, rolling into a new tune with a flourish that lifts the room like a gust of wind as Talon and Miles sprint back to the table. Out of breath, sweat trickling down their brows.

"Stop being lumps, you three, and come dance." Talon grabs Codrin's arm and pulls, but Codrin doesn't move from the bench.

"Nope. I don't dance." Codrin pulls his arm free and grabs his mug, shaking his head.

"I'm in." Athan glances between the wall to his right and Codrin and me to his left. He's boxed in unless we move. With a shrug, he plants a hand on the table and, in one swift motion, steps up onto the bench, then onto the table. The weathered wood groans under his weight, almost tipping as he hops down with a thunderous thud. He turns back with a grin. "Come on, you two."

Talon and Miles grab Codrin's arm and pull him from the bench, dragging him across the tavern.

Athan holds his hand out to me.

"Oh, no. I'm good." I shake my head, trying to wave him off.

"I'm not taking no as an answer, sweetie."

I hesitate, not really wanting to make a fool of myself, but Athan's warm smile tugs at my heart, and I cave, scooting off the bench and taking his hand as he leads me to the rest of our group. Talon and Miles bounce on their toes and sway, arm in arm. Codrin shifts his weight back and forth in a stiff motion.

Athan starts dancing, still holding my hand. He sways us side to side, feet light despite his size, the rhythm catching in our steps. He raises my arm above my head and starts to spin me like a ballerina.

Around and around and around. Faster and faster, until the tavern blurs into streaks of candlelight and motion.

Athan's hand slips from mine, and I stumble, right into a wall of pure muscle.

My vision slowly stops spinning, and Codrin smiles down at me. His six-foot-three frame of lean muscle towers over me, and I have to crane my neck to look into his gray eyes.

Strands of his dark auburn hair fall over his eyes, giving him that dark, mysterious look. And those eyes. *Damn, those eyes.* A puff of breath escapes my lips, and my heart skips a beat. His eyes are a storm I would love to get swept away in.

"Well, hello," he exhales, his body softening as he wraps his arms around my waist, pulling me closer to his broad chest.

"Hi…" I smile in return, my arms locking around the back of his neck. Athan walks by and winks as he heads over to Talon and Miles.

And just for a heartbeat, in the middle of laughter, clinking mugs, and off-key songs, there's only him and me, swaying to a rhythm that isn't the music at all. The heat of his palms against my back, the brush of his chest against mine, sends sparks skittering down my spine, and suddenly, all I can think about is how easy it would be to close the space between us and taste the smile on his lips.

"Are you okay?" The soft concern in his voice shatters the warm haze of lust clouding my thoughts.

"I'm fine, Codrin." My tone comes out sharper than I mean, so I press my head against his chest, hoping to bury the sting of it.

"Will you ever stop lying to me?" His chest vibrates with a quiet chuckle, but there's no humor in it.

My jaw tightens. *Really?* Can we ever just have a moment where he isn't badgering me over my fucking feelings?

"Explain to me what happened to your mirror." He gently lifts my right hand from behind his neck, holding it between us. The small cuts along my knuckles catch the light.

"Don't think I didn't notice this. What's going on, Ravenna?"

Shit. I meant to put some cream on the cuts after I showered but Codrin had shown up shortly after I got out and I honestly spaced it after that.

A muscle in my cheek twitches. I blow out a sharp breath and drop my other arm from around his neck.

"I don't know. I have anger issues. I let out a little rage and the mirror lost. It's not a big deal." I withdraw my hand from his grasp.

A frown tugs at the corners of his mouth. I guess my dry humor isn't cutting it tonight.

"If you're angry, then talk to me. Let me be the one you unleash it on. Don't take it out on yourself." Codrin reaches for my hands again, his fingers warm around mine. "I'm not going to sit back and say nothing while you hurt yourself."

His eyes search mine, quiet but insistent.

"Was it Zavier? Or your father? Or…" He hesitates, jaw tightening. "Alaric?"

The name alone scrapes something raw inside me, but I look away, giving him nothing.

"I said it's not a big deal," I mutter, pulling my hands from his grasp again, more forcefully this time.

He doesn't press further, but the silence between us fills with everything I won't say and everything I *can't*.

The words wedge in my throat like splinters, sharp and immovable. Rage, helplessness, and fear churn inside me, rising fast and hot, threatening to drown me. My chest tightens. The soft buzz of beer and warmth from the fire and laughter. All of it is chased away in an instant.

My fists clench at my side. I can feel myself unraveling, thread by thread. But I don't move. Don't breathe too hard. Because if I do, I might not be able to put myself back together.

As if sealing a vow, he lifts my hand and presses a gentle kiss to the cuts across my knuckles. "I know you're stubborn.

Gods, you're so damn stubborn. But you don't have to carry everything alone."

He drops my hands, only to wrap his arms around my waist, pulling me flush against his chest.

I want to argue. To push him back and tell him to stop acting like I need protection all the time.

I want to.

But instead, the fight drains from me. The words I don't have slip away.

And I sink into him, letting myself fall deeper into his hold.

I *don't* want him to let me go.

A throat clears beside us, and Codrin shifts, stepping back just slightly. My heart sinks as his arms fall away from my waist.

"Codrin, Ravenna. Sorry to interrupt," Simon says, voice low and apologetic. "But I need a hand getting Willis upstairs. That man's gone and drunk himself into a coma again." His mouth tightens with a familiar sort of regret.

Codrin hesitates, eyes flicking to mine.

"Go ahead. I'll be fine. Athan's right there." I point past him. "And so is…"

My words trail off as I glance around.

Miles is slumped at a table, head cradled in the crook of his arm, barely conscious. *Poor kid.* He's going to hate himself tomorrow.

Talon sits in the far corner, elbow propped, chin resting in his hand, making goo-goo eyes at the barmaid from earlier, who now occupies the seat across from him, giggling behind her hand.

Codrin follows my gaze and sighs. "Athan," he calls, lifting a hand.

Athan strides over quickly. "What's up?"

"I need to help Simon with Willis."

Athan glances over his shoulder to the bar, where the elderly man sits hunched over in his seat, chin resting on his chest.

"Oh, poor man Willis," Athan chuckles, turning back to us.

Willis may be the town drunk, but when he isn't drinking, he's the sweetest old man you'd ever meet. He's been Simon's most loyal customer for years, and Simon always keeps a close eye on him. He's even tried cutting Willis off early a few times, hoping to keep him from getting this bad. But after one particularly dramatic night, when Willis stormed out in a rage and stirred up trouble across town, Simon learned his lesson. Now, he just lets the night run its course, knowing Willis is safer staying here.

"Will you keep an eye on Ravenna?" Codrin's hand grazes the small of my back, a gesture that makes my skin tingle with delight.

I huff. "Seriously. I'm not a child."

Codrin just throws me a stern look.

"Of course I'll watch my girl." Athan slings his thick arm around my shoulders and draws me into his solid frame. He's built like a bull, who is inches taller than Codrin, and much broader.

I pat his chest. It feels like hitting a stone wall. "See? I'll survive. Go help Simon. I might even take this opportunity to drink Athan under the table for once."

Athan chuckles, giving me a squeeze. "Now that's the spirit."

Codrin shakes his head, but a smile tugs at the corner of his mouth. "You two behave."

He pats Athan's shoulder and heads back toward the bar, where Willis sways perilously on his stool. Codrin catches him just in time, steadying him before he can faceplant into the floor.

With practiced ease, Codrin and Simon sling Willis's arms over their shoulders and guide him toward the stairs. The old man stumbles, legs rubbery and useless, making the climb look like a circus act teetering on disaster.

They nearly lose their balance halfway up, and I go still for a heartbeat, but Codrin adjusts quickly, steadying them both.

Eventually, they make it to the second floor and disappear down the hall, toward the room Simon always keeps ready for Willis on nights like this.

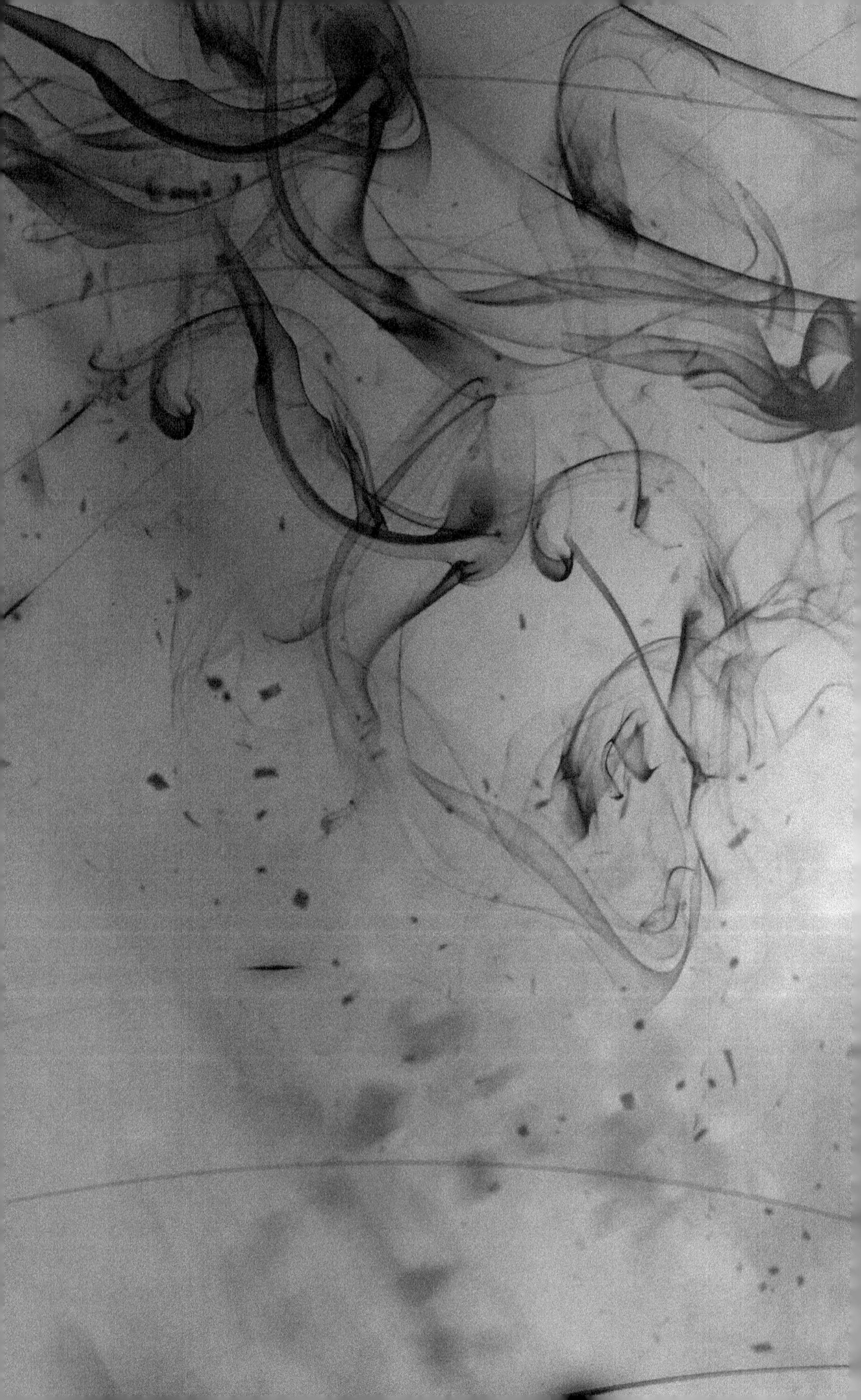

CHAPTER 11

Ravenna

The tavern thins out more as the night wears on, the boisterous noise fading to a lazy hum of soft chatter and the occasional creak of footsteps overhead. I remain close to Athan, nursing another beer I don't really want. My gaze keeps flicking toward the staircase, where Codrin disappeared with Simon and Willis. It's been a while. Longer than it should've taken to get the old man into a bed.

Something twists in my gut. It's not only worry. This is deeper. Heavier.

A low thrum starts beneath my ribs. It doesn't feel like danger… but it doesn't feel innocent either.

I glance at the stairs again. *Something's up there.* Waiting.

I shift in my seat, pulse spiking, hands curling around the rim of my mug to keep them still.

Athan says something beside me, but I'm not really listening. All I can give him is a quick *hum* in response.

A sudden gurgling noise interrupts the low buzz of my thoughts. Miles stands on shaky legs a few feet away. His face goes ash, a sickly cast to his normally rich complexion, eyes wide before he bends over and vomits all over his boots and the floor.

"Oh, gods, no," Athan groans, standing up with a grimace.

"That's it. I told him not to mix mead and ale." He slaps a hand to his forehead before jogging over to help him, muttering curses under his breath.

I stand quietly, watching Athan crouch beside Miles as he tries to steady him. Nobody else seems to care. It's just a regular night in the tavern.

No one would notice if I slipped away. And something inside me *wants* me to. Not just curiosity. Not just Codrin. A pull as if a thread is anchored to my ribs, reeling me toward a place I haven't been but somehow already know.

With Talon gone upstairs, likely tangled in the arms of that barmaid, and Athan fully distracted, the opportunity falls into my lap.

I take one last glance toward the bar. No sign of Codrin or Simon.

Sliding away from the booth, I move quietly, boots light against the creaking floorboards. I weave through tables and pass the piano, its notes now soft and haunting, like a farewell song.

The staircase looms ahead, dim and quiet, shadows pooling in the corners. My fingers brush the banister. A chill skates up my arm, featherlight, but it settles deep. Every step feels like stepping into something unseen. Something older. Wilder. And somehow, I don't want to turn back.

Candlelight flickers low along the walls as I ascend, one hand grazing the banister, my heart picking up its pace with every step. My feet move without thought now, like they know where they're going even if I don't.

Codrin should have been back by now.

Reaching the second-floor landing, I take one last glance over the railing. Athan is still preoccupied with a sick Miles, gently holding his shoulder as he sways over a bucket. No one's watching me.

I step forward. The hallway stretches out before me, lit by scattered candles mounted in wall sconces between doors that blend into the walls. I keep walking, slow and quiet. At the far end of the corridor, the hallway branches off. One path still lit, the other choked in blackness.

I pause at the split, turning toward the darker hallway. It's nearly pitch-black. No candles. No lanterns. Just a narrow window at the far end, caked in grime, letting in a sliver of moonlight that barely kisses the floor. The air is still, oppressive. Not even the creak of old wood or the moan of the tavern settling.

One door waits at the very end. Closed. Silent. But something pulls at me.

Not a sound. Not a voice. A dark and warm feeling, like velvet wrapping around my lungs.

It's not fear I feel. It's… hunger.

Not mine.

I take a step forward. Then another. My boots silent against the floorboards.

A breath lodges in my throat.

Anticipation builds deep in my gut as a low groan of wood shreds through the stillness. The door at the end of the hall creaks open slowly.

And I hold my breath as a tall figure steps out, wreathed in shadow.

It steps forward, just enough for the moonlight to catch its outline of broad shoulders that rise and fall with every breath it takes.

And its face…

Two glowing silver eyes. Burning like twin moons in a starless sky.

They lock on mine.

Every instinct screams for me to run. But I don't.

I *step closer.*

One foot in front of the other. The silence deepens. The air feels heavier now, thick with something ancient. Not danger. Something else. Warmth?

My pulse pounds but not with fear. With recognition.

The figure tilts its head. I mirror the motion, mesmerized.

Another step.

I don't even realize I've raised a hand until it's hovering midair, as if reaching for something I don't understand.

"Ravenna."

Did it just whisper my name? I'm not sure.

"Ravenna."

There! Now I know I heard my name. But it sounds like it's coming from farther away. I slowly tear my gaze away from the figure, looking over my shoulder.

Nothing.

I whip my head back to the dark hallway to find it empty. The door is still cracked open, but the figure is gone.

I swear I'm seeing things.

Shoulders dropping, I stumble back, colliding into something hard.

I feel the heavy breathing of someone behind me as strong hands clamp my shoulders.

"What are you doing up here?" Codrin's voice whispers in my ear.

I spin out of his grasp to face him and shrug a shoulder. "Just roaming around."

"In a dark hallway? Seems a bit dangerous. Don't you think?" Codrin steps into me, his arms snaking around the small of my back, locking me into his hold.

I tilt my head back to meet his storm-gray eyes. "Hmm… maybe I like the danger."

"Careful." His voice drops lower. A warning, but there's heat beneath it… a challenge.

His hand curves around my neck, fingers firm but gentle. His thumb grazes along the side of my jaw, keeping me exactly where he wants me.

"You never know what could be lurking in the shadows."

"I already found it," I want to say, but the words don't leave my mouth.

He leans in, lips ghosting mine, his breath warm, but he doesn't close the distance yet.

My hands find his chest, meaning to push him back. Instead, they fist the front of his shirt.

His touch steadies me as I lean into it. The weight of his hand isn't a threat. It's an anchor. Only with him could I bare my throat and feel no fear.

Codrin's other arm tightens around my waist more, drawing me flush against him. Unyielding. Certain. A silent promise that he wouldn't let me go unless I asked.

I don't.

I won't.

His nose grazes mine. His voice is a whisper, hazardous and intimate. "Tell me to stop."

I don't breathe. I don't blink. "Don't you dare."

My pulse pounds.

His mouth claims mine.

And I let him.

Gods, I want him.

The pressure is firm, commanding, but not cruel.

Because with him, giving in never feels like weakness. Only

strength shared.

I part my lips beneath his, a sharp gasp catching in my throat as his teeth graze my lower lip. It's a warning, a promise, and a challenge all in one. I answer the only way I can. I kiss him back, matching his hunger, refusing to back down even when he deepens the kiss and takes the lead again.

Sending me into submissive darkness.

"RAVENNA!"

My name drags me back to reality. Codrin pulls away and my shoulders drop as Athan's voice thunders against the tavern walls, laced with concern and a hint of annoyance.

"He has the worst timing," I murmurer.

Codrin releases me from his hold. "Tell me about it," he grumbles.

I pivot on my heel and rush back into the light as Athan calls my name again.

"RAVENNA!"

Gripping the railing, I lean far over, spotting Athan pacing the main floor, his neck craning as he scans the second floor for me.

"What?!" I hiss.

"Damn it, woman! Are you trying to give me a heart attack?" Athan's large hand slams to his chest as he takes a dramatic exhale. "You are really testing the strength of my old heart."

"Your old heart, really?" I roll my eyes. "Sure, Athan. I'll try to be better about not killing your ancient heart. So, overdramatic."

I mutter the last bit under my breath.

"What are you doing up there?"

Before I can answer, Codrin comes up behind me, his hand sliding along the small of my back as he leans over the railing, grinning down at his friend.

"Oh… never mind." Athan shakes his head.

"What's up, Athan?" Codrin asks with a little sternness in his tone.

"I need to get Miles back to the barracks." He makes his way toward Miles, who is still slumped over in his chair. "Poor kid has been puking nonstop." He groans as he hoists Miles to his feet and slings an arm around his shoulder.

"Need a hand?" Codrin makes his way toward the stairs.

"Nope. I got him. I'll see you all in the morning." Athan winks and heads out of the tavern.

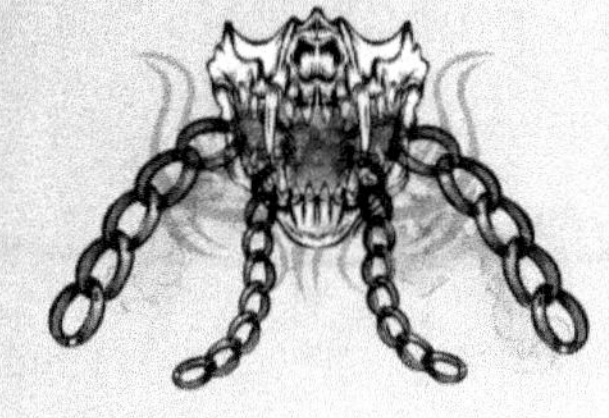

CHAPTER 12
Codrin

We set out early, the sea breeze rolling in from the coast, keeping the morning air sharp and clean. But the streets of Theiahold are far from calm.

For the past five days, word of the missing girl spread like wildfire. Fear clings to the air, and the tension is palpable. People murmur in hushed voices, glancing over their shoulders as they go about their routines. Parents keep their children close, and shopkeepers linger at their doorways, eyes wary.

I haven't let go of the missing girl either. Even after talking with General Hawk and requesting an audience with King Zephyr, both of them brushed me off, insisting Lieutenant Ulric Hollowstone has it handled.

I doubt that.

No one says it aloud, but everyone's treating her disappearance like a closed case. Forgotten.

So, I took a patrol shift today. Unofficially.

We pass four slayers, laughing loudly with their arms slung over each other's shoulders, swaying as they stumble back toward the barracks after what I'm sure was a full night of drinking. A few more rush past us, one calling out, "Good morning, Captain!" with a quick wave before they round the corner ahead. Heading toward the main café, making the most of a rare morning without training.

Our boots echo softly over the cobblestone streets as the squad around me falls into easy chatter and laughter.

"I'm telling you, we fake her death," Miles says, deadpan. "Boom. Funeral, ashes, Ravenna sneaks out on a ship with you, Codrin."

I give Miles a half-smile and a distracted nod, his words slipping past the weight crowding my thoughts.

"I'm telling you," Athan chuckles, clapping a hand on Talon's back and nearly knocking him off balance. "We just throw Talon here into a wedding gown and send his cute ass down the aisle in her place."

"Talon would make a beautiful bride." Miles twirls one of his blades with a grin.

Ravenna exhales a small laugh, shaking her head. "Maybe we'll call that plan B… or plan C."

What started as a serious conversation about finding a way out of her arranged marriage has now completely devolved. But I don't mind the shift. At least she's laughing. Even if her smile doesn't quite reach her eyes. She catches my eye for a moment, just long enough for something unreadable to flicker there, then looks away like nothing happened.

A part of me knows we're grasping at straws, and the truth sits like a stone in my gut. There's no easy way out of this. We can joke about disguises and fake deaths, but none of it changes the reality. Alaric isn't the kind of man to be easily fooled, and there's no telling what lengths he'll go once he's made up his mind. The others don't get it. They can't.

"Or poison the wedding wine and let the bastard drop mid-vow," Talon mutters.

My jaw tightens. That one doesn't sound like a joke. And a darker part of me, one that knows more than I'll ever admit, wonders if even that would be enough.

As we near the bakery, Warren Bullock, the baker, leans against the doorframe, his arms crossed over his chest, his brown eyes scanning the streets, settling on me as we near.

"Good morning, boys… and lady," he tips his head toward Ravenna, who returns the gesture. "What brings you all here?"

I plant a foot on the entryway step. "I'd like to talk to you about the girl who went missing a few nights ago."

Warren drops his arms and lets out a sigh as he pushes off the doorframe. "Didn't think investigating things like this was in a slayer's job description…" He arches a brow, fingers lacing over his round stomach.

"It's not," I admit. "But curiosity's gotten the better of me. I would like to know more about what happened that night."

He scratches the side of his neck. "Well, like I told Lieutenant Hollowstone, she came by just as I was closing. Asked for some loaves of bread. I gave her a couple. She left."

"Did she say anything? Hint where she was going? Was anyone with her?"

Before he could answer, movement behind him catches my eye.

He steps aside as his wife steps into the doorway, a beaming smile lighting up her face. "Codrin!" she says, flour dusting her apron and streaked across the dark skin of her right cheek and forehead. Her curly dark hair is bundled in a bright wrap, and the scent of fresh, warm biscuits fills my nostrils from the tray resting in her hands like an offering from the gods.

"How are you, sweetie? Here… you all want some?" she offers. "Fresh from the oven."

Before I can respond, Athan and Miles swarm her like starved hounds.

"I love these!" Miles says stuffing one in his mouth and grabbing for a second one.

Athan just gives me a smug look with half a biscuit already in his cheek. I roll my eyes as he steps around me.

Azalee's smile widens as she brushes past me. "Of course. What are you all up to this fine morning?"

"They're here about the missing girl," Warren answers.

Talon and Ravenna reach for a biscuit, just as her smile quickly falters and she looks over her shoulder to her husband with a crease of concern.

"Delia?" she asks softly.

I pivot toward her. "Yes, her."

She nods, turning fully to me. "I spoke to her for a little bit." She holds the tray out to me.

"What about?" I ask, taking a biscuit, but I don't bite into it.

"Not much, really. She said something about needing to find her brothers. Was planning on heading north."

I open my mouth to speak but an uncontrollable choking cough interrupts me from behind.

"Whoa, easy, man. Don't choke." Miles pats Athan's back as he leans forward, hands on his knees. Bits of biscuit flying as Athan tries to catch his breath.

"You, okay?" Talon says, rushing to Athan's side.

Athan straightens slowly. "Yep…fine," he gasps, still red in the face.

Ravenna silently steps up beside me.

Talon turns away from the recovering Athan and narrows his eyes on Azalee. "Why north?"

Azalee shrugs. "She didn't say. But she seemed… determined."

"Like she knew where her brothers could have gone off to?" My voice drops to a whisper.

She nods her head slightly, her eyes glued to mine with concern.

"You told the royal guards you never spoke to her," Warren says sharply, stepping closer and resting a gentle hand on her arm.

She shoots him a stern look. "Those guards couldn't track a breadcrumb trail in a bakery. And I trust these ones more." Her deep brown eyes scan softly over us.

"We'll figure this out," I promise her. But a part of me suspects that was a lie. If Delia really went north, she would've had to pass through the Nothingness Forest. Beyond that? The endless snowy mountains of Nivalis Requiem Summit.

And Veilstead.

No. She wouldn't go there. Why would she? Even crossing the forest alone is suicide. It doesn't make sense.

"I know the guards found a shawl and a half-smashed lantern in the alley," Warren adds, pointing across the street. "Just over there."

"Thanks," I say. "We'll check it out."

We say our goodbyes, Athan and Miles snatching the last biscuits from the tray as we cross the street toward the narrow alley between two shops.

The shadows feel cooler here, boxed in by tall buildings. Scrap wood, rusted pipes, and bent metal litter the edges. We spread out along the alley, moving carefully.

Ravenna tosses aside a board. "Do you think she was with someone?"

Miles kicks an empty can aside, eyes sharp as he scans the ground ahead. "If she wasn't, someone took her."

"Could've been both," I murmur. "Someone pretending to help her. Or she met up with the wrong person."

I sweep my hand along the side of one wall, searching for

marks, blood, something. But the guards were too thorough or maybe purposefully careless. No signs of struggle. No drops of blood. Just a cleaned-up echo of where a girl might have vanished.

I make a mental note to review Ulric's report again when we get back. At least Azalee gave us something. It isn't much, but it's more than we had before. And maybe a step closer to finding Delia and her brothers and their friend.

We spend nearly an hour scouring the alley, checking gutters and shadowy corners. But it's like she vanished into mist. The end of the alley opens into the outskirts of town, to a worn back road that slopes gently toward the main gates. Out of town and into open fields toward the border of the forest.

I stare at the road for a long time before we turn back, re-tracing our steps out of the alley and to the main center.

But there are still too many questions.

And not enough answers.

We wander the town silently, killing time and pretending we're not all frustrated and exhausted.

The sun hangs high in the afternoon sky, casting long gold shadows that cling to the edges of the buildings. The air now thick and hot, the kind that sticks to your skin and saps your patience.

We spread out along the stone fountain in the town's center.

I lean against the edge, catching my breath and find myself watching her again.

Ravenna stands feet away, chatting with Talon and Miles.

With everything going on my eyes still wander to *her*.

She's radiant. Even when she's not trying to be.

The light catches her hair just right, and for a moment, she almost doesn't look like a slayer or a princess, just a girl standing in the sun, free for a breath.

She catches me staring. Just a flick of her eyes.

But it's enough.

She smiles. Small. Barely there. But it's for me.

And just like that, everything else disappears. The heat. The mission. The ache I've been carrying in my chest for days.

This moment, Ravenna, is all I need.

An arm suddenly loops around my neck, yanking me into a headlock.

"Look at this lovesick bastard." Athan laughs, grinding his knuckles into my scalp. "Someone get a bucket, I think he's about to start reciting poetry."

"Get off me, you overgrown ox." I grunt, struggling as he laughs and finally lets go.

I rake a hand through my tousled hair and glare. "You're an ass."

"And if you drool any harder, you'll flood the city." He wipes fake tears from his eyes. "It's honestly impressive how pathetic you look."

"I'm not even doing anything," I mutter, though my eyes stray back to Ravenna just in time to catch her laughing at something Talon said.

"Right. 'Watching.'" Athan chuckles under his breath.

I don't respond.

Athan steps up beside me, hammer slung over his shoulders. "Seriously though… it's different between you two."

I glance at him. "What do you mean?"

He nods toward her. "She fights harder when you're watching. You," he gestures at me, "go soft whenever she's near. You think it's subtle. It's not. The whole squad is noticing."

I say nothing, because what the hells can I say? He's right.

Athan drops his voice so only I can hear. "Just don't get so lost in those icy blues that you miss the enemy's blade swinging your way."

I smirk. "She can handle herself."

"I know she can," he says, his grin fading slightly. "But I also know you'd take a blade for her without blinking. That kind of loyalty doesn't go unnoticed."

I glance sideways at him. He raises his brows like he's daring me to deny it.

"Just saying." He shrugs, then backs off as the others approach.

Talon leans against the fountain's ledge. "Damn, this heat. Can we head back now?"

I let out a deep sigh. "Sure. There's nothing else we can do here for now."

I can feel Athan watching me again. Measuring. Waiting to see if I'll break.

Hells, I shouldn't care so much what him or any of them, for that matter, think. I've led this squad for years, and I trust them with my life. But they're not the ones I'm truly worried about. One slip, and it could all unravel. Not just my position but hers too. I shouldn't have kissed her. Should've kept that distance I worked so damn hard to maintain. But now that I know what it's like to feel her lips on mine…I can't go back.

Her eyes meet mine.

Just a moment.

Just enough.

Tonight.

That word passes between us without breath or sound. My heart stutters. My lips betray me with the faintest smile.

I've lived in Theiahold for years, trained in its fields, fought in its shadows, but I've never once called it home. Not until she smiled at me that first time years ago.

Athan claps a hand on my shoulder, leans in, and murmurs, "And there it is."

Shit.

I clear my throat and shift my stance.

My eyes stealing one last quick glance at her. I watch her face drop and a slight satisfied smirk cross her lips her as her eyes drift past the group. My gaze follows and I spot Lucas and Zavier, who's supporting his arm in a sling, stroll by. The moment Zavier's dark gaze locks onto Ravenna, every muscle in my body seems to flex with tension as I fight back the urge to go plow him. But as the captain, I hold myself back.

"Alright," I say, stepping forward with a stretch to relieve my muscles but keeping a watchful eye on Ravenna as her gaze drifts away from Zavier and back to the group. "Let's eat."

"Sweet!" Athan pipes up as he steps beside Talon, whose head is resting on the fountain's ledge, and gives a slight punch to his arm. "Hey! What's up with you? Your barmaid lady keeping you up late?"

"No. Just some stupid dreams…" His voice trails off. "Actually, I could get some food."

"Didn't you eat two breakfasts this morning?" Athan arches a brow.

"I've been burning calories like no other these past few days of training." Talon stretches his neck side to side, cracking it once before slanting me a hard look. "Unlike watching your friend flirting from the sidelines."

My eyes widen, but before I can say a word, Athan jumps in, mouth full of fake shock.

"Wait! Who was *flirting*?" He glances between me and Ravenna like he doesn't already know.

Ravenna rolls her eyes. "You're all idiots."

She turns and starts walking toward the cafe. And of course, all four of us follow. Her protectors never far from her side. I open my mouth, probably to say something dumb just to keep her smiling.

We freeze. The entire town stills.

The sound punches the air like a war drum.

CLANG. CLANG. CLANG.

The town's bells. Loud and unrelenting. The alarm that every slayer has been trained since childhood to recognize.

Danger. Immediate. Close.

Nearby, a townsperson shouts, voice cracking over the wind, "Slatier demons! IN TOWN!"

How? Its daylight. No demons have ever wondered far from the forest. So, why are there Slatier demons in town now? I can feel my stomach twist with an uneasy tightness. Some-thing isn't sitting right and I don't like it.

The town erupts into chaos around us, drowning out my every thought and question as iron sings and boots slam stone as the squad rushes toward the pounding heart of it all.

Ravenna, axe in hand, charges into the madness without a second thought.

Before I can shout out to her, she is already gone. Vanishing into the crowd of frantic townspeople.

I curse, sword flashing from its sheath as we all sprint down the street. Rounding the corner, I'm hit with a tidal wave of screams and smoke.

My team splits off as more slayers join.

Rounding the corner to screams and smoke.

A house is already ablaze, flames licking the sky as people run in every direction. A woman with a child in her arms sobs as she's pulled away by a guard. The acrid stench of burning wood mixes with something far fouler. Demon blood, sharp and sulfurous, like rotting meat soaked in brimstone and iron.

I scan the square. Too many civilians. Too many Slatiers. We don't have time for fear. No time to think.

Muscle memory kicks into full gear and I lift my blade, voice cutting through the noise. "Alpha squad. Clear civilians and hold the line! Bravo squad, with me! We drive them back from the east!"

The slayers snap into motion. Weapons drawn. Orders obeyed. No hesitation.

We move.

My blade tightens in my grip as the first Slatier comes into view, tall, hunched, claws dripping red. Its yellow eyes find me through the smoke.

I don't wait. I run straight for it. My blade clashes with the demon's claws, iron meeting bone with a high-pitched shriek. It lunges, snapping its jaws, wild and rabid, and I sidestep, burying my sword into its ribs.

I rip the blade free, black blood sprays my face and across

the stone, and I spin just in time to see another one charging toward me.

This one's smaller. Faster. Screeching with laughter like it's playing a game. I meet it head-on, swinging hard.

Ashenbane iron cleaves through its shoulder, severing the limb completely but it doesn't stop. Hissing with a grin of razor sharp, jagged teeth it charges at me again.

I swing my sword. Slicing through its midsection like butter and it skins across the stone, lifeless.

A woman's scream of pure terror pierces the air farther down the street.

I glance that way just as a home collapses in flames.

Villagers scatter in the street, some pointing, others shouting.

"Someone's still in there!" a man yells, his face pale, eyes wide with horror.

Another woman sobs uncontrollably, clawing at a neighbor's arm.

"Please, my son. He's inside!" she cries.

My pulse spikes.

Someone is trapped beneath the wreckage.

Three guards rush past me to help the woman's son.

Across the town square, Athan barrels into a demon, slamming it through a wooden post. Miles isn't far, blood streaming down his face, but he's swinging like a madman.

I whirl around at a shrill, agonizing scream, only to witness a slayer being ripped apart at the waist by an oversized Slatier.

The demon lets out a roar as it tosses the slayer's body parts toward me.

"Fuck!" I duck at the last second as guts and blood shower me.

Where the fuck is Ravenna?

We have been on hundreds of patrols. We have fought many demons over the years. And yet something deep within me tightens in my stomach over her safety right now.

I know she would be pissed if she knew how worried I was.

Another Slatier leaps from a rooftop, crashing onto a wagon behind me. I spin and drive my sword up through its gut, its blood gushing along my arm.

Smoke thickens in the air. Another scream. This one younger. A child.

Talon, eyes blazing, slashes through two demons at once, shirt torn, blood on his blade. He yells something as he leaps forward, slides along the dirt, and scoops the child into his arms.

More demons leap from rooftops, climbing walls, dragging civilians from hiding. The body of another slayer flies past me, thrown like a ragdoll.

My boots skid over blood as I scan the hell that has taken over the town.

Where is she?

"Ravenna!" I call out, knowing she won't answer.

A second demon barrels toward me. I sidestep at the last

second, swinging my sword low, the blade slicing through its leg. It collapses, snarling, and I finish it with hard stab through its gut before it can rise again.

I turn on my heel and freeze. My eyes widen, and I hold my breath as I witness another slayer's final moments. His screams echo in my ears as he's thrown from a rooftop by a Slatier. They're cut short as he lands face down on a metal pipe sticking up from the rubble. It drives through his face and out the back of his skull.

A knot drops to the pit of my stomach as I scan the grounds once more for her. These tragedies and horrors aren't anything new. We've fought in countless battles together, but somehow, this one just doesn't sit right.

My mind flashes to her laughter echoing across the courtyard, the way her eyes catch the light when she's scheming something reckless. The press of her body as we danced at the tavern. The taste of her lips. That fire. That light. Gone.

Smoke thickens around me. Screams blend together until they're a chorus. I fight on, feet moving without thought, cutting down whatever gets too close. But my focus is fractured. Shards of panic slice through every breath.

What if she's hurt?

What if I'm too late?

"I can take care of myself," her voice echoes in my head.

Yeah. I know she can. But I still fucking worry.

Another demon roars from a rooftop, leaping into the street.

It lands on a merchant's cart with a crash, splintering wood and scattering terrified townsfolk. I charge, blade raised, blood already painting my face. But through it all, my eyes keep searching. My heart keeps pounding.

I cut through another demon, panting hard, sweat and blood stinging my eyes. Smoke swirls through the air, thick, choking. It clings to my skin and fills my lungs.

And then, I see her.

Through the haze, barely twenty feet away, a flash of silver hair catches the firelight.

She stands her ground, axe clenched in both hands, facing off against a Slatier demon that has to be at least seven feet tall. Its dark flesh stretches over bone, a grin carved into its grotesque face like it's enjoying this.

"Ravenna!" I scream, shoving through debris and bodies, sprinting toward her. But she doesn't hear me. Doesn't look. She's locked in the fight.

A perfect block. A sharp swing. A clean slice across the demon's arm. It howls.

Gods, she's holding her own.

The demon doesn't stagger. Doesn't back down. In one quick breath it lunges but Ravenna sidesteps, swinging her double-bladed axe in one fluid arc. The blade bites deep into its chest, but the demon doesn't even flinch.

It's too fast. Too strong.

Its clawed hand swishes through the air and crashes into her side and she flies. Hits the ground with a sickening thud. Her axe clatters from her grip. She doesn't move. Not a twitch.

"Nooo!"

I run faster.

The demon gathers up her axe in one hand and then turns its attention to her. Looming over her, breathing hard, it stoops down and scoops her up like she weighs nothing. Slinging her over its shoulder, limp like a broken doll.

"RAVENNA!"

I throw myself forward. Iron in hand. Blood in my mouth. I slash at the demon's leg, but it turns, and its massive claw arcs through the smoke.

The crack of the impact crushes into my chest and I fly backward, slamming into a collapsed wall of rubble. Stars flash behind my eyes. Pain explodes through my ribs. I gasp for air but get nothing but fire.

No. Get up. You have to get up.

I try to move but my body doesn't listen. My fingers twitch uselessly in the dirt.

The demon vanishes into the smoke with her still slung over its shoulder.

A roar erupts from deep within my chest A ragged, broken sound.

A calming, yet cold and heart stopping familiar voice comes

from behind me.

"You might want to sit this one out."

Footsteps crunch under the rumble. Every step nearing closer with a delicate steadiness.

"Don't worry," the silhouette slowly stepping through the smoke, the outline long and lean, half shadowed by firelight, "he'll save her…"

Golden eyes blaze over a fang-lined smile.

"…baby brother."

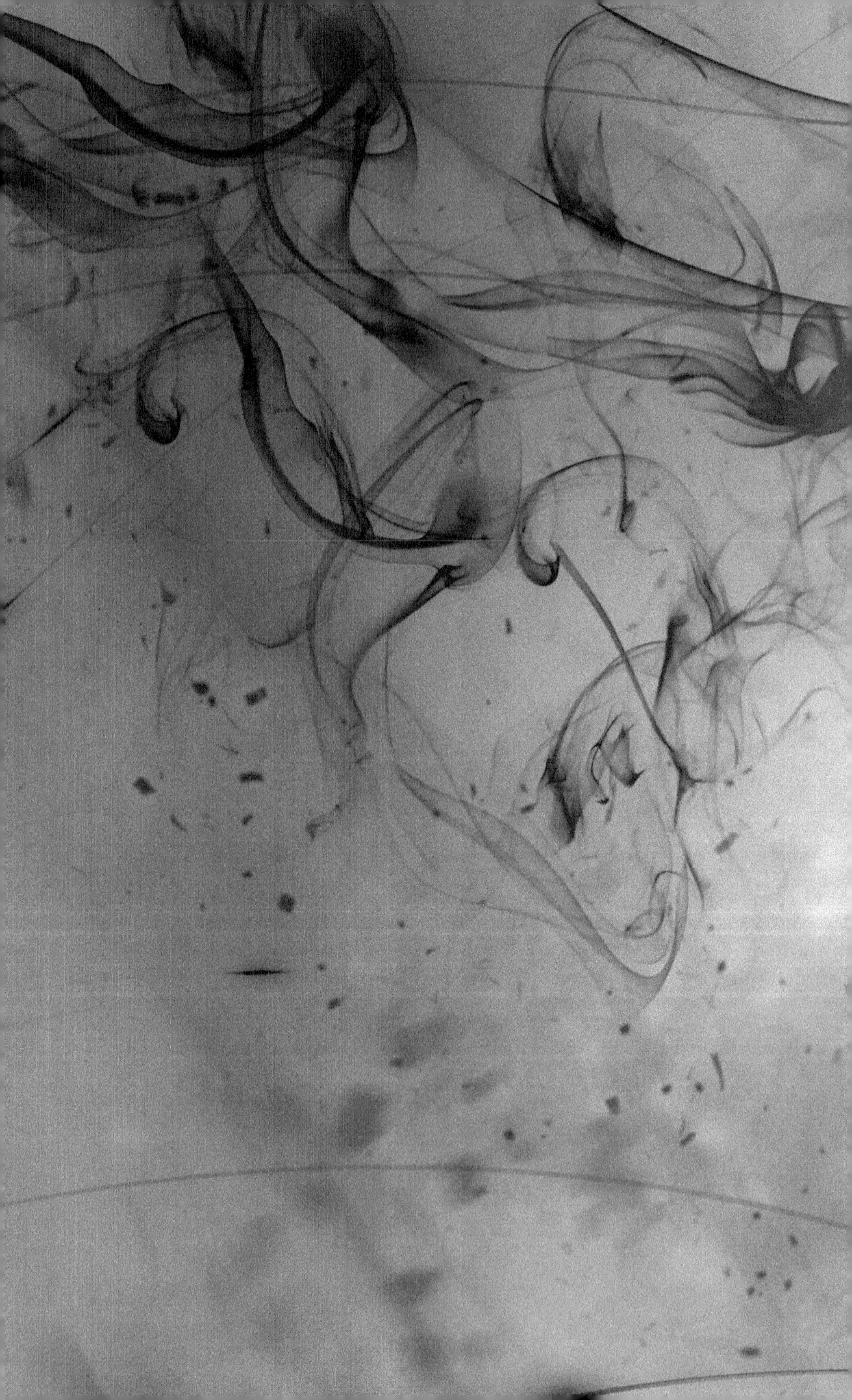

CHAPTER 13

Ravenna

A soft shuffling pulls me from the dark. My fingers twitch and brush along the thin, small blades of what could only be grass. The pounding in my skull keeps me and the pain in my chest escalates with every breath I take.

The last thing I remember was fighting that godsdamned demon. I had it, until it caught me off guard with a surprise swing. Then, nothing. Maybe I heard Codrin's voice, distant and wild with panic. Or was that just a dream?

Leaves crunch near my head and my eyes snap open, every nerve braced for battle. Only to be met with… boots?

Polished black boots with not a speck of dirt on them. They step out of view, and a twig snaps. The ground shifts as someone lowers beside me.

"You're awake." The voice is calm. Smooth. Unfamiliar. "How are you feeling?"

I sit up slowly, hissing through my teeth. My body protests with a low throb in my ribs as I reach for my pounding head. My fingers brush over a small gash caked in dry blood along my hairline and forehead.

I catch a glimpse of a man at my side, watching me from just feet away. He's dressed in elegant black. A silk blouse hangs open slightly at the collar and fitted pants cling to strong legs like they were stitched to his skin. He runs a hand through shaggy, shoulder-length, jet-black hair, like ink poured from a bottle.

I hate to admit it, but he's kind of handsome in that dangerous, untouchable way. That square jaw and sharp cheekbones. But it's his eyes that have me hooked.

Elegant gold. Like suns set in stone. Warm at first glance, but with a darkness behind them that makes my skin tighten.

"Who the fuck are you?" I bite out, my slayer instincts faster than my princess manners.

A low chuckle slips from his lips. "I was warned you had a mouth on you."

I don't respond.

Instead, I keep my gaze steady, my breath even, as my fingers inch behind my back. Slow and silent my fingers move toward the small leather sheath hidden beneath my shirt. My bear claw knife. A gift from Talon. A last-resort kind of weapon.

I grip the hilt. But before I can even think about moving.

"I wouldn't do that if I were you, Princess." His voice is smooth. Confident. Laced with amusement. His head turns, and those golden eyes find mine. They're not soft anymore. They're molten steel. And my entire body locks up.

"Especially since I'm the one who saved your cute ass."

In half a breath he's on me. My back slams against the earth, breath knocked from my lungs. One hand clamps my wrist to the ground, the other plucks the knife from my grip with infuriating ease.

He leans down close, lips curved in a smug grin.

"Don't need you killing the one person who saved you."

My pulse stutters.

Who is this man?

His face is too perfect. Too controlled. The way he seems to carry himself is like power that loops around him like a second skin. Slick and cold, like mist sliding over stone, yet somehow pressing in on me from all sides. The feel of his body against mine prickles my skin, unnatural and suffocating. And those glowing eyes watching me with a stillness that feels ancient. And predatory.

He releases my wrist, standing with the smooth, silent power of someone who's always been the hunter, never the hunted. My knife dangles from his fingers before he casually slides it into his belt.

I stay on the ground for a moment too long. Breathing too hard. Trying not to show it.

My eyes flick around the clearing. Trees. Mist. Silence.

I can tell we are on the outskirts of the Nothingness Forest but I'm not sure how far we are from Theiahold.

And Codrin? Why isn't he here? My throat tightens. Where is he?

He's not coming, says the voice deep within me. It's slick. Cold.

Twisted with hatred. *He let you go. Didn't even bother chasing after the demon. And now…*

My blood chills.

Now a stranger has done what he couldn't. What he didn't. Saved you.

Something shifts. Just at the edge of my sight.

I turn sharply, but nothing's there. Only my own shadow, cast long against the mist-laced ground.

Except… I swear it looks as though it doesn't match me.

It's angled all wrong. Elongated in a way that defies the light.

And then, so faint I almost miss it, it moves. A twitch. A stretch. A slow, deliberate curl of the fingers.

I don't move. I *know* I'm not moving.

A chill creeps along my neck. I blink, and it's still again. Normal. Harmless.

Maybe I imagined it. Maybe I'm just… disoriented.

I shake away the tension gripping at me, trying to shake loose the voice… and whatever the hells I just saw of my own shadow.

Alaric chuckles low under his breath, and my attention darts back to him.

"It's been quite a day," Alaric says, his tone so calm it grates against my skin.

He steps away from me, slow and deliberate, giving me space, I hope. As if that will make me feel any safer.

It doesn't.

He crouches a few feet away, brushing a fallen leaf from his knee.

"I was nearby when I saw *it*," he says casually, like he's commenting on a dinner party gone dull. "A Slatier demon, dragging a woman's limp body through the trees like a sack of grain. I'll admit, curiosity got the better of me." He glances at me. "Imagine my surprise when I realized who it was."

"You followed it?" I ask, voice hoarse.

"I hunted it." His gaze sharpens. "Watched it slither its way into the Nothingness Forest. Did you know it was heading straight for the edge? Past the ward line?" He doesn't wait for an answer. "It would've crossed. And once it had, you wouldn't be sitting here, Princess."

My tongue sticks to the roof of my dry mouth.

"I killed it," he adds softly. "Before it killed you."

The words fall like stones into the clearing.

A thousand replies burn on my tongue, but I can't get a single word to form. I should be grateful. I *should* feel relief. But all I feel is that creeping unease again, like a trap has just sprung shut. Then he lifts his chin and gives me the kind of look that wraps itself in silk but cuts like a knife.

"No need to thank me," he says with a tilt of his head. "Though I'd be lying if I said I wasn't hoping for some sign of appreciation."

"Why?" I manage, my voice like gravel. "Why help me?"

He studies me for a long moment, the corners of his mouth twitching with something unreadable. "Let's just say," he murmurs, walking slowly toward me again, "I have a vested interest in keeping my bride alive."

The word slams into me like a blow.

My stomach flips, nausea curling low like I've swallowed poison. *Bride…*

I stare, wide-eyed, lips parting as the words tumble out.

"King Alaric Vyrenhartmire," I whisper.

His smile deepens, slow and mocking. "At your service."

He stops just short of me. So, close I can smell the faint trace of something sweet and dark clinging to his collar like wine and blood and something colder beneath.

He leans in, voice low and rich, like a secret whispered in the dark. "And between us, I rather enjoyed saving you."

Before I can spit a reply, something slithers into my mind. Soft and feminine, like a feather brushing across the inside of my skull.

Of all the people… The voice giggles. *I mean of all the vampires in the world. He saved you.*

A hollow ache blooms in my chest. My spine arches as I force the agony down.

It wasn't Codrin who came for you. It was Alaric. He followed the demon. Fought it. He's here. And Codrin…?

"Shut up," I mutter under my breath.

Alaric's brows lift slightly, curiously but I ignore him.

Codrin seriously left me to die. I fingers tore at the blades of grass, ripping them from the ground at the root. *He would be here if he truly cared.* My heart hammered against my chest to the thought as it boiled within me with every breath.

"Are you okay, Princess?" Alaric's voice shakes me out of my rage.

I snap to my feet, breath ragged with the anger I was feeling more toward Codrin, not Alaric. "Don't stand there like you're some fucking savior."

Alaric just smile and says in a soothing, gentle tone. "Well, I believe I did *rescue* you," he says, smoothing a nonexistent wrinkle from his sleeve. "You were unconscious. Bleeding and alone. The demon had plans for you that would've made even the old gods weep. So, in a way yes. I will say I am your savior."

"I don't need your fucking act," I snap, eyes blazing. "You swoop in with your smug smiles and perfect timing. What, you want me to fall at your feet for not letting a demon rip me apart?"

Well, if it wasn't for him. That's exactly what would've happened to me. But the fury I'm feeling I know isn't all directed at him. Right now, he is the only one standing in the crossfires.

His grin grows, slow and knowing. "No, Ravenna. I don't want you at my feet." He steps closer, just once, gaze steady. "I want you standing… at my side."

Because Codrin doesn't. He never did.

I shake my head again, heart thundering against my ribcage with confusion. Anger. Pain.

He wants me. The words race through my mind. Codrin *always wanted me. Didn't he?*

If he did, then where is he? The voice echoes louder now. It doesn't feel like just a thought. It has *weight*. Presence.

My chest seizes around the thought.

Where *was* he?

If Alaric followed the demon into the Nothingness Forest. Fought it, killed it. And where was Codrin?

Why hasn't he come?

Why isn't he here now?

My eyes drift, unwillingly, to Alaric. Standing there like he belongs in the shadows. Too still. Too patient.

He says nothing and he doesn't have to. Because I'm already unraveling. Because a small broken piece of me is starting to believe the voice that swirls in my head.

What if… Codrin really didn't care?

This vampire. This man I'm meant to hate. Is the only reason I'm still alive.

Alaric shifts as his hand disappears into the tall grass, only to reappear a split second later with my axe in hand.

"Here. You might need this," he says with a soft grin, handing the axe to me.

I take it, fingers slowly closing around the handle. It feels heavier now. Or maybe it's the weight of betrayal and truth that has finally broken inside me.

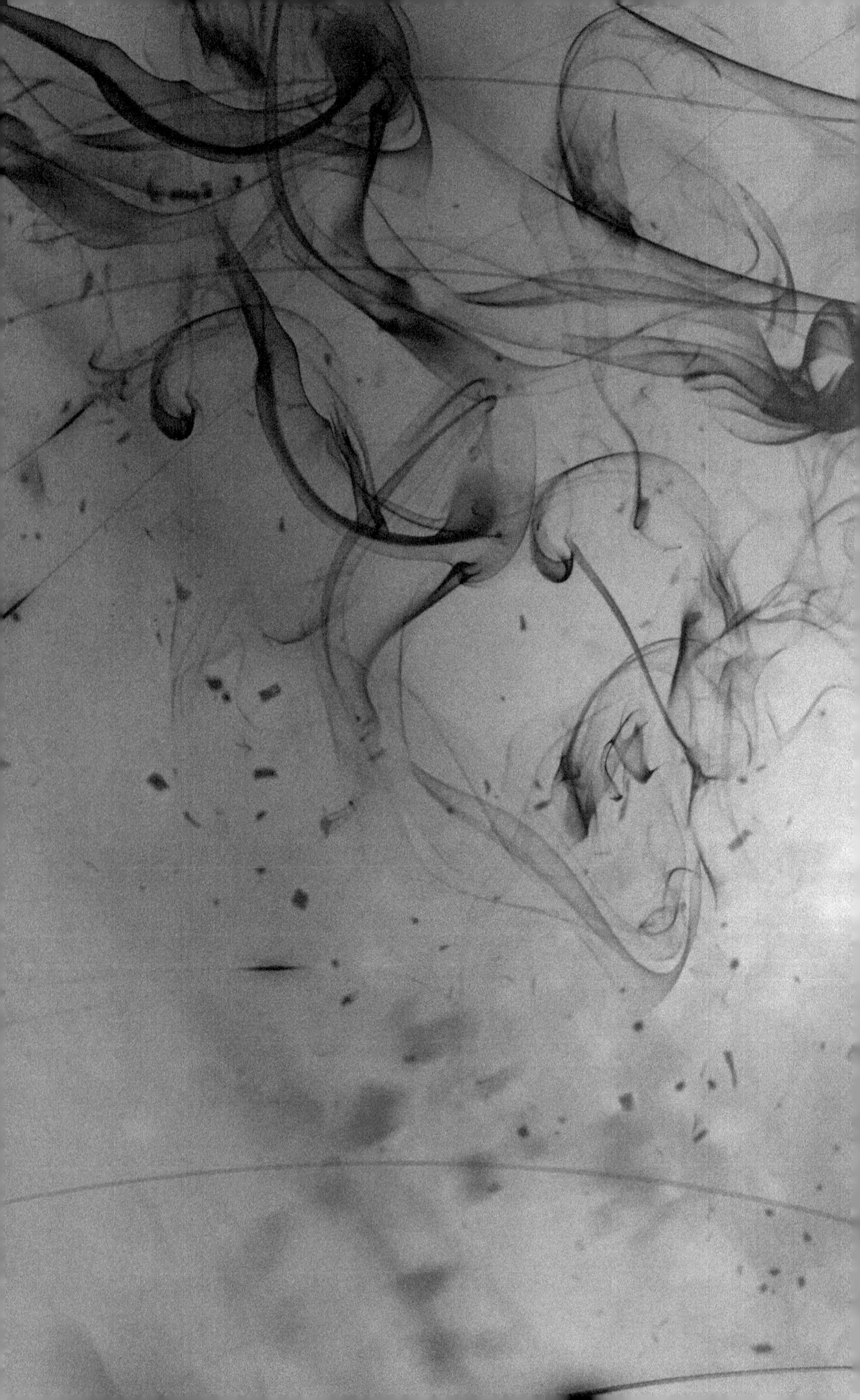

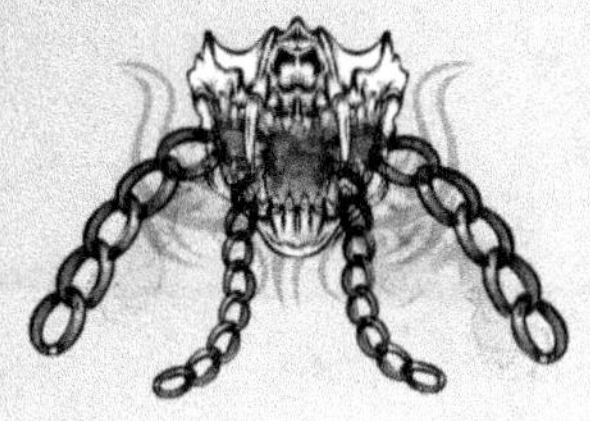

CHAPTER 14
Codrin

"Get the fuck up, Codrin!"

Talon's voice cracks like a whip. But I don't move.

"Why isn't he moving?" he growls, turning to Athan "And who the fuck is this guy?!" Talon jabs a finger toward the man standing off to the side, hands in his front pockets, a smirk on his face.

The town quieted not long after Ravenna was taken. The Slatiers had scattered back into the Nothingness Forest shortly after Ravenna was taken. Leaving behind the silence of the destruction and loss.

But nothing quieted in me.

I haven't moved from the rubble where the demon dropped me with my body buried and soul gutted.

The screams have faded, replaced by sobs and prayers.

I know she'll return. I know Alaric is out there, tracking the demon and that he'll bring her back. But it should've been me. I should've chased it. I should've torn it apart.

But the second I saw Darius…

I froze. Now stuck in a loop of uncontrollable failure.

Athan grabs the back of Talon's collar. "Knock it off."

"Fuck, no!" Talon jerks his shoulder from Athan's grip. His voice is tight, cracking at the edges.

"My sister is gone." He turns in a frantic circle, jaw clenched, eyes wild. "We don't have time for this! I'm getting the guards. We need to track that thing. Now!"

He storms off without waiting for an answer, rage masking the fear that I know is eating him alive.

Athan exhales through his nose, slow and tense.

"I'll deal with him."

He doesn't wait for my response, just turns with a tight glare in Darius's direction, eyes flashing with a warning he doesn't bother putting into words.

Then he strides after Talon.

Silence lingers around me, but the soft crunch of debris behind me announces Darius is stepping closer.

He looks exactly as I remember, and somehow, worse. Darius Vyrenhartmir wears his usual elegant black attire that hugs his lean frame, his dark hair hanging in tousled waves to his cheekbones, sharp enough to cut glass. His golden eyes gleam with amusement, but there's always something calculating behind them. He moves like a shadow that knows it's being watched and enjoys every minute of it.

"He seems a little overly dramatic."

"Fuck off, Darius," I rasp, wincing as I push off the rubble, pain shooting through my side.

"Oh, Codrin, it's been ages." He takes a step closer, arms lifting like he's about to pull me into a hug, then stops short with a sly smile. "What's it been? Five years? Ten?"

I level him with a look. "Forty."

"Forty years! Wow! Has it really been that long?" Darius taps his chin, expression full of false longing. "Feels like just yesterday you turned your back on us and *poof*… just vanished."

His hand drops to his side, eyes narrowing. "And for what? This gods-forsaken, sun-soaked little kingdom?" He casts a slow look over the smoldering wreckage, lip curling. "I don't see the appeal."

"It's better than Veilstead ever was," I growl, taking a step toward him. "Now tell me, what are you doing here?"

Darius calmly brushes a bit of dust off his shoulder, completely unfazed. He lets the question hang before replying.

"I just came to say hi."

"Don't play dumb." I step closer, fists clenched. "Why are you and Alaric *really* in Theiahold?"

Forty years I've stayed hidden from them and I know all this time neither of them tried to find me. So, why now? I know Alaric is set to marry Ravenna. But there must be more behind it.

"Oh, sweet, sweet baby brother. Alaric has his reasons. I'm just here for the entertainment." Darius's smirk widens.

My jaw locks. If Alaric's history has taught me anything, it's that he never does *just one thing*. There's always more beneath the surface.

"And by the looks of things, he'll be getting what you will *never* have."

Fury radiates through my veins to Darius's words. Not thinking, I charge at him, but he's too quick. He springs to the side and across the fallen rubble with immortal speed and I slam into it with a bone crunching blow to one knee and chest.

"Someone hasn't been feeding as much, have they? *Tisk... tisk.* That is such a shame."

"Stay away from her," I snarl through clenched teeth, springing to my feet to face him.

Darius furrows a brow; his steps unhurried as he approaches me. "And what do you plan to do?"

We're chest to chest, I might have the height, the strength and also the fury but Darius always knew how to hold his ground. He rocks on his heels, hands loosely clasped behind his back as he lifts his chin with a huff breath. So help me, I want to knock that fucking smug expression clean off his face.

"We both know what Alaric desires. And when he sets his mind to something, he achieves it. As for you being here?" He taps my chest, like I'm nothing more than decoration. "Well, that's just a delightful little bonus. Just remember, where you are standing *now* Codrin... and where he is."

Darius points past me. Beyond the buildings, beyond the field, toward the distant forest and everything that lies past it.

I swallow hard. The panic clawing up my throat to the very thought of Ravenna in Alaric's arms. Or possibly wounded? Confused or worse…alone.

I should've chased that demon. I should've been the one who brings her back.

I should've saved her.

I know just how true Darius's statement is. Alaric knows how to get the things he wants. He sweet-talks his victims, overpowering them with his abilities.

One hand resting casually on his lower back while the other brushes his pronounced cheekbones, Darius wanders, shooting a sidelong glance at me but I stand firmly, my shoulders aching with tension. A smirk plays at the corners of Darius's lips.

"If I were you, Codrin, I wouldn't go meddling in things and risking your life over some princess." A glint of amuse-ment dances in Darius's eyes as he reveals his fangs.

"Good thing you're not me," I snap with a snarl.

If Darius doesn't want me involved, then that's exactly where I belong, especially if Ravenna's in the middle of it.

Darius rolls his eyes and tilts his head back, releasing a bored huff before turning his full attention back to me, his golden eyes piercing into my dull gray ones. I blink, uncertain I'm reading him correctly. Was that sympathy that crossed his features for a fleeting moment? Does Darius even know what sympathy feels like?

"You're truly pitiful. Even those once gorgeous eyes of yours have dimmed from neglect," Darius says, straightening his vest like this is just another day.

He pivots and disappears into the smoke, leaving me alone to drown in the ash, and sharp burn of guilt that won't let go.

I haven't stopped pacing. Hours have passed, and every second that has passed, scrapes across my nerves like broken glass.

Ravenna is still missing.

The sun has started to set. The town has gone eerily quiet after the chaos. The king sent guards out in waves in search of Ravenna. Patrols scoured the streets and the border of the Nothingness Forest.

But no report. Not one fucking report on her whereabouts. Not a signal trace.

I wanted to search with them, but General Hawk called me back to the castle to organize the others and to stay put for further orders.

So, here I am trapped in my room at the barracks with the unknowing, weighing on me with every second.

Footsteps pound down the hall outside my room, pulling me from my agonizing thoughts. I pause, flexing my fingers at my sides, trying to breathe through the rising tension. How some of these squad boys could still be wired from the attack and now sprinting laps like idiots is beyond me.

But the steps don't fade. They get louder. Faster. Closer.

My door explodes open.

"You son of a bitch!"

Her voice hits like a shield slammed into my chest. Her arms reaching high above her head. "You never fucking came for me!"

At the last second, I notice the axe soaring through the air and coming straight at me. I dive to the floor just as the weapon swooshes past my head and impales itself into the wall behind me.

"Fuck, Ravenna! You could've taken my head off." I scramble to my feet just as she charges at me. Her hands hit my chest, and she shoves me against the wall, the axe mere inches from my face.

Her hand slaps across my face, and my head whips to the side.

"Where the fuck were you?" She slaps me again. "You left me. You left me to die." Her voice cracks with a raw rage that was slowly breaking to the surface.

"No, I didn't." I try to say but her hand slaps across my cheek, leaving a sting of her own pain in its wake.

"I don't recall seeing you out there. You know who was out there?" Her eyes wail with tears as she takes a quick breath. "A vampire. A fucking vampire was out there saving me." A tear falls from the corner of her eye, trickling slowly down her cheek. "And where were *you*?"

"Ravenna…" I take a step toward her, only for her to shove me back against the wall.

She raises a hand, ready to slap me again but I grab her wrist mid-swing. It trembles in my grasp. My eyes lock onto her icy blues and I swear not only do I see the pain she is feeling but the rage that she has towards me. I don't know what to say. I have no excuse. I have failed her and she knows it. Her eyes darken, almost crimson with fury to the reality of it all.

What have I done?

My chest constricts. I've seen her angry before. I've seen her fight godsdamned monsters. But I've never seen her like this. Eyes brimming with betrayal, voice shaking with heartbreak she's trying to mask as hate.

I did this to her. I caused this pain. How can I explain to her why I couldn't be there for her without telling her everything?

"I'm sorry," are the only words that slip through my lips.

"Fuck your sorry." She pulls her arm from my grasp and rips her axe from the wall, not even looking at me. "Fuck you, Codrin."

And just like that, she's gone. The door slams shut behind her, but the echo of my failure lingers, louder than her rage.

"Fuck!" I roar, swinging my fist into the wall. The sharp crack of bone meeting stone is satisfying in the worst way. Pain blooms through my knuckles, but I welcome it. At least it's something I can feel. Something I deserve.

Leaning into the cold wall, my forehead pressing against it

as I try to slow my breathing. But it's no use. Her voice still rings in my ears. Her eyes. Her shattered eyes. And it's my fault.

I push myself away from the wall and drag my feet across the room to collapse onto the worn, overstuffed leather couch, face buried in my hands as the weight of everything presses down on me.

Taking a couple of deep breaths. Its not just today that haunts me. But forty years crashing into me like a tsunami.

Hiding in the forests and caves, surviving like an animal after I fled Veilstead. The long, desperate journey to Theiahold. A teenage Simon finding me in the gutter, offering a hand when no one else would. Odd jobs. Long nights. Then the day I saved a guard's life. Everything changed after that.

Climbing my way up the ranks of the king's guard, then the slayers. And Ravenna. Gods, Ravenna. The first time I saw her across the training yard, her arms trembled under the weight of her axe, but her eyes burned like frost fire. Fierce. Unyielding. Watching her become everything her father said she couldn't be… it was like watching a star forge itself from ash. I knew even then that she would be the death of me.

Fingers laced behind my neck, elbows propped on my knees, a quiet curse slips past my lips as the walls close around me.

My gaze drops to the throw rug at my feet. Its vibrant blues, beiges, and reds blurring together, like everything else these days.

Like a flame I cupped too tightly, snuffed out by my own hands.

I lift my head, eyes scanning the room.

The cherrywood desk and chair off to the side are half-buried beneath stacks of unfinished reports, training schedules, and worn maps marked in ink. A tall bookcase looms beside it, one shelf buckled under the weight of old battle manuals, loose scrolls, and a few well-thumbed novels hidden between the mess.

To the left, a small hearth sits cold, the ash swept clean. My leather armor and slayer mask hang on a wooden stand near the window, the dark iron of the mask battered and scarred, casting a long, silent shadow across the floor.

At the back, a narrow doorway opens into a separate bedroom, the door ajar. Just beyond: a single bed with rumpled sheets and the edge of a nightstand, nothing more.

This isn't just a room. It's a war camp masquerading as a home.

This space, my so-called sanctuary within the Slayer Squad barracks, is a monument to the trust I earned when I became captain two years ago.

So much for noble. A breath huffs out between my teeth, bitter and sharp.

I shake my head, trying to chase away the memories. So much has happened since then. And just this past week, it finally felt like everything was falling into place for Ravenna and me.

If I were you, Codrin, I wouldn't go meddling in things and risking your life.

Darius's warning drums through my thoughts. Did Alaric come here for revenge? Was this really about me after all these decades?

Sunlight still pours through the windows, golden and warm. But it can't thaw the chill gripping my heart. I kick off my boots, the heavy leather thudding against the floor. Reaching down, I unbuckle the knife strapped to my right ankle and toss it onto the side table.

My fingers find the inner seam of my other pant leg. There hides a pocket, stitched by my own hand.

From it, I pull the gem.

Cool in my palm, even after being tucked against my skin all day. I run a thumb over its smooth surface, then hold it up to the fading light. Sunlight flickers through its translucent body, catching the deep blue core like a solar eclipse, the moon's shadow wrapped in silver-white light.

A piece of my past I was never meant to take with me.

I stole this shard when I left Veilstead. As long as I carry this stone, I can walk in daylight like any mortal. Free. I press the gem to my chest for a brief second before tucking it back into its hiding place.

I sink back into the couch, the cushion groaning beneath me as I stretch out. Tomorrow, I'll tell her everything. No more secrets. No more lies. She deserves the truth. Even if she never forgives me.

Even if it's the last thing I do.

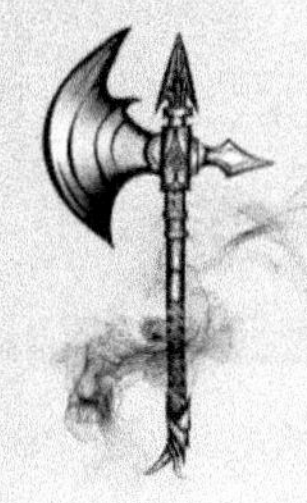

CHAPTER 15
Ravenna

His eyes find me the moment I enter the dining hall.

King Alaric stands in the doorway as though he owns it. And maybe, in his mind, he does. Conversations falter when he turns. Goblets hover midair, laughter dips into silence. His golden gaze snaps to mine, steady, searing, blazing with something that almost looks like delight.

Even dressed in his finest all-black attire, trimmed in subtle gold thread, I can see the sharp outlines of muscle beneath.

He extends his arm out to me. A gesture to those looking in from the outside see as genius and noble. As for me I see as caution and dangerous.

After a breath laced with reluctant curiosity and under the weight of far too many eyes, I take it.

"You are a breath of scattered stars," he murmurs into my ear.

I answer with a cruel twist of my lips.

The dark royal-blue gown I wear does resemble the night sky. The bodice hugs every curve like it was poured on, while smoke-gray beadwork curls along my chest and waist. Puffy sleeves hang elegantly off my shoulders, exposing my collarbone and draping sheer clouds of fabric down my arms. It screams too romantic. Too staged.

He escorts me to the table like a man presenting his prize. The grand dining hall is ablaze with candlelight, the chandeliers dripping with crystal. Long banquet tables overflow with roasted meats and glazed fruits, wheels of cheese and silver bowls brimming with sweets.

Applause rises. Too loud. Too long.

Over-the-top cheers echo through the room, fueled by full bellies and flutes of wine. Cups clink. Forced laughter returns. Fevered over a celebration not for survival. Not for healing.

But for *him*.

The King of Darkness. The man who *rescued* me.

Musicians along the far wall play a lilting, triumphant melody that twists beneath the noise like a thread pulled too tight. Servants glide between tables. Nobles toast with flushed cheeks and gleaming smiles.

Once again, I was kept in the dark about when King Alaric was due to arrive. And looking around the dining hall, it's obvious my parents knew.

I should've known. I should've seen it coming.

The demon attack was the perfect smokescreen of a *hero* swooping in to save the princess. And now, I'm expected to smile through this evening's feast like I should be thankful of him. Thankful he showed up when he did.

I slump into my seat between Talon, dressed in a formal white blouse, soft-gray vest, and black trousers, and Mother, radiant in her glittering sky-blue gown. Both flashing the proud colors of Theiahold.

Alaric circles around to take the seat across from me, next to his brother Darius, who lifts his goblet to me in a silent toast, a thin smirk curling at the edges of his mouth like he knows more than anyone else in the room. He's draped in all black, a living silhouette of the night sky. His tousled hair looks like he combed it with his fingers, and I can't tell if that was intentional or just carelessness turned effortless.

I don't return the gesture.

Something about him unsettles me. The way his golden eyes, resembling his brother's, shift, tracking every movement, scanning the crowd of dancers behind us, lingering on conversations without ever joining in. He shifts in his chair, half-turned from the table like he's already bored, more fascinated with the performance around him than the so-called honored guests.

Watching with a glint of amusement in his eye.

I shift my gaze away and prop my elbow on the table, head resting in my hand. I don't give two shits how unprincessly I look as I let out a bored yawn. I am already ready for this so called party to end.

Father sits at the head of the table, draped in his usual sharp-edged blue and gray regalia. He and Alaric fall into talks of practiced diplomacy about kingdoms and good fucking fortune.

"Don't you agree, my dear?" Father glances my way.

I nod, managing a faint smile. Resisting the urge to roll my eyes.

My mind's too full for niceties. Too raw to care to what he is saying.

Sweet, sweet child, the voice slinks in, its poison-wrapped words curling through me like smoke.

I lift my head from my hand and catch my reflection in a polished fruit bowl beside me. The reflection waves her fingers. My own resting flat on the table.

Still moping over him. Why? What has he truly done for you? the reflection whispers. *He's nothing but a coward who ran the moment things got hard.*

I squeeze my eyes shut, taking in several slow deep breaths before I open my eyes again to the fruit bowl. Finding the reflection mirroring my every move.

"You, okay?" Talon leans in, voice low.

"Yep." I swallow hard, running a finger between the tightness of the lace choker and my throat. The deep blue sapphire pressing hard against my skin.

I ignore Talon's stare as I lift my goblet and take a long drink. Watching my every move with a sharp, silent worry.

The music swells around us, but it feels like background noise and my eyes fall a distant hum beneath the weight of Alaric's attention.

"You look remarkably well," Alaric says, voice just loud enough to rise above the din. "Considering the earlier circumstances."

I glance sideways at him, wine untouched in my hand. "You mean the part where I was nearly gutted in the woods?"

His mouth curves slightly. "That would be the one."

I hum in response, neither confirming nor denying the near-death bit. "Well, Your Majesty, we slayers are trained not to scare so easily."

"Hmm." His gaze flicks down my chest and back up. "Most princesses I've met don't throw themselves into such danger."

I tilt my head. "Then you've met the wrong kind of princess."

He chuckles. "You know, I've heard stories of your time on the Slayer Squad. But I didn't expect them to be so… understated."

I arch a brow. "What do you mean?"

"You held your own against that demon for far longer than most men could."

Talon leans forward. "Funny. I don't remember you being there for most of that."

I shoot my twin a sharp look, but he just sips his wine with studied indifference, eyes locked on Alaric.

"And what stories have you heard?" I ask turning my attention back to Alaric.

His lips part but before he could speak Father interrupts, his voice carrying with a fake cheerfulness from the head of the table. "How are you liking Theiahold so far?"

Alaric lifts his goblet to his lips, giving me a quick wink as he takes a long sip.

I fight the urge to roll my eyes. Of course, Father would want to know that. No reason to ask how his travel was or if he and his men had any trouble getting here. Oh no. That's not important. It's all about Father's kingdom. It's always about his fucking kingdom.

"You have a lovely home, Zephyr." Alaric replies with a clearly forced smile as he sets his goblet down, his fingers loose along the stem. "I'm saddened to hear what occurred in town earlier today, but I hope some of my men were able to help out."

"Yes, it is very unfortunate, but that is the price we pay for having the Nothingness Forest right outside our gates." Father lets out a half-hearted chuckle. "Someday, we shall get rid of the monsters roaming there once and for all."

"We can only hope." Alaric raises his goblet to Father.

Father returns the gesture. "With our kingdoms coming together, we won't need *hope*. Speaking of…when shall the wedding take place?" Father's voice punctures my chest with pointed precision, casual on the surface, but sharp beneath.

My head jerks up, eyes wide. There it is the question I'd known was coming, hovering on the tip of his tongue all evening.

"Actually, Your Majesty," Alaric says smoothly, leaning in with his fingers interlaced on the table. "Before we rush into the ceremony…"

His gaze drifts to me, locking on the disarming intensity.

"…let's hold off for a little while," he rests his chin on his steepled fingers, "I'd like the chance to get to know this exquisite young lady first. And I believe she would like to get to know me before saying yes."

I choke on a breath.

"What do you say to one week, princess?" His lips curl up slightly.

Father's jaw clenches, his goblet pausing midair. "I see," he mutters, and takes a long drink.

I exhale, stunned that he doesn't throw the goblet across the table.

Seated beside Alaric, Darius lets out a quiet snort. The first sound he's made all evening. One look from Alaric and he's silent again, the smirk still lingering.

Talon remains silent, his attention fixed on his plate. I can't tell if he's hiding his reaction from our parents or still reeling from earlier, of me missing for over four hours.

"Well, I see no problem with that," Mother interjects, trying to smooth the tension rising across the table.

Her easy acceptance surprises me, though I know the performance is likely for Alaric's benefit. She'll hear it from Father after supper.

"Indeed, as long as it is no problem for you, Princess Ravenna?"

My name in his mouth is both velvet and thorns. A shiver crawls down my spine, pooling low in my belly before I can stop it.

I stiffen in my chair, tearing away from his gaze and nodding slowly. "One week."

Is he really giving me a choice in this arranged marriage? I have to get to know him for one week…and then I can say no? The breath rushes from my chest at the thought. I've spent the last week agonizing over being forced to marry a vampire, and now I am given a choice in the matter.

I narrow my eyes on Alaric, who tilts his cup toward me. It can't be that easy. Nothing in my life is *ever* that easy. Even if Alaric isn't just pretending to give me a choice as a means to win me over, which I have my doubts about, there's no way Father will let me out of this. Not when this marriage is the key to furthering his power.

Talon shifts beside me, his chair scraping across the stone floor as he stands from the table. "I'm going to go…mingle." He takes his goblet and heads into the crowd, swallowed up by dancing couples and swaying drunks.

A grin curls Alaric's lips, goblet in hand he stand and makes his way around the table to take Talon's empty seat.

"Is he always that subtle?" Alaric asks tightly, once Talon is gone.

"He's protective," I say. "We're twins."

Alaric arches a brow, taking a sip of wine. "Ah. That explains the glare."

Darius snorts into his goblet.

My gaze shifts back to Alaric as he pulls his goblet away, a drop of wine lingering on his lower lip. He licks it away, slow and deliberate.

"So, Princess, tell me something about yourself."

"What do you want to know?" The words leave my lips without thought, too fast, too open.

My cheeks flush. My breath falters.

"A little black bird told me you like to read." His voice is soft but screams danger. "What books have captured your heart?"

Mother and Father too distracted in hushed conversation, utterly oblivious to the undercurrent threading between Alaric and me.

I lick my lips, words catching in my throat. "I like to read a little of everything, but… dark fairytales are my favorite."

Alaric's brows rise, amused. Or maybe intrigued.

I take a long sip of wine, my head spinning from more than just the alcohol.

"And what do you like to do for fun, besides rescuing princesses?" I ask, the question sounding more flirtatious than I intend.

"Me?" His grin deepens. "A king hardly has time for fun. Running a kingdom is… consuming. But I enjoy music. Violin, especially. Stargazing."

Alaric turns in his chair and in one swift motion reaches out, grabbing the seat of my own chair. The legs scrape across stone, and a soft squeal escapes my lips as he pulls me toward him.

Resting an arm on the back of my chair, he leans in, his lips grazing my ear. "Want to know my favorite pastime?" He grins revealing a flash of fangs.

"What's that?" I ask, trying to take another sip of wine and hoping he doesn't notice the tremble in my words.

"Hunting."

The word slips off his tongue slow with hunger.

Choking mid-sip, wine spills from my mouth, and down my chin. I quickly set the goblet down and reach for the cloth napkin sitting on my lap. But its Alaric's hand that stops me, cupping my chin, and turning my head to meet his golden gaze. My breath catches as his thumb brushes along my chin and wipes away a drop of wine.

He runs his thumb along my bottom lip, and I involuntarily part my lips, letting the tip of his thumb slip between my lips. The taste of wine mixed with the cold, sweet taste of him touches my tongue, sending a wave of heat down my spine and between my legs.

My chair scrapes against the floor as I shoot to my feet.

"Ex-excuse me for a moment." I gather my skirts and flee the dining hall, heart pounding behind my ribs like a snare drum.

Out in the corridor, I press my back against the cold stone wall. *What the seven hells was that about?* I curse as the chill bites my skin, a welcome relief to the heat rising beneath my skin. My head falls back, and I close my eyes, willing my breath to steady.

I feel a shift in the air to a presence that lingers over me, but I don't dare open my eyes. My breath catches to a warm breath that grazes the side of my neck, and for a heartbeat, my mind reaches for Codrin.

My eyes flutter open to find Alaric standing before me just barely out of reach. His tall and composed figure shadowed in the golden flicker of the wall sconces. Every angle of him seems carved from night and firelight. Sharp cheekbones, squared jaw, those golden eyes pinning me in place.

"Are you alright, my little princess?" His voice is low, smooth, like the finest silk dragged across bare skin as he closes the space between us.

His hands press the wall on either side of me, boxing me in. Not harsh. Just… inescapable.

"I'm not your *little princess*." My chin lifts in defiance, though my voice comes out softer than I'd like. "And I'm fine."

His eyes bore into mine, slowly, deliberately. Like he's searching for something buried deep beneath the surface. Or maybe peeling it away.

"Will you marry me, princess?" His voice is barely above a whisper. And yet I hear every syllable as if they're stitched into my chest.

My heart pounds louder than the cheerful chatter, laughter, and music that fill the corridor from the grand dining hall.

"Why are you asking?" I cross my arms over my chest. "You

made a deal with my father. I'm yours no matter what I say."

"But I want you to have a say in this."

"I don't have a choice in my future." The words spill from my lips, sharp and real, bitter as the cold stone against my back.

"I have offered you one week," he says. "Let me show you who I truly am within that time. I am not the monster everyone has set me out to be."

Narrowing my eyes, I stare up at him through my lashes, my lips pressed, my jaw tight.

"I'll give you until the end of the week to decide if you want to marry me."

"And if I say no?" I lift my chin higher.

He leans in closer, perfectly calm. "Then I leave without a bride."

I arch a brow, trying to read the truth in his eyes. "My father will never allow this."

"I'm a king too," he says. "What I say matters just as much as your father's. If need be, I will take the heat if we do not marry."

"Why?"

He responds with a devilish grin.

What is he playing at? I know I will not marry this man. This vampire. This monster. I can suck it up for a week with him, play the part, and before I know it, it will all be over. He will go back to Veilstead *without* me, and I can go back to living my own life…and deal with the repercussions of Father's wrath.

"Hm." His lips curl. "You're shaking."

He leans in more, his breath skimming my collarbone. A whisper of heat where there should be distance.

"Maybe I can help," he says softly. "Something to ease that storm I see brewing inside you."

His fingers trail down the side of my waist, slow, and calculated. A cold breeze touches my leg as he gathers the edges of my skirts and raises them higher.

My body tightens but the heat between my legs rages up into my chest, taking my breath. My head falls back, my eyes flutter shut as I shamefully let the arousal of his touch take control.

Gods help me.

A shiver ripples down my spine as his fingers graze my thigh and slide high until they press against the warmth between my legs.

I suck in a breath.

What in Hella's fire am I doing?

His lips brush my collarbone, then trail upward, a phantom heat ghosting across my neck, setting my skin ablaze.

The fingers of his other hand trace up my arm, featherlight. Over my shoulder. Then around my throat.

"You're trembling," he whispers, slipping a finger between my legs.

I let out a startled gasp as he slides his finger into my heat. My hips jolt against the intrusion, a soft moan slips past my lips before I can stop it. My body, traitorous and aching, responds before my mind can make sense of what's happening.

His thumb finds my clit, pressing. Circling ever so slowly.

A rush of sensation I *shouldn't* want shoots through my entire body.

He withdrawals, and I quickly try to steady my breath. Gathering the tattered pieces of what little self-control I feel I have left.

But then he presses forward again, body pinning mine to the wall, and all the space I need to think, to *refuse,* is crushed out of me. Caught between the stone behind me and the heat of him in front of me, I have no space left to think.

Two fingers slide into me this time, and my breath catches on a silent gasp as he slides deeper and unrelenting.

My knees falter, shame curling hot in my gut as my body betrays me, chasing the heat he has ignited inside me.

Pleasure spears through me like lightning as his thumb returns to my raw, sensitive clit. I try to contain the wild and reckless feeling sweeping over me. But the humiliating rush of it all is too sweet to let go.

Through the haze of sensation, my body shudders with uncontrollable desire, betraying me as I start to explode from within.

A throat clears behind us.

Snapping me back to reality like a whipcrack.

Alaric stills. His fingers slip from me in an instant, though his other hand remains hovering around my throat, his body still flush against mine.

"What?!" he snarls, head whipping over his shoulder.

Darius stands casually at the end of the corridor, hands tucked into his pockets, rocking heel to toe like he didn't just walk in on something he'll never let either of us live down.

"Dessert's being served," he says mildly, his lips curling into a grin. "But it seems you've already started on yours."

My cheeks flushed, mortified to that thought as to what I must look like right now. To what this whole scene looks like. What the seven hells was I thinking? Letting Alaric corrupt me in such a way.

Alaric lets out a growl. Lower this time, more warning than rage. Pushing off the wall, he turns to fully face his brother.

"Watch yourself, Darius."

His brother simply smirks, adjusting Alaric's collar. "Have fun," he says lightly, patting Alaric's chest with a teasing pat, and strolls off as though he hasn't just shattered the moment.

I exhale slowly, trying to steady myself as I smooth my gown with trembling fingers, praying I don't look as disheveled as I feel.

Alaric turns back to me, his eyes melting into mine.

He raises the two fingers that I know were just inside me and licks them clean of my juices with a low hum of satisfaction.

"Mmm… delicious."

I stop breathing.

And like nothing happened at all, he offers me his hand. "Shall we return to the agony of this evening, little princess?"

I don't argue with the nickname as I take his arm, the truth sinking in.

I know this man is dangerous. I know I should push him away and forget about what just happened here.

But all I can think about is how bad I want to go upstairs with him. The thought hits before I can stop it, heat rushing into my core. But right now, I'm not sure I care. Because a part of me doesn't want to walk away.

CHAPTER 16

Ravenna

I shouldn't be here.

The thought pounds in my head as King Alaric leads me deeper into the maze garden, farther from the entrance, farther from the guards I can't even see anymore. If they're still nearby, they're silent shadows now.

The winding hedges stretch taller than I remember, their leafy arms bending inward like they're trying to swallow the sky. Only slivers of light filter through the gray, grim clouds above.

I want to feel grateful for the solitude. No guards in sight. No Talon. No Codrin. Just the sound of our steps on the stone path and the quiet rush of distant wind.

But I don't.

I try to take a deep breath, but my dress makes it impossible.

Despite its elegance and the soft blue hue that flatters my skin, the low-cut, formfitting bodice clings too tightly. The delicate beaded straps keep slipping off my shoulders, as if the dress itself wants to be rid of me. The satin skirt flows like water, graceful, yes, but it defines every curve, every line of my body, and the short train behind me does nothing to make me feel any less exposed.

I hate it.

I hate that my mother made me wear it.

I hate that it makes me feel seen.

And worst of all. I hate that *he* is the one seeing me.

Alaric walks beside me in silence. No smug grin. No lingering toughness. Just… stillness. Like he's waiting for something.

"I thought you might not come," he says finally.

"I never said I wouldn't," I answer, eyes fixed ahead. Not like I had much of a choice.

I catch a flicker of amusement cross his face. Not gloating but possibly knowing. Which makes it worse.

He knew I would show up this afternoon. Even since our heated moment together in the corridor three days ago. I have shown up to everything he had planned. Making sure he found the time throughout each day to spend with me.

From sharing an afternoon tea together, to lounging in the library while I read him one of my favorite fantasy tales, all while he stares at me with a sparkle in his eyes, to now wandering the maze gardens alone together. He was even so kind as to return my knife to me with a small bouquet of wildflowers he picked himself.

He has been treating me like…well, a lady. And honestly, I have been quite enjoying it.

We stop near a stone bench choked in ivy. Neither of us sits. He turns to me fully.

"I want to ask you something," he says. "And I'd like you

to answer honestly, for once."

"For once?" My jaw tightens. "You don't know me."

"I know enough." His voice is soft. Not mocking. But firm. "You wear strength like armor because it's the only thing *they* haven't taken from you. You speak like fire because silence feels too much like surrender. And I know...." His eyes sharpen. "You hate how much I affect you."

My mouth opens; however, nothing comes out. Only a flash of heat that flares low in my gut, followed quickly by shame.

"I scare you," he adds, voice lower now.

"You don't scare me," I snap and proving my point by giving him my back.

"I know I don't scare you. But it's not because you think I'll hurt you." He steps closer. Not enough to touch but near enough to be felt.

"You're scared because when you're with me, you feel something that isn't rage or duty or even guilt. You feel like...maybe you could stop running. Like someone might actually see you for more than the role you were forced into."

My heart thunders in my chest.

He speaks of me as though he has known me for years. He speaks of me better than anyone ever has...even Codrin.

"You don't know what I feel," I whisper.

He fingers wrap my bicep and he spins me around to face him.

"No," he says. "But I know what I *see*."

His eyes search mine like they're peeling me apart, layer by layer. And gods help me…I don't want him to stop.

Does he truly *see* me? He has spoken more truth of myself, even I wouldn't admit to.

"You think you can win me with words?" I ask, voice tighter than I intend.

"No." He steps in, just enough to brush the hem of my skirt with his boots. "If I wanted to win you, I would've taken you already."

Something wild pulses through me, with equal parts of fear and desire.

I lift my chin, defiant. "Then why haven't you?"

His answer is quiet. Weighted.

"Because I don't want to own you, Ravenna. I want you to choose me. And I want you to know that if you do…I won't be the one who breaks you."

I want to say something sharp and cruel. But I don't. I just freeze.

Alaric closes the last inch between us. His scent wraps around me, like something dark and woodsy, threaded with spice and storm. His fingers rise slowly, brushing the underside of my chin as he tilts my head upward. Gentle but deliberate, forcing me to look at him. To really see him.

His eyes lock onto mine, and suddenly, the air feels too tight. My breath falters in my lungs.

"I wasn't lying," he says softly, his voice low enough to drown in. "When I said I wanted to wait one week. I meant it." His thumb grazes just beneath my lower lip, barely touching. "I want to get to know you, Ravenna. Just as much as I want you to get to know me."

His words linger between us, as dangerous as the way his touch still cradles my chin.

A part of me wants to believe him.

Not the king. Not the monster. But the man beneath it all. The one whose voice dips into softness when he says my name. The one who looks at me like he sees more than just a crown. A duty. A bride-to-be.

And that part of me?

It's terrifying.

Because trusting him might be the most foolish thing I've ever done. But I'm starting to wonder if it might also be the most honest.

A loud boom cracks through the sky as the storm breaks without mercy. Lightning cleaves the sky above, jagged and violent, followed by a bone-deep roar of thunder. The clouds crack open and release their fury. Rain pours in sheets, cold, immediate, and blinding.

"We should find shelter," Alaric says, his hand suddenly grasping mine.

We run through the wet grass. My skirts tangle around my legs, soaked through within seconds. Mud clings to the hem, grass stains the once-elegant blue satin. Every step is a fight to stay upright as the storm swallows the garden.

Ducking beneath the pergola, both of us are breathless and drenched.

Rain drums a war rhythm on the wooden slats above us. My dress, soaked, leaving nothing to the imagination. The thin fabric turns sheer, plastered to every inch of my skin. I clutch the fabric around myself, trembling. My cheeks burn. My hair hangs heavy and matted down my back, no trace left of the polished up-do from earlier.

I can't look at him.

Not like this.

Water drips steadily from Alaric's black hair onto the floorboards as he peels off his all-black swallowtail coat. He squeezes out the water, the thick velvet dark and slick in his hands.

"Here." He steps forward and places it over my shoulders. "It'll keep you a little warm, and, well, covered."

I nod, wrapping it around myself like armor, though I'm all but defenseless beneath it. His scent clings to the fabric. Warm. Rich. Spiced. Too easy to sink into.

When I finally dare to glance up, he's already watching me. His eyes soften, but no less intense. A quiet smile tugs at his mouth.

"No need to be so flustered," he says gently, tilting his head.

"I'm not flustered," I lie.

He chuckles, low and rough, the sound sending another shiver through me that has nothing to do with the rain.

His gaze dips to my lips, then returns to my eyes.

"I think you are," he murmurs, closing the space between us, slow and sure. "And it suits you."

I open my mouth to argue, to deflect, to say *something* sharp.

But there's hunger in his eyes now, that cautions me to speak.

His hand finds my waist, firm and deliberate and I gasp as he pulls me in close, feeling the shape of him through the soaked fabric between us.

He leans in. "You're still afraid of what you want," he says, his breath brushing up my neck.

"I'm not," I breathe, though my frantic pulse betrays me.

His lips graze the curve of my ear.

"Prove it."

The storm roars behind us, thunder rattling the earth, but I only hear the sound of my own breath quaver against his touch.

"You don't scare me," I lie.

His mouth curls into something between a smirk and a snarl. His fingertips brush under my chin, tilting my face to his. His thumb traces the shape of my lower lip.

A tremor tightens in my chest.

"Good," he whispers. "Because I won't pretend I don't want you."

His gaze dips to my lips, then returns to my eyes. Those golden eyes lock onto mine, stripping away everything I have been pretending to be.

"End of the week," his voice low and reverent, "if you choose not to marry me, I'll go without a fight. And you will never hear from me again."

"You promise?" I ask, not wanting to leave his touch. A part of me *wants to be chosen*. But more so, I *want* to choose.

"I promise," he vows on a whisper.

Then his lips claim mine.

Soft, at first, just a press of warmth. Then deeper, hungrier, as if sealing his vow with more than words. As if this kiss holds the weight of something ancient and aching.

And I let it.

Hella help me, I let it.

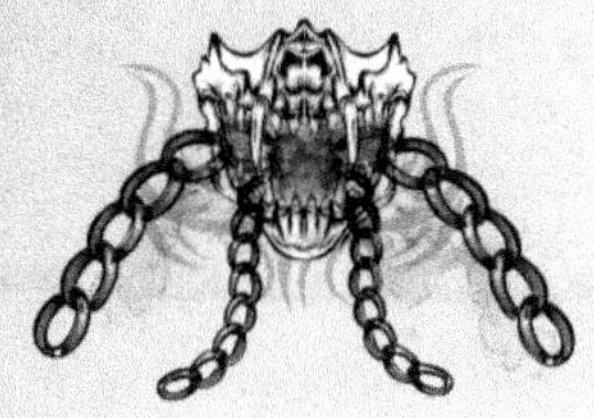

CHAPTER 17
Codrin

The air inside the tower is thick with the scent of damp stone and old rot. The wood has soaked in years of humidity, and now it reeks of decay, like the bones of a place long abandoned. The occasional breeze brings in traces of salt and sea from the coast, but it is never enough to clear the stench.

I'm not supposed to be here. But I need to get away. Away from the training field. Away from the court. And mainly, away from *her*.

I lean forward, arms bracing on the windowsill, the tower's arched window framing the gray, rain-slicked world below. The storm has passed, leaving the town soaked and quiet, a thin mist crawling between the rooftops. Most of the townspeople are still inside, the streets half-empty and shining with rainwater.

But it isn't the streets I'm watching.

It's the garden.

The pergola.

Nestled at the edge of the maze, hidden to nearly everyone but perfectly visible from the tower's height, stands the small ivy-wrapped structure. My eyes lock on the figures beneath it. Two shadows framed by the wet wood and thick vines. One dressed in all-black as night attire. The other clad in silver-white.

There is no mistaking her.

Ravenna hasn't seen or even spoken to me since she left my room the night she buried her axe in my wall. But I have been watching her from a distance for these past couple of days as she strolls the grounds, arm in arm with *him*. Looking at him the same way she used to look at me.

I know I'm torturing myself, but I can't tear myself away. Two days after the Slatier attack in town, I canceled training due to the loss of our three comrades. And today I had Athan take over the slayer training. Too obsessed to keeping a watchful eye on Ravenna and all while I keep hidden from Alaric.

My blood boils every time I see him touching her, and it takes everything in me not to charge after him and slice him to pieces.

Her black slayer attire has long been replaced.

Now, she dons elegant dresses. Each day, each small gathering, she wears a different color. From lilac purple to a soft, cheery blossom pink. Today, it's a periwinkle blue. Even her hair has been replaced by its normal braid, to a stylish up-do with loose curls streaming down her back.

She looks so different.

She looks like a princess.

My heart breaks seeing her like this. Nothing about her hints that she picked up a weapon and slaughtered demons only days ago. This isn't her. This isn't *my* Ravenna.

Talon, at least, started talking to me the day after the attack, informing me he of his true option of not trusting Alaric. Right there with you, buddy; however no matter how much I want to tell Talon everything. I still can't seem to get the words out. Not yet anyway.

My grip tightens on the edge of the windowsill as I watch Alaric's hand claim Ravenna's waist. My breath stops, eyes narrow, and a growl escapes my lips the moment their lips meet.

Time doesn't slow. It stops completely. All I can hear is my own blood rushing to my ears. My chest rises and falls with shallow, broken breaths.

That kiss was mine. Just days ago. And yet here she is, surrendering herself to a stranger, a king, as if *we* meant nothing.

I shut my eyes for a moment, trying to block out the scene before me.

But it doesn't help.

The image has seared itself behind my eyelids, there to torture me for all eternity.

I thought she felt something for me. The way her body leaned into me, the way her lips parted beneath mine. The way she looked at me. Had it all been a lie? Had I misread everything?

I know she's avoiding me. From skipping training, to turning around and walking the other way when she sees me in the corridors. And now this?

I slam a fist into the stone before I can stop myself. The pain barely registering. I want to scream. To rage. But what's the point?

"You know. Jealousy really doesn't suit you," comes a low voice from behind.

I spin around, startled, not with my hand on my sword, but with fury barely chained behind my eyes.

Athan steps through the doorway and makes his way toward me, soaked from the rain, his dark, shoulder-length hair slicked back, and hammer slung lazily over his shoulder.

He glances past me to the window, his gaze following the invisible thread of heartbreak that still connects me to the pergola below.

A knowing look passes between us.

I turn away, my voice cold. "Don't."

"I wasn't going to say anything," Athan replies quietly, stepping to the other side of the window.

The silence stretches between us, thick as the storm clouds still crawling over the horizon. Only the soft tap of water dripping from Athan's soaked clothes breaks it.

He leans against the opposite wall. His eyes stay fixed on the window, on the spot where I still see her, even though she's no longer there.

"You going to tell me what you're really doing up here?" Athan finally asks, his voice low, not unkind.

I don't answer.

Athan exhales through his nose and scrapes a hand through his wet hair. "Alright. Let's pretend I'm too dumb to figure it out. That maybe you climbed up to this old watch tower to do some soul-searching and not, say, torture yourself by watching her kiss that bastard from half a mile up."

My jaw tightens.

He nods slowly. "Yeah. That's what I thought."

A tremor runs down my spine as I turn back toward the window. The mist has thickened now, swallowing the garden in silver fog. Part of me is grateful. At least I can't see them anymore.

"She made her choice," I say. The words feel like ash in my mouth.

Athan doesn't respond right away. He just steps closer, finally setting his hammer down with a soft clunk beside the stone wall. "She made *a* choice. That doesn't mean it's the one she wants."

I throw a guarded glance at him.

He tilts his head slightly. "Oh, come on, Codrin. You've known Ravenna for how long? Even I've seen her wear a lot of faces. That one she wears now?" He shakes his head. "It's a mask. And a heavy one."

"She doesn't look like she's struggling," I mutter bitterly.

Athan arches a brow. "Oh, no, she looks radiant. Like a fucking jewel. That's the point." He folds his arms and leans beside me now, his voice softening. "She's surviving, Codrin. And right now? Playing nice with the enemy is the safest move she has."

I say nothing. Because if I speak, I might break.

Athan lets out a heavy sigh and bumps his shoulder lightly into mine. "You should talk to her."

"She doesn't want to talk to me."

"Maybe not. But that doesn't mean you shouldn't try."

I look down at my knuckles, bloody and bruised from punching the wall. "I don't even know what to say."

He studies me for a long beat. "Then start with the truth. That's usually a good place."

"Yeah… sure." I huff, my shoulders dropping as I watch Ravenna, smile so brightly, hand-in-hand with Alaric, leaving the garden maze and heading back toward the castle.

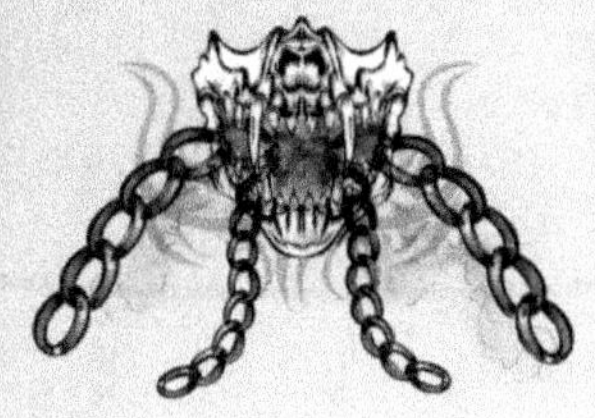

CHAPTER 18
Codrin

I sit on the end of the couch in the far corner of the tavern near the fireplace, nursing a beer. The Royal Pub, located outside the castle gates, is far nicer than Simon's place as it caters to wealthy patrons.

I don't care for the place, but I've been avoiding Simon's… and everyone else. So, this is the next best option.

I don't know if I promised more to myself or Athan that I would talk to Ravenna, but I failed terribly at that too. My stomach dropped to the floor seeing her laughing in the early afternoon light as she had walked, arms linked with Alaric out of the maze garden. I shattered, and now, I'm unable to pick up the broken pieces to put myself back together.

I sit here tonight as mishmash scents of pine and citrus and rich brandy, and sweet cigars from countries across the sea, engulfs my senses and invades my thoughts. Trophy heads line the wall, and the paintings framed in gold glow against the kingdom's colors of light-blue and silver wallpaper. It all makes me feel out of place.

The dark oak baseboards blur along the walls, each one hand-carved, each one whispering money and power. Fine velvet couches stretch out along the windows like thrones, smug and heavy. Crystal glasses clink together in a soft, pretty melody that gnaws at the edges of my nerves, mingling with the low hum of laughter and empty chatter.

Just like Simon's tavern, this one has an upstairs as well. However, the ladies here dress in their finest satin and velvet dresses of deep reds, bright greens, and soft pinks, their hair done up with feathers and small jewels. Some ladies wearing oversized jewels around their necks of rubies and emeralds and sapphires I assume are gifts from some very happy customers.

A young barmaid, possibly in her early twenties, golden-blond hair held up in a loose bun, her blush-pink dress and white apron clean of stains, weaves her way around the tables and chairs with a tray full of beer mugs balanced on one hand.

She sets the tray on the table centered among the couch and a few chairs. Men grab for the beer, not so much as a thank you to the young lady. I take the last one, giving her a quick smile of thanks as I lean back in the couch and start downing the bubbly, cool liquid.

The guards and slayers swap stories about women, travel and who'll outdrink who tonight.

I almost laugh. If Athan were here, he'd drink them all under the table.

Normally, I'd enjoy the banter. Tonight, it scrapes against me like broken glass. Four days of shit piled up, and I'm drowning in it.

My mind flicks to Ravenna. To that night.

No. I shove the thought down so hard it nearly chokes me.

The older guards light cigars, laughing like they own the fucking world. I roll my eyes so hard it hurts.

Gods, I hate this place.

Some of the younger ones start slamming shots of Hella's Kiss, betting who can drink the most. My money's on the slayers. At least they know what real fire feels like.

I fake a smile here and there, toss a few hollow laughs into the noise, but every second that ticks by frays my patience thinner.

Just leave me the fuck alone.

I slam back the rest of my drink, the burn doing nothing to numb the feelings, and wonder how fast I can disappear before I lose it completely.

A giggle from across the room catches my attention, and I spot the back of the golden-blond-haired barmaid. She seems to be enjoying a friendly conversation with a gentleman she's blocking from my view.

Another shy giggle leaves her lips, her cheeks flush, and her body shifts to the left, revealing the man responsible for her delight.

Arms sprawled across the top of the royal-blue velvet couch, leg resting over his knee, sitting with a toothy grin upon that damn mischievous face of his, my brother. Darius.

It takes everything in me to not jump from this damn couch

and throw his ass out of here.

Darius leans forward, gently grabbing the girl's hand and pulling her onto his lap, whispering into her ear. Her cheeks redden as she laughs at whatever he says to her.

I grip the handle of my beer mug to the point of breaking. Darius has a way with sweet-talking young mortals, and with those hungry eyes of his, I know he's trying to snag himself a meal.

As the barmaid gets up from Darius's lap, waves goodbye, and heads toward the back kitchen, I sit back with a relieved exhale. But my brows furrow as Darius watches her every move until she finally disappears from sight. His dark gaze slowly turns to me, those devilish thoughts of his flashing across his diamond-shaped face.

I stare him down like a hunter fixed on his prey.

Darius brushes a long strand of black hair from his face as he leans back and pats the seat beside him.

I hesitate, glancing around at the others. No one even looks at the prince. No one has a clue what kind of monster lurks right before them. Briefly, I try to ignore his invitation and think of just leaving.

But I toss the thought aside, stand, and straighten my shirt before making my way across the tavern toward him.

Instead of sitting next to Darius, I take a seat in the chair across from him.

"If looks could kill." Darius lets out a deep chuckle, placing a leg over his knee.

"Don't even think about trying anything, Darius."

He responds by letting out an overdramatic yawn.

"Don't worry, Captain. I fed enough to last me this entire miserable trip." He responds with an overdramatic yawn. Swishing a glass of brandy in his hand, he takes a swig, his golden eyes locked on me over the rim of his glass. "Speaking of which, when was the last time you *truly* fed?"

Heat flares beneath my skin. "That's none of your concern."

"Well, my concern or not, I do have a little something special for you." He sets his glass down on the small side table.

"I don't want anything. Especially if it's coming from you."

Darius's tone softens as he leans toward me. "Hold that thought for now."

Ravenna pops into my mind. Does Darius know of her and me? Would he stoop so low as to hurt her? My heart drops to my stomach at the thought of her being in danger.

"Don't worry. It has nothing to do with your precious princess." Darius rolls his eyes.

"I don't need you crawling through my guilt like it's yours to touch," I growl.

He smirks, knowing he can feel the anger bleeding off me. That's always been his thing. He doesn't need to hear your thoughts to twist the knife. He just *feels* it, reads the ache beneath your skin and knows right where to press.

"Whatever." His eyes shift around the room as though the scene around him is more interesting than our conversation. "Anyway, it's just a little gift to *help* you out."

"Help me with what? What is it?"

Darius claps his hands together with excitement as he jumps to his feet.

"Follow me!"

"I never said I wanted whatever it is you have." I say, crossing my arms as I lean back into the chair.

"Get up. Let's go." Darius snaps his fingers.

I have a feeling I'm going to regret this.

I hesitate for a couple of breaths before finally getting to my feet and following Darius across the tavern and up the stairs to the second floor. The darkness grows thick as we silently make our way down the long hallway to a closed door at the end. Without a word, Darius opens the door, revealing a dark room lit only by a few candles on the nightstand.

My eyes slowly adjust as I step into the room. Darius walks in behind me and closes the door with a soft click.

I freeze, noticing someone lying on the bed. They're on their side, their back to us. I whirl around to face Darius. "What the fuck is this?"

"It's time to feed, Codrin." He leans against the door; arms crossed over his chest.

I stumble back as though Darius just bitch slapped me. "No,"

I snarl, stalking to the other side of the bed.

I stagger back as the person's face comes into view.

A young royal guard lies unconscious on the bed; dry blood crusted on the side of his head where something hit him to knock him out. The coppery tang hits my nostrils, and a shiver runs through me as I clamp a hand over my mouth and nose, trying to keep the smell out.

But it's too late.

My mouth instantly starts to water.

Gods, it's been so long. Too long, since I've tasted fresh young blood. My teeth ache with the desire to sink into the guard's flesh.

The intensity of my thirst shocks me. Normally, I can keep myself under tight control. A little blood is commonplace during training. I can't lose control every time someone gets a cut.

Shaking, I stumble back from the bed.

"I won't."

"Oh, come on. I even made sure it wasn't one of your *Slayer Squad buddies*." Darius stalks forward. "You can deny it all you want. But I can see it in those dull, hungry eyes of yours. You *want* this."

I shake my head, my eyes fixed on the unconscious guard.

Images flash through my mind. Fleeing Veilstead. Becoming a ghost in Theiahold. Hiding my secret. Surviving, my curse that writhes in my veins. Crouching in a dirty alley, feeding off a rat. Simon approaching me.

He didn't run. He offered me a deal: drink just enough to live, only from those he brought me, and never take a life. In exchange, he would keep my secret.

I swore I wouldn't.

I kept that promise, even as it starved me, dulled my senses, weakened my strength. But a promise, especially one made in blood and gratitude, means everything to a man's honor.

I stand over the young royal guard. Imagining the taste of that clean, *fresh* blood. Knowing it will be better than the stale bitterness of Simon's drunk patrons.

Swallowing down the knot in my throat.

My fangs slowly extract.

The guilt of a forty-year promise shatters before me as I try to control the craving building up and the animal inside clawing to be released.

My stomach cramps, and I break into a cold sweat.

I'm so hungry.

Though I just fed last week, it still isn't enough. It's never enough. I want fresh blood. I *crave* fresh blood.

I stumble back, shaking my head, but the guard's scent wraps around my senses, a sweet, brutal lure that drags claws down my resolve, making it harder and harder to remember why I should walk away.

Darius moves with immortal speed to my side, whispering in my ear, "Do it, Codrin. You need this. Do it for your princess."

I take an involuntary step closer to the bed. Darius nudges me further. "Do it, Codrin. You know you'll feel so much better."

Hunger rips through me, raw and savage, and I tremble from the effort it takes to hold myself back. I shouldn't have let myself get this bad. Maybe if I just have a taste. Just a little bit to take the edge off.

I take a step closer, mouth ajar, my fangs out on full display.

Alaric is here to steal Ravenna away from me. I can't let that happen. I need the strength. Alaric has taken everything from me once before.

Not again.

Not this time.

I need all the strength I can get to keep that fucking King of Darkness away from the woman I love.

That's right.

The woman I love!

I won't take much. Just a few sips. This guard won't even know come morning.

I kneel at the side of the bed, hovering over the guard. The large vein in his neck pulses with every breath he takes, blood running through it like a river roaring in my ears.

I lick my lips. My tongue glides over my fangs. Taking a deep breath, I lean over the guard, open my mouth, and sink my teeth deep into his neck.

I close my eyes and groan as the warm, rich taste of blood

rushes into my mouth.

Hells, I've missed this taste so much.

The guard flinches, his eyes popping open wide. He flails, a feeble punch thrown with all the strength of a drowning man, and I barely feel it glance off me.

He tries to throw another punch but I'm too quick for him. I grab his arm, holding it down with one hand and wrapping my other arm around his body like a boa constrictor, locking him in place.

I just need a little more.

The guard kicks and struggles against my weight. I press all my weight down harder on him, willing him to stop struggling. His heart races, his breathing coming in loud pants.

Stop. Stop fucking struggling.

His struggles only trigger something deep within me. Something I have locked away for forty years. The blood rushes into my mouth and down my throat, and the young guard bucks like a wild animal. The monster in me roars to life, sinking its claws into my spine, dragging me deeper into the frenzy. With every blow he tries to make, I feel him weaken in my arms.

Just a little more, I order myself.

Darkness devours me as I lock my teeth down harder.

I sit on the floor, leaning against the wall. The young royal guard lies motionless on the bed, his dead eyes staring blankly at me.

Darius crouches down in front of me, blocking my view of the guard's lifeless body, and hums with pleasure. "There's those beautiful eyes."

I glare at my brother, flashing my fangs with a growl. "Get away from me, Darius."

Using the wall for support, I struggle to my feet. Darius steps aside as I stagger over to the small mirror hanging on the wall across the room.

I stumble and catch myself; my hands planted along the wall on each side of the mirror.

I lift my head slowly. My reflection peers back at me.

Now that I have fully fed, my irises have transformed from forty years of dull, stormy gray clouds into an enchanting shade of moonlight silver.

"Don't worry about this mess. I'll take care of it," he says, watching him in the mirror as he strolls over to the overstuffed chair in the corner. Sitting, he smiles back at me. "As for you, baby brother, go enjoy the rest of your night."

I peek over my shoulder at him as he gives me a wink.

I scan the nearly dark room, as though seeing for the first time. Every detail of the room is clear as day. The thrill of fresh blood sings through my veins, the muscles in my body tighter and more toned. My strength, powerful.

And my speed.

Oh, how I have missed the feeling of running as though soaring through the wind like a bird flying through open sky.

Ignoring Darius, who sits silently watching my every move, I make my way over to the window, opening it wide. The cool night air wraps itself around me. Calling out to me. Begging me to come out and play in the star-scattered night.

With the high of the kill racing through me, I feel little for the young man lying dead just feet away. I know from experience that will probably change when the high wears off a bit. But for now, I feel like myself again for the first time in so long.

I take a deep breath of fresh air, ready to take on the night.

Gazing over the town, my glowing moon-silver eyes fall upon the castle. Setting my sights directly on the northwest tower window.

Ravenna's room.

A warm craving slithers through me.

CHAPTER 19

Ravenna

I pace around my dark room, the night air refreshing as it plays in the long curtains around the open window and cools my tired mind.

These past few days have been long and agonizing torture, getting dolled up in these uncomfortable, too-fucking-tight dresses. I swear yesterday's dress cracked a rib. It still hurts to take a deep breath.

And my cheeks. Oh, my poor cheeks and jaw.

Plastering a smile on my face all day like some simpering court pet…

Yeah, I prefer my jaw hurting for better reasons than a fake smile.

But it's working, isn't it?

Mother hasn't scolded me once. Father's been too busy basking in political approval to notice my sarcasm. And as for Codrin.

I know he's been watching. I can feel his damn presence lingering like a lost soul unable to move on. Pathetic. But whatever. Let him stew a little.

Still, the longer I play this game, the more tangled I feel. Alaric gave me a choice… and I've seen a different side of him these past few days. Measured and dangerous… sure, but not cruel. Calculating, but not careless.

If I do marry Alaric, that means I would become queen. But I don't want to be a queen.

I don't want to belong to anyone, not even Codrin right now.

His name is a whisper in my head. I longed for him to step out from the shadows, swoop me in his arms, and take me away. But that never happened. It will *never* happen. Codrin proved that days ago. I am not enough for him to save.

Codrin can seriously go fuck himself now.

A shift in the air halts my pacing. Scanning the room, nothing seems odd. But something is there. I feel it. But what?

In the far corner, where the shadows dwell the most, a set of glowing eyes stares back at me.

Breath snags in my chest.

I stand there frozen in the middle of the room, unable to tear myself away from the shadow figure staring back at me. Instead of fear, a strange stillness settles over me, as if the world has gone silent, every frantic thought dulled to a hush. Is this the same shadow figure I saw at the tavern? It has to be. I know it is.

It shifts, taking a slow step toward me.

My heart accelerates.

The figure stops.

I blink and it's gone. Before I have time to react, everything happens in one quick blur.

The figure looms behind me. Its hand clamps over my mouth,

cutting off all words. Cutting off the scream rising in my throat. Its broad chest of hard muscle rises and falls as it presses itself against my back.

Tilting my head back, I feel the cold, sharp blade of my own axe against my neck. The shadow figure leans into my ear, its breath warm against my skin, sending chills of unknown pleasure I can't explain along my spine.

I want to be scared. Want to fight back. But my body has disconnected from my mind and now I am paralyzed.

Its chest rises on a deep inhale, then exhales… "You know, it's not very fucking nice to throw things at others." The words end on a deep, rumbling growl.

That voice. It's so familiar. There's no mistaking it.

I know it's him. But it can't be him. Can it?

The shadow figure's hand presses harder over my mouth, pushing my head back further, the blade pressing deeper against my neck, but it still doesn't pierce my skin. It's lips part as they ghost along my ear.

My breath hitches in my throat.

I'm trapped. At its mercy. And yet I am willing to let this mystery figure take me however it wants.

And in one swift movement, its hand shifts from my mouth, and the axe falls to the ground. I take a quick breath before it spins me.

Fuck. But before my eyes can even catch up with how fast I

was spun. I am gasping for air that is cut from my lungs as its hand wraps tightly around my throat, pulling me in close and I am met with glowing silver moon eyes narrowed on to me.

"Cod-rin…" I gasp, wriggling in his hold, but his grip only tightens, sharp and punishing, a low growl rumbling from his chest.

What's gotten into him?

Just remember he is the one who left you. Left you… to die.

My brows drop at the thought. My vision focuses, and I am faced with his snarling glare. His lips part parts and two sharp, pointed canines line the top of his teeth.

I let out a choked gasp.

Codrin has fangs?! But how?

I'm trapped in the killing hands of… Codrin? A vampire? I should be terrified. I should be fighting, screaming, scrambling to get away.

But I'm not. Even with his fangs inches from my face, even with his vampire eyes burning into me, there's no fear. There's only…

"That wasn't very nice…" his voice low as it interrupts my thoughts.

"You fucking deserved it," I spit, baring my teeth at him.

His grip tightens, and I gasp, my hands flying up, gripping his massive forearm as he constricts the last of what little air, I have left from escaping my lips.

He doesn't love you, the voice hisses in my ear. *No reason to care. No reason to love.*

"Shut up," I whisper to the voice.

Codrin arches a brow, causing me to stand on my tip-toes. "Don't toy with me," he snarls, yanking me up to his eye level, causing me to stand on my tip-toes.

"Well then, next time I won't miss," I say gasping out each breath.

"Don't threaten me with a good time, *Ravenna.*"

"Or what?"

Before I can argue more, the ground shifts beneath my feet. I'm airborne for a split second, and the next, crashing down on top of my bed. Codrin's body pressing against mine, trapping me as his lips slam to mine. His fingers loosen around my throat, and I take in a quick breath through my nose as our lips stay locked together.

His hand shifts from my neck, snaking around the back and sliding into my hair. Gathering a handful of my hair, causing a shriek to escape my lips as he yanks my head back hard exposing my neck. He presses me deeper into the mattress. His lips move from mine down my neck, and I'm finally able to take a full breath of air, filling my lungs and exhaling on a moan as I feel his tongue slide along my neck, his lips kissing the skin every so often.

Is he planning to bite me? Drain me of my blood?

I plant my hands on his chest, ready to push him off me but the thought is quickly forgotten as my fingers stroke the wall of muscle through his shirt, and my hips betray me as they grind against him.

Hot, hungry pleasure races throughout my whole body as his fangs glide across my skin. I shouldn't want this. He's a vampire. Dangerous and deadly, everything I've been taught to hate. To kill.

Did he let one of the Veilstead guards turn him into a vampire?

Did he change into this monster for me? Because I'm engaged to a vampire king?

Or has he always been a vampire?

No, that's not possible… isn't it?

Either way, I should be fighting back, shoving him away, remembering who I am. A slayer. Sworn to fight the creatures of the night.

But I don't.

Gods, help me, I don't want to.

My hunger for him runs just as deep as his does for me.

"You were made to destroy me," he whispers against my ear, voice thick with something darker than lust. "And I gladly let you. As long as it gives me something real to feel. You are mine. You are my rapture, Ravenna."

A rush of heat curls in my belly. And all I can think is, *and you are mine.* "I hate you," I say instead.

He snarls, but before he can say anything, my bedroom door creaks, and the moment shatters around us. Before I can steal one last touch from him, he's gone.

I jolt up in bed as my door opens and Talon's head pokes into the room.

"Hey, you still awake." It isn't really a question, and he doesn't wait for an answer from me as he steps inside, closing the door behind him.

"What, Talon?!" I don't even try hiding my annoyance. My heart is still racing, my skin still burning from Codrin's touch.

I glance at the open window, at the curtains dancing from the night breeze or is it from Codrin leaving out my window?

Talon's eyes narrow. "Rave, are you okay?"

My head snaps back to my brother. "I'm fine. I'm trying to get some sleep, and you just barge in here like I owe you a conversation." I hop from the bed, stomping toward him, more annoyed with him for interrupting a heated moment.

"I wouldn't barge in if I wasn't fucking worried about you, Rave." He steps further into the room. His shoulders tense, fists clenched. "I haven't really had a chance to talk to you since the attack. And honestly, it seems lately you've been… off. And I'm not sure how to reach you anymore."

I scoff, folding my arms tight across my chest. "Oh, I'm sorry. I didn't realize you had the right to analyze me."

"It's not about analyzing. It's about giving a shit. And clearly, you've been too busy playing princess with King Alaric to notice the people who actually care about you."

The words hit me like a slap. And the worst part is a part of me wants to believe him. To let the anger in his voice wash over me and drown me in guilt. I know he cares. I know he worries. Sometimes too much.

But does he really? The voice hisses in my head.

A spark ignites in my chest. A spark fueled by so much fucking frustration.

Crossing my arms in front of my chest, I let the words spill from my lips with no regret. "Don't act like you give a shit."

"I give a shit." He lashes back, stomping a foot as he widens his stance.

"Oh, please," I huff out a laugh, shifting my weight to one side. "Just because you've been hovering around me like a shadow doesn't mean you care."

"Think what you want. But I know what I see," Talon snaps as he takes two hard stomps toward me.

My arms fall to my side, head falling back with a deep exhale as I give him my back.

"I see you enjoying yourself as you hang off his arm, all dolled up and giggling like he's the best damn thing that's ever happened to you. I see you letting him get close to you. Too close."

He says that last part like a warning, like he's trying to protect me. And it just pisses me off more.

I spin on my heel to face him. "Oh, so you can *enjoy* yourself," I point a finger at him, my eyes piercing straight into his. "While being dragged upstairs by the barmaid that night. But gods forbid I have even the slightest joy in my own life without being criticized for it."

His jaw clenches, a muscle twitching in his cheek. "This isn't about me."

"No, of course it isn't." My voice rises, my hands trembling at my sides. "It's about what you or Codrin *think* I need." I take a step toward him. "What's best for me." Another step and this time Talon takes a step back. "What I should or shouldn't be doing. Because Hella forbid any of you give two shits and actually ask me. That would be too easy, now wouldn't it."

"That's why I'm here." His voice low with his arms out, palms up.

I stop mid-step; my shoulders slump and I shake my head. "No, you're not."

"Yes, I am," He tries to take a step forward, but I stop him with a narrow glare.

"No, Talon," my voice low but laced with a fiery wrath that grows with every step I take toward him. "You stand there and say you're worried about me. That you care about me. But when was the last time you asked me how I feel? Hmm? Neither you, nor Codrin truly care."

He looks at me, wide-eyed, mouth slightly ajar as if to argue, but no words come out.

"You all treat me like I'm some stupid little girl who needs constant guidance. Like you all know me better than I know myself. But you don't. None of you do." My voice cracks. Just once. But I swallow it down as I close the space between us. "You see what you want to see." I jab my finger at his chest. He flinches a step back. I step closer. "You hear what you want to hear." Another jab. Harder.

The air around me hums. Thickens. Something stirs in the corners of the room.

Talon's brow lowers, his hands fisted tightly at his side.

"I just… I don't want to see you get hurt."

My head tilts to the side. "Oh, I'm already hurt, Talon." My voice drops to a cold whisper. "And none of you seem to give a damn about that."

He takes a deep inhale, readying himself to speak but before he can get a word out, I shove him back. Not because I want to. Because I *need* to. Because if I don't, I might break in his arms instead of breaking him apart.

He stumbles, catching himself with a hand on the dresser. A flicker crosses his face. Guilt, maybe. Regret. Who the fuck knows?

The shadows along the walls stretch. Just slightly. Crawling, reaching. I see them move. I *know* I see them move.

But I don't care.

I welcome them.

The voice in my head hisses like smoke. *They don't under-*

stand you. They never have. They only want to control you. Tell you what to feel. Who to be. What you should feel. They don't care about you… not really.

Talon lets out a shaky breath, taking a step toward me with what little determination he has. "Rave, I—"

I cut him off. Both hands slam against his chest, and I shove him hard toward the door.

"Get. *Out!*"

I push again.

He collides with the wood, wincing as the doorknob digs into his lower back.

I step closer, my fury sharper than fangs.

"I don't care for what you have to say. Now get the fuck out of my room."

"What the fuck has gotten into you?" Talon tries to step forward, but I drive him back with my wrath. His back slams against the door once more.

"Nothing has gotten into me." My voice twists with something sharp. Cold. "You are just finally seeing the *real* me."

Talon drops his head. "Whatever you say, Rave."

"Just get the fuck out." I turn and stalk back toward my bed, rage in every step.

He opens the door. Hesitates and looks back.

"But this isn't the real you," he whispers. "I know that much at least."

I freeze. Just long enough to let the words cut me.

Then why does it feel so fucking true?

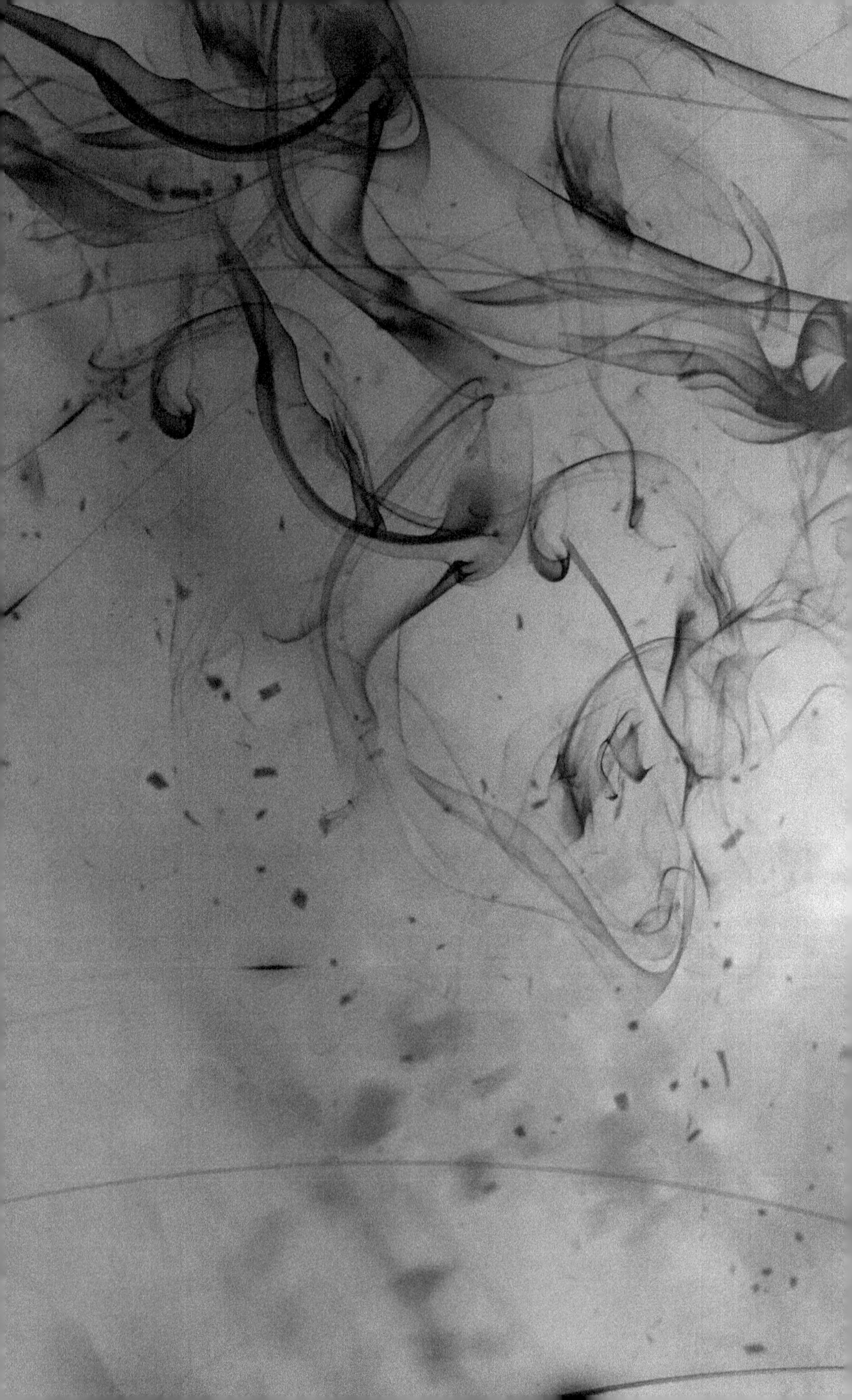

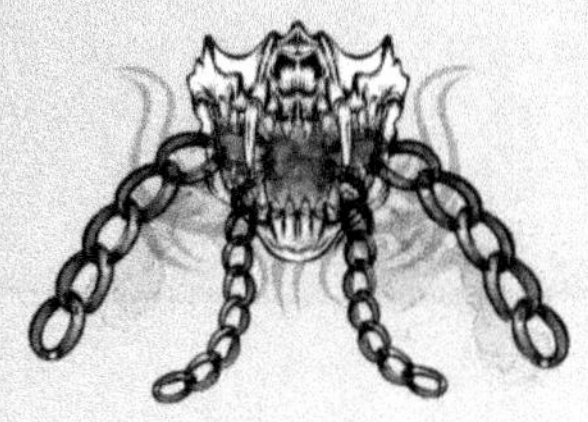

CHAPTER 20
Codrin

The walk back to my room is a blur.

Every thought tangles into a knot, winding tight enough to snap. The feel of her skin, the heat of her body pressed against mine, it's etched into my senses like a burn that won't heal.

I pace the length of my room, boots still on, tracking mud and dust across the floor. My blood is still singing from the high of a fresh feeding, my strength buzzing beneath the surface.

But Ravenna's taste… damn, I can still taste her on my lips.

I can still feel her heartbeat against my chest, wild and frantic, but not with fear. Not with terror. She said she hates me, but I know it's not true. Not with the way she looked into my silver, predatory, monstrous eyes and instead of pushing me away, *she pulled me closer.* A slight grin crawls up the side of my face to the thought.

It thrills me. It terrifies me. And now she knows. Maybe not the full truth. Maybe not everything I've kept locked away for decades. But she saw what I am. She saw the monster behind the man. And she didn't run.

I laugh under my breath, the sound ragged, unhinged. She didn't fucking run.

She wanted me. Even after what I did.

I press my palms to my temples, fingers lacing through my hair as I pace my room replaying every second of what just happened, over and over until it's a web of heat and desire tangled with her voice and her touch.

But as the high starts to fade, doubt creeps in. I was reckless. Beyond reckless. Her brother walked in, and I barely had time to vanish before he caught me.

A creak from the shadows cleaves through my focus, swift and ruthless.

I freeze. The walls in my mind going up. Every muscle snapping taut.

Shit.

The fresh blood still pulsing in my veins heightens my senses, sharpens the air. I draw a deep breath, picking apart the scents threading through the room. Wine and blood. Pine and citrus.

My head drops to my chest, as I let out a deep sigh.

I can hear every near-silent step he takes, moving out from the shadows and into the open space of the room. I lean against the desk with my arms crossed.

"Hello, brother," I say through my teeth.

A man steps forward, dressed in sharp, midnight-black attire, his eyes glinting gold beneath the shadows. Those stupid golden eyes I want to pluck from his fucking skull. Mister King of Darkness, Ruler of Veilstead. My older brother, Alaric.

His grin is lazy, casual, like he's already won something I haven't even begun to fight for.

"Baby brother." His voice is smooth, too smooth, that it makes my bones rattle beneath my skin. "What a pleasure it is to finally find you."

Has he been standing there this whole time? Fuck, I was so wrapped in my own thoughts I didn't sense him when I entered the room.

"Is it?" I growl, forcing my shoulders to relax even as every muscle wants to tense. "Because I'm pretty sure you've known where I was this entire time."

"Oh, I did," Alaric concedes with a shrug, his hands clasped behind his back like he's inspecting a particularly dull piece of art. "But there's something exhilarating about letting the hunt stretch on. Wouldn't you agree?" He flashes an enigmatic smile.

I bite down on the snarl rising in my throat. "You're just pissed I walked away."

He raises a brow, his grin twitching wider. "Walked away?" he echoes as if testing the words. "You didn't walk away, Codrin. You ran. And here you are, still running."

"Then why are you here, Alaric?" My voice drops, the words scraped raw. "What's the point of this little visit? To gloat?"

"To gloat? No." Alaric chuckles, but it's hollow, taunting. "Perhaps I just wanted to congratulate you. It's not every day my wayward brother decides to build himself a new life under my nose. And you've been so careful to keep your little secret. Quite the act of restraint, truly." His gaze sharpens. "Until tonight."

My fists clench. "You were watching."

"*Always*," he hisses. "I must admit, it was quite the performance. Your rage. Your hunger. Your… devotion." His smile dances, sharp enough to split bone from marrow. "I see now what kept you tethered to this place."

I hold his gaze, my fists clenched so tight my knuckles ache. "Stay the seven hells away from her."

"Or what? You'll stop me? *Kill* me? After everything you've already given up?"

I swallow hard, but the words stick, frozen in the back of my throat. Alaric catches the hesitation, his smile twisting into something darker.

"Tell me, Codrin, how does it feel to be so pathetically predictable?" His words slither into the air, curling like smoke. "Risking everything for a girl who can never truly understand what you are."

I push off from the desk but reach back to keep my hands planted on the surface of the wood, bracing myself from lunging at him. "She understands enough."

"Oh, does she?" Alaric's head tilts, eyes blazing. "And when she discovers the full truth? When she sees the depths of what you are, what you've done, do you honestly believe she will look at you the same way?"

My jaw clenches until it aches. "Get to the point, Alaric."

"The point, brother, is that you're clinging to a fantasy. You think you can protect her. That you can be what she needs. But the truth is, you're nothing more than a shadow playing at being human. And shadows," he leans forward, his voice lowering to a whisper, "always fade when the light comes."

The air clings to my skin, thick and stifling, carrying the sharp bite of his taunting presence. But there's something else too. Something lurking just beneath his words.

A challenge.

A warning.

"What the hells do you want, Alaric?"

"What I've always wanted," he says, stepping close enough that I can feel the heat of him. "For you to return home. To be what you were meant to be. To stop hiding from the truth of who you are."

"If you want me to return then what does this have to do with Ravenna?"

Alaric shrugs a shoulder. "I have my reasons."

My nails dig into the surface of the desk. "Stay away from her," I growl through clenched teeth. "Also, I'll never go back to Veilstead."

"*Never* is a dangerous word, Codrin." Alaric waves a finger in my face like some disapproving parent. "Especially when you're not the only one with secrets."

What the seven hells is that supposed to mean?

He turns on his heel, making his way to the door with the same infuriating calmness he arrived with.

"One more thing. Your princess." Alaric pauses at the doorway. "She's fascinating. I can see why you're so taken with her." He gazes at me over his shoulder, eyes glinting. "It would be a shame if something happened to her. Especially with how delicious she tastes. I would hate for you to lose that."

He licks his lips, and I snap.

I lunge at him.

But he's faster. With one swift movement, Alaric spins around, snatching me by the throat and smashing me against the wall. His fingers clamp around my throat, squeezing with little effort.

My hands grasp the muscle of his forearm as he slides me up the wall and off my feet, lifting me to his eye level. Alaric is taller and stronger than me. Even at my full strength, I have never been able to outmatch him.

"She will never love you. She will only see you for the monster you are," he growls, his fangs glowing in the moonlight. "Soon, I will have her, and I will make you watch as she enjoys the taste of me."

"I will kill you." I claw and wrench at his arm, every muscle straining to break free from the chokehold crushing me against the wall.

Alaric leans closer to me, pressing me harder into the stone wall. "I'd like to see you try."

His hand clamps tighter around my throat, constricting the air to my lungs. I kick with all my strength, but with my limited range of motion, Alaric stands like a boulder, unmoved.

My lungs burn. My vision blurs. I can't get myself out of this.

Spots dance across my vision, and everything around me starts to go black. I hear pounding in the distance, unsure if it's my own heart or something else.

Something charges hard into Alaric. His hand rips from my throat, and I fall to the ground, gasping for air.

"Sorry I'm late to the party," Athan says, brushing dust off his sleeves as he stands. "Got held up at a tea gathering with some chatterbox mermaids. They insisted I stay for a second round; however, I couldn't exactly say no without offending royalty. You know how it is." He grins wide. "Alaric, buddy, fancy seeing you here. Did you miss me?"

Alaric jumps to his feet, rage flashing in his eyes. "Do you ever shut the fuck up?"

He charges Athan at full speed, lifting him off his feet and slamming him to the floor on his back.

Athan coughs for breath. "I take it we'll catch up later then."

Alaric grabs his ankle and swings him around, throwing Athan across the room like he's nothing more than a doll. He hits the wall and falls onto the desk, splitting it in half under his weight.

I try to rush to my feet, but Alaric catches me by the toe of his boot with a hard kick to my chest. Grabbing a fistful of my hair, he pulls me to my knees and throws a punch to my jaw. Another across my cheek. And another. My lip splits, and blood fills my mouth. Alaric drives his knee into my face, throwing me back.

Another vicious punch to my ribs, and the crack of bone echoes through the room.

I cough hard, blood spattering the floor and agony spiking through my ribs with every shallow breath, each inhale like knives sawing through my side.

"Is that all you've got, Codrin? Forty years, and you still haven't learned your place." He drives his boot into my side, sending me crashing to the floor once more. The pain is sharp, electric, but my fury burns hotter.

Athan manages to pull himself up from the wreckage of the splintered desk, a dazed but determined grin plastered on his face. "Damn, Alaric. Was it something I said? Because that was just plain rude."

He leaps forward, grabbing Alaric by the arm and twisting it behind his back with a strength that surprises even me. But it only lasts a second.

Alaric jerks free and backhands Athan across the face, the impact sending him reeling into the wall. Athan slumps to the ground, eyes hazy, but somehow still grinning. "Yep… definitely rude."

Alaric's golden eyes snap back to me, murderous and fiery. "I will tear everything you care about apart." He steps forward, looming over me. "Starting with her."

Rage floods me like wildfire. I surge to my feet, the sudden motion catching Alaric off guard. I lunge at him, slamming my shoulder into his gut and propelling him backward into the wall with a bone-rattling thud.

But he's too fast. Before I can pin him, he twists away and sweeps his leg into mine, toppling me back to the floor.

The door flies open.

"What the fuck is going on here?!" Talon's voice shatters through the chaos, his silhouette cutting through the moonlight spilling in from the hall.

I expected the guards. Hells, I even expected Darius. But not Talon. Not now. There's no hiding it now. He sees it. He sees me with glowing silver-moon eyes and fangs. And I can see it in his wide icy blue eyes the slayer trained to kill.

Alaric's gaze narrows. For a moment, his eyes flicker to Talon like he's debating whether to kill him right here and now. But then he grins. It's all teeth and malice.

"Another time, little brother." Alaric sneers as he pushes past Talon out the door.

Silence stretches, thick and heavy. My chest heaves as I suck in air, the taste of my own blood sharp on my tongue.

"Is the party over already?" Athan whines.

"Athan. Codrin?" Talon's voice is tight with hesitation as he says my name, his fists clenched at his sides. "What the fuck did I just walk in on?" He darts his gaze to Athan but still closely watches me from the corner of his eye.

"Something that needs to be discussed far away from here." Athan groans as he drags himself upright. His eyes flick to me. "We need to move. Now."

I nod, pushing aside the pain and the rage and focusing on getting us the hell out of here.

"Where?" Talon demands, his gaze bouncing between the two of us. "What the hells is going on?"

"Not here," I rasp, clenching my side. "Simon's tavern. Let's go."

"Good idea." Athan staggers to his feet. "I need a drink anyway."

"Simon's?" Talon snaps. "You're out of your fucking mind. After all that noise, the guards will be here soon."

"That's why we need to leave now." Athan limps to the doorway, shoving Talon out into the hall as he goes. "Unless you'd rather stick around and explain to the guards why King Alaric was about to rip Codrin's head off?"

Talon looks past Athan to me, expression torn between fury and something like fear, but nods. "Fine. But when we get there, you're going to explain every-fucking-thing."

"As long as you buy the first... couple of rounds," Athan says, patting him on the back.

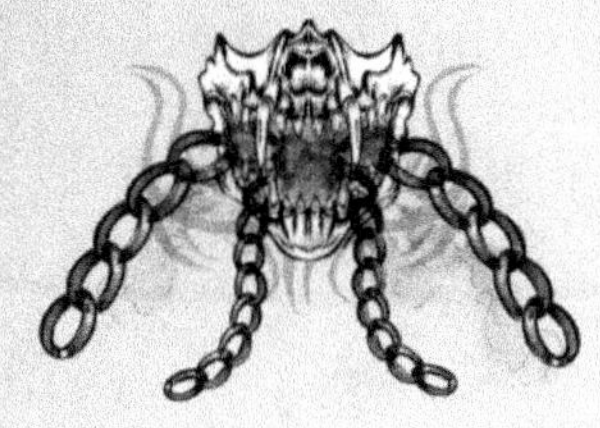

CHAPTER 21
Codrin

We move fast. Too fast for the guards to even notice as we tear through the castle grounds and into the town's shadows.

I keep pace with Athan, my side burning with every step, but I suck in a sharp breath and push through the pain. Talon charges behind us, not wanting me at his back. His curses cutting the air as we weave through narrow streets and back alleys, heading straight for Simon's tavern.

Athan kicks open the door and we all pile in, slamming it shut behind us. The scent of roasted meat and ale hits my nose, mixing with the familiar earthy musk of old wood and worn leather. The main room is crowded, laughter and conversation drowning out the madness we left behind. No one notices us as we cross the room and flee up the stairs.

Ducking down the hall, we slip into one of private rooms Simon leaves open for us when we get too plastered. The door shuts with a creak and a thud, and I finally allow myself to collapse into the nearest chair. My chest feels like it's been ripped open and stitched back together with broken glass.

Athan flops onto the couch, wincing as he props his legs up. "So, that was fun. Can't remember the last time I got my ass handed to me so thoroughly. Really brings back the nostalgia."

"Shut up." Talon stands in front of the door, fists clenched, eyes wild with fury and confusion.

"What the fuck was that?" Talon's voice rises with each word. "Why did Alaric attack you?"

"Oh, we were just catching up." Athan puffs out a chuckling breath.

Talon shakes his head. Ignoring the remark. "Why did he call you brother?" His eyes narrow on me, burning with an intensity I haven't seen in him before. "And…and what is up with your eyes?"

Athan lets out a low whistle, lounging back on the couch. "Well, Codrin. You heard the man. I do believe this is your moment of *truth*."

I glare at him, his words digging under my skin.

Talon's gaze is still pinned on me, his breathing heavy and ragged.

"You want the truth? Fine. You're not going to like it." I push to my feet, ignoring the fire screaming through my ribs.

Talon snaps into a fighting stance, his hand shooting for his sword but he doesn't draw it.

I drop my gaze to the floor and throw my hands up. Talon slowly lowers his hand from the hilt of his sword, but his stance remains as I take a step back from him.

Lifting my gaze, I lock eyes with Talon and say in one quick breath. "Alaric is my older brother."

Talon stares like I've just spoken another language. "Brother? What the fuck are you saying?"

"Vampire," Athan mutters, unhelpfully. "Just like Codrin."

I shoot him a look.

Talon's jaw tightens. His entire body goes still. "You're what?"

"Vampire," I repeat, quieter now. "Born in Veilstead. I left over forty years ago."

Talon takes a step back. "But how? You're our captain. You're a slayer. You trained me. You stood beside me. You fought with us all these years. And you never said anything?"

"I couldn't."

"Bullshit!"

I brace myself against the sharp bite of his fury. Of course he's angry. I lied to him. Hid what I am. But it's more than that. We're Slayers. Trained to hunt monsters like me. To kill them without hesitation. And now he's looking at me as he realizes he missed one hiding right under his nose these past seven years.

"I was hiding," I admit. "From Alaric. From what I used to be. I crossed the border and swore I'd never go back. I survived for years thanks to Simon."

"Wait! Simon knows?" Talon's mouth drops, his brow raised.

I nod. "When I earned my way into the king's guard, into the slayers, and I felt I had finally built a life. I never intended to get close to you and Ravenna. I never planned on staying this long."

Talon's head falls back against the door as his hands covering his face. A muffle grumble of choice words is heard as he runs his hands down his face. "You've been lying since the day we met. To all of us."

"Actually. I've known for a while." Athan raises a hand with a casual shrug.

"Not helping," I snarl at him.

Talon drops his hands to his thighs with a sharp slap, shaking his head, like he's trying to dislodge the truth from his mind.

"I know I lied. But I had to," I say, not meaning for it to sound like an excuse.

He scoffs. "And now you just expect me to believe anything you have to say? Theiahold and Veilstead have been at war for two hundred years! How do I know you're not some spy? Some plant waiting for the right moment to tear this place apart?"

"If I wanted that," I feel my tension snap, my own frustration exploding, "I would've done it years ago."

The silence crackles.

Athan breaks it with a low whistle. "Well. That went better than expected."

Talon doesn't look at him. Just at me. His eyes narrow into slits of fury.

Seconds drag by before he takes in a deep sigh. His arms flying up from his side.

"Fine." He pushes away from the door. "Tell me everything."

Stopping at my side, his eyes snapping at me from the corner. "From the beginning."

I turn my full attention to him with a nod.

He brushes past me and slumps in the chair I had occupied.

Closing my eyes and rubbing the nape of my neck as I take a second to gather myself. With a deep breath I turn on my heel to face my friend.

"Veilstead. I was raised there. Trained. Fought in the wars with Alaric. We destroyed villages together. I'm not proud of it, but I won't lie about it either."

"You were one of them." Talon jumps to his feet, the chair scrapping along the wooden floorboards.

"I was," I say, not backing down from his sudden closeness. "Until I couldn't do it anymore." Images of that final day in Veilstead flit through my mind. The blood. The carnage. I swallow hard, willing my racing heart to slow down. I'm not that person anymore.

The vein in Talon's neck throbs, his face flushed.

"We fucking trusted you." His voice comes out slow, finger pointing in my face. "You stood there and said nothing when Ravenna told us she was being married off to *your brother*."

My shoulders fall in a heavy breath, each word slicing me deeper.

"I know. I couldn't say anything."

"The fuck you couldn't." Talon's hands swing out from his

side. "Because if you cared so much for her, then why didn't you say something then?"

"I thought I was protecting her if I didn't say anything."

"Yeah, great job you did at that." Sarcastically clapping his hands with a tight-lip smile. "Just like you *not* saving her from that demon."

The words hit me like a sledgehammer, the truth laced with bitterness.

"I was too weak… and stupid." My voice falters, guilt squeezing my throat. "The moment I saw Darius, I knew Alaric wasn't far. And if I would've gone, he would've killed me, and how would that have helped Ravenna?"

Talon's stare pins me in place, his fists clenching and un-clenching at his sides. His jaw works like he's grinding back words he doesn't trust himself to say.

His anger is clear in the tight lines around his mouth, the stiff set of his shoulders, but underneath it, a flicker of some-thing sharper glints in his eyes.

Fear.

Doubt.

Like he's warring with the urge to fight me.

"Now that Alaric's here, Talon," I take a deep breath, "I will do whatever it takes to stop him from taking Ravenna."

"Why the fuck should I believe you now?" Talon growls through clenched teeth.

Athan speaks before I can. "Because as much as Codrin's an idiot, he's a loyal idiot. If he says he's on our side. He's on our side."

"I don't need your fucking help, Athan," I snarl, but the corner of his mouth quirks up anyway.

Talon doesn't say anything as the room slowly falls into silence.

He starts pacing, his boots dragging softly over the floorboards. It's a familiar sight. One I've seen a hundred times before.

Usually, it means he's thinking.

Usually, it means he's trying not to explode.

His gaze darts between me and Athan like he's trying to make sense of a nightmare.

Athan lies sprawled out on the couch, fingers laced behind his head like this is just another shitty evening with too much beer and not enough peace.

I don't move. I just watch Talon.

His silence is worse than yelling.

Then, finally, he stops.

He turns slowly, cracking his knuckles one by one, jaw locked, but there's something different in his voice now.

Less fire. More grit.

"So… what the fuck are we going to do?" His voice is low, scraped raw. "Because if we're really doing this, if Alaric is here for my sister, then we're already behind."

I straighten, relief flickering under the weight of everything else.

"We plan," I say. "Alaric didn't come here to play king-for-a-day. He came to take Ravenna. And if we don't figure out how to stop him, he will."

Talon turns, arms folded, skepticism etched into every line of his face. "What's the plan? Stake him at the next royal banquet? Toss garlic at his feet and pray he trips?"

Athan snorts. "You really need to stop reading your sister's fantasy books."

Talon's head snaps to Athan, jaw dropping. "I don't."

"Hey, I'm just calling it as I see it," he throws his hands up in defense. "Only way you'd come up with something that mythical is if you stole it from one of those smut books."

I cough back a laugh, my fist covering my mouth in hopes Talon didn't catch it.

"It was a joke." Talon rubs a hand over his face. "Hella's fire. You two are exhausting."

"Sure, it was, buddy. Now back to reality." Athan sits on the edge of the couch, elbow on his knee, head resting in his hand. "If we want to kill a vampire like Alaric, we need something sharper. Smarter."

I nod. "We need to know what he wants. What his true plan is. It's not just the marriage. That's just the surface of his move. Alaric never plays one layer deep. He's always scheming for something bigger."

"And you think it involves Ravenna?" Talon asks.

"I know it does." My voice hardens. "He doesn't just want her. He wants what she represents. Power. Leverage. Maybe more."

Talon exhales slowly, dragging a hand through his hair. "So, what? We spy on him? Hope he slips up? Maybe it's just *you* he wants."

My body stiffens, eyes locking on his.

"He does," I admit. "If that's all he wanted, I'd be dead. There's more to it."

Athan sits up, his tone turning serious. "So, what's the next move, Captain?"

I look between them, heart pounding. No more lies. No more waiting.

"We don't wait for him to strike. We strike first."

Talon runs a thumb along the edge of his belt. Athan's brows lift, his tongue running along the inside of his lip.

And for a breath, none of us speaks.

We don't need to.

Because for the first time in days, we're not tearing each other apart. We're aiming our rage at the real enemy.

CHAPTER 22

Ravenna

I just need ten minutes. Twenty minutes tops to just feel like myself for the little time Colette is willing to give me.

When she arrived to wake me, I was already up and fully dressed in my slayer leathers. I woke early for the first time in, well, ever. But this morning, I needed a breather, and I was determined to get some time to myself.

I finish tying my hair in its usual, comforting braid as Colette walks in, breakfast tray in hand and eyes wide as they lock on me. I wait in frozen silence for her to scold me, force me out of the leathers and back into another painful dress. She doesn't speak as she makes her way across the room, setting the tray on the table. She straightens, looks me up and down with a sigh, and nods. "Well, get going, child. Don't be gone too long."

I smile, grabbing my axe leaning against the wall. "I won't be." I give her a quick kiss on the cheek and a whisper of thanks as I dash past her and out the door.

I make it out to the training field unseen. Finally able to take in a lungful of fresh air, my nerves ease with every breath as I casually swing my axe, letting my mind escape, letting my body go into the muscle memory of every swing, stance, and fighting movement.

But the silence of training doesn't last long before last night's memory sneaks its way into my thoughts. The passionate yet fiery moment with Codrin fills my every nerve with a tingle of excitement. What got into him? I mean, it was *him*, right? It was his face. His body. His lips. His touch—rougher, but not. It was all him. But his eyes? Those glowing silver full-moon eyes. They were like nothing I've ever seen before. Especially in him. And his canines? They weren't even human. They were… were… no, it's not possible. There's no way. But even with the voice silent right now, my own voice speaks.

Fangs.

I know what I saw. I swear he had fangs. But how?

Raised voices catch my attention and snap me out of my haze. "In the back alley. Just this morning. Behind the Royal Pub."

I halt mid-swing, dropping my axe to my side.

"A guard," the lieutenant's voice goes on. "Dead."

My blood turns to ice, and I race toward the voices. Stopping along the wall of the slayer barracks, I peek around the corner to find a group of guards and slayers. Their faces are tight, jaws clenched, a restless energy rippling through them as they listen intently to Lieutenant Ulric Hollowstone.

My ears strain to catch every word as I stay hidden.

"Drained of all his blood. Teeth marks on his neck," Ulric repeats, his voice low and grim. "I've already sent scouts to search the outskirts of the kingdom and along the streets. If there's a vampire loose within our borders, it needs to be found. And fast."

"How are we supposed to know which vamp did this? Because I can point out about ten of them just standing here. This place has been crawling with them all week," Lucas says, his eyes falling past the group to some of the Veilstead guards across the way.

Their words swirl around me like smoke, thick and shifting. My nails bite into the shaft of my axe. Teeth marks? Drained of blood? *Vampire?*

It can't be. My thoughts spin wildly, colliding like crashing waves. *Did Codrin? He wouldn't. He… he couldn't.*

But the suspicion twines tight and cold in my gut, feeding off every whisper, every sliver of doubt the voice has been planting in my mind.

Maybe Codrin isn't who you think he is.

Well, good morning to you too. I roll my eyes, but my shoulders drop at the voice's words, which cut the breath from my lungs, harsh with betrayal.

Ulric's voice booms over the scattered conversation. "We'll be setting up a patrol outside the gates. I want eyes on every inch of land between here and the village. If you see anything, anyone, out of the ordinary, you report it. Immediately. Dismissed."

The guards and slayers disperse, but their murmurs continue, carried on the breeze like scattered ash.

"Drained dry…"

"Never seen anything like it."

"I'm telling you it was one of those Veilstead guards."

"No. It's gotta be a rebel vamp."

My legs feel like lead, my breath shallow and jagged.

Codrin's silver eyes flash in my mind. Glowing. Predatory. Did he do this? Could he have?

The voice hisses through my thoughts, sharp and cunning. *Why not find out for yourself, Ravenna?*

My palms start to sweat at every word, hitting like a punch to the gut.

Codrin wouldn't have done this.

You know what he is. You saw his eyes, his fangs. Why do you insist on lying to yourself? The voice slithers through my thoughts like smoke.

I press my back further into the wall, the world tilting around me as if the ground itself is shifting. I need to find him before anyone else does. I need to warn him and possibly get some damn answers to all these questions racing through my head.

I know he didn't do this. Codrin would never… not to one of his own men, not to a royal guard. Not to anyone.

But the doubt loops tighter, fueled by the images seared into my memory. His glowing silver eyes. The rage of hunger radiating from him like heat.

And I can't get the voice in my head to shut the fuck up for two seconds so I can think straight.

Are you sure you even know him at all? You have studied vampire ways for years. You know the truth. Stop denying yourself.

I push off from the wall and head toward the front of the barracks.

Where the hells are Talon and Athan?

Panic grips me tighter with each passing moment. Talon wasn't near the training grounds when I arrived there earlier. As thankful as I was at the time, now I'm starting to wonder where he could be. Knowing him, he's still pouting in his room over our little fight last night. But Athan isn't lounging by the barracks door, flirting with every young maid that passes by. They're *always* here. Always within sight, always making their presence known.

But not now. Not when everything feels like it's coming apart at the seams.

My pulse pounds so hard I can barely hear anything else. The guards' whispering voices fade into a low hum, and my focus narrows to a single thought. *Find him. I need to find him.*

I storm through the slayers' barracks, ignoring the questioning looks of passing slayers.

The hallway to Codrin's quarters feels longer than usual, the air thick and cloying. Every step intensifies the thudding in my chest, dread clawing its way up my spine.

As I reach his door, I notice it's slightly ajar. Taking in a deep breath, I push the door open all the way with the blade of my axe. And freeze.

Splinters of wood and shredded fabric litter the floor. The overstuffed leather couch is ripped to shreds, one of its cushions gutted and spilling its insides across the rug.

The cherry desk has been split clean in half, its broken legs jutting at awkward angles like snapped bones. Reports, ink bottles, and quills are scattered everywhere, mixed with shards of glass that stop me cold.

Splattered along the walls, smeared across the floorboards, are dark, ugly stains. Blood.

This can't be…

A chill seeps into my bones, paralyzing me in the doorway.

"What… what the fuck happened here?" I whisper to the empty air.

And where the hells is Codrin?

"Codrin?" I step inside, my boots crunching over broken glass. "Talon? Athan?"

Only silence, broken by the occasional creak of wood as I tread over the wreckage responds.

A glint of something catches the corner of my eye near the edge of the broken desk. I sheath my axe to the holster on my back and kneel down. Brushing away torn papers, I pick up the familiar silver coin size pendant and place it into the palm of my hand.

My heart drops to the pit of my stomach. This is Athan's. There was no mistaking it. I have seen him wear this all the time, never taking it off. I run my fingers along the darkened soot grooves that stand in sharp contrast to the worn silver. Its hammered surface burnished yet faintly scarred from years of wear. At the center of the pendant is a snarling wolf, its detailed lines etched deep into the metal, their grooves darkened with soot making the wolf head stand out more. Inner twine lines wrap around the edge like a circle that cannot be broken. A once sturdy silver chain hangs with a now broken clasp.

I clutch it tight in my palm, my breath coming quicker. This tells me Athan was here. And if the state of this room is any indication, something went very, *very* wrong.

Codrin wouldn't have attacked Athan? Would he?

Why wouldn't he? The voice adds to my growing thoughts of cold, terror.

No, Codrin wouldn't. I know in my heart Codrin would *never* hurt Athan. There is more to this. I know there is.

Getting to my feet, I place the chained pendant into my pocket and dash toward the door only to be blocked as Father storms into the room, followed closely by General Hawk, Lieutenant Ulric Hollowstone, and Zavier Walheld, his arm free of the sling. *What the fuck is Zavier doing here with them?*

"We need to find Codrin." The words rush from my mouth.

Father's dark eyes scan the wreckage, with pressed lips, before settling onto me. "I couldn't agree with you more, daughter." His lip curling slightly as he nudges broken bits of furniture aside with his foot. His gaze is cold and accusatory. "One of my guards was found dead. And I have reports stating the captain of my Slayer Squad was the last seen with him and is now missing. That seems guilty to me. Wouldn't you agree, General Hawk? I mean what do you think of all this?"

The general steps further into the room, standing tall in his polished silver-white armor, the gray cape around his shoulders swaying down his back. His hand rests on the hilt of his sword.

That same fucking blade he held to my brother's throat.

"I agree, Your Majesty. I think we have a killer on our hands. And would order a full manhunt before he kills another innocent." Hawk side-eyes me with a sneer.

"What!?" I yell, shaking my head in disbelief. He can't be serious.

But it's evident from the expressions on my father's and the general's faces that they came to this agreement before they even walked into the room. They don't care about the wreckage of this room. I know they won't question it. They want to find someone guilty and somehow Codrin happens to be the brunt of it all.

My gaze darts to Zavier who chuckles under his breath. I grind my teeth and fist my hands tightly at my side, holding back the urge to not punch that damn devilish grin off his so-called pretty boy face. I wish I had broken his fucking neck when I had the chance.

"Codrin is innocent." I stomp toward my father and gesture to the ruined room. "How could you say that? Look at his room. Something happened here. To him."

"Just a cover-up." My father brushes past me with a wave of his hand as he takes a couple of long strides into the room. "Lieutenant Hollowstone," he turns on his heel, giving me his back. "It seems you have been promoted."

"Are you serious!?" I gasp. "That's bullshit! He's a guard. Not a slayer. He can't take Codrin's position."

Ulric steps forward, his posture rigid with deference. "Your Majesty," he places his right fisted hand to his chest and bows his head. "I am honored to accept this new position. What are your orders?"

Zavier still stands in the doorway, hidden behind Ulric and Hawk, baring his teeth in an unsettling smile. Like he's enjoying the dramatic scene unfolding before him.

Father turns his attention back to me, his eyes almost black as a bottomless pit as he narrows them on me. He speaks but not to me. "General Hawk, *Captain* Hollowstone, assemble your men in a search for Codrin Hardtblade. Bring him in alive." A cold, vicious glint sparks in his gaze as he watches my jaw drop. His voice then drops to a poisonous whisper. "I want to take the pleasure of executing him myself."

My eyes go wide. I want to ram him. I want to take my axe and slice it straight into his oversized belly and spill his guts to the floor.

"Enough," a voice cuts through the room as a shadow of a beast strides into the wreckage of Codrin's room, dressed in pristine black attire, and golden eyes that glow under the sunlight pouring through the shattered window.

"King Alaric." Father straightens stiffly, his hands curling into fists at his sides, the arrogance draining from him like blood from a wound.

Alaric carries the authority of a man who's never had his commands questioned, his sharp gaze zoning in on my father.

"Your Majesty." General Hawk snaps into a rigid bow. Ulric follows suit, his face pinched.

Only Zavier remains unfazed, arms crossed over his chest as he leans against the doorframe.

"I couldn't help but overhear your… accusations." Alaric's gaze sweeps across the room, pausing briefly on me before fixing back onto my father. "How quick you all are to condemn a man without proof."

"The proof is the dead body of my guard!" Father lifts his chin as he steps over a shattered chair. "Found drained of blood. You know what that means. The signs are obvious. Unless it was one of *your* men."

"Are you pointing your finger at me and my men?" Alaric snarls revealing his fangs. "Watch yourself, Zephyr."

"No, of course not. It is that I have plenty of witnesses' placing Codrin at the scene. I'm just saying, if the creature—"

"Choose your words wisely, *Your Majesty*." Alaric steps closer, his muscles tensing and hatred blazing in his golden eyes.

Father looks as though to coward back half step, then stiffens his spine. "I meant nothing by that. I am saying if *Codrin* is responsible and not brought to justice, more will follow."

Alaric inhales slowly, shoulders easing as if forcing down words best not spoken. "I see. Perhaps this is true. But we must not mistake haste for justice. The captain of your Slayer Squad deserves a fair trial, does he not?"

Hawk's jaw tightens. "With all due respect, Your Majesty, we cannot risk waiting. If he's dangerous—"

"*If,*" Alaric echoes with a smirk. "So much certainty in your tone and yet so little proof. As it stands, Codrin is a man who served your kingdom loyally for years. Any investigation into his alleged crimes should be thorough, fair, and just. Is that not how things are done here? Or is that not how things are done for *my kind*, if he is a… what did you call us?" Alaric turns to Father. "*Creature,* was it?" The word slides off his tongue like a challenge wrapped in diplomacy.

A tick starts in Father's jaw, barely visible but I know the storm it hides.

"Allow me and my guards to assist in the search." Alaric's eyes slide to mine, something close to concern buried beneath their deep golden depths. "I can ensure that Codrin Hardtblade is returned safely and treated fairly. If he is innocent, then the truth shall prevail. And if not…" A faint smile tugs at his lips but disappears as quickly as it came. "Then justice shall be served."

Father's graying brows drop. But with Hawk and Ulric hanging on the king's every word, he can do little but nod. "Very well, King Alaric. You may join the search."

"Excellent." Alaric clasps his hands together, his smile widening. "General Hawk, Lieutenant Hollowstone—"

"It's Captain, Your Majesty," Ulric says with pride.

Alaric snaps a narrow eye to the man, who's pride swiftly fades, dropping his gaze to the ground.

"General Hawk, *Captain* Hollowstone," Alaric's sharp stare still fixed on Ulric as he grumbles the rank before looking away and continuing. "Gather your men. I'll have my own guards spread out as well. Let us ensure a thorough search. And I would prefer if no one dies in the process. Understood?"

Ulric and Hawk nod.

"Now." Alaric turns his full attention to me, his voice lowering as he reaches his arms out to me. "Princess Ravenna, are you alright?"

My hands tremble with the force of everything I can't say, but I shove it all away, swallowing hard as he takes me into his arms. "I know Codrin is innocent."

"I'm sure of it and I will ensure he has his chance to prove it," He replies with a steady and certain tone as he presses me into his broad chest. "I will personally see to it that no wrong comes to him." The feel of his fingers gracefully start gliding up and down my back, almost making me want to crumble right then and there. "You have my word."

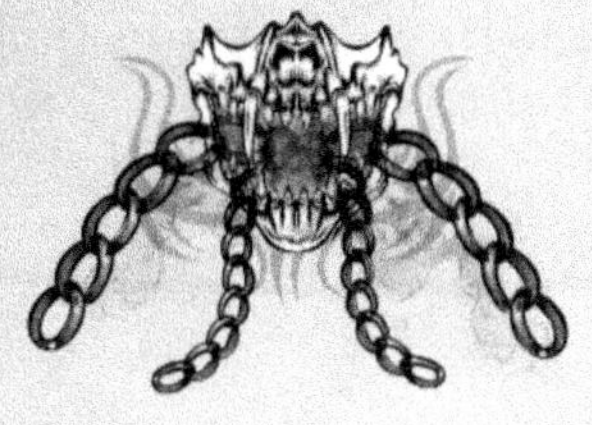

CHAPTER 23
Codrin

than drags his boots across the room to the blanket-covered window. Drawing back a little, he tucks a piece of his wavy hair behind his ear and peeks out. A light sigh escapes his lips as he looks over his shoulder at me. "Sun is down."

"Thank gods." I jump to my feet and stretch, my arms high over my head, my spine cracking along each vertebra.

All day I've been trapped in this room. Waiting impatiently for the sun to finally go down.

As the sun rose over the horizon this morning, its rays pouring through the curtainless window, hitting my skin with a sizzle. I had hurried to the closet, covering the gap along the door and floor, doing my best to not let any sunlight in until Athan and Talon were able to scrounge up some blankets to cover the window. When I reached down to the hem of my pants, I realized the makeshift pocket was torn down the center. My Eclipsis Gem is gone, disappeared sometime between now and when my brother tossed me around my room like an old shoe.

Simon bursts through the door, his chest rising and falling in a heavy breath.

"Sun is down."

"Yeah, we know." I interlace my fingers behind my back and stretch my arms up as I lean forward.

"You boys need to get out of here." Simon shuts the door and tosses Athan a sack. "Here."

Athan catches the sack in both hands with a huff as it slams into his chest.

"There's some food and supplies in it."

"What's going on?" Talon jumps to his feet from the bed.

Simon's gaze locks on me. His brow arches like a disappointed father and points a stern finger. "Codrin, you are a wanted man. You need to get your ass out of here. Fast. Guards from both Theiahold and Veilstead have been on a wild manhunt for you all day."

"What for?" I straighten, dropping my arms to my side.

He doesn't say a word. His eyes drop and he shakes his head.

My heart drops to the pit of my stomach. He knows what I have done. I have broken a forty-year promise to him, and the disappointment is written all over his face.

I close the distance between us, placing my hands on his shoulders, my forehead resting against his. "I'm sorry." It's the only words I can find. I want to explain myself, but it would be pointless. But I was foolish for believing Darius would "take care of the body." Did he actually set me up? Making sure someone found the guard I drained. But how would anyone know it was me who had done it? Unless Darius threw me to the wolves when the body was discovered. I should've known. I knew not to trust him.

"I understand your reasoning," Simon says in a low whisper, placing a hand on my shoulder and giving it a slight squeeze. "No need to explain."

But the need to explain gathers on my tongue. Simon knows a lot about me, but once again, he's another person in my life who doesn't know the *whole* story.

Simon lifts his head away from mine, our eyes meeting. "I always knew you'd cause me trouble, boy. Just didn't think it'd be this kind." Shaking his head, he pats my shoulder.

A stab to the heart, but he meant well. I know he won't hold it against me for long. But I will hold it against myself until my last breath.

Simon brushes past me and steps into the middle of the room.

"There's a cabin ten miles south. You know where." He glances at me, and I nod as I reach for my sword lying on the bed and strap it to my belt. "Head for the open fields, past the hills. It's not much, but it's safe. I'll send word when things settle."

"Hold on! Why the hells are they hunting Codrin?" Talon's voice shakes slightly, but he keeps his cool, pulling on his boots.

No one answers him.

Athan moves past him, lifting his war hammer from where it leans against the wall.

"Come here beautiful." He plants a kiss on the head of the

hammer. "Time for a road trip."

"Wait!" Talon jumps to his feet, grabbing my arm and spinning me toward him. "What the seven hells is going on, Codrin?"

Anger, fear, and confusion all tangled together in his eyes as they search mine. One more truth I buried. One more line I crossed. He stayed with me all day, never once letting me out of his sight since Alaric attacked us. But maybe he stayed because he doesn't trust me. I told him everything I could. Well, almost everything. I didn't have the heart to tell him this.

I meet his gaze, swallowing down the lump in my throat. "I drained a royal guard… last night."

Talon's hold drops. He steps back, shaking his head, the betrayal cracking away everything we had built over the years.

He might as well stab me now. It wouldn't hurt nearly as much.

Athan breaks the silence. "We can deal with this later. Right now, we run."

He throws the sack over his shoulder and charges out the door.

"You don't have to come," I tell Talon, my voice low. I wouldn't blame him if he stayed behind. Not after this.

He doesn't look at me. "We will deal with this later," he says, echoing Athan's words but lacing them with steel. He brushes past me and disappears out the door.

We slip out the back of the tavern. The sting of the seawater air hits my face as we step into the night.

Talon keeps his distance from me, not even so much as a side-eye glance in my direction as we make our way through the alleys, ducking into the shadows to hide from passing guards. At every corner, we hold our breath. Only when the coast is clear do we move, slipping through town and toward the fields.

The moon stays hidden behind a shroud of clouds, casting the land in near-total darkness as we cross the fields in silence. Only the occasional silver glow leaks through, just enough to outline the rolling hills and the narrow path we follow.

Wind brushes through the tall grass, soft and cold against my face. Every so often, a low, sharp, raven call comes from the trees in the distance. Its cruel sound filling the dark.

Talon doesn't say a word the entire time. Not even when Athan tries to make a joke about the mud sucking at our boots. Not even when I stumble once, cursing under my breath. He just keeps walking, a shadow between us.

It takes nearly three hours to reach the cabin.

By the time we arrive, my legs ache, my shirt clings to my back with sweat, and the only thing keeping me upright is the fear of being seen.

The place looks worse than I remember.

The roof is intact, but barely. The front porch sags to the left. Athan pushes the door open, and a thick cloud of dust rises from the floorboards. Cobwebs stretch across the corners like old lace.

We step inside, boots echoing against the wooden planks. No candles. No fire. Just stale, summer air and the scent of mildew.

No one's lived here in the past six years. After Simon's mother passed, he stopped coming as often. Chose the tavern instead. Still, he used to come by from time to time, clean it up just enough to keep it standing.

I remember being here once. I was still raw then, still figuring out who I was pretending to be. I can still recall the first time I met Simon's mother, welcoming me with open arms and making me tea. It tasted awful, but she smiled when I drank it.

Her ghost isn't here. But the memory of her clings to the walls.

Athan drops the sack near the old stone fireplace and I start searching for dry wood. Talon lingers near the door, arms crossed, his silence somehow louder inside these walls than it was out in the fields.

I pile the driest logs I can find into the hearth.

"You think making a fire is a good idea?" Talon snaps, his words edged and brittle.

Athan and I glance at each other.

"He's right," Athan says with a sigh. "We can go without fire."

He kneels and rummages through the sack, pulling out a loaf of bread. Tearing it apart, he tosses a piece to me and another to Talon. "But we *do* need to find you a good dark place to hide come dawn." His words are muffled by a mouthful of bread.

I nod but say nothing.

Without my Eclipsis Gem, I have to hide from the sun like any other vampire. It's only been a day, and already I miss the warmth of sunlight on my skin.

But more than that...

I miss Ravenna.

I hope she's okay. I know she can handle herself, but with Alaric and his ways. I snarl at the thought, trying to shake away all the things racing through my mind, and make my way to the kitchen. I open cabinet after cabinet, knowing they're empty. But it's better than letting my thoughts spiral, better than letting the questions eat me alive.

"I know there's an old barn out back," I say opening and closing a cabinet without even bothering to look inside it. "I bet I can hide in there." I turn, leaning and resting my hands against the dusty countertop. "What about you two?" I nod to Athan and Talon.

"Oh, I was thinking of cuddling up with you tonight. To keep warm, of course." Athan chuckles, standing and making his way over to a chair sitting in the middle of the room.

The chair groans, threatening to break, and a cloud of dust flies up around him as he drops his oversized body into it.

"So, did anyone by chance think to bring any beer?" he says, coughing and waving his hand in front of his face to shoo away the dust around him.

My mouth opens to speak, but Talon moves. He steps away from the wall, his face hard, his eyes like iron.

"You going to explain yourself, Codrin, or what?" He takes a step and places a hand on the hilt of his sword, slayer instinct overriding everything else.

I push off the counter and make my way to the open area of the room, my eyes never leaving Talon's glare.

Athan sits up, rubbing at his still-bruised ribs, and positions himself on the edge of the chair. Readying himself to stop either one of us from doing something we might or might not regret.

I shake my head at Athan, signaling him to stand down.

We are trained for this.

Trained to spot the monster beneath the skin, no matter how human it looks. And right now, no matter who I am to Talon, all he sees is something he should have killed the second he found out.

Maybe he's angry at me. Or maybe he's furious with himself for never seeing the truth about what's been right beside him all these years. Slayer instinct doesn't care about the face it wears. It only sees the monster beneath.

"What do you want me to explain?" I start with a deep breath. "I'm still the same person I've always been. Vampire or not."

"Vampire or not? You killed a royal guard! Why?" His fists clench the hilt of his sword so tightly his knuckles go white. For a moment, I think he's going to draw his sword and honestly, I don't doubt it.

"I had to!" I growl, my patience already fraying. "If you want to stand here and act like I'm suddenly some fucking monster, then go right on ahead. But I'm telling you right now, Talon. Ravenna is in more danger now that we're trapped out here. And if you can't get past your own bullshit long enough to see that, then you're a bigger fool than I thought. I did what I had to. To protect her. If taking a life after *forty fucking years* is what it took, then so be it. I'll do it again without hesitation."

"Look what good it's done, Codrin." Talon's arms fly up, gesturing around the room. "*You're* the reason we're out here."

I flinch at his words, the truth of them cutting deeper than I'd like to admit.

"No one told you to come. You could've stayed."

I don't have time for this shit again. Alaric's out there hunting me, and now Talon wants to start another fight over something I didn't mean to lose control of but did and I don't think he's willing to listen to my reasoning this time.

"I didn't come for you." Talon's voice is low, steady, but every word lands like a strike. "I came because she trusted you. And now that trust is going to get her killed." He takes a step forward, his jaw tightening. "So, yeah. Maybe I should've stayed behind. Would've saved us both the fucking disappointment."

"What, protecting your sister isn't a good enough excuse to

kill a royal guard for his blood? I would've drained anyone to make sure I was at full strength for her. I would've drained the *whole* royal fucking guard and the slayers!" I stomp a couple of steps toward him. My muscles tense, the vein in my neck pulsing.

Talon takes a step toward me, hands fisted tight, jaw locked with rage.

"I would've drained this whole fucking town for her."

My eyes burn silver. My fangs flash, on full display.

Let him see me. Let him see the monster he thinks I am.

Talon doesn't back down. Doesn't flinch.

He moves fast, and I don't see the punch coming until it crashes into my jaw, snapping my head to the side. I stumble back as pain shoots through my skull. Catching myself, I focus on the ground, letting the wave of shock and dizziness subside. The taste of iron fills my mouth, and I spit blood onto the dusty floor at Talon's feet.

Good. Maybe if I bleed, he'll remember I still can. I lift a narrow, sharp gaze to him. Only to be met with his even sharper gaze as he lowers his chin and bares his teeth. Theres not even a hint of regret that crosses his face as his knuckles whiten in tight fists at his side. His shoulders rise and fall, the muscles in his arms tensing. Ready to throw another punch.

I straighten. My muscles coil, every inch of me begging to retaliate. But before either of us can move again, Athan shoves himself between us, arms outstretched, breath ragged.

"You two want to beat the shit out of each other, fine. But *not* tonight."

He turns to Talon. "Not while your sister's out there with *him*."

Then to me. "And not while Alaric's hunting *you*."

Silence falls around us, broken only by the wind groaning through the cracks in the cabin walls. I wipe my mouth with the back of my hand and back away from Athan and Talon.

Talon's still fuming, chest rising and falling like he just sprinted a mile. But he doesn't move.

Athan lowers his arms, exhaling slowly.

"We need to pull our shit together and focus on the whole *'Alaric wants to tear us all to shreds'* thing instead." He lets out a low chuckle. "Now, as much as I'm enjoying this dick-measuring contest—"

"Shut up, Athan," Talon and I snap at the same time.

"Aww, I love when you two bond." Athan grins, but it's tight. His eyes stay wary, watching both of us closely.

The room quiets after that. No one says a word. Athan moves to sit near the hearth, chewing on the last bite of tasteless bread. Talon drops into a chair near the wall, arms crossed, jaw still tight. I stay on my feet, pacing the room once or twice before sinking down on the floor against the far wall, away from both of them.

An hour crawls by. Outside, the wind howls. Inside, it's the kind of silence that presses on your chest. Long and heavy.

I don't look at either of them. I just sit with my back against the wall, eyes on the dusty rafters, each breath dragging harder than it should.

One of my ribs still isn't healed, not fully. I feel it with every inhale, like something sharp grinding behind my lungs. Alaric did more damage than I let on. Shattered my nose. Cracked three ribs. Left me coughing up blood and barely breathing. Along with a concussion and a little internal bleeding to top it off.

I forced the healing, pushing every drop of strength I had left into knitting bone and sealing blood, but it wasn't enough, not all the way.

Now it's taking everything just to stay upright. My limbs are heavier than they should be. My balance is off. My vision still flickers at the edges when I stand too fast, like the world keeps blinking out.

I haven't had a chance to feed to make up for it all. And I haven't told them. But every so often, I catch Athan watching me. That subtle side-eye he thinks I don't notice.

Like he's tracking every uneven step. Like he knows. Of course he knows. He's always known. And he's letting me pretend.

I shift my jaw. The ache is still there, sharp, steady, and earned. Talon's punch wasn't just rage. It was a reminder. A consequence I know I deserved.

"Does she know?"

The question lands flat in the air, rough and sudden after so much silence.

I look up to see Talon turn my head toward Talon staring straight ahead at nothing unparticular. Just breathing like he's been holding it in all night.

"Rave," he says, more quietly now. "Does she know what you are?"

I draw in a breath, slow and tight. "She knows. I kind of paid her a visit last night before you showed up to her room."

Talon's head snaps to me, his brows furrow, lips tight. I force a half-hearted grin to him as I watch him shift his shoulders and flex his fingers once before curling back into fists. Probably wasn't the smartest thing for me to say at this moment but I was trying to lighten the tension in the room.

"How did she take it?"

"Better than you did." I huff out a laugh.

A smile tugs at the corner of his mouth.

"Yeah... well..." he leans forward, arms on his knees. "I take it she still trusts you?"

"Yes. Or so I hope."

He looks away again. A soft curse under his breath.

Not at me this time. At himself. Maybe at the world.

"I swear my sister..." he mutters, shaking his head. "She always did have a damn stupid heart."

"Yeah. And it's the only thing that's kept me alive." I say, giving a small, hollow laugh.

The silence creeps back in, but it's different now. Not as sharp. Not as hostile. Just tired.

Talon leans back in the chair, fingers interlaced, resting against his face. He doesn't say anything else. He doesn't have to.

Athan shifts where he sits, his eyes on the boarded-up window.

"Sun will be up soon," he says, quietly. "You should get moving before that pretty face starts sizzling."

I let out a low breath, dragging a hand down my stubble jaw where Talon's punch still throbs.

"Right."

I push myself up slowly, muscles aching, mind heavier than my limbs. I glance toward the others. Talon drops his hands from his face, Athan watches me with a tired half-smile.

"Try to get some sleep," I say, even though we all know none of us will.

The air bites hard as I step out of the cabin. The sky is softening, just barely, hints of blue bleeding into the black.

The barn stands at the edge of the trees, slouched and forgotten. I trudge through the damp grass, boots sinking slightly into the soil.

When I push the door open, the hinges groan in protest.

Dust dances in the pale gray light. The smell of old straw and weathered wood wraps around me like a memory. There's an empty stall near the back. It's dark, quiet, just enough space to vanish in.

I settle down in the corner, pulling my coat tighter around me. It's not sleep I'm after. It's distance.

From the guilt.

From the things I've done.

And still holding on to the way Ravenna looked at me the last time I saw her… like she still believed in me. I'll be damned if I let that fade. I will do anything to make sure Ravenna is safe. Even if it means ending my own brother. I close my eyes and let the barn swallow what's left of me.

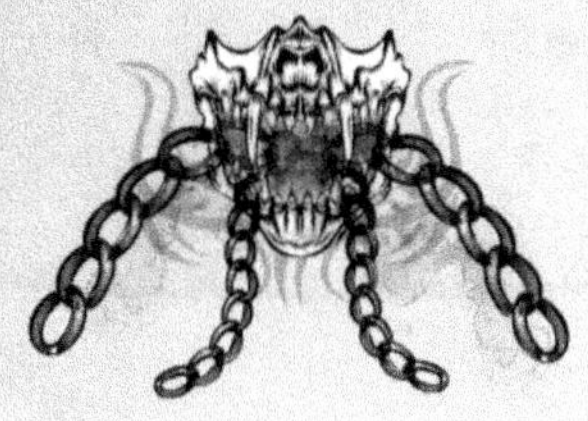

CHAPTER 24
Codrin

We've rationed out the supplies, barely. Athan started complaining about the lack of meat on day one. Talon hasn't spoken to me much since the punch. I didn't expect him to.

The cabin stinks of sweat, dust, and frustration. Every board creaks. Every gust of wind makes me glance toward the window like a paranoid dog waiting for the gate to open.

I sit on the floor, back against the cold stone hearth, arm resting on my propped-up knee as I idly flip a dagger in one hand. Athan digs through the sack for the third time tonight.

"Gods bless you, Simon," he breathes dramatically, holding up a bent, stained deck of cards like he just found the Holy Relic of Boredom.

"Boys, who's ready to lose?"

Talon doesn't answer, but he doesn't protest either. We settle into the wobbly chairs around the table. I take the seat with my back to the kitchen, better to keep the room in view. Talon to my right. Athan strolls over, sets the only lantern in the center of the table, and drops into the seat across from me.

He starts shuffling. His motions are loud, exaggerated. The cards slap the wood like thunder in the stillness. And we start playing. Kind of. Mostly, we just go through the motions.

"Whoa. No. I win." Talon gestures to his four of a kind, raising a brow at Athan's full house.

Athan strokes his thick beard, squinting at the cards like they've personally offended him.

"Fine." He throws his hands up. "I'll let you have this round."

Talon smirks. "Have this round? Bro, I *won* this round."

"Sure… whatever you say, buddy." Athan gathers the cards with mock defeat, then slides the deck across the table. "Your deal then."

Talon gives him a part glare, part half-hearted grin as he takes the deck and starts to shuffle.

I lean back in my chair; arms crossed over my chest, watching the two of them banter like everything isn't falling apart outside these walls.

Like we aren't trapped.

Waiting.

It's been three days, and Simon's silence is starting to feel louder than anything else. Maybe he's lying low. Maybe he's—

Nope. I'm not going there.

I've been so restless these past couple of days. Unable to sleep. Unable to really focus. My mind is racing with so many what-ifs on how every time I close my eyes, I see her face. Always the same look in her eyes. Scared and worried. How my dreams are an endless cycle of me running to her but no matter how close I think I am she is still out of reach.

I rub my thumb over the edge of the table, catching on a splinter. The game has been a nice distraction, one I should be thankful for, however it's nothing but noise to me. It's a way to keep our hands busy and our minds on something other than Ravenna and all the shit that has fallen on us.

The last time we were all together, sitting around a table at Simon's tavern, full of laughter and life. Was what? Almost two weeks ago. Damn. Feels like a lifetime. Fuck, so much has happened since then. Too much.

Simon offered to send word to Ravenna to let her know we didn't abandon her. We would *never* abandon her, and she knows that. But it was too risky. I couldn't take the chance of Alaric reading her thoughts and finding out where we were.

She's okay.

She has to be.

I keep drilling those words into my head, hoping they'll start to feel true.

But they don't.

Athan knocks softly on the table in front of me, pulling me out of my thoughts. My eyes drift slowly to meet his.

"You doin' alright, man?"

"I'm good." I huff, sitting up straighter, and taking the cards. Hoping to hide behind the cards I have fanned out in front of me as we roll into another round.

The night carries on with some jokes, laughter, and Talon calling Athan out for trying to cheat for the second time.

Athan stretches far back in his chair, balancing on the back two legs. He lets out a deep breath and pressed his hands to his abs. "Damn, I'm getting hungry."

"Any food left?" I ask, shuffling the deck.

"There are some apples." The upper half of Athan's lip curls up in disgust.

His chair tips back too far, nearly toppling, but he catches himself, grabbing the edge of the table with a grunt.

"This is why we don't lean back in our chairs," Talon says dryly, lifting a brow. He pushes his chair back from the table, its legs scraping the rotting wood floor. He makes his way over to the counter and grabs the waterskin on the table.

"Gosh, Mom. You're no fun." Athan sticks out his tongue like a bratty kid, then lets the chair thump back onto all fours.

Talon lifts a middle finger without looking back, raising the waterskin to his mouth.

Athan starts rambling about some five-course meal he wishes he could have.

I nod at every other word he says but my mind drifts slowly out of focus.

Talon coughs suddenly, then chokes, spluttering water across the floor.

"You good?" Athan leans forward, half-rising from his seat.

"Talon?" I ask, straightening in my chair.

Talon wipes his mouth, eyes wide, still coughing as he jerks a hand toward the window.

"I saw something," he says, breath catching. "Outside."

That's all it takes.

Athan moves first. He blows out the lantern, plunging us into darkness. The soft hiss of the flame vanishing is followed by silence, except for the pounding of my pulse.

Athan grabs his hammer from beside the door and stands ready. Ensuring that if anything dares to come through the entryway, it's not going to get far.

Talon's blade is already in hand; his back braced against the wall next to the window on the left.

I draw my sword.

The floorboards groan beneath me with every step, but I move slow, calculated. I keep my weight low, my breath held. A part of me is hoping it's Simon with good news. But the other part of me knows there's no such luck. I creep toward the window, pressing my back to the wall opposite Talon.

Talon peeks through the slats. He looks back at me, shaking his head. "I don't see anything."

I take a look, pressing my eye to the slats, my vampire eyes scanning through the dark. At first, I don't see anything. Just trees. Grass swaying. The moon behind the clouds. Maybe it was just a shadow of a tree branch. Maybe it was just a bird soaring by.

But movement catches my eye from the left.

A hulking figure steps from the trees; its black armor catches the moonlight in jagged silver slashes.

There's no mistaking one of Alaric's hybrids.

For years, he's taken mortal men and twisted them into almost seven-foot, bulking beasts. Turning their flesh, bone, and blood to bend to his every will. No one knows how he does it. Hells, I'm not even sure I want to know. As for why he does this? I could name a hundred reasons, none of them good, I know that.

Its shoulders bulge unnaturally wide. Its head nearly brushes the low-hanging branches. Another emerges to the right, just as massive. Both move like shadows wrapped in iron, their steps slow and deliberate. Their heads tilt in eerie unison like they're *sniffing* the air. Hunting.

My throat locks up.

"Well, shit."

"What?!" Talon whispers, taking a look out the window.

I exhale. "We've got company. And not the friendly kind."

I glance over my shoulder. "Two beast guards. Veilstead's finest monsters. Tall as trees. Armored like walking fortresses."

Athan huffs. "Great. Just what I needed. I was getting bored just sitting around."

I look back through the slats.

And that's when I see him.

Shadows in the clearing ripple and pull back. And out of the darkness, Alaric steps into view.

Moonlight trailing off him as though it's a part of him. Calm, cruel eyes scanning the cabin like he already knows we're watching.

A chill licks down my spine.

He's not just searching.

He's waiting.

I turn back to the others. "Well," I mutter, gripping my sword tightly. "Looks like our plan is being set in motion for us."

"How kind of him," Athan says, voice dry as dust. "We didn't even have to send an invitation."

Talon rolls his shoulders, cracking his neck. A wicked grin pulls at his mouth. "Let's bring these bastards down."

I nod toward the window. "One's flanking left, the other right. They're covering the exits. Alaric's front and center."

Athan lifts his hammer. "So, they're surrounding us like we're scared little mice." He smirks. "Let's give them a reason to regret that."

Outside, the night holds its breath.

Then, his voice cuts through the stillness. Smooth. Cold. Like honey over broken glass.

"Codrin."

He says it like a greeting. Like a prayer. Like he's savoring the weight of my name on his tongue.

"You always did have a talent for running. It seems you didn't make it far this time."

A pause.

"But hiding in an old shack on the edge of nowhere?" He clicks his tongue, mock disappointment. "Hardly the legacy of a prince."

My jaw tightens.

"Come out." His voice lowers but still sharp. "Let your slayer brothers see you for what you really are."

Another pause.

"Or perhaps you need motivation."

A long silence follows before Alaric speaks again.

"She misses you, you know."

My blood runs cold.

"Your sweet little *Ravenna*." Alaric's voice curves around her name like a song. A secret. A possession.

I look over to see Talon as he grinds his teeth at the mention of his sister's name. The overprotective brother out in full force.

"She still dreams about you. Still clings to that foolish hope that you *might* save her."

Fucker knows exactly where to cut. But I will cut him deeper. He doesn't have to shout. Doesn't have to threaten. Just the way he says her name is enough to make my heart hammer and my hands burn. I don't know if Alaric's bluffing, or if he's been toying around in her mind, twisting it like a thread between his fingers. Or if she really is still waiting. Still hoping. Still believing in me.

I watch Alaric through the slats, his head bows, hands in the front pockets of his pants, as he swings the toe of his boot at the ground.

My breath catches as his head snaps back up with a twisted grin and his golden eyes staring directly at me. "But don't worry, sweet brother. I've been keeping her… extra comfortable."

My grip chokes the hilt of my sword until my knuckles ache. The veins in my arms pulse, my blood shifting from cold to boiling. If he has laid even one finger on *my girl*. I will rip his arms from his body with my bare hands and shove them down his damn throat.

Athan lets out a low growl beside me, as he shifts the long shaft of his hammer in both hands. He crouches, ready to lunge through the wall at any given second.

Gods. Please let her not hear this.

Let her not know I'm about to face the devil himself, with nothing but guilt in my chest and a sword in my hand.

My grip loosens just enough for breath to return to my lungs.

"Hey…" I whisper on a breath. "If I go down… please. Get your asses out of here."

Athan snorts, but there's no humor in it. "If you go down,

I'm dragging your undead ass out with me. Even if I have to throw you over my shoulder like a sack of turnips."

Talon doesn't smile. Doesn't blink. His sword gleams in the dim light. His voice is quiet. "You're not going down." He takes in a deep breath. "Not while we're still standing."

I look at them both, wanting to say more but the words won't form on my lips. Both have been by my side these past seven years. They might not be blood; nonetheless they will always be known as my brothers in everything.

From the corner of my eye, I catch movement. I turn back to the window.

Alaric lifts one pale hand. No words. No theatrics. Just a simple, silent command.

And the world shatters.

A thunderous crash explodes from the left side of the cabin, inches from where Talon is standing.

Talon doesn't hesitate. He hits the floor in a roll, knees digging into the wood as the beast guard swings its massive sword in a deadly arc, metal shrieking through the air. Talon brings his blade up just in time. Ashenbane iron clashes with steel. The sheer force of it nearly knocks him flat.

"GET DOWN!" Athan roars as he lunges into the fray. His hammer gripped tightly in both hands as he arcs it through the air with a deep, brutal swing.

CRACK.

The head of the hammer slams into the guard's side with bone-crunching force, denting the armor. The creature goes flying, crashing through the table and chairs with a thunderous roar. Wood shatters. Cards scatter like autumn leaves in a storm. The floor shudders beneath our boots.

Talon is already back on his feet, charging after the guard as it stumbles, crashing into the far wall. He doesn't give it a chance to recover.

Athan pauses for a split second, his eyes soften onto me, years of friendship held in them. "Don't die on me."

I can only give a quick nod before he barrels through the gaping hole in the wall, straight toward the second guard, who's now charging from the right flank. I step through the ruins of the cabin, sword gripped, boots crunching over broken stone and glass. My eyes lock on Alaric, who stands casually shifting his weight as he draws his sword from its sheath and smiles with fangs.

The sharp, quiet night stretches between us as Alaric takes slow, deliberate steps forward, his boots silent against the grass. His eyes never leave mine.

"You've grown bold, baby brother," he says, pointing his sword at me. "Hiding in plain sight. Leading slayers. Falling for the girl."

My sword lifts, the point angling toward his chest. The air between us thrums like a drawn bowstring.

"You really think they'll follow you when they see what you are?" He steps closer. "A traitor. A liar. A monster just like me." He places a hand to his chest with a devilish smirk.

"I'm *nothing* like you." My muscles tense with adrenaline.

He laughs, low and hollow. "No. You're worse. You crawled away after what we did, put on a mask, and played a penitent little slayer. But I remember, Codrin." His eyes flash with conviction. "I remember how you *smiled* when we hunted."

My breath catches. Shame, fury, and guilt, flares in my gut. He sees it. I know he does as he leans in with a satisfying grin.

"You loved the kill," he whispers. "Don't pretend you didn't."

His voice sharpens. "She doesn't know that about you, does she?" He chuckles darkly.

"She knows enough," I snarl through my teeth.

"She knows what you are, but she doesn't know *who* you truly are. She thinks you're some noble savior now. Not the blood-drenched hound who once dragged a priest's head back to my feet like a gift."

I raise my sword and charge at him. Lunging straight for his head. Our swords slam together with a shriek of steel. He's fast. Faster than I remember. But I've been waiting for this. I twist low, aiming for his ribs, but he parries with inhuman ease. We lock blades again. His face inches from mine.

"She'll learn eventually," he murmurs in my ear. "I wonder what she'll think when she finds out. Or maybe I'll just tell her myself. While I'm under her skirts *again*."

I shove him back a couple of steps. "Fuck you, Alaric."

He tilts his head. "I gave you a chance, Codrin. Years ago. I would've let you kneel beside me. And now?" His golden eyes darken with rage. "Now you're *nothing* but a crack in my kingdom. And I intend to seal it shut."

"It's not your fucking kingdom." My voice roars across the field.

His eye twitches and he lets out a deep snarl between clenched teeth. Looks like I struck a nerve.

My heels push off the ground as I lunge first but I feel the delay in my footing as my body betrays me. My jaw locks, biting down the pulsing pain of fire that rips down my ribs from the swing of my sword. I quickly recover before Alaric has a chance to notice but I know he

Our swords slam together in a burst of rage, the impact ringing in my ears. My boots dig into the ground as I push all my strength and weight against Alaric's.

"I should've killed you the night I left." A roar tears out of my throat as I slam forward with everything I have.

"But you didn't." He shoves harder my boots sliding across grass and mud and we break apart, circling.

His next move comes quicker. He feints left, then slashes right. Our blades scream across each other.

I duck under his next swing and drive my elbow into his ribs.

He stumbles back a couple of steps, hand gripping his side where my elbow hit. "You *couldn't*." His breathing staggers. "Because even after everything, you still wanted my approval."

"I don't give a damn about your approval." My voice is a growl. "I couldn't kill you because you don't fight fair."

"Fair? Nothing in this world is fair. We had built an army together, and you abandoned it. *Abandoned me*." His eyes blaze with less triumph and more like betrayal.

"You left me to rot in the ashes of everything we built." His voice rising with fury on every word.

"I didn't leave. I *escaped* because you were trying to kill me, or did you forget about that part, Alaric?"

His head falls back in a deep laugh, then slowly lowers again as he points his sword at me. "If I wanted to kill you, you would've been dead forty years ago."

I smirk. "Or it's just your old age catching up to you."

Alaric snarls as he leaps toward me, blade heading straight at me.

I sidestep at the last second, feeling the wind of his blade graze past me. I pivot and lunge. But he swings with surgical precision, every movement sharp, elegant, practiced.

I know these strikes. I trained beside them. I counter one, barely deflect another, my muscles burn as my grip starts to slip. A dull, growing ache rises in my side where the unhealed rib threatens too fully snap. I force the pain down and push forward, lashing out with a downward strike meant to split his shoulder.

Alaric sidesteps like smoke, twisting behind me. His elbow slams into the back of my neck.

I stagger forward as the ground seems to tilts sideways, then roll beneath my feet. A wave of nausea churns in my gut as the world spins, colors blurring at the edges. Black and white spots burst across my vision, pulsing with my heartbeat. My knees almost buckle. I blink hard. Once. Twice.

Everything feels far away. Like I'm watching myself from across the field.

I can't afford to fall.

But Alaric doesn't let up.

Before I can recover, I feel his massive boot to my side. Pain erupts in my ribs again. I hunch over, one arm clutched across my ribs, breath caught, eyes squeezed shut as fire tears through my side.

He clicks his tongue. "Sloppy," he says, shaking his head with a disapproving sigh, twirling his sword as he circles me like a predator. "You're slowing down."

"Fuck you," I snap, trying to cover the wince as I force myself to my full height on shaky legs.

"Is that any way to speak to your king?" He stops and leans slightly on his sword, its point digging into the ground.

He smirks, but it fades as I lunge again, without giving it a second thought.

This time, I don't hold back.

The fury in me boils over.

"You will never be my king," I snarl, fangs flashing, rage lighting a fire in my blood.

Alaric blocks at the last second as I strike wild and savage. Blow after blow meant to kill, to maim, to erase him.

He blocks the second. Parries the third, but the fourth grazes him. A shallow cut across his jaw. Blood wells. He touches it with his fingers. Looks at the red and smiles as he licks his own blood from his fingers.

"There's the beast." His voice is like a storm rolling in from the sea. "I knew you were still in there."

We circle again.

My breath comes harder now. Shoulders tight. Arms shaking. I can feel the edge coming closer. The edge of my strength. I just need to hold out a little longer.

I steal a glance toward the cabin, where Athan's hammer crashes into one of the guards. The blow connects, but the creature doesn't fall. It grabs him by the chest and hurls him like a sack of grain across the field. He slams into a tree and goes still.

"Athan!"

My head snaps the other way toward Talon. His blade dances with precision, slicing into the second guard again and again, but the thing's too big, too strong. It catches his leg with a backhanded swing and up, slicing at his side. Talon drops onto his back with a hard thud and doesn't move. Is he still breathing? Gods, please show me some sign he's still breathing.

My heart pounds, pain and fury knotting together in my gut. They're down. Both of them. Athan, thrown like he was nothing. Talon, cut down mid-strike.

Because of me. All because I dragged them into this. Because I couldn't stay dead. Because I thought I could outrun him. I can't let this be where it ends for them. If anyone dies tonight, it'll be me. Not them. Never them.

I bite down hard, jaw aching with the pressure, blinking past the blur in my vision, I turn back to face the evil I no longer see as a brother.

His fangs are exposed now. "Don't worry," Alaric sneers. "You'll all be together soon."

I crouch low, arms unsteady under the weight of my sword. Each breath scrapes my throat like fire. Every strike I've thrown feels heavier than the last.

Alaric is relentless. Calm. Precise. He's not fighting to kill me quickly. He's savoring it. Drawing it out like a symphony. His blade swings through the air.

I quickly sidestep it but I'm not quick enough. I let out a hollow scream as a flame of pain slices across my side, dropping me to my knees.

My sword slips from my fingers. My palms hit the dirt, nails clawing uselessly at the cold earth like I could dig my way out of this. Blood drips from my side, soaking into the mud.

I steal one last glance over where Athan and Talon had fallen. Both spots now empty. I let out a relieved breath knowing they had recovered in time and were able to escape. Because *if anyone dies tonight, it'll be me.* The words sing through my head like a lasting song of melody. Soothing my nerves. Drowning out the pain that rips through every part of my body.

The ground beneath me vibrates as Alaric steps forward.

"You knew this was never going to end any other way, brother." Alaric raises his sword, the edge catching the moonlight.

I feel my body gradually start to shut down. Unable to move. My strength and power drains from my fingertips. *If anyone dies tonight, it'll be me.* I take a soothing breath in, my head lowering as calm washes over me. My friends are safe, probably half-way down the field by now and I know Athan and Talon will keep Ravenna safe. My fate is sealed, and I accept it as my eyes grow heavy and slowly close as I wait for death to take me.

The air splits like lightning ripping the world in half.

My eyes snap open. A blur of iron and steel slams in just above my head. I look up to find Athan, eyes blazing, teeth grinding, muscles trembling as his hammer catches Alaric's blade mid-swing, blocking the death blow. The force drives

Athan down to one knee, the shaft of his war hammer groaning beneath the pressure, but he holds.

"Told you not to die on me, Captain."

I can't help the smile that tugs at the corner of my mouth. That son of a bitch should've ran but didn't.

Alaric snarls, pressing harder, his strength monstrous.

That's when a blur moves in from the darkness.

Iron tears across flesh.

Alaric lets out a deathly roar but doesn't fall as Talon's blade bites deep into his back. One clean, brutal arc that splits fabric, skin, and silence. Blood sprays in ribbons.

In a fluid, furious motion, Alaric shoves Athan flat to the ground, whipping around and swinging back, slamming into Talon's chest with a deathly crack.

Talon flies several feet back, hitting the mud hard face down, the wind knocked clean from his lungs.

He gasps, and tries to rise, catching over his shoulder a guard charging toward him. Palms and feet slip along the mud as he tries to push himself up, only to fall back to the ground. He reaches for his sword and rolls onto his back, eyes wide as the beast descends.

Talon raises his sword just in time. The blade punches through the beast's gut and bursts out its spine with a sickening, wet crunch. Blood vomits from the wound, dark and steaming, coating Talon's face and chest. The thing screams as it convulses on Talon's sword. Talon rolls clear as the body crashes to the ground, trapping his sword beneath it. He scrambles up, breathless and now unarmed.

In one swift move, Athan jumps to his feet, blood smeared across his temple. He lets out a snarl that sounds more beast than man as he swings his hammer upward. The crack of bone splinters the air. Fangs snap shut mid-roar as the vampire king sails backward, hitting the ground hard enough to make the earth scream.

Dust kicks up around Alaric's body as he lands, hair whipping across his face. But he rolls to a crouch almost instantly, fangs bared, rage burning in his eyes.

Athan grabs me by the upper arm, breath ragged.

"This has been fun," he growls. "But it's time to go!"

We run, Talon close behind, his sword left buried beneath the dead beast guard.

We limp. Bleed. Stumble through the trees. And behind us, Alaric's voice cuts through the night. Low and cold. "Run, Codrin! Run while you still bleed. Next time, I won't just kill you."

A pause. A breath.

"I'll slowly carve your name into her screams."

CHAPTER 25

Ravenna

The castle has become a living maze of silver armor and all-black leathers topped with harsh commands. Guards and slayers swarm the grounds, scouring every hall, every shadowed corner, and along the town, while Alaric's men sweep the outskirts.

Father raged for hours about turning this into a rescue search as soon as he found out Talon was missing from the castle too. Athan's absence was equally noted, though Father assumes he teamed up with Codrin.

While they're all supposedly searching for Codrin, Athan, and Talon, I still can't take a single step without eyes on me. The walls of my own home have become my prison. Trying to tear myself from the confines of the castle and move beyond the gardens or attempt to slip through the gatehouse, there's either a Theiahold or Veilstead guard waiting. Father's order, no doubt. His paranoia is really starting to tighten around me like iron chains. And worse, is running into one of Veilstead's beast of a guard with his unnerving, shadow-dark gaze fixed on me like a bird of prey.

Where did Veilstead conjure up these guards anyway? With their overly broad muscular bodies and immortal height of at least reaching seven-foot. I mean, I know Athan is tall but damn, these guards really define the meaning of the word "beast." Either way, I'd rather take on a Slatier than one of these *things*.

I push away the thought as I watch two beast guards walk across the corridor and out the front double doors of the castle. I honestly hope those things don't find Codrin, Athan or Talon.

Why do you worry for them? They're the ones who left you.

I squeeze my eyes shut, ignoring the voice whispering at the back of my mind. The same voice that's been keeping me company as it grows louder, more incessant, with each passing day.

"They didn't leave me," I whisper, my words swallowed by the empty corridor. "They wouldn't just abandon me."

Wouldn't they? Codrin didn't even say goodbye. Not a note. Not a word. After everything, he just ran.

A snarl rips through my chest. "He was attacked. They all were. It's not… It's not what you're saying."

But even as I say the words, doubt twists itself around my ribs. Maybe Codrin realized he was finally caught. Finally exposed. Maybe he did run to save himself. And Athan… well, I suppose loyalty only stretches so far when you're faced with death.

But Talon… No. Talon wouldn't just leave me. He wouldn't just run. Would he?

My chest tightens, the voice's venomous words sinking deeper.

Of course, he would. Why not? Everyone else has.

"Stop." I clutch the sides of my head, my nails digging into my scalp. "Just fucking *stop*."

But it never stops. Not anymore. It whispers and curls deeper, twisting my thoughts until I can't tell where my fear ends and the truth begins.

My steps slow then stop at the sound of my father's voice roaring down the stone corridor.

"It has been nearly two weeks! And you all still haven't found that *monster*." His voice rises on every word. "What good are you all? Find him, or I will have every one of your heads on a spike come dusk. I want him found alive… NOW!"

Footsteps thunder toward me. I flatten my back against the cold wall just as three royal guards burst out of the throne room. None of them notice me. They're too focused. Too urgent.

Inside, his voice rises again but calmer.

"I'm glad to see you're doing better today."

"Yes, much. It has been a trying couple of days since their attack on my guards," Alaric's cold voice answers, smooth and unbothered.

My breath catches as I inch closer, peeking around the corner.

Father paces the center of the throne room, hands twitching at his sides. Alaric stands at the dais, still as stone, with a calm, patient look in his eyes as he watches him.

"My poor wife has been beside herself with worry for our

son. You're sure he wasn't with them? Could they be holding him hostage elsewhere?"

Alaric drops his head. "Sadly, I didn't see the prince."

Father curses under his breath, dragging both hands down his bearded face.

"But we will find your son. Do not give up hope."

"The nerve of… of that traitor. I should've known. I should've never let that monster into my castle."

"This is not your fault, Zephyr," Alaric says smoothly.

That's when I see it. My eyes widen as they lock onto the dry blood covered blade of the sword in Alaric's hand. Something inside me snaps tight, and before I can even think I step forward into the room.

"What are you doing with that?" My voice shaking.

Both of them turn.

Father's pacing halts. His eyes land on me, almost softening. Which is strange. His eyes never soften.

"Why do *you* have that?" I demand, pointing to the blade in Alaric's hand, unable to tear my eyes from it.

"King Alaric was attacked," Father says, stepping beside Alaric. "By that traitor, Codrin Hardtblade. And Athan Brexen. He's lucky to be alive." He places a hand on Alaric's back.

I notice Alaric flinch slightly but quickly straightens again like nothing happened.

My brow furrows as I shift my gaze between both my father

and Alaric. Father, offering pathetic show of sympathy. While Alaric, plays the part of some wounded hero.

You have got to be fucking kidding me. I roll my eyes, exhaling hard.

"But why do you have that sword?" I ask again with a snarl. I didn't know Alaric was attacked and frankly I don't give a shit. My only concern is that sword in the vampire king's hand.

Alaric looks down at it like he just remembered it's there.

"I pulled it out of one of my guards he killed." He sighs a long, heavy breath like grief that coats his lungs as if losing a guard has gutted him.

I arch a brow. I'm calling *bullshit.*

For a heartbeat, his gaze hooks mine and there, just under that grieving mask, I swear I see a smirk flicker. But gone before it lands.

Fucking bastard. I know he's not telling the full truth.

"Come, Alaric." Father's tone is gentle. "Let me get you a drink. We can talk more in the library."

They don't say a word to me, not so much as a glance as they walk past me.

I don't think. I just move as I reach out and wrench the sword from Alaric's hand.

He hisses as the blade slices across his palm, sharp and fast. Blood wells up, trickling down his wrist. He looks down at the cut. Then at me. His golden eyes flash with anger but restrained.

I mock him with a bounce of my brows, slow and deliberate. A razor-thin smile cuts across my lips as though telling him, *Go ahead. Try something.*

"Ravenna! How dare you."

Alaric lifts a hand. Not at me. But at Father, silencing him.

"It's fine. *My* dear princess has been under a great deal of stress these last two weeks." He looks at me not as a man wounded but as a predator humoring prey. "Let her keep the sword. It means nothing to me anyway."

He turns on his heel and walks out of the throne room with my father at his side.

I don't move until the last echo of their footsteps fades down the corridor.

As soon as I know they are long gone, I tear from the throne room at full speed, up the stairs, down the corridor, past stunned servants and shadowed corners. My breath is ragged, my pulse pounding in my ears.

As I reach my wing of the castle, I throw out a hand, grabbing the edge of the stone archway to swing myself around the corner. My boots skid across the floor as I whip into the final hall.

I nearly crash into my bedroom door as I shove it open and stumble inside, slamming it shut behind me and twisting the lock with shaking fingers.

My chest heaves. My muscles burn. My mind won't stop spinning as I stagger across the room and toss the sword onto the small table with a metallic thud. I collapse into the wing-back chair beside the table, sliding so low that my ass nearly hangs off the edge, arms limp over the sides. I try to catch my breath and string together a single clear thought. I let the silence of the room swallow me whole as minutes tick by slowly.

Eventually, I sit up and lean forward, elbows on my knees, staring down. I close my eyes and count to ten before I can even look at it again. When I do, I glance over my shoulder toward the sword caked in dried blood.

This isn't Codrin's sword. It's Talon's.

I sit up straighter and grab the sword from the table, setting it across my lap. My fingers trace the familiar shape, every line carved into my memory. From the pommel's crossed-blade crest to the worn black leather grip. My fingers wrap around it, and I swear I can feel the ghost of Talon's fingers still pressed into the hilt.

My gaze slides down the cross guard to the blade. Its thirty-six inches of ashenbane iron, made perfectly for Talon's height and reach.

He has a ridiculous number of swords. A different one for training, for dinners, even for wandering the castle in case something goes wrong. Honestly, I'm surprised he doesn't have one labeled for each day of the week. Maybe he does.

But this sword… this one I know better than the rest. This is his favorite. The one he brings on every patrol. The one that's saved both our lives more times than I can count.

Alaric said he hadn't seen the prince, and yet, he had Talon's sword. He lied to my father. But why?

He wants Codrin and Athan to look guilty. And by leaving Talon's name out of it, he keeps Father's hands clean. Keeps the illusion intact. The prince of Theiahold, untainted.

Untouchable.

But Talon was there. What if he fought beside Codrin and Athan?

This blade is an extension of him. And I know without question, Talon would die holding this weapon.

So why am I holding it now?

Because he is dead… the voice hisses.

"Fuck off. No, he's not."

Silence.

He killed that guard. I'm sure of it. And if he left this behind, there was a reason. He didn't drop it. He *had to* leave it.

"Alaric said he pulled it from his dead guard," I whisper to the empty room. And I know Alaric's guards are not the type you want to mess with. They're huge. They make Athan look a normal height.

I lean back in the chair, eyes drifting up to the ceiling. My mind shifts through years of training, through every fight, every kill.

I've seen demons die. I've seen guards fall. I've studied

battle wounds, learned how to read the angles, the intention behind each strike.

There are patterns. Scars. Stories told in blood and iron.

And this one? The voice echoes in my head.

"This one tells me something isn't right."

By the time evening rolls in, I still haven't left my room. The door remains locked. The curtains drawn. My fingers dig into the soft sheets on my bed as I sit curled against the headboard, spine pressed to it like I might vanish into it. Every knock is a knife to my nerves. Colette stopping by with another dress for yet another supper. Servants bringing food.

I refuse them all.

The only sounds I can stomach are the whispers of the breeze through the cracks of the window and the occasional cry of a bird in the night.

But even those sounds begin to feel like mockery.

Like the world itself is whispering just loud enough for me to hear. *You've been abandoned.*

They don't care about you. None of them do.

I curl tighter into myself, refusing to let the tears fall. I've been racking my brain for hours over Talon's sword. But it's the voice's whispers that make my stomach churn.

Why did they leave me?

Why did *he* leave me?

Just as all hope crumbles around me, a soft knock breaks me out of my despair.

"Princess," Colette's voice calls gently through the door. "I brought a tray of nightly sweets and your favorite bottle of wine." I can hear the smile in her words.

I drag myself from the bed and make my way to the door. Unlocking it, I find Colette standing there smiling, tray in hand with a bottle of red wine, a goblet, and a plate filled with an assortment of cheeses, crackers, and a few slices of bread.

When she says *sweets*, she never means actual sweets. I've always preferred cheese and wine on nights I can't sleep.

She knows me so well.

"Thank you, Colette." I take the tray.

She offers a quick nod and scurries off down the corridor.

I close the door with my foot and lock it behind me. Stepping over a boot I kicked off earlier, I cross the room to the small table and wingback chair. I set the tray down on the table next to Talon's sword, flop into the chair, and pour myself a glass of wine.

When I lift the cloth napkin from under the plate, a small piece of parchment flutters loose, drifting to the floor. I catch it mid-fall.

Tears well in my eyes as I recognize the handwriting. But

the singular word, written with the kind of certainty only *he* carries, that makes my breath catch.

Tonight.

I spring to my feet, wanting to burst from my room and chase Colette down, ask her if she had seen him. When she might have seen him. I know this is Codrin's handwriting but I also know I can't go running down the corridor to ask Colette of this. It isn't safe. There are still too many eyes watching.

I press the parchment to my chest and breathe in deeply. I knew he wouldn't leave me. My muscles slowly begin to unwind. A smile tugs at my lips as I relax back in the chair and take a sip of wine, letting the taste bloom along my tastebuds. The dark berries and oak unfolding in quiet layers with each sip.

After nearly three full glasses of wine, my mind grows fuzzy, my nerves unraveling from soothed calm into an agonizing knot. The goblet in one hand, a piece of bread in the other, I pace the room. My eyes flick to the door every few seconds, hoping and foolishly desperate, for the sound of a knock.

But hours have crawled by.

I have no idea when Codrin might show up. Or if he will at all. Maybe the note was just to say he's alive. That he's safe. He wouldn't risk coming here. He can't.

My breath shortens into shallow pants as the walls seem to close in around me. Sweat trickles down my brow. I swear the fire has been burning for hours, untended and relentless, flooding the room with suffocating heat. I need air. I set the goblet and bread on the table and rush to the window. Throwing it open, I drink in lungfuls of cool air, that kisses at my flushed skin. But the heat rising inside me barely fades.

I take in another deep breath as I lean my arms on the windowsill, staring out over the quiet town. Guards shuffle through the streets, but the townspeople sleep soundly in their beds. My gaze climbs to the half-moon hanging high above, nestled in the dark, stars scattered like tiny shards of hope.

I catch myself watching the shadows. Watching for even the slightest movement of a Codrin shaped figure to emerge from the shadows. That small hope clinging to my chest.

I shake my head and push away from the windowsill, leaving the window open. Damn it. He's not coming. He was never coming. *It's safer if he doesn't*, I tell myself.

I cross to the table, pick up the goblet, and take one last long sip. The curtains flutter as a breeze slips through the room. With the goblet still to my lips, I turn to head for bed.

I freeze.

My breath catches on a gasp as the goblet slips from my hand. Red wine splashes across the rug, sinking into the threads like blood.

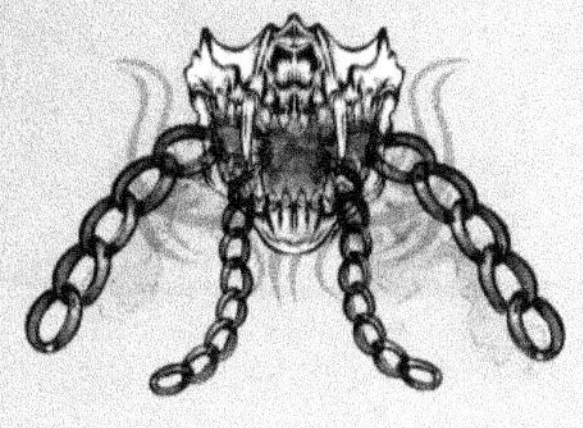

CHAPTER 26
Codrin

y grin stretches from ear to ear as my eyes take in every inch of her.

Before I can speak, Ravenna launches herself across the room and straight into my arms. Pain stabs sharply through my ribs, but I don't care. I catch her midair, wrapping my arms around her waist as she locks her legs around me. Her arms cling tight around my neck, pulling me closer just before her lips crash into mine.

Heat explodes through my body like a lightning bolt. I smile into the kiss, unable to stop. I've imagined this moment a hundred times, but nothing compares to having her *here*. Alive. Safe. In my arms.

"Did you miss me?" I murmur against her lips.

"Where the fuck have you been?" she breathes, the words hot and half trembling with anger and relief, before she kisses me again.

"I've been out," I say, teasing. "You know… just roaming around."

She pulls back just enough to raise an unimpressed brow.

I speak in fragments, lips brushing hers between each word. "I'll explain… everything… later."

She holds me tighter, clinging like she's afraid I'll vanish if she lets go.

"I'm still mad at you." She pulls back fully, jabbing a finger into my chest, her glare fierce and familiar. "But I am sorry—"

I silence her with a kiss, fierce and hungry, my hands tangling in her hair, tongue sweeping into her mouth like I've been starved of her. I don't care what she was about to say. I just need her. I need *this*.

"I know…" I whisper against her lips, arms tightening around her.

My hands slide down, finding her hips, palming the curve of her body with a low groan.

Damn. I've missed this. I've missed her.

It's been twelve days since I last saw her. Twelve agonizing, brutal days.

We've been hiding out in an abandoned barn just beyond the farmlands, far enough to stay unseen, close enough to watch the town. After Alaric found us at Simon's old cabin, I barely made it out alive with two ribs shattered, a gash in my side that still won't close right. It took nearly a week before I could even stand without collapsing. Now, I'm just strong enough to move. Just reckless enough to try.

After Athan and Talon are passed out in the hay, worn to the bone from rotating *day* watches and running on scraps. I slipped out while they slept, silent and selfish. They'd kill me if they knew.

But gods, she's worth it. Worth the risk. Worth breaking every rule of survival I've ever followed.

I've watched over her for years, kept to the shadows, kept my distance. I told myself it was enough just to keep her safe. Even when it tore me apart. Even when she was promised to another.

And now… now she knows.

She knows what I am. The secret I've buried deeper than blood. I came here tonight prepared for her to scream, to spit, to cast me out with the same hatred I've seen in every slayer's eyes when they look at the Veilstead vampires. I would've accepted that. Still protected her. Always.

But instead… she's in my arms.

Clinging to me like I'm not a monster. Like she wants me. Like maybe, gods help me, she's *always* wanted me.

The relief that crashes through me nearly brings me to my knees. I don't deserve this. I don't deserve *her*. But here I am with her, holding her. And now I'll never let her go.

"Take me, Codrin." Her whisper is a gift sent from the gods themselves.

You don't have to tell me twice.

She lets out a little squeal when I squeeze her ass, lifting her and carrying her to the bed. But before I can toss her down onto the mattress, her fingers find my jaw, tugging my face toward her. Her piercing, icy blue eyes search mine.

She hesitates, brow furrowing. "Your eyes… they're faded." Her fingers tremble against my cheek. "What happened to you?"

I swallow hard, the truth clawing its way out. "Alaric happened… twice. The bastard's little love taps took everything out of me." I brush my thumb across her lower lip, a hunger charging through me that I can barely hold back. "It took everything I had to heal myself. Nearly drained me dry." My hand trails up her back. "But it's not going to keep me away from you."

A spark of something dark and determined flashes through her eyes. Without another word, she hops out of my hold and pushes me back a step, our bodies parting just enough for her hands to find the hem of her shirt and tug it over her head. The fabric falls to the floor, leaving her bare before me.

"You need to feed," she says, her voice steady but edged with need. "Take what you need. All of it."

My breath catches as my throat tightens. "Ravenna…"

"I mean it." She steps forward, pressing her bare chest against me. The heat of her skin sears into mine. "You're hurting. You need strength. I won't lose you, Codrin. Not again."

Her words unravel something deep in my chest. I crash into her lips, kissing her with the kind of desperation that borders on worship. My hands roam her body, savoring every inch of her skin. I push her back against the bed, lowering her down as I follow, bracing my arms on either side of her.

I pause, hovering just above her pulse, the warmth of her skin calling to every buried hunger inside me. I don't hesitate but I *do* feel the weight of it. The meaning.

She's offering this freely. Her blood. Her strength. *Herself.* Not from pity. Not from panic. But from something far deeper. Trust.

My hand slides to the back of her neck, holding her like she might vanish. I press my forehead to hers, my voice a low rasp against her lips. "Are you sure?"

Her answer is a breath against my skin. "Yes."

I press a kiss to her collarbone, then another, higher. My lips graze the place where her heartbeat thrums the loudest. A sacred place. I plant a trail of reverent kisses across her skin, savoring the tension coiling between us like a drawn bowstring.

Before I can let myself back down, I press my body firmly into hers as I sink my fangs in.

Her gasp breaks against my shoulder, shattering into a moan that pulls me deeper into her. Her fingers dig through the back of my shirt and into my skin, anchoring me. I draw from her slowly, every drop burning like lightning through my veins. Power, yes but it is more than that.

And the taste. Gods help me the taste of her blood.

It floods me with strength and warmth and desire. It's a taste unlike anything I've ever known. Pure, rich, intoxicating. It coils through me like wildfire, not just feeding me, but changing something. Awakening. Unleashing. A dark craving demanding to be sated and something else, far deeper and older, stirring inside.

I pull away just enough to meet her gaze, my fingers tangling in her hair.

"Ravenna…" Her name breaks from my lips, husky and rough. "I need more of you."

I devour her with a desperate and unrestrained kiss. The urgency between us builds like a firestorm, every touch, every kiss, every breath feeding into the hunger we share.

Her fingers tear at my shirt, and our lips part briefly as she yanks the shirt over my head before throwing it aside. Her hands roam over my chest, her nails scraping along my skin, igniting every nerve with raw, burning need.

Her touch lightens, soothing as she traces her fingers along the scars on my chest. The ones etched deep, silent witnesses to a past I've never dared to speak of. And somehow… she touches them like she intends to claim each one.

She doesn't ask. She doesn't force me to explain. Just feels them with a gentleness that makes my chest ache. As if her touch alone could ease the torment that birthed these scars.

Mapping me like a cartographer of pain, her fingertips skim the thick seam along my lower right side, tracing upward toward the left along the jagged lines across my chest. There, her fingers glide with softness up to the scar around my shoulder. Her touch lingers there the longest. Tracing, memorizing every bit of my scar.

I slip my fingers under her thighs, and she lets out a slight squeal as I pull her to the edge of the bed. Her legs wrap around my waist, her body pressing against mine with a force that sends a shudder through me.

I lean over her, my lips trail down her neck, over the fresh bite mark. The taste of her remains on my tongue, a sweetness I can't get enough of. I kiss my way across her collarbone, down to the swell of her breasts.

Her breath hitches, a soft gasp slipping from her lips as my mouth finds her nipple. I circle my tongue around the hardened peak, slow, deliberate, savoring the way she trembles beneath me. My hands tighten around her hips, anchoring her as she arches into me, like she's trying to fuse our bodies into one.

But it's more than the way she tastes. More than the way her skin responds to my touch.

She's the one I've waited for. Protected. Longed for in silence. The one I almost lost, more than once.

And gods help me, I love her.

I don't say it. Not yet. But it's there in every touch, every breath, every kiss pressed to her skin like a prayer. She's holy to me. And tonight, I worship every part of it.

"Codrin…" she whispers, her voice tangled with want and desperation. "I *need* you."

"Not yet, my little rapture," I feel her body tremble as I growl against her skin, kissing lower, nipping gently at her ribs before dragging my tongue along her stomach. "I want to taste all of you."

She moans, her fingers threading through my hair, tugging just enough to send a pulse of pleasure straight through me.

My hands slide up her thighs, pushing her legs apart. I settle between them, pressing my lips to the sensitive skin along her inner thigh. She trembles beneath me, her breath coming in short, uneven gasps.

"Gods… Codrin…" she pants, her voice a fractured plea as she bucks her hips up.

"I've missed you so much," I murmur against her skin. "Every part of you."

I lower my mouth to her core, my tongue sweeping over her with slow, deliberate strokes. Ravenna's back arches off the bed, a cry escaping her lips as I taste her, savor her, pushing her further and further until she's writhing beneath me.

"Codrin… please…"

My cock presses hard against my pants from her plea. *Not yet, buddy. Patience.*

Her fingers grip the sheets, her body rocking against me, chasing the release I'm purposefully withholding.

I slide a finger into her, then another, curling them just right, my tongue never ceasing its torment. Her cries fill the room, her body straining, tightening, her thighs trembling against me.

"Let go, Ravenna." My voice rumbles against her wetness, my gaze locks onto her flushed, beautiful face. "Let me have *all* of you."

Her back arches higher as her orgasm crashes over her like a wave, her entire body shaking as she cries out my name. I keep my mouth on her, drawing out every shudder, every gasp, until she's left breathless and shuddering.

Her body relaxes with exhaustion.

But I'm far from finished.

I pull myself up, my lips crashing into hers, letting her taste herself on my tongue. Her hands are already at my waist, fingers working my pants loose, pushing them down over my hips. I kick them off, the last barrier between us finally gone.

I press her deeper against the mattress, our bodies tangled together, her legs hooking around my waist as the tip of my cock grazes over her entrance.

"Are you sure?" I rasp, my breath hot against her ear.

Without warning, she pulls me close, and using one of our slayer training moves, she rolls me, so she is on top.

"Does this answer your question?" She stares down at me with a mischievous half-grin.

I stare up at her, breathless. Not from the move, but from *her*. The way she looks at me like I'm hers. Like I've *always* been hers. And more like her old self than I've seen in weeks.

"Gods, I've missed you," I say softly, voice rough with everything I can't say.

She grabs my wrists, holding them above my head as she lowers her lips to my neck. I feel her teeth nip at my skin, right where I bit her neck, sending a jolt through my body.

My cock pulses between her legs, begging to be let in.

"How bad do you want me, Codrin?"

"Fuuuck…" is all I can manage to get out.

She nips at my earlobe with a slight tug with her teeth.

The woman is slowly undoing me and enjoying every damn second of it. I can easily flip her back over and take control, but I love the feel of her body on top of me so much more.

She releases my wrists; her eyes locked on mine as she runs a fingernail down my chest and wraps her fingers around the shaft of my cock. She positions herself over my cock, teasing the tip over her dripping wet entrance.

Her mouth drops slightly with a moan as she slowly lowers herself onto me, her pussy sucking my cock up into her. She lets out a sharp intake of breath, her body tenses then relaxes, welcoming me in and its pure fucking heaven.

My hands grip her waist, not just to guide her, but to anchor myself to her, to this moment.

Her hips move in rhythm with mine, each roll stealing the breath from my lungs. I feel her all around me and it undoes something inside me.

Every moan she releases sets fire to my skin, but it's more than just need. It's the weight of years spent protecting her from a distance, aching for this closeness I thought I'd never have.

She arches back, head thrown in abandon, and the sight nearly breaks me. She's beautiful. Fierce. *Mine.*

Her hands brace against my thighs as she takes me deeper, and I thrust harder, chasing that closeness like it's the only thing keeping me alive.

She moves faster, her body demanding more, and I give it willingly because loving her like this is the only truth I've ever been sure of.

"Codrin. Oh, gods." My name leaves her lips on a moan.

"Fuck, Ravenna." My voice is hoarse, my body pushed to the edge with the sheer intensity of her. "You're my rapture."

She's not close enough. I need her closer.

Sitting up, I lock my arms around her, pressing her chest into mine, warm and slick with sweat. Our hearts pound as one.

Her mouth finds mine, her tongue pushing past my lips. Fevered. Frantic.

Her body arches against me, pulling me deeper.

We lose ourselves in each other, as if the world beyond this moment has been reduced to ash. Nothing else exists just the heat of her skin against mine, her breath tangling with mine, our hearts pounding like war drums.

Each thrust, each gasp, pulls us closer to something we've

both been reaching for. A breaking point of connection, of truth.

Her body tenses around me, a soft cry spilling from her lips like a prayer, and I feel her fall apart in my arms.

The sensation crashes through me, white-hot and all-consuming, my own release ripping from me with a force I can't contain. I gasp her name, not just in pleasure but reverence, like a vow whispered to the one I was always meant to find.

And in that final moment, when we shatter together, I know there is no going back. Not from this. Not from *her*.

I collapse onto the mattress, Ravenna on top of me, our bodies tangled and drenched in sweat. Her fingers drift lazily along my chest, tracing patterns I can't quite make out. My fingers lovingly thread through her silver hair.

I find solace for the first time in too long in the warmth of Ravenna in my embrace, a sanctuary I never want to leave. Her body relaxes in the security of my hold on her.

The fire in the hearth has dwindled to a mere flicker, a serene silence cloaking us, punctuated only by the soft sound of our breathing. A cool breeze wafts through the open window, carrying the salty tang of the sea.

She shifts beneath the covers, tilting her head up to look at me. She reaches up and gently tangles her fingers in the thick, tousled strands of my auburn-brown hair framing my brow. Tracing her finger down my cheek and along my jawline, my stubble prickles her fingertips. Her breath catches as she traces the outline of my lips. Each stroke provokes a shiver of anticipation, igniting a longing that stirs deep within my soul.

I part my lips and kiss her finger. "You're staring," I remark, a shy smile tugging at the corners of my lips.

Ravenna's cheeks flush, glowing in the faint light. "I'm trying to memorize you," she whispers. "Every detail."

"Don't." I shake my head, my hand cupping her cheek and my thumb stroking the delicate curve of her jaw. "I'm not going anywhere."

Her eyes flicker, doubt clouding them for just a moment before she forces a small smile. "You can't promise that."

"Yes, I can." My lips brush hers, slow and unhurried. "I promise. I'm not going anywhere. And I promise I'm not leaving you." I press a kiss to her lips, a kiss meant to soothe away the fear and hesitation lurking between us.

I slide my fingers along her spine, feeling her body respond to every touch.

Her fingers continue tracing along my chest and scars, her touch soft, thoughtful. The kind of touch that makes me forget everything else.

But the strength I gained, is fleeting. The high of the night, her warmth, her taste… it's not enough. Not enough to keep the darkness at bay.

She must sense it. Her fingers pause, her gaze burning into mine. "You're not fully healed, are you?"

"I'm fine," I lie, but my body betrays me. The dull ache in my ribs and the faint tremor in my hands return.

She sits up, the sheet wrapped loosely around her, clinging to her curves. "You need to feed."

"I told you. I'm fine." I force myself to sit up, swinging my legs over the edge of the bed, the cold air sharp against my skin.

"Codrin." Her voice is firmer now, demanding. "You're weak. I can see it. You're trying to hide it, but you can't hide it from me."

I reach for my shirt, tugging it over my head, avoiding her gaze. "I'll be fine. Just need to… rest."

"Bullshit." The word lands between us, sharp and unrelenting. "You're hurting yourself trying to protect me. Why can't you see I'm trying to protect you?"

I button my pants with unsteady hands, throwing her a forced grin. "I've managed this long, haven't I?"

She rises from the bed, the sheet wrapping her body like a gown of moonlight, her steps soundless, her presence anything but. "You've managed because you've been starving yourself. You're making yourself weak. And for what? Pride? Fear? You need strength. If you won't do it for yourself, then do it for me."

"Ravenna," I growl, my hands clenching into fists. "This

isn't… I can't just…"

"Yes, you can." Determination burns in her eyes, her chest rising and falling with the intensity of her words. "I offered myself to you once tonight. And you took it. But it wasn't enough, was it? You're still hurting. Still not fully healed. And I won't stand by and watch you suffer just because you're too damn stubborn to accept help."

Her words crack something deep within me. I want to argue. To shove the truth back into the shadows. To keep her safe from the monster I've spent years suppressing.

But I can't lie to her. Not anymore.

"You're right. But I can't… I need to go."

I turn away, grabbing my coat from the wingback chair and slinging it over my shoulders. My gaze snags on the weapon sitting beside the empty tray on the table.

"Hey… Talon's sword." I lift it carefully. "He'll be glad to see this."

Holding the blade up, I turn to face Ravenna, only to freeze at the look on her face. That flicker of guilt. Of realization.

She hasn't asked about her brother or Athan. Not once.

"Is he…?" she breathes, her voice thin and shaking, knuckles white where they grip the sheet to her chest.

I set the sword back down and stroll over to her. My hands settle gently on her shoulders. "He's fine," I say softly. "Athan too."

She exhales a breath I know she's been holding far too long. Her head bows. Her shoulders drop. That stubborn strength finally releases for just a moment.

I kiss her forehead, letting my hands glide up and down her arms, trying to warm her chilled skin. "Don't worry. They're okay. But right now, I need to go."

Her head snaps back up. Eyes narrowing. "Don't you fucking dare."

I move a step around her, but she grabs my arm and pulls me back. Her fingers tight. Her stare unrelenting.

"Codrin." Her voice quivers with emotion, but there's steel beneath it. "If you don't take what you need, you're putting both of us at risk. You said you'd protect me. How can you do that if you're only half-alive?"

The truth of her words slams into me like a blow to the chest. The hunger claws at my insides, gnawing at my restraint, and still, I hesitate because it's *her*. I have fed from her once tonight. I can't do it again. But she's right. If I'm too weak to stand, I'm too weak to protect her. And I would burn the world to keep her safe. I nearly lost her once. I won't let it happen again.

"Please." Her voice cracks, and it's that sound of vulnerability, that trust, that finally breaks me. "Let me help you. Let me be enough."

She's one to talk, but I bite my tongue.

The fight of arguing with her drains from me, the strength I clung to unraveling like thread pulled from a frayed seam. Her words are a tether, binding me to her, dragging me back from the edge of denial.

"You don't understand," I whisper, the words like rusted metal scraping from my throat. "It's not just blood. It's… you."

"Your point? Take me," she insists, her voice growing steadier, her shoulders squaring with resolve. "All of me. As much as you need."

I shake my head; my fists clenched so tightly my knuckles ache. "I'll hurt you. I can't control it. Not completely. If I lose control…" My voice cracks, my gaze dropping to the floor. "I could kill you, Ravenna."

"Then don't." She steps closer, her hand reaching for mine. Her touch is warm. Grounding. Real. "You won't hurt me. I trust you."

The words hit me like a hammer. How can she say that? After everything I've kept from her, everything I am, she still trusts me.

"I can't." I try to turn away, but her fingers curl around my wrist, refusing to let me go.

"Yes, you can." Her eyes lock on mine. Those fierce, un-yielding icy blue eyes of hers. "I know you're afraid. But I'm not. I want this, Codrin. I want you." She pulls the sheet tighter around her shoulders, her voice dropping to a softer tone. "And I want to be strong enough to protect you. Just like you've protected me."

"I'm not worth it."

"Stop. You are worth everything to me. And I won't stand by and watch you destroy yourself out of some misguided need to protect me. Not when I can help you. Not when you need me."

She slips her arms around me, the warmth of her skin through the sheet presses against me. Her heartbeat is strong and steady, a beacon in the storm of my doubt.

"Please," she whispers, her breath warm against my neck. "Take what you need."

I close my eyes. Fighting the storm inside me, as my whole-body tremors with the hunger that wants to consume, to take, to ruin. But her lilac and jasmine scent engulfs me, rich and intoxicating, making my fangs ache with hunger.

"You have to stop me. If it's too much, you *have to* stop me."

"I will." She tilts her head to the side, baring her neck to me. Her pulse flutters just beneath the surface, a steady rhythm calling to the beast inside me.

I reach for her; my hands shake as I cup her face. "Ravenna…" Her name is a plea that catches in my throat.

"Please." She whispers, her gaze remains steady, unwavering.

The hunger slams into me with brutal force. But it's not just hunger. It's need. It's the way she looks at me, with trust and want, her body pressed against mine, her heartbeat pounding in my ears.

My lips find her throat, pressing against the curve of her neck where her pulse beats strongest. I inhale deeply, her scent filling my lungs, stoking the fire raging inside me.

"Tell me to stop," I rasp, my fangs grazing her soft skin. "If it's too much, you have to tell me to stop." But I feel at this point if she did try to stop me, I don't think I will be able to.

"I'll be sure to lay you on your ass."

A chuckle escapes my lips. My fangs are pressing against her skin, and she makes jokes.

"I trust you," she says on a breath. "Just… don't hold back."

I take a breath and sink my fangs into her neck.

Her body tenses at the initial shock, but she doesn't pull away. Instead, her arms tighten around me, her fingers digging into my back as the sensation sweeps over her.

My knees nearly buckle beneath me.

I dance her backward until her back is pressed against the stone wall, my body pressing into hers. She grabs at my shirt, trying to rip it off, but I reach for her wrists, pinning them to the wall at her shoulders. More to steady myself as her blood rushes into me, hot and powerful, flooding my veins with strength and life. The ache in my ribs vanishes. The dull throb in my head fades to nothing. Every wound mended; every weak-ness purged, faster than it should be. Fiercer than it's ever been.

Gods, not even draining a whole guard made me feel this strong, this alive. This feels like something else, something… more.

It's more than just strength. It's her. The warmth of her blood. The purity of her trust. The unspoken promise tangled between us.

My hand slips to the small of her back, drawing her even closer. Her breathing hitches, but her body molds into mine, her warmth seeping into me as if she's trying to give me everything she has.

I pull back, my lips brushing her skin where the puncture marks are. My breaths come in sharp, ragged gasps, the rush of power surging through me like wildfire.

She stares at me, her eyes half-lidded, her cheeks flushed. "See?" she whispers, a ghost of a smile playing on her lips. "I'm still here."

I let out a shaky breath, the weight of my fear slowly giving way to something far stronger. "You're insane, you know that?"

"Probably." She grins, a fierce, beautiful grin. "But it worked, didn't it?"

"Yeah." I brush my thumb along her jawline, my touch reverent, awestruck. "It worked."

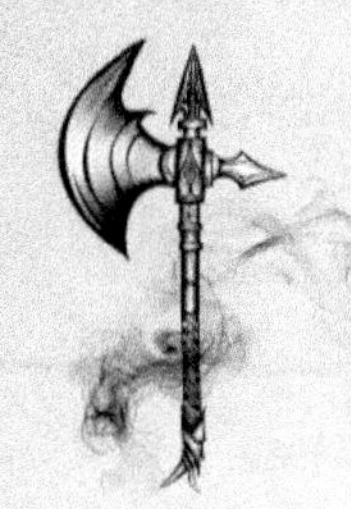

CHAPTER 27

Ravenna

Time feels as if it slows to a crawl. Codrin's fingers brush my cheek. His expression shifts, his touch vanishes. Then his body is in front of mine, shielding me from the blast of wind that tears through the room like a hurricane force.

Two colossal guards clad in pitch-black armor flash behind Codrin, grabbing him by the shoulders and tossing him back. Codrin hits the wooden floor with a teeth-rattling thud. The guards tackle Codrin to the ground, overpowering him with their immortal strength. He fights back, landing a couple of punches, kicking one guard in the kneecap, but the sheer size of his assailant overwhelms him.

I lunge onto one guard's back who's pinning Codrin to the ground and hammering on his face. I try to hook my small arm around the guard's thick neck in a desperate headlock, but another guard grabs my waist from behind and tosses me back.

The air knocks from my lungs as I land hard on my back. Unable to catch my breath in time to move, as a guard grabs my hair. I let out a choked scream, kicking the guard's armored leg as I'm yanked to my feet, the sheet falling from my body. He spins me around, clamping his massive arm across my naked chest, crushing me against his chest, and pinning my arms to my side.

I struggle and kick at its legs, but it doesn't faze him. He only grips me tighter. My ribs threaten to crack from the pressure, pressing into my lungs and constricting my breath.

I watch helplessly as the other guard pins Codrin on his stomach, his armored knee pressing into Codrin's back with enough force to make the floor groan in protest. The guard's thick fingers tighten around each of Codrin's wrists, forcing his arms behind his back. Another guard kneels, clasping iron shackles securely around Codrin's wrists.

The two guards seize Codrin by the biceps and haul him to his feet as if he weighs nothing. Neither breaks a sweat, their movements crisp and precise, like lifting him was no more effort than adjusting a chair. One of them casually brushes a fleck of blood from his armor sleeve, utterly unaffected.

Codrin, by contrast, gasps for breath, a fresh gash blooming across his right eyebrow and blood trickling from a split in his upper lip. He spits crimson onto the floor, his face flushed, chest heaving, a thin ribbon of blood sliding down his chin.

The guards standing on each side of Codrin, holding him in their grasp, loom over him, their towering frames almost monstrous in proportion. Black helmets adorned with intricate gold detailing obscure their faces. All I can see are the piercing red eyes glaring back at me.

I know these are Alaric's guards. But how dare they barge into my room like this.

All eyes snap to the bedroom door, now hanging askew on its bottom hinge, as Father strolls into the room with a satisfied smirk, his arms casually resting behind his back. General Hawk and the King of Veilstead follow close behind him.

Alaric's golden eyes fall on me, and his face contorts with rage. "Get your fucking hands off her!"

The guard suddenly releases his hold on me as Alaric storms across the room, sweeping the sheet from the ground along the way. He pulls me into him, wrapping the sheet around me. "How dare you lay a hand on her. I don't care if you're my own guard, I shall have your head for this."

Turning back to me, the anger smooths from his flawless face as his hands gently circle my shoulders. "Are you okay, Princess? Are you hurt?" He examines me head to toe. "When I heard he was attacking you, I sent my best guards to protect you. I didn't think they would be so stupid as to hurt you." He pulls me into a tight embrace, his hand brushing over my hair. "It's okay. I'm here now."

My skin crawls under his touch. The sheet wrapped around me suddenly feels too thin, too exposed.

How… how did he know Codrin was here? I bite my tongue, forcing down the bile rising in my throat.

Father claps his hands together as though he's a child in a

toy shop, a grin splitting his face from ear to ear. Standing in the middle of the now overly crowded room, he takes in the scene. "Excellent work, gentlemen!"

"Yes. Excellent work indeed." Lip curled, Alaric watches Codrin thrash against the iron grip of the guards, muscles straining and teeth clenched in defiance. They hold firm, unmoved by his resistance, like stone pillars standing steadfast in a storm.

"Now, I want to see his head on a spike, come dawn," Father says with delight.

"What?!" I spin out of Alaric's hold.

"All due respect, I do believe you promised a fair trial." Alaric steps away from me. "However," his eyes settle on Codrin, his nostrils flaring. "Tell me, Codrin, what gives you the right to fuck my betrothed?"

"I am not your betrothed." I refuse to look away, daring him to challenge my choice.

But that means nothing to my father as he stomps toward Codrin, his face red with anger. "How dare you?" He pulls his hand back and lashes it across Codrin's face. "Fuck your trial now."

Alaric clicks his tongue as he starts to paces the room. "I suppose some things never change with you. You always did sleep with just about anyone you could get your greedy hands on."

I shoot Codrin a questioning look.

Hm, I wonder what that could mean, the voice whispers. *Seems obvious to me…*

But something catches my eye from the corner of the room. A shadow twitches. A shape shifting where it shouldn't.

I blink and the shadow seems normal. It's just a trick of the light.

"Fuck you, Alaric," Codrin yells past Father, who still stands before him.

Father lashes Codrin's face again, his head whipping to the side. "Maybe I'll keep you alive and let you slowly rot in the dungeons."

Alaric stops mid-step, eyes falling on the small table next to the wingback chair. His hand reaches out, and he draws back the piece of parchment bearing Codrin's single-word note. His eyes shift over the paper, slowly gliding over me and then Codrin.

"Still using your sweet little code words?" Alaric tosses the paper back onto the table.

My head snaps back to Codrin, jaw dropping.

"Don't listen to him, Ravenna. He's trying to get inside your head. He's lying." Codrin's voice cracks as he struggles against the two guards' hold.

"Lies? What does that say about you, Codrin? From what I have gathered, you have been lying to this dear princess for years." Alaric gestures toward me.

My head drops, and my shoulders roll forward under the weight of Alaric's words.

Codrin. Lies. Secrets. He had a reason to it all but was I not enough for him to trust me with all the things he has be hiding all this time?

And clearly, there is still a lot more he hasn't bothered to tell you. After all you have just done for him, the voice hisses.

A slow slide of movement draws my gaze down. My own shadow stretches beneath me, longer than it should. Darker than any other shadow.

Then something slithers beside me. A tendril of shadow curling around my ankle like a whisper, like a touch meant to soothe.

I inhale sharply.

Codrin's brow furrows, his gaze locked on me, sharp and questioning. But I tear my gaze away from him. Did he notice? Can he see the shadows shifting at my feet? Of course not. It's just my mind playing tricks on me.

"It's okay, my sweet princess. I will not let this *monster* harm you again."

I let Alaric pull me into his embrace. Unable to speak. Unable to even move.

"Get your hands off her," Codrin growls.

Alaric ignores him as he holds me back at arm's length. His hand brushes my hair from my shoulder, and in one breath, the world around me stops spinning. Gripping my chin, he tilts my head to the side, fully revealing the side of my neck to him.

"I see." A snarl rises from deep within his chest, his eyes blazing with fury as he takes in the two bite marks on my neck.

His hand drops from my chin, and he turns sharply on his heel, launching himself at Codrin. His roar thunders through the room as he pounds his fist into Codrin's stomach again and again.

"STOP IT!" I scream, ready to pounce on Alaric's back, only to be held back by the guard.

Codrin curls in on himself, coughing out choked gasps.

Alaric's hand closes around the hilt of his sword. There's a whisper of steel against leather as he draws his blade from its sheath. "You shall die for this."

"No!" I twist in the guard's hold, my body jerking with desperation as I fight to break free, my breath ragged in my throat. I claw at his iron grip.

"I would have let you live after you bedded her, but you should have kept your fangs to yourself."

"Why don't you fight me like a true warrior, you fucking coward?" Codrin smirks as he struggles against the guards' hold.

Without a word, the towering guards force Codrin to his knees, one pressing his head down.

"Well, isn't this nice," Alaric sneers. The polished steel blade presses briefly against the back of Codrin's neck. "Right where we left off last time."

Alaric lifts the sword high, preparing to strike.

"NOOO!" My scream echoes off the stone walls.

I can't lose him. Not now. Not when I just got him back.

"I'LL MARRY YOU!" My words thunder through the room, halting Alaric mid-swing.

All eyes are on me. Alaric's sword still poised, Alaric glances over his shoulder, his brow furrowing as he narrows his eyes at me.

"I'll marry you," I repeat with a gasp.

"Ravenna, no!" Codrin shouts, renewing his efforts to get away from the guards. "Don't do this!"

Alaric lowers the sword to his side, a pleased smile spreading across his square jawline as he turns his full attention to me.

"Please, don't kill him. I'll marry you as long as he lives." My skin crawls at the thought of marrying Alaric, of binding myself to a monster, but I don't hesitate. I can't.

Because this is what love means, isn't it? Choosing Codrin's life over my own freedom. His breath over my pride. I would burn for him. Bleed for him. Break for him.

I love him. Gods help me, I love him more than anything.

"That includes Father not harming him as well. Or the wedding is off." I narrow my eyes to my father, who stands idly by not saying a word. He wasn't even going to stop Alaric from killing Codrin.

"Ravenna, don't do this!" Codrin pleads.

The room descends into a tense silence. Alaric twirls his sword, its sharp blade digging into the wooden floor as he contemplates my proposition.

After what feels like an eternity, Alaric sheathes his sword. "Take him to the dungeons," he commands without looking away from me.

A ragged, unsteady breath escapes me, torn from the deepest part of my chest. Relief crashes over me so hard my knees nearly give out. He's still alive. I stopped the blade. I saved him.

But the cost tastes like ash on my tongue. The man I love is breathing, but I've just shackled myself to a monster to make it so. I should feel triumphant, but all I feel is hollow. Shaking. Splintered.

The guards nod curtly, hauling Codrin to his feet and pulling him toward the doorway, his struggles futile against their tight hold.

"Ravenna, don't do this!" Codrin thrashes against the guards' unyielding grip, muscles straining, blood dripping down his face as he tries to break free. But he's too weak. Too broken. Still, he fights. For me.

Father's dark eyes light up, and he claps his hands together once more. "Your mother will be so pleased to hear of this news.

Come, Hawk, we have much to plan come morning!" Father practically skips out the door.

Alaric stands before me. I flinch as he cups my chin, his thumb tracing slowly over my lips as he tilts my head up to meet his gaze.

"Come tomorrow, you are mine," he whispers.

Dropping his hand from my chin, he turns on his heel and leaves the room.

My knees buckle, and I sink to the floor. My hands shake as they cover my face, my tears silent now. I've saved the man I love but in doing so, I've damned myself.

I don't even have to look up to know I'm not imagining it. I can feel the shadows stirring around me again. There is no danger. No threat. Only a steady, warmth wrapping around me like an old friend returning home.

And I let them cradle me in silence.

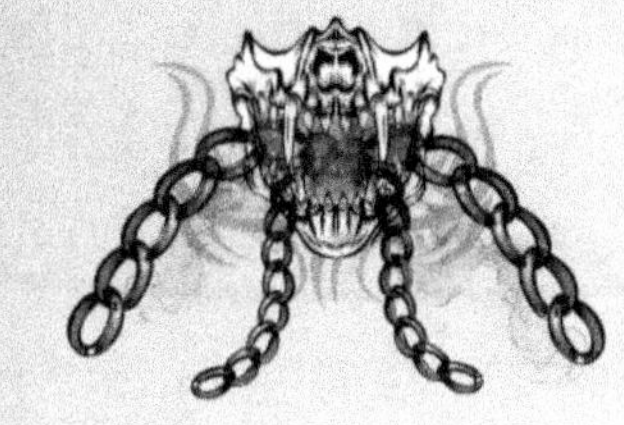

CHAPTER 28
Codrin

laric's hybrid beasts throw me into a cell buried deep within the bowels of the dungeon, where the damp chill gnaws at my bones and the air tastes of rot. But it's not the cold that's tearing me apart. It's the memory of her voice, trembling yet fierce, offering herself to Alaric to spare my life.

I should feel grateful. I should feel relieved. Instead, I'm drowning in guilt. She sacrificed everything for me. And I was too broken, too bloodied to stop her.

Also, I don't know if it was real. Maybe it was the adrenaline. Maybe it was the light playing tricks. But I could have sworn it looked like a shadow had moved at her feet. Like it was curling around her ankle. Reaching for her like it belonged to her.

And the strangest part? She seemed to have noticed the same thing, but she didn't even react. No fear. No confusion. Just… acceptance? I try to shake the image loose, but it only buries itself deeper within my mind, never to be forgotten.

The cell door groans open, the iron hinges shrieking in protest. Torchlight cuts through the darkness, flickering over the stone walls like a living thing.

Ulric stands in the doorway, flanked by two of Alaric's monstrous guards, one with iron chains glinting in its hands. The sight of them alone is a warning, a brutal promise of whatever awaits me beyond the cell.

"By orders of the king, we are to move you to a different location," Ulric declares, shoulders squared, his sharp green eyes filled with an all-righteous fury.

"Oh, good. I was just about to file a complaint about this room service." I smirk as I drag myself to my feet, catching a couple of royal guards standing off in the shadows.

Ulric's lips twitch. He doesn't bother to respond.

Alaric's beasts stomp into the cell, their heavy footfalls shaking the ground. I catch a gleam of silver woven through the links of the thick chain shackles, an extra touch of cruelty.

One clamps a hand on my shoulder, the grip vice-tight. The other seizes my wrists and yanks them behind my back, locking the shackles around my wrists.

A hiss tears from between my teeth the moment the silver bites hot against my skin, like acid poured straight into my veins.

They drag me forward like a ragdoll, forcing my arms into painful angles. The silver sears deeper with each step, burning away my strength, piece by piece. My knees threaten to buckle, but I lock my stance and brace against it. I won't give them the satisfaction.

Not now. Not ever.

We march through the dark dungeon corridor, the stones

slick with moisture and gods know what else. Light flickers from behind barred windows and torch brackets, casting long warped shadows on the walls.

Each time I even shift to resist, their hands clamp tighter like unforgiving iron bands.

The pain fades from dull to a constant sharp throb that burrows deep. I can feel the silver working its way through me, draining more than just my strength. It's trying to take my will.

But it'll have to do better than that.

We reach the end of the corridor, just feet from the door leading to the upper levels. The guards halt. Ulric steps aside as a tall, broad-shouldered figure materializes from the shadows.

"Come to join us on a nightly walk, brother?" I bite out, my smile sharp and cold. My eyes blaze silver, but I refuse to look away from him. I want him to see how Ravenna's blood, given freely with trust and true affection, has changed me. And I *am* changed. I will never be the same man again after such an act of devotion.

"You could say that." Alaric circles me slowly, his steps deliberate, a predator savoring the moment before the kill. His gaze flickers over me, assessing, taunting.

There's a madness in his golden eyes, a cruelty so sharp it's almost beautiful.

"I've been planning something special for you, little brother." Alaric's voice is calm, almost gentle. That's how I know things are about to get bad. "A fitting end for a traitor. And a thief."

I force a laugh. "What's the matter, Alaric? Upset I've been putting my hands on your precious toy? Or are you just pissed because she wants me instead?"

The smirk fades from Alaric's face, replaced by pure, murderous rage. His eyes shine like molten gold, the predator suddenly stripped of its calm.

Ulric stiffens at the shift, though Alaric's anger is not directed at him.

"Search him," Alaric orders. "Make sure he doesn't have the gemstone on him."

Ulric snaps his fingers. "Zavier. Get over here."

"You have got to be shitting me," I mumble under my breath.

Footsteps echo through the corridor as Zavier hurries forward. He stands before me, his chest puffed out like he's trying to prove something. The little bastard looks like he's won a prize.

The young slayer curls his lip, his eyes glinting with arrogance. He begins patting me down, his hands rough and invasive.

I endure it silently, watching him through narrow eyes. When he crouches to pat down my leg, his fingers prodding at my thigh, I seize the moment. I pull my knee back and drive it into his face with all the strength I can muster. The cartilage gives way with a sickening crunch. Blood sprays from his shattered nose as he crashes backward, his body skidding across the damp floor.

The other guards roar with laughter. Not a single one moves to help him.

"Idiot," Alaric mutters under his breath.

"Looks like you need to teach your men how to properly search someone, *Captain* Hollowstone," I snarl.

"Shut the fuck up!" Ulric's fist drives into my jaw, snapping my head to the side. Blood seeps from my split lip, hot and metallic.

I spit blood on his boots and grin. "That all you got?"

Ulric rears back, preparing to hit me again, but Alaric catches his wrist.

"It's getting late. And I have plans for my little brother." Alaric's smile is all teeth and malice.

Ulric nods, his expression tight with barely suppressed rage.

A groan rumbles from the floor. Zavier stirs, sitting up with a wince, one hand clutched to his bloodied face.

"That son of a bitch broke my nose," he mutters, his voice thick with pain as he stumbles to his feet.

I lean forward as best I can in the beasts' grasps, silver-moon eyes locked on him. My fangs glint under the torchlight, deliberate, undeniable.

"That was for Ravenna," I snarl. I still don't know what happened between him and Ravenna that night on patrol. But I do know whatever it was, was worth him getting a broken nose for it.

Zavier freezes. His eyes widen for a breath. Then, slowly, the recognition clicks into place. Not terror. Just cold confirmation. A twisted smirk curls his bloodied lips.

"I fucking knew there was something strange about you," he mutters taking a step toward me and spits right in my face.

The warm spray hits my cheek, sliding down slowly. I don't flinch. I just glare at him, a quiet snarl rumbling low in my throat.

Zavier wipes his mouth on his sleeve, straightens with a grunt, and turns his back like I'm not worth another word. Pride dragging him forward, he limps off to rejoin the other guards.

Alaric steps before me, holding out a black gloved hand gripping my slayer mask. Its iron surface looking crueler as the etched detail of fangs and teeth glint under the torchlight.

"I had to make some minor adjustments," Alaric purrs. "A better fit for someone like you."

He shifts the mask around in his hand. My eyes widen noticing the straps glinting in the torchlight with silver threads and the bottom lip of the mask now curls inward, which is only meant to clamp my jaw shut, I'm sure.

Alaric takes a step toward me as I struggle against the guards, but they force me to my knees. One of them shoves a balled-up rag into my mouth, silencing my curses.

Alaric slams the mask over my mouth, his fingers tightening the leather straps until they bite into my skull. The silver threads sear my skin like brands, burning into the flesh around my scalp. Agony explodes behind my eyes, every nerve lighting up at once. My body jerks, spine bowing as if struck by lightning.

My breathing turns ragged, each inhale desperate as it scrapes against the cloth in my mouth. My heart pounds so hard it rattles in my chest, each beat a fiery hammer beneath my skin. I try to twist away, but the restraints hold fast.

"There. A perfect fit." Alaric pats the iron mask, his smile broadening.

My pulse thunders in my ears, my limbs trembling with the aftershock.

A thick black fabric is draped over my eyes, plunging me into total darkness. Panic surges but not for myself. Her face flashes through the dark, pale and fierce, silver hair whipping in the wind. Ravenna. I try to grasp on to that image, but the pain surges again, stealing it from me.

"Don't get any ideas," Ulric growls as he knots the blindfold tighter. "You might as well come to terms with this is your end."

Alaric's voice reaches me like whispered poison. "Let's get a move on. We're only hours away from sunrise."

The guards haul me up to my feet. My body is fire and stone.

My thoughts are ash.

With that, I am dragged from the dungeons.

CHAPTER 29

Ravenna

The door to my room is nothing but a splintered wreck, torn from its hinges by Alaric's monsters. I can't stay here. Not after everything. Not with the twisted frame gaping wide like a broken jaw.

I rush to change and take to Talon's room across the hall. It's where I always went when I was younger. When the night terrors clawed at me from the shadows, they either sent me fleeing to the safety of my brother's room or him running into mine to fetch me. That was so fucking long ago. I grew out of that, or at least I thought I had.

But tonight… tonight I need somewhere I can close the door and feel protected. Except this time Talon isn't here.

I enter my brother's room, the stale cold air wafting around me, a heart crushing reminder that Talon hasn't been here for weeks. Wrapping my arms around myself, I make my way across the room, dropping to my knees in front of the fireplace. I fumble with some of the leftover wood still in the fireplace and with shaking hands try to strike the flint properly. It's not the fire I need to keep warm. It's the light I need to keep away the darkness.

I collapse onto Talon's bed, curling into the thick comforter and burying my face against the ghostly presence of my brother. My hands grip the edge of the blanket as if I can anchor myself to something solid and real.

But the warmth does nothing to chase away the chill sinking into my bones. My eyes burn from exhaustion, but my mind races, tangled in everything that happened. Codrin's capture. Alaric's games. The twisted satisfaction on my father's face.

I can't stop seeing Codrin's face as they dragged him away. Bloodied. Bruised. And yet, still fighting.

Fighting for me.

And I had to do what I did to save him. Right?

I can weasel my way out of this. I have with so many past suitors.

I let out a long, heavy yawn as sleep claws at my every nerve. Eventually, letting the exhaustion swallow me whole.

I wake to a suffocating weight pressing down on my chest, my arms pinned to the mattress at my sides. I try to thrash, to scream, but it's like ice encases my body. My breath comes in shallow, ragged bursts as panic seizes my lungs.

It's just another nightmare. It has to be. I just need to wake up.

But it feels too real.

Ghost-white eyes glow in the darkness above me. Empty.

Lifeless.

Thin, torn black skin covers its body as it straddles me. Flesh sloughs from its cheekbones, hanging in strips over cracked razor teeth. Black blood seeps from every open tear like tar.

"What?" my voice cracks.

It grins, stretching the ruined skin of its face. Its breath is rancid and thick, as though something rotten festers inside it.

"You are corrupted," it says, its voice wet and broken, like shattered glass dragging across stone. "You are stained. And the evil must be expelled."

The words crawl through me, sinking into my mind like poison.

Its hand clamps over my mouth before I can scream, icy cold claws crushing my lips and forcing my head back into the pillow. I buck beneath it, my legs kicking wildly. But its weight is immovable. I try to scream. But my voice dies behind the clammy pressure of its claws.

No one will ever be here for you, the voice rings through my mind.

A tear trickles from the corner of my eye, its words wrapping tight around me like chains. I am alone. Trapped beneath the weight of this creature. Unable to save myself.

In the corner of the eye, I see something glint in the moonlight.

A blade.

Curved and punishing.

The creature raises it high above its head, the moon's silver glow catching along the edge like a whisper of death.

I thrash harder, desperation tearing at me as I try to break free. But it only presses down harder, the bones in my body creaking under its weight.

"Everything inside you is rotting," it hisses. "And I will cut it out."

Wake up! I scream to myself. *Wake the fuck up. This isn't real.*

Then why does it feel like it is?

Its weight grinds against my ribs, bone groaning like splintering wood. Its wet, cold skin, reeking of decay as it sloughs against mine.

Every second, a countdown.

Not again. Not like this. Not pinned, not voiceless.

I twist and buck, but I'm just a puppet in its claws. Just a girl in a nightmare I can't wake up from.

Talon… Codrin… somebody… please…

It drives the blade down.

The cold iron pierces deep and it doesn't stop. It drinks.

My blood hisses on the metal, and the burn spreads like it's carving through more than flesh. It's slicing me down to bone and memory and soul.

I try to cry out, but its hand still clamps over my mouth. Blood pools in my throat, choking me.

I'm drowning.

Drowning in pain.

Drowning in blood.

Drowning in darkness.

My body seizes, every nerve alight with pain. Hot blood seeps through my blouse, the fabric clinging to my skin as if trying to pull me under.

The creature stares down at me, its eyes empty, unfeeling. Just watching.

I want to scream.

To fight.

But my body won't obey. I'm helpless. Completely, utterly helpless.

Like you always are.

I drown in darkness.

And somewhere in the black, something whispers, *"Finally."*

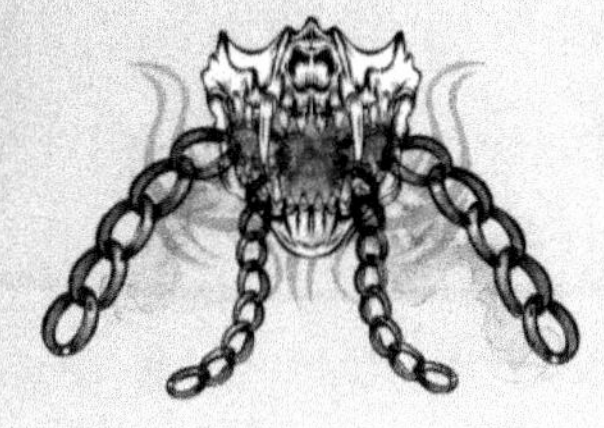

CHAPTER 30
Codrin

The creak of a door.

Heavy boots thundering against stone.

The scrape of iron chains dragging across the floor.

I can't see anything. My world swallowed in darkness beneath the thick black cloth tied over my eyes. My hands are clamped together behind me, the iron mask locked tight over my mouth.

No words can escape. No sounds. Just the silver laced in the metal seeping into my skin, keeping me weak, silent, and wide open to Alaric's voice slithering into my mind.

Just a little further, Codrin. You must be so curious to see what I've planned for you.

His amusement curls through my thoughts, like a knife on my spine. I want to rip his throat out, but all I can do is thrash against the guards dragging me like dead weight.

Your defiance is so tedious, little brother. But don't worry. You won't be needing that anger much longer.

I hear it.

In the distance, yet close. The crashing, relentless and all too familiar waves of the Astral Tide Sea turns my blood to ice.

No.

Fuck, no! Panic claws its way up my throat, tightening around my ribs. My breathing spikes, my pulse hammering behind the mask. I thrash harder, panic giving way to something worse.

They wouldn't. But what am I saying. Of course they would. *Alaric would.*

The air shifts, cooler now, sharper. I feel it seeping through the cracks of the mask, brushing across my skin like a whisper from the grave.

The blindfold is ripped away. Moonlight explodes into my vision, cruel and white, and the sight before me steals the breath from my lungs.

My wrists chained to the floor and I am faced in front of a gaping window looking out to the open endless black sea and sky beyond. Roaring waves crash below, harsh and un-forgiving. And far in the distance… a faint glimmer of gold creeps along the horizon.

Dawn.

I yank against the shackles, muscles burning, but the iron links drag me down, the chains bolted to the ground.

The cool sea air stings the raw skin of my wrists where the shackles have bitten deep. Iron alone would have been agony, but laced with silver, the metal feels like molten fire, blistering my flesh and flooding my veins with pain.

My muscles tense, rage vibrating through my bones as the

silver burns deeper. But the pain doesn't fade. It only grows worse, intensifying as the silver poisons my strength. Dragging me down like a beast caught in a hunter's snare.

Every tug on the chains scorches me like a live flame. The pain roots deep into my bones, hollowing me out with every breath.

Alaric watches, amusement etched on his face. "Surprised?"

My response is nothing but a muffled snarl as the mask grinds against my face. I lunge forward, but the chains only pull me back like a rabid dog on a leash.

Oh, how I wish I could hear you scream, Codrin. But you have such a loud mind. So easy to slip inside and pluck out all your pathetic little thoughts.

I can't shut him out. And somehow, he has even silenced my mind. Unwilling me to speak my thoughts to him.

You're thinking about her, aren't you? Poor, sweet Ravenna. I can still taste her on my fingers, you know. Grinning, he licks two of his fingers. *You might have left your little mark on her, but I'll make it mine.*

Rage tears through me, but all I manage is a strangled growl.

Alaric's grin widens. "I wanted something… poetic for your demise."

He gestures to the open window. "This tower. The very place our kind was brought to suffer. Shackled like the beasts they believed us to be. Forced to stare out over the sea as the sun rose to devour them. A slow, agonizing death."

My eyes snap to his, blazing with fury.

But you already knew that didn't you? Alaric's voice curls through my mind, his pleasure dripping from every word. *You know this tower's history. All the legends. But you never thought you'd see the inside of it for yourself, did you?*

I jerk against the chains again, the metal biting into my wrists until blood wells along my skin, hissing and sizzling against the silver. A raw, helpless groan tears from my throat.

It's useless, little brother. His taunt echoes inside my head, his pleasure prickling at my every thought. *Those chains were forged specifically for our kind. You'll never break them. You'll only wear yourself down… make the pain last that much longer.*

He moves closer, his golden eyes burning with cruel delight. *And the best part?* His thoughts sharpen like knives. *She chose me. Your precious Ravenna. She gave herself to me. To spare your worthless life.*

I thrash against the chains, my wrists burning, muscles spasming from the force of my struggles. The iron mask muffles my scream, the silver licking fire along my skin.

You can't save her. You can't even save yourself. Soon you'll be nothing but dust waiting to be scattered.

Alaric's golden eyes flash with cruelty as he steps back, his satisfaction rolling off him like a sickening perfume. "Enjoy your last few hours, Codrin. I'll be sure to make your death worth remembering." He turns and walks away, his laughter echoing through the chamber.

The door slams shut. The chains rattle. The silver bites deeper.

And I am alone.

For the first time in my life… I don't see a way out. The shackles are too thick. The silver too strong. My strength is gone, poisoned and burned from the inside out. The sun is rising, and I don't have my gem. And I'm going to die in this fucking tower. Not in battle. Not fighting.

But chained and muzzled like some wild animal. Soon forgotten.

And gods, what if no one finds me in time? What if she thinks I gave up? What if she falls… because I wasn't there to stop to catch her?

A shiver tears through me as the wind howls across the stone.

I never thought it would end like this. And I'm afraid. Not of dying. But of what will become of her if I do.

CHAPTER 31

Ravenna

The nightmare clings to me like a persistent shadow, its icy tendrils still encircling my mind as I bolt upright, gasping. Cold sweat trickles down my back. My hand flies to my chest, expecting to find a gaping wound or the cold iron of a dagger pressed to my skin. But there's only the pounding of my own heartbeat.

I draw a ragged breath.

The room is cold. No fire flickers in the hearth, just smoldering, crumbling ash. I push the covers aside and rise to my feet, my legs unsteady beneath me. The leather pants I fell asleep in cling uncomfortably to my damp skin.

I stumble to the window and shove the thin curtains back. The sky outside mirrors the weight in my chest. Thick gray clouds choke the dawn, the sun's rays nothing more than pale wisps struggling to break through the gloom.

Codrin was moved to the dungeons with Alaric giving his word he would not kill him. Even if that vile bastard can't be trusted, he'd want to savor his revenge, not end it so swiftly. Right?

I cling to that sliver of hope as I pull on my boots, tightening the laces with shaking hands.

I rush down the hallway, ignoring the curious glances from

the few guards I pass. I don't even have a plan, I just need to get to the dungeons, to check how Codrin is doing.

Maybe find a way to get him out, to escape. But how? Maybe if I can sweet-talk Alaric into letting me see Codrin, I can at least get an idea as to how to get him out of there.

Rounding the corner that leads to the south wing, I nearly run headfirst into Darius lounging against the stone wall, a goblet of wine cradled in his hand.

"Well, someone's in a hurry early this beautiful, gloomy morning." His glossy eyes hold an infuriating blend of arrogance and mischief.

"Where is your brother?" I snap, breathless. I have no time for his games.

Darius tilts his head, his expression maddeningly calm. "I have more than one brother. So, you're going to have to be more specific."

"Don't play stupid. Where's Alaric?"

He shrugs. "I would've assumed you were talking about Codrin. I guess I was wrong."

My breath snags, caught somewhere between disbelief and dread. "Wait. What?"

Oh, another secret Codrin kept from you, the voice chimes with a giggle.

Shoving the voice back into the shadows of my mind. I keep my focus squared on Darius as his grin spreads, slow and taunting.

"You didn't know?" He cocks his head, golden eyes teasing like a predator toying with its prey. "Oooh, this is delicious. I thought surely you would've figured it out by now."

"Figured what out?" I force the words out through clenched teeth, fury simmering just beneath the surface before my blood boils over at the numerous lies Codrin left me drowning in. "What the fuck do you mean Codrin is your brother?"

"Well, technically half-brother, but blood is blood, as they say. Alaric. Codrin. Myself. We all share the same loving father." He takes a long gulp of his wine, studying me over the rim. "You should see your face. Truly, it's priceless."

The floor feels like it's been ripped out from under me. My mind races, piecing together fragmented memories and conversations. Codrin never mentioned anything about family. Not Alaric. Not Darius. Nothing.

Secrets. Secrets. And more secrets, the voice hisses.

"That... That doesn't make any sense." I try to ignore the hissing, to hold my voice steady, even as it trembles. "Codrin would have told me. He would have."

"Confessed that he shares blood with the monster you're being forced to marry?" Darius chuckles. "Please. Codrin's always been a little too sentimental for his own good. Probably didn't want to hurt your precious little feelings. Or maybe he thought you'd never look at him the same if you knew."

"I... I..." My hands shake. All this time, Codrin has been

keeping this from me? The nights spent together, the secrets shared, the moments of vulnerability. And he never thought to tell me something this important? He could've told me this when I first mentioned I was being *forced* to marry *his fucking brother*.

"Are you really that surprised? We all have our dirty little secrets, Princess. But Codrin's..." Darius clicks his tongue. "Well, his might be the filthiest of all."

"Why are you telling me this?" I force steadiness into my voice, even though I feel like the world is collapsing around me.

"Because, dear Ravenna, I find your pain fascinating. And because, if I had to guess, you're on some noble little quest to go see Codrin. But how do you expect to *see* him, truly *see* him, when you didn't even know the most basic truth about him?" Darius leans back against the wall, swirling his goblet like he's lounging at some casual banquet instead of tormenting me with every word.

"He's in the dungeons..." I whisper, though the words feel hollow.

"Maybe. Maybe not." He shrugs, feigning indifference.

"Stop playing games, Darius," I snarl, my patience wearing thin.

He arches an eyebrow, swirling his wine more. "Fine," he huffs with a roll of his eyes. "Alaric had him moved last night. Not to the dungeons, though. A much more fascinating place."

My chest tightens. "Where the fuck is he?"

Darius pushes off the wall and leans in close, the rich, earthy wine clinging to his breath. "The East Tower. I overheard a couple of guards flapping their tongues about it. Apparently, your darling Codrin was tossed in there like a wild thing too broken to be of use anymore."

The East Tower? The mere mention of it sends a chill down my spine. "But… why? That tower hadn't been used in over a century. No one even knows how to reach it."

"Seems Alaric found a way. I suppose it's fitting, really." Darius chuckles, taking another long sip of wine. "Considering what happened."

"What do you mean by that?"

"Well," he drawls, eyes flicking over me like he's appraising some object of curiosity. "Your lover boy didn't just get himself thrown into the East Tower for nothing. Word has it, he lost something rather important. Something *all* us vampires hold near and dear."

"I have no idea what you're talking about."

"Oh, come on. Surely, you've read something in all those books you love to bury yourself in?" He steps forward, a glint of wickedness in his gaze. "The Eclipsis Gem. The little trinket that allows vampires to walk in daylight. Word has it, Codrin lost his. Not sure how he could lose something so valuable. Rather careless, don't you think?"

Eclipsis Gem. I've read about it, in passing. But I never imagined… "He lost it?"

"Clearly." Darius lifts his goblet, eyes glistening with delight. "And now, well, Alaric's not feeling particularly generous, from what I hear. When is he ever though?"

My heart pounds. Codrin's gem, if he lost it, he's vulnerable.

"You're a vampire. Give me your gem." I stick my hand out, palm up.

"Mine?" He pats himself down. "Hm… now where did I put that thing? I know it's here somewhere…"

"Seriously! You are an ass." I shove past him, realizing he is doing nothing but wasting my time.

"Good luck, Princess," he calls after me, his voice echoing with cruel delight. "You'll need it."

I don't look back as I throw up my middle finger and race down the hall. I only hope I can find the damn gem before it's too late. As well as, find the entrance to the tower, somehow.

I sprint through the corridors, my boots pounding against the stone floor with each step. Darius's words echo in my head, tangled with the frantic thud of my heartbeat. Codrin's Eclipsis Gem. Lost. Maybe somewhere in the wreckage of his room? If I can find it. If I can get it to him before it's too late…

My lungs burn as I race across the courtyard. Heavy raindrops start to descend from the thick gray clouds. I silently thank the goddess of the sky for concealing the sun's approach.

Clothes drenched, hair matted to my face, I make it to the barracks. I sprint down the hall to Codrin's room. I push the door open, my breath catching at the devastation within.

Nothing has been moved. Nothing has been touched.

I drop to my knees. My hands shake as I shove aside chunks of splintered wood and shattered glass. Codrin's scent lingers. Its faint, but unmistakable. Blood, mixed with him. The metallic scent stings my senses, twining with the stale rot of wood and dust.

"Come on. Come on," I whisper, my voice cracking under the weight of everything I haven't said.

I never got to tell him I love him. Not really. Not the way I want to. Not with the quiet certainty that's been building inside me since the moment I realized I could lose him. We were finally together and then he was ripped away like it meant nothing.

I tear through the wreckage, ignoring the sting of broken glass slicing into my palms, the ache in my knees from crawling. Overturned furniture, torn cushions, jagged mirror shards that reflect my desperation back at me.

What if it's not here? What if he didn't lose it here? Or what if someone already took it? What if it's gone, and with it, the last thread of hope I have to save him?

A sob claws at my throat, but I shove it down. No. I won't believe that. I *can't*. He means too much. He always has.

"Think, Ravenna," I whisper, forcing myself to breathe. "If

he dropped it, where would it have gone?"

My gaze sweeps over the mess, desperately searching for a glint of something out of place. A gemstone wouldn't simply vanish. It has to be here. It has to be.

My fingers brush something hard and cool among the torn cushions. My heart leaps as I dig deeper, pushing aside the fabric until I see it.

A faint glimmer of deep, blue.

The Eclipsis Gem.

I have never seen anything so beautiful. How could something so small hold so much power for a vampire?

A ragged sob escapes me as I clutch the gemstone in my palm. Its surface is smooth and cold against my skin. Relief floods me, swift and overwhelming. But the feeling crashes as a beam of warm morning sunlight hits my face through the broken window. The rain has stopped, and the sun is starting to break through the clouds.

Shit! Now how am I going to find the tower?

"Princess?" a voice tinged with uncertainty interrupts my thoughts.

I turn to the door to find one of the royal guards standing there, his brows drawn together.

"What?" I snap. I don't have time for this.

The young guard shuffles his feet, glancing toward the shattered window. "I know how to get to the East Tower."

I spring to him, grabbing the collar of his shirt, and shaking him. "How?"

The guard's eyes shift, his jaw drops open, quivering, but no words escape his lips.

"Either spit it out or get the fuck out of my way." My grip tightens around his collar as I shake him harder.

His words stutter but spill from his lips on one quick breath. "Th-there's a door behind the s-sunrise tapestry in the throne room."

"Thank you."

I almost shove him aside and burst through the door into the hallway, then sprint out of the barracks and across the slick cobblestones of the courtyard. Rain still lingers in the air, but above me, the clouds are breaking apart, the first hints of dawn beginning to bleed through the cracks in the sky.

My feet slam against the polished wooden floors as I fly through the castle's winding halls, my heart pounding in my throat. The windows I pass grow steadily brighter with dim gray giving way to pale gold and every slant of sunlight stretching across the floor feels like a ticking clock.

Servants dart out of side rooms with trays of fruit and bundles of linens, blinking in shock as I whip past. I nearly crash into a wide-eyed steward rounding a corner, barely twisting in time to avoid a collision.

The air sharpens with the scent of morning bread and hearth

smoke, normal life waking up all around me, but nothing about this moment is normal. With every second, the light grows stronger. With every second, Codrin inches closer to death.

I shove open the heavy doors to the throne room.

It's deserted. Silent.

I take a sharp left, past the large pillars I face the stone wall. My chest tightens as I stand in front of the sunrise tapestry. I've passed by it a thousand times, admired its intricate weaving, the sun rising over the sea in swirls of gold and crimson. Once, it filled me with a sense of promise and hope for new beginnings. Now, its intricate design mocks me, taunting me with uncertainty as to what I might face beyond its woven artistry.

I tear back the heavy tapestry with both hands. The fabric shudders with the force, nearly ripping from the hooks holding it in place. Behind the tapestry, an iron-banded door stares back at me. Rusted with age but still sturdy.

My fingers tremble as I reach for the handle.

What if I'm too late?

No. I can't think like that. I have to keep moving.

I push the door open and step into the dark passageway, the air thick and musty. Stone walls close in around me as I follow the narrow corridor, the only sound my ragged breathing and the echo of my own footsteps.

I am so close.

I reach the end of the passage. Two paths stretch out before me. One to the left, the other to the right.

Fuck, which way leads to him?

I clench my fists, my nails biting into my palm. There's no time to check both. No time for mistakes. My only hope is to trust my instincts.

I veer left, sprinting down the passage to a spiraling staircase. Without hesitation, I dart up the stairs, toward the heavens. My heartbeat trips and stumbles, hoping each step brings me closer to him.

Just keep the sun concealed a little longer. Please.

The stairs wind upward, seeming to twist endlessly around themselves. My legs ache with every step, but I refuse to slow down.

I can't slow down.

I'm almost there.

The air grows unbelievably colder the higher I climb, cooling the sweat beading on my forehead. My breaths are harsh and shallow, but I press on, ignoring the burning in my lungs.

Just a little farther.

I reach the top of the staircase, and my heart plummets at the sight before me.

A solid iron door. No handle. No lock. Just a smooth, impenetrable surface mocking my desperation.

"No…" I whisper, my fingers tracing the icy metal. "No. No. No."

I pound my fists against the door, pain shooting up my arms. "Codrin!" I scream his name until my throat burns, the sound swallowed by the thick stone walls.

He can't be gone. Not now. Not when I'm so damn close.

"Please." My voice cracks. "Please be alive."

Fighting back the tears building in my eyes, I force myself to think. I step back and look around. The corridor narrows into nothing but dark stone. There's nothing here. No guards. No noise. No signs of anyone who could stop me.

Which means they expect the door to be impenetrable.

Sealed off.

A final, cruel barrier between me and the man I love.

"Fuck this." My fingers curling tightly around the gem still clutched in my palm. "I'm not giving up."

I reach for the dagger I keep hidden in my boot. Without hesitation, I drive the blade into the thin gap between the iron door and its frame, twisting and wrenching until I hear a faint, metallic groan.

Come on. Come on.

I throw my weight against it, muscles straining, jaw locked tight. The blade quivers beneath the pressure, threatening to snap. My shoulder burns with every shove, and a jagged bolt of pain shoots through my arm as the edge bites into the tender flesh of my palm. Blood slicks the hilts, but I don't stop.

The door groans, slow and reluctant.

I force it to move. Inch by painful inch.

Every sliver of progress feels like a war won, but the resistance is brutal. The hinges screech like wounded beasts, and my hands are raw, trembling. My chest heaves with effort and desperation. He's just on the other side. I can feel him. I *have* to get to him.

I shove harder, a low, feral noise escaping my throat as I twist the dagger one final time and throw my shoulder into the frame.

The door shifts again.

Almost there.

I throw all my weight into the door and suddenly, the door jerks open, swinging inward with a low, grating moan. The force of it nearly sends me sprawling forward, but I catch myself just in time, bracing my shoulder against the stone wall.

Light. Blinding, searing light pours into the chamber beyond.

I squint against the brightness, the intensity of it so over-whelming I almost stagger back. But I steady myself, my breath catching as I take in the room before me.

It's a circular chamber of stone walls and one tall glassless window looking out to the sea. And in the center of it all…

My breath seizes. My mind struggles to process the scene before me. The iron shackles lie in a tangled heap on the cold floor, their heavy chains twisting like serpents. Scattered among them is Codrin's slayer mask, its iron surface scorched and blackened.

Ash.

It's everywhere.

Spread like a dark stain across the floor, mingling with the metal bindings. A gust of wind slips through window, salty and cold from the sea beyond, and it kicks ash into small spirals that dance across the stone like ghosts. It clings to the broken chains. To my boots. It's all that's left.

He's gone.

The gem slips from my fingers into the ashes. I drop to my knees, a strangled sob tearing free from my chest. My fingers plunge into the ash, sifting through the remnants of him. My heart fractures under the weight of the truth seeping into my soul.

He's dead because of them. Alaric and my father might have brought him here. But Talon and Athan were not here to save him. They all let him burn.

Even I've failed him. I should've pushed him out of my room the second he appeared last night. But I was too selfish to let him go. I should've known he would get caught. I should've known Alaric would not have let him live.

The thoughts twist through me, sharp and suffocating, like thorns wrapping around my heart. I can't get air in fast enough. My hands go numb. The world tilts, too bright and too dark all at once, like my body doesn't know how to hold itself together.

My body trembles as I stare at the pile of ashes before me.

Scorched remnants of cloth and the warped glint of a belt buckle lie half-buried in the dust of a cruel echo of what once was.

Codrin.

The man who protected me, loved me, fought for me…

Reduced to nothing but ash.

A screaming sob tears through my throat, raw and broken. It feels like my soul is shattering apart, each fragment burning in agony. But no matter how hard I scream; it doesn't ease the crushing weight.

I dig my fingers into the ashes, the grit cold and rough against my skin. My hands shake as I clutch Codrin's remains, crumbling through my fingers like sand, as if the world itself is mocking me.

Telling me I am too late.

Telling me I have failed.

"But you promised. You *promised* you wouldn't leave me."

My hands tremble as I stare down at the gray dust staining my skin. This was Codrin. His life, his strength, his love. *Gone.*

I press my fists to my chest, the ashes smudging my blouse as I clutch at my own heart, as if I can somehow force it to keep beating. The air feels thin, like I can't draw in enough to fill my lungs. I wheeze like I'm drowning on dry land.

The voice in my head purrs softly, its smooth venom comforting. *They took him from you. You gave everything, and they took him anyway.*

"Shut up," I whisper, my voice shredded. But the voice doesn't listen. It never does.

You were never meant to save him. You were meant to be broken.

The words sting. Because deep down, I know they're true. I have failed.

I lift his iron mask from the ashes, the one he wore while pretending to be something he wasn't. A shield against the world's cruelty. And now, it's nothing but a twisted, useless relic.

The blood from the cut on my palm drips over its surface, painting it with my grief. My nails bite into the metal's sharp edges, but I don't loosen my grip. Pain is the only thing keeping me from completely shattering as the darkness whispers to me, urging me to unleash it. To use it. To become something else. Something stronger.

The air thickens with the scent of salt and death. The sea breeze stirs the ashes across the stone floor, sweeping them toward the open window. As if the wind is trying to carry him away from me. Trying to erase what little remains of him.

"No..." My voice cracks, but the rage beneath it is fierce. "No, you don't get to take him from me."

I reach out, trying to gather the scattered ashes as if my hands could somehow put him back together. But the wind only laughs at me, scattering the fragments of him into the morning air.

He's gone. I'm alone. And there is nothing I can do now.

No one's here to hold me up. No one's here to help me put the pieces back together.

I feel the darkness curl her grasp tighter around my soul, wrapping itself around me like chains. But these chains… they don't feel like imprisonment.

They feel like power.

The voice murmurs again, the words cool and enticing. *Embrace it, dear. Let it consume you. You don't need anyone. You never have.*

The mask's sharp edges bite into my grip. A singular, burning purpose consumes my mind. They will all suffer. The ones who took him from me. The ones who stood by and did nothing. They will pay for their viciousness.

I rise to my feet, the mask's sharp edges bite into my grip as a single drop of blood slips free, falling to the ash covered floor. The chamber darkens around me as shadows stir in the corners of the tower, slithering across the walls. One shadow brushes lightly against my hand and I don't pull away from its cool, weightless touch. Instead, I let it comfort me as though I belong with it. As though it's been patiently waiting for me.

CHAPTER 32

Ravenna

I stumble through the passageway, barely registering the cold stone scraping against my palms and knees. The ash clinging to my hands, hair, and clothes mixes with the sweat and tears along my cheeks. It chills. Seeping into my skin like frostbite.

Because whatever warmth I had is gone. Hollowed out. Replaced with something sharp and frozen that coils in my chest and refuses to let go. And I don't want it to let go. I never want to let, whatever this is, go.

I can't feel my legs, but they keep moving, forcing me forward until I reach the narrow door hidden behind the tapestry. My fingers shake as I shove it open and stagger out into the throne room.

Voices filter through the air, casual, even cheerful. Their laughter strikes me like blades, slicing deeper with each passing second. The world tilts and sways, but I refuse to fall. I refuse to collapse in front of them. Not after what they've done.

"…the day has cleared up. Let's hope the gods will grant us the same sunshine tomorrow."

My father's sickeningly bright voice fills the room as if nothing at all is wrong.

The shadows crawl along the wall beside me as I round the corner, my fingers tightening around Codrin's mask. My boots drag along the marble, leaving blackened smudges on the pristine surface.

My father and Alaric stand in the middle of the throne room, their conversation light, pleasant like two old friends making plans. Chatting like they didn't just murder the man I love.

"Zephyr, you truly are generous," Alaric muses with that infuriatingly calm smile. "I imagine tomorrow's ceremony will be as grand as we've all hoped."

"Yes, yes," my father booms. "And with such good fortune today, the timing couldn't be more perfect."

A feral roar tears from my throat.

Both men turn, eyes widening as they take me in.

"Ravenna…" my father begins.

"This fucking wedding is off!" I scream, my voice raw and cracking. "You murdered him! You both murdered him!"

I can't imagine what I must look like to them. Coated in ash and possibly some smeared blood on my blouse from the cut on my palm. But I don't care. Let them see. Let them know what they've done.

Alaric's eyes scan me with detached curiosity, but my father looks utterly bewildered.

"What are you talking about, my dear?" Father's tone is a fake calm. "You've been running around all morning, haven't you? Perhaps some rest would do you well."

"I made a deal with him!" I point at Alaric, with Codrin's mask still tightly in my grasp, my voice trembling with fury. "He promised me Codrin's life in exchange for my compliance. You know this. You were there. But he lied. You both fucking lied!"

Alaric's lips curl in that infuriatingly smug smile. "You've been mistaken, princess. I did agree to spare him. But who's to say what accidents might occur when a man is kept in the dungeons? Tragic, really. Yet entirely out of my hands."

"Liar."

Alaric steps forward, his voice as smooth as silk. "It was your father's decision to move the timeline forward. Not mine. He is the king of this land, after all. I simply abided by his wishes."

My father arches a brow, feigning confusion. "Ravenna, you are being hysterical. We simply moved him to a more secure location, given his… condition."

"Learn to lie better than that, Father. You both will pay for what you've done." My voice shakes, but not from weakness. From the rage. From hatred so intense it leaves me trembling.

Alaric's smirk deepens. "Sometimes, only fire can strip away the lies and leave the truth behind."

"Fuck you," I growl through my teeth.

My father steps forward, his tone turning cold. "That's enough, Ravenna. You will go to your room and prepare for tomorrow's ceremony. You will marry King Alaric, and you will bring honor in uniting our kingdoms. Enough of this childish rebellion."

I spit at my father's feet. "Childish? You *murdered* him."

"Codrin was a killer and a traitor." Father twists the ruby ring on his finger, a silent reminder of what happens when I stray too far out of line. "He deserved his fate."

My fist clenches tighter around the mask, its iron biting into my palm. Blood drips from the cuts left by the mask.

They think I'm broken. They think I'll just obey, like a good little girl. Not anymore. I have nothing left to lose. They have taken everything from me.

The darkness churns within me, feeding off my fury. *She* whispers to me, urging me to give in.

But I hold her at bay.

Not here. Not yet.

Without another word, I spin on my heel and storm out of the throne room, leaving them both in my wake. Let them think they've won. Let them believe their lies. I'm done. I am done being their fucking pawn. Soon they will pay for what they have done. Soon they will see the monster they have created.

CHAPTER 33

Unknown

I remain cloaked within the shadows of the towering pillars, my gaze fixed on the princess as she emerges from behind the sunset tapestry. Her voice echoes, strained and sharp, through the grand expanse of the throne room. I remain in the dark, slipping further from view as she confronts the two kings.

When her fury erupts, I seize the moment. Moving with swift, calculated steps, I slip behind the tapestry. My fingers brush the cool stone as I ease the door open and press forward into the passageway.

The air grows colder, the silence thickening as I quicken my pace. Left, then up. Higher and higher until the strain in my legs becomes a familiar ache.

The distant roar of the sea's waves greets me, whispering against the cliffs below. It carries through the cracked door at the tower's summit. My hand rests on the worn iron, pushing it open just enough to slip inside.

Golden afternoon light spills through the gaping window, painting the floor with radiant patches. My steps are slow, deliberate. Eyes searching, drawing in the details of this infamous chamber.

In the center of the chamber, shackles lie tangled and half-buried in a pile of ashes. My chest tightens at the sight, but I do not falter.

A glint of light almost hidden in shadow catches my eye.

I kneel, my fingers reaching out to grasp the gem lying on the stone floor in the ash, its glow radiant in the sunlight. It's cool and smooth to the touch. I slip it into my pocket and rise to my feet.

With the same precision I entered, I shut the door behind me, turning the key in the lock, twisting until it clicks.

The room's true terrors remain locked away.

The key disappears into my pocket alongside the gem. I descend the stairs without hesitation, my steps sure, my purpose unbroken.

This time, I do not turn right toward the throne room. I keep straight, slipping through the shadows of the long corridor, my path leading me to the other side of the castle.

The secret now in my possession.

CHAPTER 34

Ravenna

Scalding, angry tears streak down my face. My body trembles as I stand in the doorway of my room. The damaged door was removed, its debris swept away, leaving no trace as to what occurred here late last night. Of course, Father would replace the door so quickly.

Ash and blood still clings to my skin, caked beneath my nails. Codrin's mask is cold and heavy in my grip, its edges biting into my palm. My body shifts, rage rising from my toes and up my spine. My nostrils flare as I breathe through my nose. If only it were that easy. To fix the true damage Father has done.

I step inside, closing the door behind me and I don't flinch as the shadows welcome me. Curling around the corners of the room like waiting arms, slithering along the ceiling, the walls. Familiar. Faithful. Watching.

Footsteps pound down the corridor. Fast. Urgent. The door bursts open, and he rushes in, breathless.

"Rave! I've been looking for you." Talon's steps slow, hesitant, as his eyes land on me, then on the blood, the soot, the mask clutched tight in my hand.

"Gods, Rave. What happened?" His voice cracks. "What are you covered in?" His face twists with confusion, with dread like I'm some ghastly creature risen from the depths of a nightmare.

Maybe I am, but I say nothing.

For a heartbeat, my gaze runs over his disheveled, blood-stained and clearly battered appearance. A part of me wants to throw my arms around him. To weep into my twin brother's chest.

But the other part of me… doesn't care that he's standing at all.

"Get away from me." My voice is low. Feral. Even I don't recognize it.

He steps forward. "Rave…"

"Where the fuck were you?!" I scream, hurling Codrin's mask at him with everything I have. It smashes into his chest and clatters to the floor.

He jumps back, stunned. "What the hells?"

He blinks, staring down at the mask where it lies on the floor. His brows furrow as he looks back up at me.

Does he see it? Does he see the madness in me? The rage. The suffering.

"Codrin is dead." Heat surges through me, boiling beneath the surface. "Burned to ash. And you," I stomp forward, snarling. "Where the fuck were you?"

Talon's body stiffens as he stares at me as though I slapped him. "No, that's not possible."

"Not possible?" A raw and broken laugh escapes my parted lips. "He's gone. While you were off doing fuck knows what."

Talon shakes his head. "Athan and I woke up and he was gone. We've been out looking for him. I assumed he'd come here…"

"Don't," I snap. "Don't you dare try to explain." I take a step back, wanting to get as far from him as possible. I can't look at him without nausea curling in my stomach.

I catch movement in the corner of my eye, and I can't help but grin with mischievous delight as thick shadows slide higher along the wall.

Talon's voice trembles through my thoughts. "What happened, Rave?"

My gaze lands back on him. "Why does it matter now? You're too late. I was too late." I feel a sharp pain stabbing my heart at the words; *I was too late.* "What, do you think you're still some great protector? Some noble hero?" I stalk toward him, head held high, voice dropping to a venomous whisper. "You're neither."

"That's not fair!" he fires back, fists clenched. "He made his choice. He came here knowing it was too dangerous. He knew…"

"Shut up!" I scream, lunging forward and slamming him into the wall before I even know I've moved. My hand locks around his throat. His body jolts. I squeeze.

I can feel my brother's pulse drumming against my palm. His face goes pale. His mouth opens but no words escape his lips.

"You left me," I growl in his ear. "You left *him*. You let him die. And you left me to mourn him."

He claws at my wrist. "Rave… this isn't… my fault…"

I slam him against the wall by his neck. "Isn't it?"

"Rave, please," his voice cuts off as I squeeze harder. My vision narrows until all I see is this pathetic, useless brother who failed me when I needed him most. The shadows throb behind me like a second heartbeat.

"They understand me," I whisper, eyes locked on his. "They've always understood me."

"What… what the fuck… are you talking about?" His face reddens, veins bulging at his temples as his lips lose color.

I squeeze harder. The shadows gather behind my back like wings, stretching wide and furious.

His mouth opens in a strangled, desperate whisper. "Your… eyes…"

"What of them?" My voice is cold steel.

"They're… crimson…"

For a moment, I pause.

"Good…" The word slips from my lips with satisfaction, my fingers refusing to release their hold.

The shadows ripple with approval. Their hiss is soft as satin. *At last,* they seem to say. *At last, you see.*

Talon stares at me, real horror in his eyes now. "You're not my sister," he whispers.

A slow, knowing, dangerous smile forms along my lips, and I release him. Talon crumples to the floor, coughing, clutching his throat.

I crouch before him, grabbing a handful of his tangled hair. He grits his teeth as I pull his head closer to me. "No," I murmur. "I'm not." I shove him away, his head almost hitting the stone wall.

Pushing off from my knees, I stand over him, my hands on my hips.

The last piece of who I was cracks, crumbles, turns to dust.

"You're just like the rest of them." I shake my head, revulsion curling in my gut.

Talon reaches out for me, hand shaking. "Rave, please…"

I roll my eyes in disgust and turn my back on him.

"Stop begging. It's pitiful. Even for you."

I stalk across the room and disappear into the washroom. The door slams behind me. Shutting out Talon, on the light, on everything that made me human.

The shadows stay with me.

They *always* stay.

CHAPTER 35
Alaric

The iron door groans beneath my grip, its rusty hinges protesting as I force it open. A sound of neglect, of ancient brutality, as I step inside.

Dim moonlight filters through the cell, slashing the chamber with ghostly shadows. And there, at the center of the room, the remains of my brother's defiance lie scattered. A pitiful offering to the darkness we once ruled.

I kneel, my fingers trailing through the ashes. Cold. Lifeless. Nothing left of him but dust and silence.

"Oh, little brother." The words spill from my lips, heavy with something dangerously close to nostalgia. "You were always so stubborn."

I lift a handful of his remains and squeeze, the brittle ash crumbling against my palm. A fitting end. He chose his path. Chose betrayal. And now all that's left of him clings to my skin like dust.

"It didn't have to end this way." The phrase is meaningless. A hollow thing I whisper to the dead. But amusement stirs in my chest, threatening to break into laughter. I release the ashes and watch as they sift through my fingers, caught in the moonlight like scattered stars.

I rise and cross the chamber to the open, gaping window. The sea rages below, waves crashing against the cliffs with the fury of the gods. The same cliffs that swallowed our enemies whole centuries ago. When mortals trembled at our feet, bowed to us, knowing our power was absolute.

But you, Codrin… you chose to be weak. You chose their world over ours.

"Fool," I whisper, shaking my head. The wind brushes my face as I extend my hand, releasing the last remnants of him into the night air. His ashes scatter, carried by the chill wind over the endless sea.

We fought side by side once. A brotherhood forged in blood and darkness. We ruled with unmatched strength. Unyielding. But as time wore on, you craved their acceptance. Their fragile, pathetic world. And in the end, that's what killed you.

I wipe my hand against my pants, the ash smearing across the fabric.

"But you got in the way, little brother." I straighten my shoulders, spine rigid and proud. "And now there's nothing left of you but dust."

CHAPTER 36
Unknown

The hood of my cloak conceals my face, my steps barely more than whispers against the cobblestone as I glide through the dimly lit alley toward the tavern's back entrance. I cast a cautious glance over my shoulder, eyes sharp for any sign of pursuit before gently pushing the door ajar and slipping inside unnoticed.

The cacophony of clattering dishes and frenzied shuffle of cooks and barmaids surrounds me, but none pay me any heed. They're too absorbed in their work to notice the shadow threading its way through their midst. Their ignorance serves me well.

I descend into the basement's shadowy depths, the air growing cooler, thick with the scent of damp stone and stale ale. In the farthest corner, outside the dancing light of the lone candle, a solitary figure waits, swathed in darkness.

I take a seat across from him, the weight of my mission pressing down on my chest. My hand slips into the folds of my cloak, producing a deep blue gem no larger than a half-dollar. I place it on the table between us.

"This should suffice for the task at hand," I say, my voice low and edged with urgency.

The shadowed figure reaches for the gem, his fingers pausing above it, reluctant to believe it's real. "Is this...?"

"Yes. An Eclipsis Gem." I make sure no tremor, no hint of doubt, sullies my voice. I need him to understand I'm not one to be trifled with.

He turns the gem over in his palm, a sparkle of greed mixed with disbelief in his eyes. "And here I thought such treasures were mere myth. How did you come by it?"

"That's not important. Our agreement is." I lean in, letting the shadows cling to me, using them to emphasize the seriousness of my demand.

"Agreed." He extends a hand, his palm rough and calloused as I clasp it, sealing the deal with a handshake.

I rise to leave, but not before delivering a final warning. "The wedding must not proceed."

"It won't."

I give a sharp nod and turn away, allowing the darkness to consume me once more. As I slip from the basement, the gem's absence feels like a burden lifted. Now, all that's left is to wait and hope the chaos I've set into motion will do the rest.

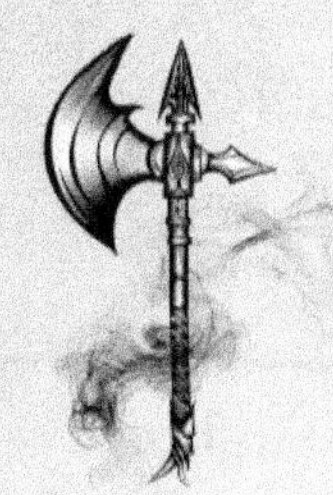

CHAPTER 37

Ravenna

I release a heavy sigh as a gentle knock sounds at my door. The newly replaced door is polished and perfect, like the destruction last night never happened. I settle by the crackling fire in the plush wingback chair, my back pressed against one arm, my legs dangling over the other. An open book lies forgotten on my lap, its pages untouched for the past hour as my mind wanders far beyond the printed words.

Hours ago, I fled supper, leaving behind the endless prattle of wedding preparations, the strained pleasures forced from my own lips. My father's enthusiasm grinds me like metal on stone. I slipped away, unseen and unheard, seeking refuge in the quiet solitude of my room. But even here, with the door shut tight and the fire's warmth licking at my skin, I find no peace.

The thought is a quiet whisper in the chaos of my mind, but it screams in my chest, an agonizing truth that tears at me. I agreed to marry him. I offered myself, sacrificed my freedom, my hope, my heart, to save Codrin. But he's gone now, taken in front of me.

The darkness that has lingered at the edges of my mind moves closer now, pulling me under with the force of a storm.

I can feel it, creeping through my veins, spreading like ink in water, staining everything. I thought if I could just save him. *If I could protect him one more time.* Maybe, just maybe, I could hold on to something good, something pure.

But there's nothing left to save.

I find no peace. Not in my thoughts, not in my heart, not in the world around me. It's all slipping away. And I'm sinking into the darkness that calls to me, promising relief in exchange for my soul.

Another knock comes, firmer this time.

"Enter." I exhale an annoyed breath.

The door creaks open, and Alaric steps into the room. His presence taints the air, stealing what little warmth I have left. I keep my eyes on the book, refusing to acknowledge him. Perhaps if I pretend hard enough, he'll simply vanish.

But he doesn't. Of course not.

Instead, he crosses the room with measured steps and stands before me, silent, waiting. I refuse to look at him. I refuse to give him that satisfaction. I turn a page of the book, the rustle of paper the only sound between us.

But the silence twists tighter with every breath, stifling, heavy like a noose tightening. He wants me to break. Wants me to squirm in my own skin.

"I thought it was bad luck to see the bride the night before the wedding," I say, sharp enough to cut.

"I don't know this superstition you speak of." His voice is

steady, like he's trying to play some bullshit, civilized game.

I let the minutes drag again before I finally lift my gaze from the book, meeting his golden eyes with all the defiance I can muster. "What do you want?"

"May I sit?" he asks, already moving toward the other chair.

"Sure. You can sit on the ledge." I gesture toward the open window, the night air chilling the room. "And jump."

His laugh is quiet, almost genuine. But nothing about him feels genuine. He sinks into the chair across from me instead.

Damn.

He leans back with a casualness that makes my skin crawl. "I would like to apologize."

I slam the book shut and interlace my fingers over the cover. "Do you even know how to do that?"

Whatever this apology is, it's a lie.

"I see my orders can only go so far in someone else's kingdom." His gaze drops.

"Your orders?" I spit the words at him. "To murder an innocent man? Or your way of getting some childish revenge on your own brother?"

His eyes flash back at me. "I would never harm my brother. Even if he was a troubled soul."

"Do vampires even have souls?" I snap.

He smirks. "I sometimes like to think we do. We are creatures of the night, but that does not make us monsters. Codrin—"

His jaw tightens, and his fangs flash.

"Don't speak his name." The words spit from my mouth before I can even think.

Alaric's expression softens, his gaze turning mournful, as though he's the one who lost something precious. "Forgive me, Princess. As I said, he was my brother. But he was troubled. He caused a lot of misfortune back in Veilstead, and I feel I should apologize to you for him. For bringing that here and placing his problems on you."

I almost laugh. The gall of him to sit here and pretend to be kind, to pretend he's apologizing for something that was his fault. "What misfortunes were those?" I glare at him, sitting up straighter.

"We fought together and watched the rise and fall of the Dark War."

"Yes, and your kind demolished four of our seven kingdoms. So, forgive me for not being sympathetic."

"True. But Codrin was a soldier like no other. Over the years, he became heartless, crazed for blood. Not just to feed but to spill from anyone who got in his way." Alaric's gaze drops as if the memory actually pains him. "Forty years ago, he mur-dered our father and planned to end Darius and me for the crown."

His words drop to the pit of my stomach, mixing with the building nausea. Codrin murdered his own father? I shake my head, refusing to believe it. "Just how old are you?" I ask, if only to keep myself from breaking. There are so many questions I want to ask but trying to find the words to form seems impossible. If Codrin was a soldier in the Dark War that would make him…

Alaric smiles, a ghostly curve of his lips. "I am twenty-seven."

I roll my eyes with an annoyed sigh. "In vampire years."

"I am seven hundred and fifty-eight."

I say nothing, my mind spinning with thoughts I can't pin down. Codrin kept so much from me. Lied to me about what he was. What else did he hide?

"I never planned to send my brother to his death." Alaric's voice is soft, almost gentle. "That was not my intention. I tried to stop your father's orders. I wanted to bring him home and deal with matters my way, in hopes that he would change."

I fold my arms over my chest. "What do you mean?"

"I would have thought that after forty years, he would have turned his life around. But he didn't. Not from what I saw last night." Alaric's eyes bore into mine, full of concern and sympathy. "He was still playing his little mind games."

"What are you talking about?"

"He was not who you thought he was, Princess. He kept many secrets from you. He used you to get what he wanted. As he has always done in the past." He rises from the chair and kneels before me, reaching for my hand. I flinch but don't pull away.

"I only speak the truth," he continues, his voice shaking. "You stole my heart the day we first met. And when Codrin discovered this, he was willing to do anything to take you away from me. He has done it before."

My skin prickles. "Done it before?" And wouldn't it be Alaric who was trying to steal me from Codrin? Codrin and I had something. Didn't we? Or was that all a lie? My mind is spinning with question after question. Who can I trust? This King of Darkness who kneels before me, telling me things I can't be sure are true or not?

"I was once in love, long ago. She was my everything. But Codrin had a way with words, and she blindly walked into his arms. Then… he killed her." His shoulders drop on a shaky breath, like he actually feels something. "He took everything from me that day. My world crumbled around me. I promised myself I would never love again."

He looks at me then, his gaze so raw, so open, that my chest tightens despite everything I know.

"Until I met you."

I clamp my teeth down, the firelight skittering in my clenched fists. Lies. It *has to be* lies. Codrin wouldn't.

But my thoughts fracture.

The words *Codrin wouldn't* seems to have turned into un-raveled lies he has hidden from me for so long. He lied about being a vampire. Lied by omission, at least. He killed a guard.

What else did he bury? What else did he decide I don't need to know?

Alaric's words dig under my skin like splinters, sharp and persistent. He's told me things Codrin never dared. Too many details to dismiss. Too much conviction in his voice.

I can't breathe. I don't know who to believe. I don't know if there's anyone left to trust. I feel like I'm drowning, my thoughts pulling me under, tugging me in opposite directions until I can't tell up from down.

Still, I move. A hollow version of myself reaches out, my hand brushing away the tear on Alaric's cheek.

"You will not lose me," I whisper, the words tasting foreign in my mouth.

I'm not sure who I'm lying too anymore. Him or myself.

Because maybe… I don't know the truth at all.

CHAPTER 38

Ravenna

The following morning, the entire castle pulses with frantic energy. Servants hustle through the main corridors and dining hall, arranging flowers and sweeping away the traces of dust that dare to cling to the polished stone. Fresh linens and towels are carried to guestrooms, cooks scurry about the kitchen chopping, stirring, kneading as they prepare for a wedding feast fit for a goddess.

Father is somewhere on the grounds, overseeing the grooming of white horses for the bridal carriage, throwing orders like a king at war. Guards and servants alike are dressed to perfection. Even the slayers' uniforms are spotless.

Mother finally emerges from her rooms, where she stayed hidden away during all the *unpleasantness* as Father put it, relief over her son's safe return overwhelming her. She wanders the halls with noble guests, who swirl glasses of wine and giggle over pleasantries. Laughter clashes with the madness bubbling beneath my skin.

Madam Adelaide shoos away anyone who tries to enter my room, her voice like the sharp crack of a whip. "The bride needs quiet to prepare for her big day."

Bride. I want to fucking hurl.

I try to protest more than once, even try to look to Colette for help, only for her to bow her head, avoiding my pleading stare.

Madam Adelaide's determination overpowers my frustration. "You will see them and your brother at the Siren's Song," she insists, her expression unreadable.

At this point, I don't care if I see Talon or not.

I haven't seen him all morning. I asked one of the servants to find him, hours ago, but he has yet to show up. I think at this point, he is truly avoiding me at all costs after yesterday.

Just proving my point.

I grind my teeth as I let Madam Adelaide drag me to the vanity and I sit down with a huff.

"Colette, finish getting her ready. I am needed downstairs. I will be back shortly." She steps out of the room as Colette steps up behind me and starts pinning my hair, strand by strand. I watch her work in the new mirror's glassy surface, my own reflection hollow and distant.

"I cannot believe this day has finally come, child." Colette sniffles, dabbing the corner of her eye with a cloth.

I manage a tight smile, one that doesn't reach my eyes. My thoughts drift to Alaric's visit last night, the way his voice seized my mind, planting seeds of doubt and betrayal. Was I wrong for thinking him a monster? Was Codrin the true deceiver?

Alaric spilled so much, answered every question I asked. Codrin?

He had all that time to tell me the truth. To show me who he truly was. But he never did.

I force my gaze away from the mirror, unwilling to let the sadness seep into me any longer. What does it matter now? Everything that once made sense has been ripped away, leaving only emptiness in its place.

Colette's fingers tug at the last strands of my hair, pinning them into place with careful precision. She steps back, her eyes bright with pride. I get to my feet and make my way over to the full-length mirrors that have taken over the middle of my room.

"Well, you sure do know how to make a statement, child." Her eyes gliding up and down my dress.

Yesterday, during my fitting, I ordered the seamstress to throw the white fabrics into the fire. When she hesitated, I grabbed the fabric from her arms and threw it into the flames myself.

No white. No innocence.

The mirrors encircle me as I step closer. My eyes fixed on the multiple reflections of myself as I turn from side to side, the fabrics of the skirts swirling like shadows.

What I wear now suits the darkness that has settled within me. Good. Let them see what they've done to me.

"You did great. Thank you, Colette," I say, turning my attention back to her.

She gives me a heartwarming smile as she takes my hand in hers. "You look beautiful, child." She pats my hand softly as she lets out a deep breath. "I'm going to run to the kitchen and get something to eat. Do you need me to bring you back anything, my dear?"

"No. I'm good."

The side of her lip curls up. "Mmhmm. I'll bring you back a glass of wine."

Not waiting for me to argue, she scurries from the room, the heavy door creaking behind her, sealing me in silence.

I take another look at the mirror, my eyes gliding up and down my reflection.

My heart suddenly drops to my stomach.

So, this is it.

The mirrors reflect a stranger. Painted. Perfect. Poisoned.

I can't remember the last time I saw myself and didn't feel like I was fading. Maybe I was never meant to survive this place. Not the way they wanted me to. They've dressed me up in darkness and called it destiny. And no one's coming to stop it.

I press my fingertips to the glass, but the girl on the other side doesn't move.

Then the reflection lifts a hand and presses its palm to the glass. "I'm here for you."

I press my palm against it.

Its fingers curl through mine, warm and solid. Too real. The gentle touch soothes my nerves like safety disguised as shadow.

"I will never let you go," it whispers.

I meet its crimson eyes.

My head snaps toward the bedroom door as it slowly opens and Athan slips in, quickly closing the door behind him.

He leans his back against the door, eyes closed, his chest rising and falling like he's been running. His hair is disheveled, his clothes bloodied, his brow glistening with sweat. A fresh cut of dry blood runs down his cheekbone.

He opens his eyes, a tight smile forming as they land on me. "Hi, sweetie."

He pushes off the door and walks toward me.

My hand drops to my side. "What are you doing here?" I don't take my eyes off Athan as I speak, my gaze sharpening to glass.

He shouldn't be here. He is just as much of a wanted man as Codrin was.

"I'm here to get you out. We don't have much time. There's a carriage outside of town, waiting for us."

He reaches for my hand, but I withdraw.

Where was he when it counted? When Codrin was burning?

"I'm not leaving." Fury breathes beneath my skin. "What are you doing here?"

I take a step toward him; he takes a step back.

"I'm here to save you," his shoulders dropping, his mouth ajar. "I tried to avenge Codrin. But I'm sorry I was unsuccessful."

"Silence!" My voice slices the air like the sharpest of blades. Final. Unyielding.

He obeys. Athan's lips snap shut. His throat works as he swallows, eyes searching, for what? The woman he once knew. His friend. The girl who stood beside him on countless patrols. Who had his back as much as he had hers.

But that girl is gone. She burned with Codrin.

"Did you think you could barge in here, beg for some sort of forgiveness, and think I would run with *you*?" I take another step forward, my fists clenched at my sides. "I don't need you to *avenge* Codrin's death. I needed you; he needed you *before* his death. Now you want to *save me*? For what? So, you can feel better about yourself?"

"I'm not—"

"I said silence!" My voice cracks like thunder, reverberating up the walls.

He doesn't flinch; he plants his feet like a warrior bracing for the storm.

He leans in, close enough that I can smell the sweat and leather. "You can shout all you want, sweetie. I'm still here."

"Then where were you that night? When I needed you most?" I advance on him like a predator stalking prey, but he doesn't back down.

"I'm always here." He says it like a truth. Like a vow. But it rings hollow in the space between us.

"No. You failed." I close the space between us, shoving a finger into his chest. "You failed *me*. You failed *him*."

"I know." His jaw tightens just slightly, the only crack in his composure. "I'm trying to fix that."

I let out a strangled laugh. "Fix it?" The heat of fury rises, threatening to consume me whole. "He's *dead*, Athan. Burned to ashes. And you think you can fix it with empty words and pointless apologies?"

"I'm not here to apologize," he replies, his tone softening, a gentleness in his eyes that makes my skin crawl. "I'm here because you shouldn't have to survive this alone."

I bare my teeth, hands flexing into claws at my sides. "You think your presence is some kind of gift? You think standing there like a statue makes up for the silence? For the *abandonment*?"

Athan looks away, his shoulders tight. "We had to leave, but it was to also protect you."

"No," I snarl. "You ran. You hid. All while he burned."

He opens his mouth. Closes it again as his eyes shift over my shoulder, his muscles tense. "Sweetie, you're not the only one hurting." He looks back at me, but I catch him take another quick glance over my shoulder. "I'm here now, and we need to leave… right now." His voice shakes as he shifts his stance, his eyes now locked over my shoulder with concern.

I lean into him and whisper with a snicker, "Still trying to make yourself the hero in a story where you did nothing."

I know what he sees. I can feel them. My true protectors. My shadows.

The muscle in his jaw twitches but he says nothing.

I shove him, palms crashing against his chest. He doesn't move. Doesn't fight back. Just takes it, eyes shining with something I don't want to see.

Pity.

I want to scream. To tear something apart. But instead, I just breathe. Rage tastes like blood in the back of my throat.

"You failed me for the last time. Whatever friendship we had has died with him. Now get out."

"Sweetie, please. Let me explain."

"I said. Get. *Out.*"

His shoulders slump, his eyes filling with a sorrow that makes me want to tear him apart. But he nods, his gaze falling to the floor as he turns and walks toward the door.

Just as his hand reaches for the handle, he pauses, his voice barely a whisper. "If you ever need me, I'm right here."

The door clicks shut behind him, and I am alone again.

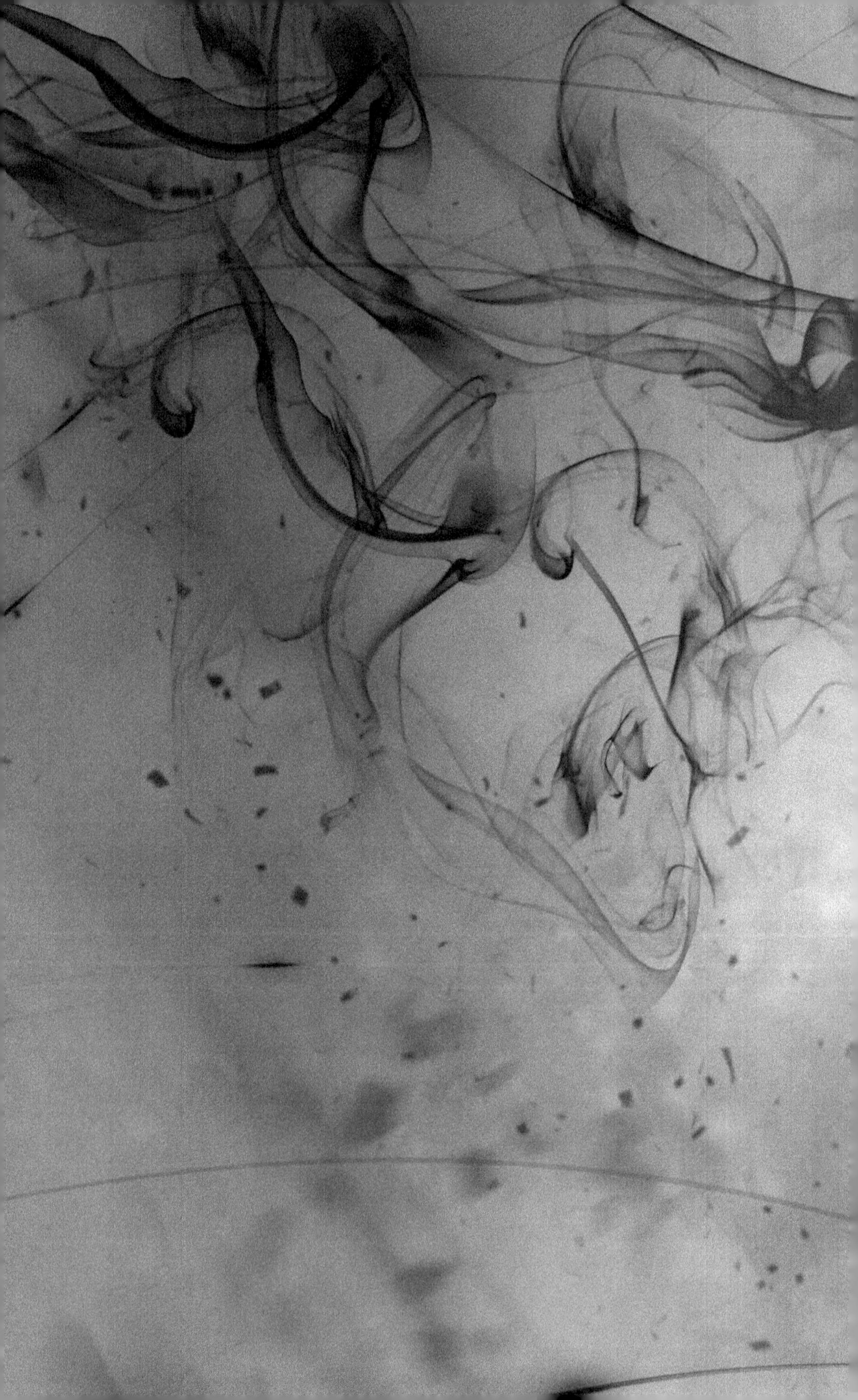

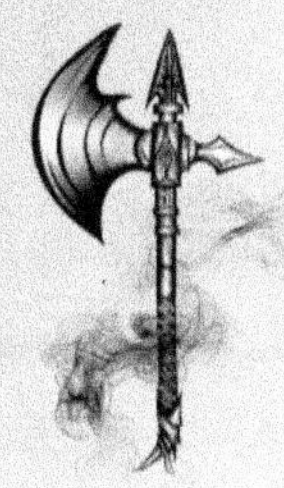

CHAPTER 39

Ravenna

The weight of my skirts drags with every step, each one echoing with a hollow thud through my chest. The Siren's Song rises from the pale stone like a grave monument, its massive doors ahead stretching high above like the maw of a beast waiting to swallow me whole.

The streets are eerily silent. The townspeople have already crammed themselves into the building to witness the wedding of their princess's glorious union to the King of Darkness.

As if any part of this could be called glorious.

The afternoon sun beats down with relentless intensity, painting the sky a vivid, mocking blue. I clutch my skirts in both hands, the tulle and lace streaming behind me like a trail of ink bleeding across the ground.

Two of Theiahold's guards stand outside the closed, towering wooden doors. Their eyes meet mine; uneasiness flickers across their faces before they bow their heads and step aside.

I have come to the realization that I am alone in all this. Athan and Talon have proved to me that I can and will never count on them. Codrin is dead and with it all the unanswered questions of lies he has left me. I have no one at my side but myself. My future is before me now and with it is the King of

Veilstead and soon I will wear the crown to its kingdom.

They want a queen? Then I will give them one.

I smooth the layers of my dress, forcing myself to take slow, measured breaths. My shoulders roll back, my chin lifts, and the icy composure I've built over the past few hours settles over me.

The guards seize the oversized iron rings of the doors and haul them open, their muscles straining with the effort. The wood groans and creaks, the sound grating on my nerves.

All conversation within the hall ceases. A suffocating silence blankets the room, followed by the soft rush of gasps and hushed whispers. Every pair of eyes turns toward me, their gazes like needles piercing my skin.

I stand framed in the doorway, the sunlight at my back painting me as a shadow against the blinding glow.

What they see is not what they expected.

"What is she wearing?"

"Is that… black?"

"She looks like death itself."

Or vengeance, I want to say. Because that's all that keeps me standing. The need to make them all pay.

I walk forward, each step precise and deliberate. The delicate black beading along the bodice of my strapless midnight-black dress catches the light like shards of glass. Deep burgundy threads weave through the fabric, swirling around my waist and hips like tendrils of blood. My train ripples out behind me, black and scarlet, pooling across the floor like shadows crawling toward their prey. The lace drapes loosely off my shoulders, whispering softly on my skin.

The spiked black tiara atop my head glitters with black diamonds, its dark brilliance ringing with the fury locked within me. Black liner outlines my icy blue eyes, making them burn brighter. My deep red lips curve into a smile that feels more like a snarl.

They wanted a blushing bride. Instead, I have become their nightmare.

At the end of the lengthy aisle stands Alaric, draped in a long black velvet and silk jacket that fits him like a second skin. His golden eyes beam, his smile wide and sickeningly charming. The very picture of darkness and allure. And beneath it all, a monster.

Talon, my mother, and my father stand to the side. Mother's face is pale, her eyes darting about, ready to faint at any moment and I know it's all because of my dress. Father's expression twists between rage and something like fear. Unable to speak his mind, I grin with delight to the sight of his hands clasped so tightly together that his knuckles are white.

Let him be horrified. Let him regret everything he's ever done.

Talon's gaze follows me, his shoulders hunched as if he's bracing for a blow. His sorrowful eyes make me want to laugh. He looks broken. And all it took was one moment of me to losing control to shatter him.

The doors groan shut behind me, sealing me in with these vultures. I force myself to walk, my boots clumping against the polished stone. That's right. Boots. Fuck wearing heels.

The whispers grow louder, like insects buzzing in my ears.

"Is this her wedding dress?"

"Who would wear something so vile?"

"She looks like she belongs at a funeral."

"I actually really like it."

I keep my head high; my eyes locked on Alaric. I won't give them the satisfaction of seeing my weakness. I won't show them my pain.

Alaric's smile widens as I approach. He holds out a hand, his eyes flaming with twisted delight. I place my hand in his, letting him help me up the four small steps to stand beside him.

He leans in, his breath brushing against my ear. "You could terrify the darkness itself in that dress."

I bare my teeth in a smile. "I am the darkness."

Alaric's eyes spark with something that almost looks like admiration. Or hunger. His grip tightens around my hand as we face each other.

"We are gathered here, on this glorious day…" the priest says, his voice reverent and thick with practiced authority. "The gods and goddesses have blessed our princess with love…"

Love. The word is an insult. A lie. It makes me want to vomit.

The priest drones on, his words blending into a haze of platitudes and promises I refuse to accept. My hand is bound to Alaric's by a red velvet ribbon.

"May their everlasting love never break."

Everlasting love. What a joke.

The priest's final words snap me back to reality. "You may kiss your bride, Your Majesty."

Alaric leans in, his lips nearing mine. I refuse to flinch. Refuse to show him the hatred boiling just beneath the surface. My eyes close, bracing myself for his touch.

But before his lips can meet mine, a thunderous crash tears through the hall.

The towering doors explode open, wood slamming against stone wall with a thunderous crack that shakes the hall.

A voice rips through the air, raw and wild and full of fire.

"ALARIIIC!"

CHAPTER 40

Ravenna

A feral growl rips from Alaric's throat, his golden eyes darkening as he shifts his attention to the silhouette backlit by the midday sun. A sword glints in the intruder's hand, the blade pointed directly at Alaric.

"Miss me, *brother*?!" the man shouts.

Gasps erupt around me. My heart soars to my throat, slamming into my ribs so hard I nearly stagger.

No. It can't be.

Can it?

Alaric storms toward my father, his movements swift and savage as he seizes my father by the throat.

"Do you take me for some kind of fool, Zephyr?" Alaric bares his fangs as he shakes my father like a ragdoll. Guards surge forward, their shouts drowned by the crowd's mounting panic.

I stand motionless on the dais, my gaze whipping between Codrin's silhouette and my father's contorted face. Talon's voice cuts through the madness as he struggles to push past the frenzied guards, their bodies pressing him and our mother farther away.

"O-of course not," Father stammers, his eyes wide, his face reddening.

"Is this why you wanted your men to help escort him?" His grip tightens, his growl deepening into something monstrous. "So, you could go behind my back and betray me?"

"Of course not." Father repeats as he claws at Alaric's wrists. "You… saw the ashes. He… was dead."

"Maybe you need a refresher as to what death should look like."

Alaric's roar reverberates through the air as his hands clamp down harder. Father's face turns a hideous shade of purple, his eyes bulging, his mouth open and gasping for air. Talon lunges forward, but he's too late.

The crack echoes through the hall, sharp and wet like a branch snapping underfoot but far more final.

The world goes silent.

Father's body crumples to the floor, a lifeless heap. His eyes unblinking and hollow staring through me.

The hall erupts with screams. Panic consumes the crowd as townspeople climb over one another, their terror driving them toward the exit like a stampede of cattle.

Mother shrieks, a high-pitched wail of grief as she collapses to her knees, clutching Father's body to her chest. Sobs rack her form, the sharp, shrill sound of her heartbreak slicing through the uproar.

Talon drags her back to her feet, shoving her into the arms of a guard. "Get her out of here!" he yells.

As the guard ushers Mother away, Alaric's monstrous guards ambush the crowd. Talon draws his sword, his eyes wild as he charges into the mayhem. His ashenbane iron blade clashes against steel, deflecting a strike from one of Alaric's guards before spinning to meet another attacker head-on.

"Ravenna!" Talon shouts. "Get out of here!"

But I can't move. I'm rooted to the dais, frozen as I stare down at our father's corpse. His sightless eyes fixate on me, the horror etched into his face a grotesque mask.

I wait for grief. For rage. For something that feels like loss. But there's nothing. Just the cold creeping through my chest, a chill so deep it leaves frost in my veins.

I should feel something. Anything. But my heart is a locked box, and the key was burned with Codrin.

A smirk curls the corner of my bloodred lips, a hint of cruel amusement whispering through me.

"Good riddance, old man."

I turn from his body, the chaos of the hall stretching before me like a living thing. Fear thickens the air, sweet and intoxicating.

I raise my arms high, breathing it in, letting it settle in my lungs like smoke. Shadows spread along the ceiling, slithering down the walls, answering my breath. The icy pleasure of vengeance coils through me like silk and steel.

I want more.

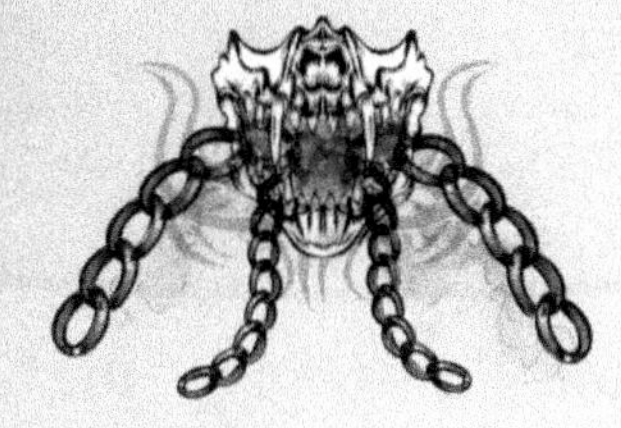

CHAPTER 41
Codrin

I wade through the sea of terrified guests, their screams and panic crashing against me like waves. I shove past them, my shoulders battering against frantic bodies, only to be shoved back as they flee. The press of them is maddening, their fear thick and suffocating. I've only made it a quarter of the way up the aisle. Not nearly close enough.

"Will you just stay fucking dead?" Alaric's eyes blaze as he points a finger at me. "Guards! Kill him!"

More of Alaric's monstrous guards emerge, their swords glimmering under the pale light. Their movements are mechanical, ruthless. And they're all coming for me.

A familiar voice booms from somewhere to my left.

Athan stands atop a bench, hammer raised high, a wild grin on his face and fire in his eyes.

"IT'S TIME TO DANCE, BOYS!"

Slayers, Theiahold guards, and townspeople let out a rattling roar as they all surge forward, pouring into the fray like a flood breaking free from a dam. Blades clash with bone-rattling ferocity, metal shrieking as it meets metal.

The air thickens with blood, sweat, and the screams of dying men.

One of the townsmen wielding an axe, slashes clean through a Veilstead guard's stomach. The weak point in the armor splits like paper, and the guard's insides spill to the ground as his body crumples.

Talon's silver blade beams as he rushes to Athan's side, blocking a sword that nearly takes off Athan's head. They move as one, standing back-to-back with their weapons held ready. Their legs brace wide, knees bent, as two hybrid guards charge at them.

I keep moving, keep forcing my way through the tangle of bodies. I have to get to her. She's only feet away, up on the dais. My gaze locks on her, but the crowd surges between us, blocking my view.

"Ravenna!" I shout, the roar of battle swallowing her name.

A sudden wave of dizziness slams into me, hot and blinding. The world blurs, and my vision narrows to pinpricks of light. My fingers tingle, heat swimming through them like fire.

What the fuck?

I grit my teeth, shaking my head to clear the haze. I can't lose focus now. Not when I'm this close. My knuckles whiten as I tighten my grip around the hilt of my sword.

A monstrous guard steps into my path, his eyes glowing red beneath his helmet. He's a mountain of muscle and steel, his blade swinging toward me with brutal speed.

I duck beneath the blow, my sword flashing as I drive it deep into his side. His roar echoes around me, the sound rattling my bones. I twist the blade and yank it free, blood spraying hot and thick across my face.

Another guard charges with his blade raised high, only to be cut down by Talon. He moves with a savage precision I've never seen before, his sword cleaving clean through the guard's neck. Blood fans across Talon's face in a red crescent as the body falls forward, its head rolling to his feet.

He stumbles slightly, but steadies himself, eyes wild and frantic. But he clenches his jaw, plants his feet, and tightens his grip on the blood-slick hilt before surging toward the next guard.

I lunge forward, shoving aside bodies and dodging strikes, my blade carving a path through the chaos. Blood spatters, iron screams, and the air thrums with the frenzy of war. I'm closer now. I can see her. Standing beneath the crumbling arch. She looks like a queen carved from ice, fierce, untouchable, and terrifyingly still.

But the distance between us feels insurmountable.

Not just the gauntlet of guards and flying iron and steel. Not just the broken bodies between us. It's something deeper. Heavier. A chasm gouged wide by grief, by betrayal, by the monstrous choices we've both made.

Her eyes find mine across the madness. For a split second, everything slows. I see the girl I once knew. The one who laughed in the wind, who pressed her forehead to mine and whispered promises in the dark. But that girl is vanishing. Slowly slipping away like smoke.

There's something cold in her now. Something vast and unrelenting. I feel it like frost on my skin, creeping in through every crack in me.

Then I catch movement. Not from her. From behind her.

The shadows on the wall. They're wrong. Slithering down like ink spilled across stone, thick and deliberate, stretching toward the floor as if drawn to her. Just like I saw the other night.

It's like they're feeding off her. Or answering her.

I don't know which.

And still, I run toward her, desperate to hold on to whatever's left before it disappears entirely.

But Alaric's guards keep coming. And so does the darkness.

CHAPTER 42

Ravenna

nce again, he lied to you, the voice whispers in my ear.

Codrin cuts his way through the chaos, his sword flashing with ruthless precision. Blood splatters across his chest and arms. His movements are powerful, frantic, and fueled by something darker than fear.

Why is he here? How is he here? He was dead. I saw the ashes. I held the ashes of what was him in my hands. I held his scorched mask in my hands.

Yet there he is, fighting his way toward me. Something sharp and disorienting lurches inside me, like the floor has tilted beneath my feet.

The crowd writhes like a living, breathing creature, clawing at him, fighting against him. And still, he pushes forward, cutting down any who stand in his way. Determination burns in his eyes, their silver glint cutting through the madness. For a moment, my chest tightens. He is fighting his way to me.

You think he's here to save you? the voice taunts, a cruel laugh rippling through my mind. *You are nothing but a pawn to him. A means to an end.*

Icy tendrils of doubt wrap around my heart, squeezing it tight. Codrin's words of love, of devotion echoes in my mind.

Were any of them real? Or just another lie spun to keep me beneath him?

He hid from you. He lied to you. You never truly knew him. The voice slithers deeper. *You loved him. And he betrayed you. Even now, he would use you for his own gain.*

I blink, fists curling tight. Rage pulses through me like molten fire, searing away the ache threatening to surface. He is between the man I loved and the stranger who kept so much hidden.

"Lies," I breathe. The word spits from my lips, like a rotten apple. "All of it."

I barely register Ulric until he lunges into Codrin's path. Their swords clash with brutal, bone-jarring force, and my lungs seize at the sheer force of it.

He fights so fiercely. But is it truly for me? Or just for himself?

My mind fractures under the weight of doubt. I want to believe in him. I want to run to him, to feel his arms around me, to bury myself in the familiar scent of him.

But the darkness curls tighter.

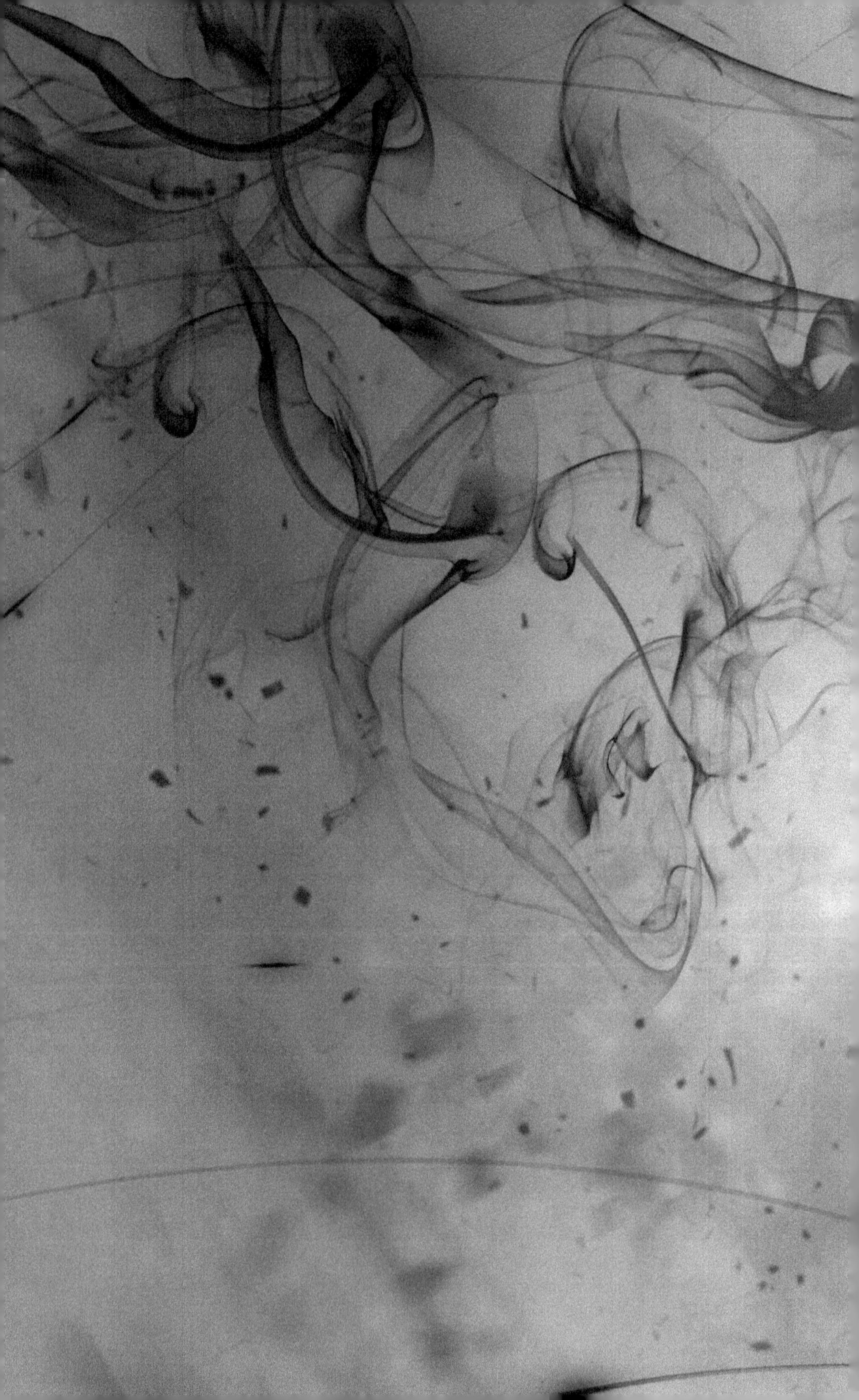

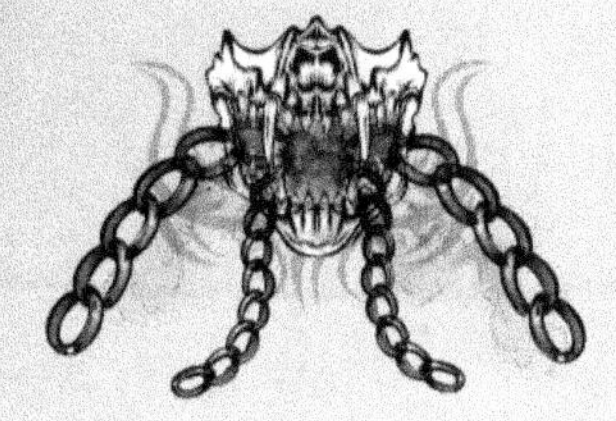

CHAPTER 43
Codrin

"**I** am really going to enjoy killing you myself, *monster*." Ulric's words drip with spite, his sword twirling in his hand, an extension of his rage.

His eyes burn dark and unrelenting. This isn't duty. This is personal. And I can't say I blame him. Not when I've made an enemy of everyone in this room. They trusted me with their lives, and I lied to them about my true identity, my true nature, and killed one of their own.

"I don't want to fight you, Ulric." I drop into a fighting stance anyway, legs bracing beneath me as I circle him. He dances back and forth, his steps quick and lethal.

Every movement dares me to misstep.

Every breath slinks like a warning waiting to strike.

"You're going soft now?" Ulric's lip curls in a sneer, his fingers tightening around his sword. "I will never understand how you became captain. You never deserved the rank, you weak bastard."

His insult pierces deeper than it should. Once, we fought side by side. Trained together. Bled together. And now, he's here to end me. His voice carries the kind of bitterness that burns slow, like uncured firewood.

"You can keep the rank, Ulric. Just know you'll die with it." I keep my gaze locked on him, every muscle tensed, ready to spring.

A spark of doubt crosses his face. I see it, just for a heartbeat. But then it's gone, replaced by blind, unrelenting fury.

Ulric charges, his roar splitting the air like a beast uncaged. His sword comes down with brutal force, the blade aimed to cleave my head from my shoulders.

I block the strike just in time, the clash of iron against steel reverberating through my bones. The impact jars my arm, my fingers stinging from the force. I push back, driving him away, my boots scraping against the blood-streaked floor.

But he recovers quickly, his rage propelling him forward like a battering ram. Again, he lunges. Again, I evade, my body twisting out of his reach. I spin on my heel, my sword cutting through the air as I pivot to face him.

"You should have stayed dead, Codrin." His breath comes in sharp, ragged bursts. "This kingdom would be better off without you."

"Maybe so." The words spill from me before I can stop them, but I refuse to let the truth of them sink in. Not now. Not when Ravenna's life depends on me. Not when her name beats in my chest like a second heartbeat.

Ulric's hatred is a living thing, a beast that drives his every movement. His strikes grow wilder, sloppier, as his anger twists his focus. I know his style. His weaknesses. His arrogance.

He thinks this fight is already won. That I am the same man who once held loyalty to the kingdom above all else. That I am the same man who once called him brother.

But I am not that man. Not anymore.

I am a shadow crawling through the darkness. A storm waiting to break.

I am death itself, and I will cut through anyone who stands between me and Ravenna.

Ulric lunges again, his sword aimed for my throat. I deflect the blow, twisting my wrist just enough to send his blade skittering to the side. His eyes widen, his snarl faltering. I strike, my blade slicing through his arm, blood spraying across the floor.

He staggers, clutching at the wound with a choked gasp. But he doesn't back down. Even as his blood stains his shirt, he readies himself for another strike.

"I will not die by your hand, you filthy creature." The pain trembles from his lips, but there's steel there, buried deep.

"You're already dead. You just don't know it yet."

He dives, but I'm faster. My sword cuts through the air with brutal precision, slicing across his chest. Blood pours from the wound, and he collapses to his knees, his sword slipping from his grasp.

The fire in his eyes flickers. Falters. Dies.

I leave him there, gasping for breath, his blood pooling beneath him. There's no time to linger. No time to grieve what's been lost.

Ravenna is all that matters now.

CHAPTER 44

Ravenna

I watch with bated breath as Codrin's blade slices through the air, a deadly arc that meets Ulric's with a clash fierce enough to split the sky. Codrin moves like a shadow come to life, fluid and relentless, every motion carved from fury. His silver-moon eyes burn with the need to reach me, to rip me from the chains of this nightmare.

The air thickens with the metallic tang of blood and the sharp cries of dying men. Screams wrap around me like serpents, but my eyes never leave him. Every heartbeat, every breath is measured against his brutal dance of survival.

But a blur of motion catches my eye from the left. I drag my gaze away from Codrin to find Alaric kicking the body of the same guard who had told me the way to the East Tower. The young guard's body crumples to the floor, limp and lifeless, a crimson pool spreading beneath him like ink spilled across parchment.

My stomach twists, my throat tightening as I turn my head away, forcing my eyes back to Codrin still fighting Ulric. Their blades colliding with a viciousness that borders on madness.

The voice's words seep into my mind, it's venom seeping into an open wound.

He managed to escape that tower, leaving you none the wiser. The voice crawls through me like a living thing, barbed and merciless. *Leaving you to suffer alone. Abandoned. Forsaken.*

"But he wouldn't leave me."

He is a prince. A prince! You two could've been together. But he chose to keep that from you. He chose to keep so much from you.

The thought claws at my insides, tearing through muscle and bone until all that's left is a hollow, gaping void.

"But he's here now," I whisper, not truly believing the words myself.

The voice cackles. *Oh, sweet, sweet princess. Do you truly believe he is here for you? He's only here for himself. He saved himself. He left you behind. He let you wallow in pain, believing he was dead.*

"But he—"

My words die as a cold but comforting shadow brushes along my hand.

He did this all for himself and you are nothing more than a worthless pawn in everyone's way.

"No, I'm not." I choke back a breath.

Then show them. Show them all who you truly are. The voice purrs with satisfaction, curling deeper into me like a spiteful lullaby.

My fingers tremble, nails biting into my palms as the words echo like a curse. A relentless drumbeat that splinters my mind.

Release.

Every moment of agony, every drop of blood spilled, it all comes crashing down in a wave of fury so violent it steals my breath. Darkness curls tighter around me, choking, suffocating, until the air itself feels like poison.

Release.

Pain lances through me, ripping at my sides as though claws are tearing me apart from within. My body spasms, doubling over as I clutch my stomach. My breaths come shallow, sharp, but the pain only stirs the rage boiling beneath the surface.

And then, there's nothing but fire.

It pulses through my veins like molten lava, scorching away doubt, fear and everything else. It roars through my blood until there's nothing left but the need to destroy.

The scream that leaves my throat isn't mine. It's something ancient. Something broken. And it echoes like the crack of a world splitting open.

The red fog swallows me whole.

It devours my pain.

My sorrow.

My hope.

All that remains is… nothingness.

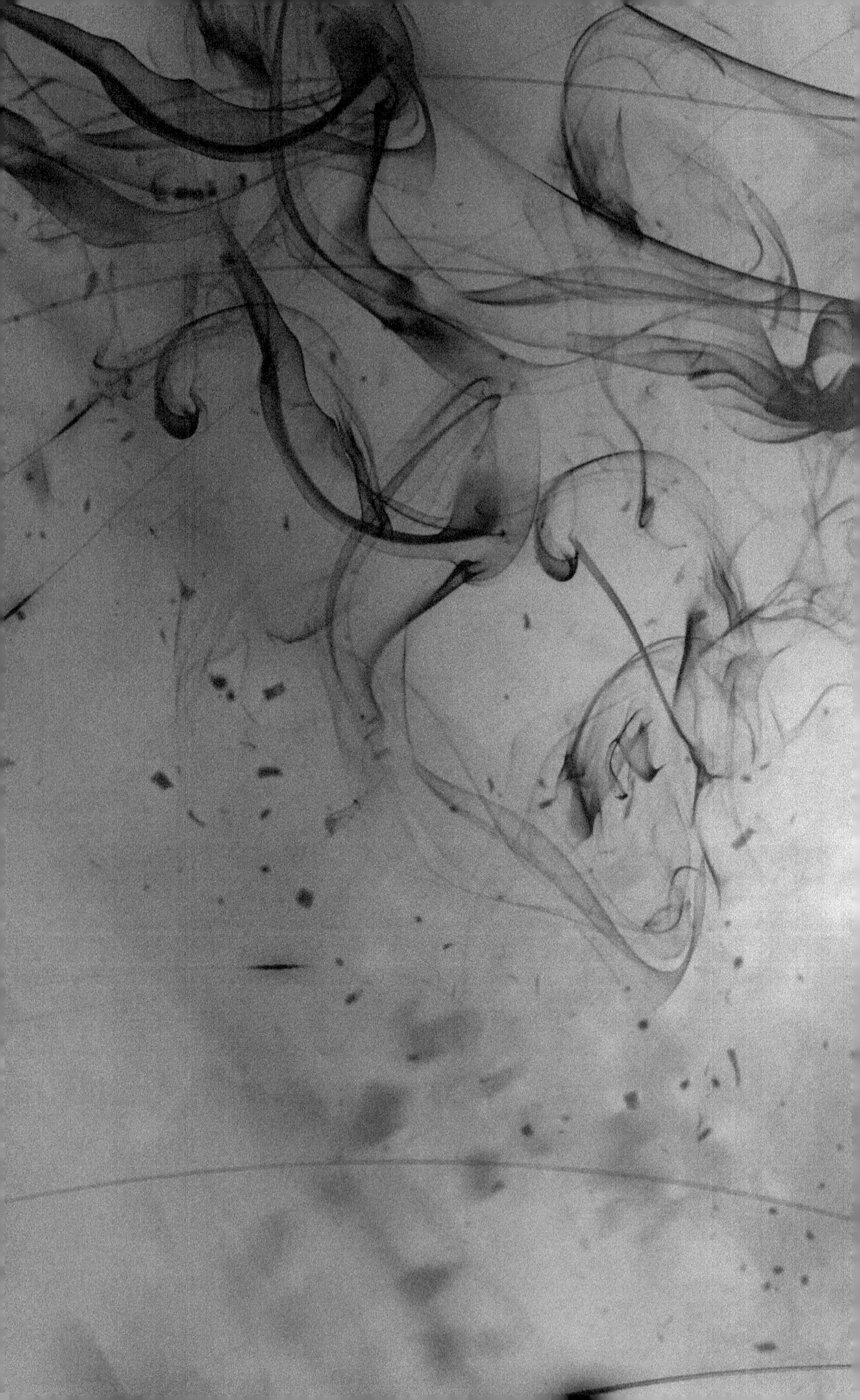

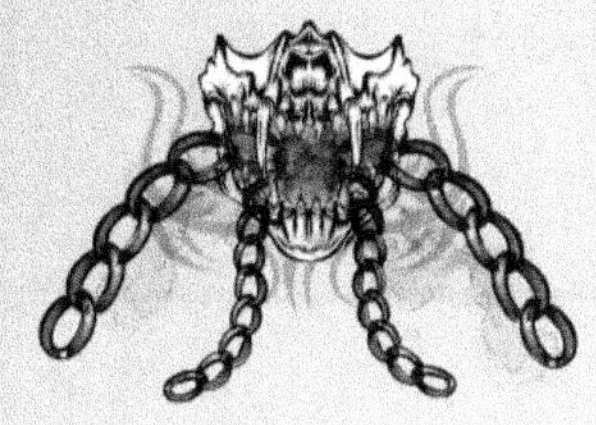

CHAPTER 45
Codrin

The air shifts.

Subtle at first. Like the room itself is holding its breath. An invisible ripple tears through the chaos, bending the very weight of the world. It's magic. But it's unlike any kind of magic. It's something deeper. Something older.

My head snaps up.

And there she is.

She doubles over on the dais, clutching her stomach, her face twisted in agony.

A cry rips from my throat. "RAVENNA…"

The world narrows to her. Nothing else matters. Not the screams of the dying. Not the blood-soaked chaos surrounding me.

Only her.

I charge toward the dais.

I am so close.

"Ravenna!"

Only feet away but I suddenly feel the ground beneath my feet disappear as a hybrid guard crashes into me from the side.

My sword flies from my grip as I'm slammed to the stone floor. Pain explodes through my ribs, knocking the breath clean out of me.

The beast snarls, massive and wild, pinning me down with its full weight.

I fight, kicking, clawing, writhing beneath its massive weight. But it's no use.

I see her stand on shaking legs. Her body sways, her face pale, her eyes stretched wide.

I thrash harder, blood smearing under my nails as I claw at the stone and the beast's armored chest. I don't care about the pain lancing through my side, or the copper in my mouth, or the bruises forming beneath my skin.

I pour every breath, every drop of strength, every desperate thought into breaking free.

Because if I don't, if I fail now, I know she will be gone.

I'm almost there, Ravenna.

So close, I swear I can feel her heat against my skin. But then, she freezes. Rigid, like her soul just ripped free from her body. Her eyes snap to mine, and they are no longer the icy blue I know so well.

They're a burning crimson.

My breath seizes in my throat, and then I see him. Fear like I've never known floods my veins.

Alaric emerges from the shadows behind her like a phantom conjured from darkness. His arm snakes around her waist, pulling her into his chest, his touch possessive and infuriatingly gentle.

Ravenna melts into him, her crimson eyes locking onto mine, and something breaks in them. Or perhaps it's me that's broken. Maybe I broke the moment I watched them rip her from me.

"NOOO!"

The roar rips from my throat, deeper than breath, louder than thought.

My body fuels, not by strength but by something wild and electric, something ancient and unrelenting.

Every nerve lights up. Every muscle coils and burns.

I hurl the guard off me. Its massive body sailing through the air and slamming into a pillar with a sickening crunch.

I roll to one knee, breath rasping, pain searing through my side.

My hand finds the hilt of my sword. I grip it like it's all that's keeping me tethered. Because letting go would mean letting her go.

The beast rises, impossibly fast. A snarl rips from its throat. Its eyes blaze as it charges, sword drawn, the blade glinting like a promise of death.

I hurl myself sideways, boots sliding over blood-slick stone.

The beast's sword misses by inches.

The wind of it burns my cheek.

I rise with the roll and drive my blade into its gut. The blade bites through muscle and bone, shuddering in resistance as it sinks to the hilt.

The creature chokes, blood spilling from its mouth, its teeth stained crimson.

Its eyes widen. Its breath catches.

I twist the blade.

It jerks once, then collapses. Its body convulses and goes still. Lifeless.

I wrench the sword free, breath heaving. Blood spills in thick rivulets across the floor, blooming like ink in water. My hands drip red. My face is streaked with it. The scent of death clings to me like a second skin.

I turn back to her.

To the dais.

"Ravenna!"

My body surges forward, raw and unrelenting that refuses to let me fall behind.

Black fog rises around them like a living beast, writhing and thick, a monstrous veil that threatens to steal her from me.

I charge up the dais steps, lungs tearing, legs screaming.

I'm right here, Ravenna.

So close. Just one more step. One more breath. One more heartbeat.

My heart slams against my ribs as I barrel into the fog. But it parts for me. Spitting me out on the other side.

She's gone.

It hits me like a blade to the chest. My sword falls to the ground with a clatter. My knees slam into the stone, the impact echoing louder than the screams around me.

The world tilts. Breaks.

My hands splay against the floor, trembling. Shattered breath stabs from my throat as I watch the last wisps of the fog fade. Leaving behind nothing but the gaping emptiness where she should be.

No footprints. No blood. No fog. Nothing.

As if she never existed at all.

My vision burns. My chest collapses inward.

"No," I whisper, barely a sound. "No. No, no, no. NOOOO!"

My scream tears through the hall, raw and feral, echoing like a death knell ripped from the gut of the world.

He took her.

He took her from me.

The thought repeats, splintering inside me like glass.

She was right there. I could have saved her.

But I was too slow. Too weak. Too late.

My hands ball into fists. My breath snarls through clenched teeth.

I slam my fists into the stone floor.

The impact splits the surface beneath me, cracks spidering out like veins of anguish. Pain rockets through my arms. I welcome it. I crave it. It's the only thing I can feel over the hollow scream in my chest.

I failed her.

I fucking failed her.

She was right there, my hands inches from hers, and I lost her again.

A scream tears loose from somewhere deep inside me, but it's not just grief this time.

It's something… else.

Blinding, white-hot pain surges up my spine like lightning, seizing every nerve.

Exploding through my back, like molten metal poured straight into my spine, ripping down each nerve like claws through sinew. My body arches violently, muscles locking, tendons straining to their limits.

What is happening?

My scream shreds into something animal. Savage. Unrecognizable. It bounces off the blood-slick walls in twisted echoes. I can't tell if I'm screaming from heartache or agony. Maybe both. Maybe more.

The pain is evolving. Spreading. Something buried deep inside me. Something feral and brutal as it claws its way out.

It wants free.

And it won't stop until it *has* me.

My shoulders feel like they're being ripped apart from the inside, each muscle stretching, shredding, like wings of bone trying to burst from a coffin of flesh. My vision blurs at the edges. My mind floods with static.

Is this death?

My fingers gouge into the stone. Nails split. Blood smears across the cracks. My entire body convulses; a puppet of torment strung on the threads of something I was never meant to unleash.

Another guttural roar tears from my throat, steeped in rage and ruin.

I hear bones cracking.

My bones.

I feel them breaking, reshaping.

The sound is wet, wrong. Like the world is snapping in half.

And I can't stop it.

I'm unraveling. Coming undone.

This isn't a choice I've made. It's a consequence given to me.

The torture builds, heartbeat by heartbeat, a crescendo of agony so unbearable, I want to beg for death, but even death has abandoned me.

Please…

Please, make it stop…

The world blinks white. The pressure tears outward in one vicious release as everything breaks around me.

My back splits open with a sickening, wet rip.

Flesh peels. Blood pours.

And from within me, something ancient erupts out into the world.

The world blurs and tilts, my vision darkening at the edges. My chest heaves as I collapse forward, trembling from the aftershock. The pain lingers, but it's different now.

Cold and powerful.

I force my eyes open, my breath still ragged.

And there I see them. I feel them.

Two massive, midnight wings stretch from my back. Their leathery skin is lustrous with an unnatural, ethereal sheen. They twitch and flex, as if testing their newfound freedom. As if they've been waiting to be unleashed.

Every pulse of pain only strengthens them, the power thrumming through my veins is intoxicating.

All-consuming.

Is this my punishment? My price to pay for failing Ravenna? Or is it something more? Something I've kept buried, shackled by fear and doubt.

This is what I've become. This is what I am now. The darkness I've tried so hard to hide now lies bare for all to see. And I welcome it with open arms.

With a final, shuddering breath, I rise to my feet, the wings spreading behind me, carved from blackened midnight sky itself. Their expanse consumes the room, tendon and bone flexing like they carry the weight of reckoning itself.

My reckoning.

The blood-stained hall stretches before me, the scent of death clinging to the air. The echo of my voice screaming her name still lingers, the pain of her absence bleeding into every heartbeat. I feel her slipping away, buried beneath the darkness they've forced upon her.

But I also saw it in her eyes. A flicker.

It wasn't fear. It was something *else*.

And I swear by every drop of blood spilled, I will burn Veilstead to the ground and all that lies in my way to get her back.

To reclaim what is *mine*.

Even if it means unleashing a wrath this world was never meant to survive.

ACKNOWLEDGMENTS

Where do I begin? There are so many people I want to thank for all the love and support they have given me while writing this book. First, I want to thank my husband, who never stopped believing in me writing this book. You never gave up on me, even during the times when I was ready to give up. Thank you for listening during all the times I would blab your ear off about the plot. Thank you for being my biggest support. Thank you for just being you.

I want to thank my two awesome children, who both have kept me on track. To my daughter, who gave me the name Athan, and to my son, who would always ask, "You working on your book, Mom?" with a side-eye glance of "get on it." Honestly, it helped keep me going.

And to my parents for all the love and support they have always given me.

I also want to thank my amazing friends: Chantel, Megan, Lexi, Amanda, and Keith, you all are the best of friends a girl could ask for. You all have seriously been not only supportive but have been willing to read and give me your input and so much more.

To my editor, Emily Kline, girl, you are the best. You have really helped me find the right words when I felt lost on certain parts. You have helped me so much with your input and suggestions. I can't thank you enough for all the emails you have answered right away and dealing with my constant change of this and that.

Thank you to Atra Luna Design for the cover design. I can't put into words how you have truly captured the heart of this book. Working with you has really been wonderful, with all the back-and-forth emails asking for even the smallest of changes. You took the image from my mind and brought it to life. Your artwork is astounding. Thank you!

ABOUT THE AUTHOR

When not zoned in on writing, T.M. is either out spending time with family and friends or snuggled up on the couch with her two dogs trying to crochet another project to keep her idol hands busy while watching movies or having quiet time reading with a glass or two of wine.

Follow T.M. Carucci:

tiktok.com/@t.m.carucci

instagram.com/author_tmcarucci/

www.ingramcontent.com/pod-product-compliance
Lightning Source LLC
Chambersburg PA
CBHW060809120726
47909CB00006B/1842